THE POOLBEG BOOK
OF
IRISH GHOST STORIES

Shane Davis
McKen

GW00359722

THE POOLBEG BOOK
OF
IRISH GHOST STORIES

Edited by David Marcus

POOLBEG

A Paperback Original
First published 1990 by
Poolbeg Press Ltd
A Division of Poolbeg Enterprises Ltd,
Knocksedan House,
Swords, Co Dublin, Ireland.
Reprinted 1993
Reprinted May 1995

ISBN 1 85371 112 8

A catalogue record for this book is available from the British Library

Cover design by Peter Knuttel
Typeset by Typeform Ltd
Printed by The Guernsey Press Company Ltd,
Vale, Guernsey, Channel Islands.

CONTENTS

INTRODUCTION

Without wishing to beg a question one can say that ghosts are almost as old as man. To be exact, the first death gave birth to the first ghost—hence the phrase "to give up the ghost".

Ghosts, then, are spirits of the dead, and they have populated folk-belief from prehistoric times up to today. It follows that the ghost story has a history older than that of most literary species. However, by the time the written ghost story in the English language became popular, ghosts somehow had acquired a bad name. All because they did what ghosts must do—they haunted. The spirits, so to speak, had become flesh, albeit insubstantial flesh, making the mistake of materialising—so we are assured by many citizens attested sane and level-headed—as wraiths, headless torsos, transparent figures, ectoplasmic emanations, and assorted sheet-flappers. They struck terror into all who witnessed, or thought they had witnessed them, often reducing them to gibbering loons. Their preferred outer abode was a dark wood; indoors they inhabited rambling old castles or, more latterly, unsaleable houses, stalking creaky corridors and draughty bedchambers to the accompaniment of howls, shrieks, moans, plods and clankings. It goes without saying that they were largely nocturnal creatures, preferring the small hours and often the most inclement of weather in which to conduct their business. Daylight, electric light, gaslight were eschewed. Candlelight, because they had the capacity to extinguish a candle and so create the maximum horripilatory effect, was welcomed. Assuredly, nobody loved them.

That was the situation up to and including the nineteenth century. The nineteenth century was the ghosts' hey-night when, even if nobody loved them, most readers loved reading about them. Ghost stories were best sellers in Victorian times, and many of the writers of such stories—most of whom now haunt nothing more exciting than reference books—were household names.

Came the dawn, i.e., the twentieth century. Ghosts, it would appear, were very much out of their element in the new age of technological materialism, and so they proceeded to de-materialise. Laying aside almost *en masse* those apparitional powers they had previously possessed, they reverted to their original spiritual essence. The old head-tucked-underneath-the-arm image was spurned, the old haunts abandoned. Now the ghost was an idea, a feeling, as insubstantial as breath, as obsessive as thought. It no longer waited upon man's death to be given life. Invading the citadel of his mind, it took up permanent residence in a subliminal lair from which it could permeate his whole being, host and ghost becoming almost as one.

The short story, having itself by this time developed into a highly sophisticated medium, grippingly reflected the transformation, so that the modern ghost story offers a range and subtlety to both author and reader more testing, more disturbing, and eventually more persuasive than its nineteenth century predecessors.

Irish writers have always been especially well equipped, both historically and temperamentally, to excel at writing ghost stories. The following selection represents many of the best Irish writers and their best Irish ghosts, past and present.

David Marcus

ELIZABETH BOWEN

Hand in Glove

Jasmine Lodge was favourably set on a residential, prettily wooded hillside in the south of Ireland, overlooking a river and, still better, the roofs of a lively garrison town. Around 1904, which was the flowering period of the Miss Trevors, girls could not have had a more auspicious home—the neighbourhood spun merrily round the military. Ethel and Elsie, a spirited pair, garnered the full advantage—no ball, hop, picnic, lawn tennis, croquet or boating party was complete without them; in winter, though they could not afford to hunt, they trimly bicycled to all meets, and on frosty evenings, with their guitars, set off to *soirées*, snug inside their cab in their fur-tipped capes.

They possessed an aunt, a Mrs Varley de Grey, *née* Elysia Trevor, a formerly notable local belle, who, drawn back again in her widowhood to what had been the scene of her early triumphs, occupied a back bedroom in Jasmine Lodge. Mrs Varley de Grey had had no luck: her splashing match, in its time the talk of two kingdoms, had ended up in disaster—the well-born captain from a cavalry regiment having gone so far as to blow out his brains in India, leaving behind him nothing but her and debts. Mrs Varley de Grey had returned from India with nothing but seven large trunks crammed with recent finery; and she also had been impaired by shock. This had taken place while Ethel and Elsie, whose father had married late, were still unborn—so it was that, for as long as the girls recalled, their aunt had been the sole drawback to Jasmine Lodge. Their parents had orphaned them, somewhat thoughtlessly, by simultaneously dying of scarlet fever when Ethel was just out and Elsie soon to be—they were therefore left lacking a chaperone and, with their gift for putting everything to some use, propped the aunt up in order that she might play that role. Only when her peculiarities became too marked did they feel it necessary to withdraw her: by that time, however, all the surrounding ladies could be said to compete for the honour of taking into society the sought-after Miss Trevors. From then on, no more was seen or heard of Mrs Varley de Grey. ("Oh, just a trifle unwell, but nothing much!") She remained upstairs, at the back: when the girls were giving one of their little parties, or a couple of officers came to call, the key of her room would be turned in the outer lock.

The girls hung Chinese lanterns from the creepered veranda, and would sit lightly strumming on their guitars. Not less fascinating was their badinage, accompanied by a daring flash of the eyes. They were known as the clever Miss Trevors, not because of any taint of dogmatism or book-learning—no, when a gentleman cried, "Those girls have brains!" he meant it wholly in admiration—but because of their accomplishments, ingenuity and agility. They took leading parts in theatricals, lent spirit to numbers of drawing-room games, were naughty mimics, and sang duets. Nor did their fingers lag behind their wits—they constructed lampshades, crêpe paper flowers and picturesque hats; and, above all, varied their dresses marvellously—no one could beat them for ideas, nipping, slashing or fitting. Once more allowing nothing to go to waste, they had remodelled the trousseau out of their aunt's trunks, causing sad old tulles and tarlatans, satins and *moiré* taffetas, to appear to have come from Paris only to-day. They re-stitched spangles, pressed ruffles crisp, and revived many a corsage of squashed silk roses. They went somewhat softly about that task, for the trunks were all stored in the attic immediately over the back room.

They wore their clothes well. "A pin on either of those two would look smart!" declared other girls. All that they were short of was evening gloves—they had two pairs each, which they had been compelled to buy. *What* could have become of Mrs Varley de Grey's presumably sumptuous numbers of this item, they were unable to fathom and it was too bad. Had gloves been overlooked in her rush from India?—or, were they here, in that *one* trunk the Trevors could not get at? All other locks had yielded to pulls or pickings, or the sisters found keys to fit them, or they had used the tool-box; but this last stronghold defied them. In that sad little soiled silk sack, always on her person, Mrs Varley de Grey, they became convinced, hoarded the operative keys, along with some frippery rings and brooches—all true emeralds, pearls and diamonds having been long ago, as they knew, sold. Such contrariety on their aunt's part irked them—meanwhile, gaieties bore hard on their existing gloves. Last thing at nights when they came in, last thing in the evenings before they went out, they would manfully dab away at the fingertips. So, it must be admitted that a long whiff of benzine pursued them as they whirled round the ballroom floor.

They were tall and handsome—nothing so soft as pretty, but in those days it was a vocation to be a handsome girl; many of the best marriages had been made by such. They carried themselves imposingly, had good busts and shoulders, waists firm under the whalebone and straight backs. Their features were striking, their colouring high; low on their foreheads bounced dark mops of curls. Ethel was, perhaps, the dominant one, but both girls were pronounced to be full of character.

Whom, and still more when, did they mean to marry? They had already seen regiments out and in; for quite a number of years, it began to seem, bets in the neighbourhood had been running high. Sympathetic spyglasses were trained on the conspicuous gateway to Jasmine Lodge; each new cavalier was noted. The only trouble might be, their promoters claimed, that the clever Trevors were always so surrounded that they had not a moment in which to turn or choose. Or otherwise, could it possibly be that the admiration aroused by Ethel and Elsie, and their now institutional place in the local scene, scared out more tender feeling from the masculine breast? It came to be felt, and perhaps by the girls themselves, that, having lingered so long and so puzzlingly, it was up to them to bring off (like their aunt) a *coup*. Society around this garrison town had long plumed itself upon its romantic record; summer and winter, Cupid shot his darts. Lush scenery, the oblivion of all things else bred by the steamy climate, and perpetual gallivanting—all were conducive. Ethel's and Elsie's names, it could presumed, were by now murmured wherever the Union Jack flew. Nevertheless, it was time they should decide.

Ethel's decision took place late one spring. She set her cap at the second son of an English marquess. Lord Fred had come on a visit, for the fishing, to a mansion some miles down the river from Jasmine Lodge. He first made his appearance, with the rest of the house party, at one of the more resplendent military balls, and was understood to be a man-about-town. The civilian glint of his pince-nez, at once serene and superb, instantaneously wrought, with his great name, on Ethel's heart. She beheld him, and the assembled audience, with approbation, looked on at the moment so big with fate. The truth, it appeared in a flash, was that Ethel, though so condescending with her charms, had not from the first been destined to love a soldier, and that here, after long attrition, her answer was. Lord Fred was, by all, at once signed over to her. For his part, he responded to her attentions quite gladly, though in a somewhat dazed way. If he did not so often dance with her—indeed, how could he, for she was much besought?—he could at least be perceived to gaze. At a swiftly organised river picnic, the next evening, he by consent fell to Ethel's lot—she had spent the foregoing morning snipping and tacking at a remaining muslin of Mrs Varley de Grey's, a very fresh forget-me-not-dotted pattern. The muslin did not survive the evening out, for when the moon should have risen, rain poured into the boats. Ethel's goodhumoured drollery carried all before it, and Lord Fred wrapped his blazer around her form.

Next day, more rain; and all felt flat. At Jasmine Lodge, the expectant deck chairs had to be hurried in from the garden, and the small close rooms, with their greeneried windows and plentiful bric-à-brac, gave out a stuffy, resentful, indoor smell. The maid was out; Elsie was lying down with a migraine; so it devolved on Ethel to carry up Mrs Varley de Grey's tea—the invalid set very great store by tea, and her manifestations by door rattlings, sobs and mutters were apt to become disturbing if it did not appear. Ethel, with the not particularly dainty tray, accordingly entered the back room, this afternoon rendered dark by its outlook into a dripping uphill wood. The aunt, her visage draped in a cobweb shawl, was as usual sitting up in bed. "*Aha,*" she at once cried, screwing one eye up and glittering round at Ethel with the other, "so what's all this in the wind today?"

Ethel, as she lodged the meal on the bed, shrugged her shoulders, saying: "I'm in a hurry."

"No doubt you are. The question is, will you get him?"

"Oh, drink your tea!" snapped Ethel, her colour rising.

The old wretch responded by popping a lump of sugar into her cheek, and sucking at it while she fixed her wink on her niece. She then observed: "*I* could tell you a thing or two!"

"We've had enough of *your* fabrications, Auntie."

"Fabrications!" croaked Mrs Varley de Grey. "And who's been the fabricator, I'd like to ask? Who's so nifty with the scissors and needle? Who's been going a-hunting in my clothes?"

"Oh, what a fib!" exclaimed Ethel, turning her eyes up. "Those old musty miserable bundles of things of yours— would Elsie or I consider laying a finger on them?"

Mrs Varley de Grey replied, as she sometimes did, by heaving up and throwing the tray at Ethel. Nought, therefore, but cast-off kitchen china nowadays was ever exposed to risk; and the young woman, not trying to gather the debris up, statuesquely, thoughtfully stood with her arms folded, watching tea steam rise from the carpet. Today, the effort required seemed to have been too much for Aunt Elysia, who collapsed on her pillows, faintly blue in the face. "Rats in the attic," she muttered. "*I've* heard them, rats in the attic! Now where's my tea?"

"You've had it," said Ethel, turning to leave the room. However, she paused to study a photograph in a tarnished, elaborate silver frame. "Really quite an Adonis, poor Uncle Harry. From the first glance, you say, he never looked back?"

"My lovely tea," said her aunt, beginning to sob.

As Ethel slowly put down the photograph, her eyes could be seen to calculate, her mouth hardened and a reflective cast came over her brow. Step by step, once more she approached the bed, and, as she did so, altered her tune. She suggested, in a beguiling tone: "You said you could tell me a thing or two . . . ?"

Time went on; Lord Fred, though forever promising, still failed to come quite within Ethel's grasp. Ground gained one hour seemed to be lost the next—it seemed, for example, that things went better for Ethel in the afternoons, in the open air, than at the dressier evening functions. It was when she swept down on him in full plumage that Lord Fred seemed to contract. Could it be that he feared his passions?—she hardly thought so. Or, did her complexion not light up well? When there was a question of dancing, he came so late that her programme already was black with other names, whereupon he would heave a gallant sigh. When they did take the floor together, he held her so far at arm's length, and with his face turned so far away, that when she wished to address him she had to shout—she told herself this must be the London style, but it piqued her, naturally. Next morning, all would be as it was before, with nobody so completely assiduous as Lord Fred—but, through it all, he still never came to the point. And worse, the days of his visit were running out: he would soon be back in the heart of the London Season.

"Will you ever get him, Ethel, now, do you think?" Elsie asked, with trying solicitude, and no doubt the neighbourhood wondered also.

She conjured up all her fascinations. But was something further needed, to do the trick?

It was now that she began to frequent her aunt.

In that dank little back room looking into the hill, proud Ethel humbled herself, to prise out the secret. Sessions were close and long. Elsie, in mystification outside the door, heard the dotty voice of their relative rising, falling, with, now and then, blood-curdling little knowing laughs. Mrs Varley de Grey was back in the golden days. Always, though, of a sudden it would break off, drop back into pleas, whimpers and jagged breathing. No doctor, though she constantly asked for one, had for years been allowed to visit Mrs Varley de Grey—the girls saw no reason for that expense, or for the interference which might follow. Aunt's affliction, they swore, was confined to the head; all she required was quiet, and that she got. Knowing, however, how gossip spreads, they would let no servant near her for more than a minute or two, and then with one of themselves on watch at the door. They had much to bear from the foetid state of her room.

"You don't think you'll kill her, Ethel?" the out-of-it Elsie asked. "Forever sitting on top of her, as you now do. Can it be healthy, egging her on to talk? What's this attraction, all of a sudden?—whatever's this which has sprung up between you two? She and you are becoming quite hand-in-glove."

Elsie merely remarked this, and soon forgot: she had her own fish to fry. It was Ethel who had cause to recall the words—for, the afternoon of the very day they were spoken, Aunt Elysia whizzed off on another track, screamed for what was impossible and, upon being thwarted, went into a seizure unknown before. The worst of it was, at the outset her mind cleared—she pushed her shawl back, reared up her unkempt grey head and looked at Ethel, unblinkingly studied Ethel, with a lucid accumulation of years of hate. "You fool of a gawk," she said, and with such contempt! "Coming running to me to know how to trap a man. Could *you* learn if it was from Venus herself? Wait till I show you beauty.—Bring down those trunks!"

"Oh, Auntie."

"Bring them down, I say. I'm about to dress myself up."

"Oh, but I cannot; they're heavy; I'm single-handed."

"Heavy?—they came here heavy. But there've been rats in the attic.—I saw you, swishing downstairs in my *eau-de-nil*!"

"Oh, you dreamed that!"

"Through the crack of the door.—Let me up, then. Let us go where they are, and look—we shall soon see!" Aunt Elysia threw back the bedclothes and began to get up. "Let's take a look," she said, "at the rats' work." She set out to totter towards the door.

"Oh, but you're not fit!" Ethel protested

"And when did a doctor say so?" There was a swaying: Ethel caught her in time and, not gently, lugged her back to the bed—and Ethel's mind the whole of this time was whirling, for tonight was the night upon which all hung. Lord Fred's last local appearance was to be, like his first, at a ball: tomorrow he left for London. So it must be tonight, at this ball, or never! How was it that Ethel felt so strangely, wildly confident of the outcome? It was time to begin on her coiffure, lay out her dress. Oh, tonight she would shine as never before! She flung back the bedclothes over the helpless form, heard a clock strike, and hastily turned to go.

"I will be quits with you," said the voice behind her.

Ethel, in a kimono, hair half done, was in her own room, in front of the open glove drawer, when Elsie came in—home from a tennis party. Elsie acted oddly; she went at once to the drawer and buried her nose in it. "Oh my goodness," she cried, "it's all too true, and it's awful!"

"What is?" Ethel carelessly asked.

"Ethel dear, would you ever face it out if I were to tell you a certain rumour I heard today at the party as to Lord Fred?"

Ethel turned from her sister, took up the heated tongs and applied more crimps to her natural curliness. She said: "Certainly; spit it out."

"Since childhood, he's recoiled from the breath of benzine. He wilts away when it enters the very room!"

"Who says that's so?"

"He confided it to his hostess, who is now spitefully putting it around the country."

Ethel bit her lip and pm down the tongs, while Elsie sorrowfully concluded: "And your gloves stink, Ethel, as I'm sure do mine." Elsie then thought it wiser to slip away.

In a minute more, however, she was back, and this time with a still more peculiar air. She demanded: "In what state did you leave Auntie? She was sounding so very quiet that I peeped in, and *I* don't care for the looks of her now at all!" Ethel swore, but consented to take a look. She stayed in there in the back room, with Elsie biting her thumb-nail outside the door, for what seemed an ominous length of time—when she did emerge, she looked greenish, but held her head high. The sisters' eyes met. Ethel said, stonily: "Dozing."

"You're certain she's *not* . . . ? She *couldn't* ever be—you know?"

"Dozing, I tell you." Ethel stared Elsie out.

"If she *was* gone," quavered the frailer sister, "just think of it—why, we'd never get to the ball!—And a ball that everything hangs on," she ended up, with a scared but conspiratorial glance at Ethel.

"Reassure yourself. Didn't you hear me say?"

As she spoke Ethel, chiefly from habit, locked her late aunt's door on the outside. The act caused a sort of secret jingle to be heard from inside her fist, and Elsie asked: "What's that you've got hold of now.?" "Just a few little keys and trinkets she made me keep," replied Ethel, disclosing the small bag she had found where she'd looked for it, under the dead one's pillow. "Scurry on now, Elsie, you'll never be dressed. Care to make use of my tongs, while they're so splendidly hot?"

Alone at last, Ethel drew in a breath, and, with a gesture of resolution, retied her kimono sash tightly over her corset. She shook the key from the bag and regarded it, murmuring, "Providential!", then gave a glance upward towards where the attics were. The late spring sun had set but an apricot afterglow, not unlike the light cast by a Chinese lantern, crept through the upper storey of Jasmine Lodge. The cessation of all those rustlings, tappings, whimpers and moans from inside Mrs Varley de Grey's room had set up an unfamiliar, somewhat unnerving hush. Not till a whiff of singeing hair announced that Elsie was well employed did Ethel set out on the quest which held all her hopes. Success was imperative—she *must* have gloves. Gloves, gloves . . .

Soundlessly, she set foot on the attic stairs.

Under the skylight, she had to suppress a shriek, for a rat—yes, of all things!—leaped at her out of an empty hatbox; and the rodent gave her a wink before it darted away. Now Ethel and Elsie knew for a certain fact that there never *had* been rats in Jasmine Lodge. However, she continued to steel her nerves, and to push her way to the one inviolate trunk.

All Mrs Varley de Grey's other Indian luggage gaped and yawned at Ethel, void, showing its linings, on end or toppling, forming a barricade around the object of her search—she pushed, pitched and pulled, scowling as the dust flew into her hair. But the last trunk, when it came into view and reach, still had something select and bridal about it: on top, the initials E. V. de G. stared out, quite luminous in a frightening way—for indeed how dusky the attic was! Shadows not only multiplied in the corners but seemed to finger their way up the sloping roof. Silence pierced up through the floor from that room below—and, worst, Ethel had the sensation of being watched by that pair of fixed eyes she had not stayed to close. She glanced this way, that way, backward over her shoulder. But, Lord Fred was at stake!—she knelt down and got to work with the key.

This trunk had two neat brass locks, one left, one right, along the front of the lid. Ethel, after fumbling, opened the first—then, so great was her hurry to know what might be within that she could not wait but slipped her hand in under the lifted corner. She pulled out one pricelessly lacy tip of what must be a bride-veil, and gave a quick laugh—must not this be an omen? She pulled again, but the stuff resisted, almost as though it were being grasped from inside the trunk—she let go, and either her eyes deceived her or the lace began to be drawn back slowly, in again, inch by inch. What was odder was, that the spotless finger-tip of a white kid glove appeared for a moment, as though exploring its way out, then withdrew.

Ethel's heart stood still—but she turned to the other lock. Was a giddy attack overcoming her?—for, as she gazed, the entire lid of the trunk seemed to bulge upward, heave and strain, so that the E. V. de G. upon it rippled.

Untouched by the key in her trembling hand, the second lock tore itself open.

She recoiled, while the lid slowly rose—of its own accord.

She should have fled. But oh, how she craved what lay there exposed!—layer upon layer, wrapped in transparent paper, of elbow-length, magnolia-pure white gloves, bedded on the inert folds of the veil. "Lord Fred," thought Ethel, "now you're within my grasp!"

That was her last thought, nor was the grasp to be hers. Down on her knees again, breathless with lust and joy, Ethel flung herself forward on to that sea of kid, scrabbling and seizing. The glove she had seen before was now, however, readier for its purpose. At first it merely pounced after Ethel's fingers, as though making mock of their greedy course; but the hand within it was all the time filling out . . . With one snowy flash through the dusk, the glove clutched Ethel's front hair, tangled itself in her black curls and dragged her head down. She began to choke among the sachets and tissue—then the glove let go, hurled her back, and made its leap at her throat.

It was a marvel that anything so dainty should be so strong. So great, so convulsive was the swell of the force that, during the strangling of Ethel, the seams of the glove split.

In any case, the glove would have been too small for her.

The shrieks of Elsie, upon the attic threshold, began only when all other sounds had died down . . . The ultimate spark of the once-famous cleverness of the Miss Trevors appeared in Elsie's extrication of herself from this awkward mess—for, who was to credit how Ethel came by her end? The sisters' reputation for warmth of heart was to stand the survivor in good stead—for, could those affections nursed in Jasmine Lodge, extending so freely even to the unwell aunt, have culminated in Elsie's setting on Ethel? No. In the end, the matter was hushed up—which is to say, is still talked about even now. Ethel Trevor and Mrs Varley de Grey were interred in the same grave, as everyone understood that they would have wished. What conversation took place under the earth, one does not know.

CONALL CEARNACH

The Homing Bone

Professor David Gillespie was a distinguished anatomist. It is scarcely necessary to add that he was a Scotsman; for has not a wise Providence ordained that the principal products of Caledonia shall be marine engineers, metaphysicians, and anatomists? Equally brilliant on what are technically known as the "hard" and "soft" parts of the human frame, he was particularly strong on the subject of the skeleton; and to hear him lecture on the petrous portion of the temporal bone was a revelation to the unsophisticated first-year student of medicine. In the lecture theatre he would stand at the rostrum, of a morning, and taking a bone for his text, he would hold forth for a full hour. Common "grinders" could point out foramina and muscle-insertions well enough for examination purposes; but their instruction was dry and uninteresting. In Gillespie's hands a bone became a thing of beauty. His lecture was not a lecture; it was not a sermon; it was an oration. He would wax eloquent as he went along, and his enthusiasm was infectious. Not infrequently, when his peroration closed with some apposite quotation from the poets, a spontaneous burst of applause went up from the crowded benches; and students, as they wended their way to pastures new, would remark to one another: "Man, but Gillespie's just great!"

Professor Gillespie came of Highland Gaelic stock; a stock which is far from materialistic; and his grandmother was reputed to have possessed the gift of "second sight." Many a time young Davy had shuddered as he listened, by the fire of the crofter's cottage, where he first saw the light, to the weird, uncanny tales of the Highlands; but five years' hard work at the Edinburgh School of Medicine had knocked the nonsense out of him in more ways than one. Now, at the age of fifty-four, one of the leading anatomists of Europe, he could afford to bestow an indulgent smile on the narrator of tales pertaining to the supernatural. A man who, for twenty years, has spent most of his waking hours in the atmosphere of the Dissecting-room, is almost as much at home with the dead as with the living. His stock-in-trade, so to speak, being corpses, the creepiest story about "corpse-candles" naturally leaves him unmoved. Yet the fear of the supernatural is so deeply ingrained in human beings, and the stories, heard in boyhood days, sink so deeply into the subliminal self, that the acquired scepticism of later years is, after all, the merest veneer, which may vanish in a moment; if only circumstances arise, in which a sufficiently strong appeal is made to those hereditary instincts and pre-historic beliefs that slumber beneath the surface.

So much, by way of preface to the secret history of the curious happenings which led to Gillespie's resignation of his Chair of Anatomy, and his retirement into private life; a step which astonished all who heard of it, for he was regarded as being but at the zenith of his powers. I now tell the tale as it was told to me by Cochrane, who heard it from the lips of Gillespie himself.

When the British Medical Association held its annual conference in Dublin, Gillespie was invited to preside over the Anatomical Section; and his address at the opening meeting of the section was as brilliant as might have been expected from one of his reputation. The conference over, Gillespie devoted his time to sight-seeing. He spent a day visiting the Cathedrals, and, in the afternoon, he prowled about the quays and back streets of the city. Half an hour was given up to viewing the vaults of St. Michan's, with its celebrated mummies, and crossing over the Metal Bridge he wended his way through Cook Street, that home of undertakers, where every shop resounds to the stroke of the coffin-maker's hammer.

Having passed through this gruesome quarter, he wandered further afield, until he came upon the old church of St. Walburgh's. The ground about the church had long been closed to burials, and he found some workmen engaged in levelling the churchyard. The tombstones had been removed and arranged along the churchyard wall; for, since the inscriptions they bore were no longer legible, they had served their purpose, and were mere cumberers of the ground. During the levelling process some relics of mortality had become uncovered, and in one corner there lay a jumble of odd assortments of skulls and some large bones.

Gillespie's professional eye detected, amid the heap, a splendid specimen in a perfect state of preservation. It was a thigh-bone, or as an anatomist would more accurately describe it, a left femur; that of an adult man, for, by the trained eye, the sterner sex can be distinguished even in the bony structures. The Professor coveted the bone, and foresaw in it the material for an interesting and instructive paper. He had no qualms of conscience about securing it; only, in deference to any susceptibilities on the part of the Irish workmen, he did so quite unostentatiously, and walked away with the coveted femur concealed beneath his overcoat.

Arrived at his lodgings, he stowed it in his bedroom until after dinner; when he proceeded to brush away the adherent earth from the bone with a clothes-brush, and settled down to gloat over his treasure. From the great length of the femur, and the powerfully developed trochanters, he deduced the fact that the man who had owned it must have been an exceptionally tall and muscular individual; and the professor fell to wondering whether the said individual had been an Irishman, or one of the old Norse stock whose descendants among the Dubliners retain somewhat of the Viking characteristics. He sat in his dressing-gown until eleven o'clock, and strove to visualise the appearance which the owner of the bone must have presented in life; then he yawned sleepily, and dropping the femur into his portmanteau, lest he might forget it in his hurry to catch the morning boat, he tumbled into bed and fell fast asleep.

His sleep had not lasted for long when he was visited by a horribly vivid dream. In his dream he seemed to be awakened by a sound of knocking at his bedroom door. Before he had time to say "Come in!" the door opened, and four skeletons entered, carrying a coffin on their bony shoulders. They deposited their burden on two chairs beside his bed, and stood like waiting mutes. Suddenly the lid of the coffin flew open, and its occupant, a tall skeleton, sat up and pointed first at the professor, and then to its own lower limbs. Following the gesture, Gillespie looked and saw that the left femur was missing. Still sitting up in the coffin, the tall skeleton leaned forward towards the bed and clutched the professor by the throat with a vice-like grip of its bony fingers.

Gillespie gasped for breath, gave a strangled scream, and woke up in a fright. It took some little time for him to realise his surroundings. He sat up in bed to find his heart palpitating violently, his brow wet with perspiration, and about his scalp a curious sensation associated in the lay mind with the phenomenon known as "the hair standing on end." It was decidedly a novel experience for the professor, for he boasted that he never dreamed dreams, or that if he did, they were so unimportant, that his waking moments contained no recollection of them.

The explanation was perfectly simple, he told himself. During the conference his meals had been more irregular than they would have been at home. Some of the dinners, too, were more elaborate than those to which he was normally accustomed. Why, he wondered, could not a party of grave and learned scientists foregather without over-eating and over-drinking like a lot of schoolboys at a picnic? Then the material of his dream had been supplied by his afternoon saunter through that extraordinary street of coffin-shops, and the bone purloined from the churchyard completed the tale.

Yet, in that dark room, in the small hours of the morning there were stirrings of the hereditary fears—the fear of the dark and the fear of the dead; and he fell to moralising over the fact that Providence had for some reason or other seen fit to endow the human scalp with a set of "*erector pili*" or hair-raising muscles, and the further curious fact that that particular set of muscles could only be called into play by supernatural (or superstitious) terrors. Did not the pious Aeneas' hair stand on end at the apparition of his beloved dead wife, Creusa? But the professor's classics were decidedly rusty, and while attempting in vain to complete the line "*Obstupui, steteruntque comae*"—he fell asleep once more.

However, he was not destined to enjoy his resumed slumber for long. The ill dream was repeated with variations. Once more the door opened, the four skeletons entered, bearing a coffin which they placed on chairs by the bedside; but this time the lid did not fly open. Instead, the professor found his gaze directed by the bony forefingers of the skeletons to the name-plate on the coffin-lid; and, to his horror, he saw the name of the deceased was set forth as DAVID GILLESPIE.

While he still gazed in horror-stricken silence, a troupe of skeletons came crowding into the room, and circled round his bed in a dance of death, their bones rattling like castanets, and their grinning jaws gnashing as though chanting a hymn of hate. Closer and closer they circled, until one gigantic skeleton halted, and raising an enormous thighbone, aimed a stunning blow straight at the professor's head. Gillespie instinctively put up one arm to ward off the impending blow, and the effort awoke him.

This time he was indignant. He had refused several offers of hospitality from Dublin hosts, preferring to select quiet lodgings for himself. That was one of his idiosyncrasies; for he strongly objected to sitting up into the small hours, smoking and talking "shop"; and experience of many Medical Congresses had proved such dissipation to be the normal sequel to accepting the hospitality of professional colleagues. And now here he was faring no better, or rather worse. Confound it all! His digestion must be completely upset. If only he had strolled into the country, instead of through those unhealthy back streets adjoining the Liffey. His head felt decidedly queer, too, and he reflected that it was probably that queer feeling which had coloured the finale of his second nightmare. Could it be something more serious than indigestion?

Gillespie had read somewhere that Chinese physicians attached great importance to the prognostic interpretation of their patients' dreams. Did the curious variant by which he distinctly saw his own name inscribed on the coffin-lid portend a dangerous illness? Such gruesome visions reminded him of the creepy tales heard in his childhood days. His grandmother, who was popularly credited with "second sight," used to tell of how she had seen a coffin, with her husband's name on it, carried past in the moonlight, three days before he died.

One story recalled another. There were stirrings in the subliminal mind. As a boy he firmly believed in ghosts. Why exactly had he lost that belief? Like the Missionary, in one of Robert Louis Stevenson's fables, he began to think that after all there might be something in it. The French called ghosts "*revenants*," folk who came back. Came back for what? If he told his dream to any of the old wives in his native village they would roundly assert that the dead Irishman, or Dane, as the case might be, had come back for the femur that had been stolen from the churchyard. This introduced another train of thought; consecrated earth. Yes, the bones which had served him for purposes of lecturing for the past twenty years, were bones that had been taken from the dissecting-room, macerated and bleached. They had never been interred; had never lain in consecrated earth. Should he, in deference to sentiment, restore the femur to the churchyard, after first making a neat sketch and recording the exact measurements?

Needless to say, Gillespie in his normal waking mood, and in broad daylight, would never have soliloquised in this strain; but, as I have already hinted, the dark brings back forgotten fears and scruples, and the professor was by no means in a normal mood. His thoughts were running on this long unused track for some minutes, when he dosed asleep again. But did he? For that is a question which no man living can answer—not even the intelligent reader. Gillespie stoutly denied that he did. Cochrane declared that he only dreamt that he did not; that, in point of fact, what followed was part of the same dream, and that it was a part of the dream to dream that he was awake.

Be that as it may, let us abide by Gillespie's version for the present. He was (let us premise) still awake, and following out this line of thought, when he heard a dull knocking sound in the room. It was a muffled tapping, repeated at regular intervals, and appeared to proceed from the closed portmanteau which lay on the floor close to the dressing-table. Although the room was quite dark, Gillespie instinctively glanced in the direction from which the sound proceeded, and as he did so he became aware of a faint, hazy luminosity of rectangular form. The luminosity increased in brilliance, until it became quite evidently the outline of the portmanteau, with a distinct view of its interior, as though it had been placed against a fluorescent screen, under the action of exceptionally powerful Rontgen Rays; and the object which stood out most clearly, as in an actual skiagraph, was the purloined femur. So sharply was it defined that it appeared to impress a photograph of itself on Gillespie's brain; and then the fluorescence died away, and the room was plunged in darkness again.

By this time, the professor was (so he asserted to Cochrane) as wide awake as ever he had been in his life; his every sense strung to the highest pitch of expectation; but thenceforward he was obliged to depend solely upon his sense of hearing for information as to subsequent events. He distinctly heard, he alleged, a noise as of someone fumbling with the catch of the portmanteau; the click with which it opened; and a dull, thudding sound, as of someone walking in the room with a wooden leg or crutch. Next, his bedroom door swung ajar, and the someone or something stumped slowly down stairs and along the matting of the hall. The front door opened slightly—enough to send a current of air sweeping up the stairs and into the bedroom—and closed again noiselessly.

All this time, Gillespie was mentally alert, and experienced no abnormal sensations, except for a tense feeling about the head, and a curious inability, or even unwillingness, to move or speak. Then came a blank in consciousness, and he remembered no more until he awoke to find it broad daylight.

A knock at his bedroom door heralded the arrival of no more supernatural a visitant than the maid-of-all-work with his boots and shaving-water. He rose with something of an effort, and the act of stooping for his boots and hot water caused his head to throb violently; while the singing in his ears almost deafened him. But, like Macbeth, the terrors of the night being gone, he felt himself a man again; and he was in a humour to explain his present, as well as past, experience in terms of materialistic philosophy. Dyspepsia; that was the explanation in a nutshell. Dyspepsia, coupled with a restless night.

Shaved and dressed, he hastened to complete his packing, and opened his portmanteau to stow away his shaving tackle and toilet brushes. As he opened it, he recollected with a smile how he had debated with himself in the watches of the night the advisability of returning the stolen bone to the churchyard; but he decided that such an action would be a concession to a temporary aberration of superstitious weakness; better keep it as a memento of his visit to Dublin.

Now if Professor Gillespie had been an untidy, unmethodical man, this story would not have been told; but the fact remains that nothing would do him but to empty the contents of the portmanteau on the floor, in order to pack away all his belongings neatly. And then it was that he made the discovery that caused him to abandon the idea of catching that day's boat, and sent him instead to consult Cochrane in Merrion Square. He discovered that the bone was missing!

It was only when he had thoroughly satisfied himself that it really was missing, by replacing the contents of the portmanteau, article by article, repeating the process several times, and making a thorough inventory of the objects in the room, that he decided that there was something wrong. Had he at his time of life begun to indulge in day-dreams, or was he the victim of hallucinations? He would have sworn in any court of law that he had conveyed the bone to his room the night before, brushed it clean, and placed it in his portmanteau. Was that waking experience on a par with the visions of the night? Was he taking leave of his senses?

He toyed with his breakfast, and informing his landlady that he had changed his mind, and intended to leave by the evening boat instead, he made a last desperate effort to regain his normal bearings. Mid-day found him once more standing in the churchyard of St. Walburgh's. The workmen were still engaged in levelling the surface, but one of their number was re-interring the heap of bones which had been laid aside in the corner. Only one portion of skull and a few long bones were left uncovered; and among the latter, in precisely the identical position which it occupied when Gillespie's eyes first lighted upon it, was the great left femur!

There was no mistaking it; for, apart from the size and abnormal development, it was as free from churchyard mould as though it had been freshly washed and dusted. Instead of throwing light on the subject, this only complicated matters still further. What was the meaning of it all? His head sang and throbbed so much that it was with difficulty that he made his way as far as his lodging.

In the afternoon he went to Cochrane's, and sent in his card. It had the opposite effect to that which he intended; for, instead of seeing him immediately, Cochrane kept him waiting until he had seen the last of his patients, hoping to settle down to a long chat on subjects arising out of the Conference.

When Gillespie's turn did eventually come, and he had finished relating his strange experiences, both in dreaming and waking states, Cochrane put to him a few questions, and set about a thorough examination. Every medical consultant has his own particular fad; and Cochrane's fad was blood-pressure. Once he adjusted the sphygmomanometer, and found that the professor's blood-pressure stood at 210, he cared nothing about reflexes or pupil-reaction. Blood-pressure explained everything, and in Cochrane's opinion the whole matter was simple.

Gillespie, like most anatomists and other specialists, had forgotten all he ever knew about the ordinary practice of medicine. He thought that, so long as he was oblivious to the flight of time, his arteries were in a similar state. As a matter of fact, they were prematurely senile and sclerosed from the routine of his life and the mental preoccupation which had caused him to neglect precautions suitable for a man of middle age. It was highly probable that the bursting of a small arteriole in the brain had given rise to the sensation of a "stroke," metamorphosed into a blow aimed at his head by the skeleton of his dream fancy.

The upshot of the consultation was that Gillespie was prevailed upon, under stress of warnings as to the serious consequences of disobedience, to resign his Chair of Anatomy and retire from public life. He took a quiet bungalow in his native air, and persevered in the gentle exercise treatment prescribed by Cochrane; but rest had come too late, for he was carried off by a severe stroke within seven months of his resignation; so that Cochrane's diagnosis was not very far wrong after all.

I first heard Cochrane tell this story at a clinical lecture on arterio-sclerosis; but at the time he mentioned no names. It was since I qualified that I wormed the whole tale out of him, with full particulars, as well as he could remember them. Still, blood-pressure will not explain everything; and I firmly believe that Gillespie did remove the femur from the churchyard, and stow it in his portmanteau. To my mind, the only question that remains unanswered is this: "How did it find its way back again?"

TERENCE de VERE WHITE

One of the Family

"Mother, if you could see your Richard now!" was his filial thought as he drove in his newly purchased car in his newly purchased riding clothes to his first hunt. He was passing the gate lodge of Ballyorney Park where she had been born and brought up and had left (in circumstances that had never been made perfectly clear to him) to marry his short-lived father, another dependent of the Templeton family, needless to say.

Ballyorney was a ruin now; the present Lord Templeton lived in the Isle of Man safeguarding what was left of the family fortune. The selection, signing and dispatching of a greeting card for him was the focal point of Christmas when Richard's mother was alive. When he gave up acknowledging them (with good wishes for the New Year) she absolved him from blame. No Templeton could do wrong; and, if one seemed to, you may be quite sure there were always extenuating circumstances.

Richard's first lesson from his mother in their two-roomed basement lodging was about the family. Before he could safely dispense with diapers he knew the names of the successive Templetons and their wives and children, as a precocious little English boy might his country's kings and queens. Lady Caroline, Lady Lucy, Lady Elisabeth, and many more—of these was composed his mother's litany of the saints. And in her pinching poverty her one regret was that there was no family now for her son, brought up in loyalty and reverence, to serve. With his brains and accomplishments and well-bred appearance he might even have been recommended to a bank or brewery by the reigning earl. She remembered how Lord Templeton's father was for ever having applications made to him by needy respectable people.

Although Ballyorney and the Templetons became eventually the whole matter of her conversation, his mother had only once taken Richard to visit her first home. The expedition was quite an enterprise, with a child of seven, and it took all of a wet Saturday getting there and back. The house he had pictured as a fairy castle had been burnt so thoroughly to the ground that now only a screen of granite with holes where windows should have been recalled its former glory. Ruined glass-houses in the garden where weeds were shoulder-high; roofless stables in the yard; paths choked with grass and moss; lily ponds coated by green slime—Ballyorney was depressing beyond belief. Those names that had sounded so arcadian when his mother recited them—the yew walk, Lady Catherine's garden, the top meadow—would stand in his mind henceforth as symbols of waste. For one sublime moment on that mournful day the sun came out, and he would never forget the paddock ablaze with scarlet poppies. These owed nothing to tradition. They shot up on their own. Fresh recruits for a defeated army.

Was it this experience—never repeated, never referred to—that freed him from the thraldom of generations to the Templetons? He would make his own world. His one memorable row with his mother took place when he began to show the flair for pictures which was to make him quite rich so quickly; she closed her eyes, rolled her head reminiscently, and said, "I can hear Mr Charles." He had great taste, she remembered, but married unfortunately. "Am I never to do anything without your dragging in one of that bloody family?" he had blurted out then, and at once was sorry when he saw her face crumple. Blasphemy hurt her.

There was too much on his mind to allow him to dwell for long on nostalgia evoked by a bolted gate; if not exactly frightened, he was acutely nervous at the prospect ahead. It was one thing to show off at a riding-school, quite another to charge across country on a hired horse he had never seen or sat on before.

A mare—he knew enough to distinguish—she was waiting for him, saddled and bridled, with a girl at her head. Kind of eye and sleek of coat—the mare; he could not say as much for her attendant. With a nice economy she undermined the little confidence he was clinging to by telling him the hireling was "a bit above herself and inclined to play up", and advised him to "stand no nonsense if she was inclined to rear". The horse-box would be waiting here at five o'clock, by which time the light would have gone in any event. She helped him into the saddle, slapped the mare on the neck, and slouched away. Richard would have gladly paid her to stay until the hunt moved off. The mare was as restless as a child in church, shaking her head up and down as if she hoped to escape from the bridle; embarrassing him by a way she had of half-turning and presenting her rear to passing traffic.

Why was he submitting himself to this trial by ordeal? To realise some fantasy? To give colour to a self-portrait he had in preparation? The gods have a short way with hubristic antics of this sort, and one of them was assessing his presumption, judging by the insolence of his stare when Richard was apologising to a child with whose pony he had come into collision. A well-mounted man of Richard's own age—a stranger—but with something so familiar about his face that his failure to give any salute was painful. A humiliating admission. But for the moment Richard wished himself anywhere else than ill-at-ease in a milling crowd of excited horses.

The horn sounded at last. The concourse sorted itself out; a general shuffle gradually became a procession; there was a jingling of harness and a hurry of hooves as the hunt moved out of the village.

On a side road the horses began to trot; then a halt while the Master put his horse at a ditch. Richard was hardly aware of how his own arrived eventually in a green expanse over which the pack was spread out, running fast, followed by the Master and his huntsman. Behind them came the lucky few who had avoided the pushing and cursing and apologising that had dogged Richard's progress from road to field.

But now, seated firmly in the saddle, his mare's neck upright and steady at last, he found the cheerful pounding of her shoes on the firm turf sweeter than any music. Life will never be better than this. And his good feeling extended to the concentrated faces galloping beside him. At first there had been a good deal of overtaking when cavaliers who had been for some reason held back asserted the supremacy of their mounts; but by now a hierarchy had been established. Richard looked for the insolent witness of his incompetence but could not see him among the front runners.

Down one hill, up another; at the top, a fence— the first obstacle. Richard's heart stopped, but only for an instant. He must not let his mare feel the disquiet with which he looked between her ears at the barrier ahead. Over it went the hounds, with swinging tails; the Master took it in the manner born; on his heels went three in a row. All over, safe and well. It was Richard's turn; the mare had seen the fence, and there was considerable reassurance in the asthmatic roar she gave, as if she had dealt with its like before. He let her have her head, and as she left the ground leaned forward, grasped her mane, closed his eyes, and offered up a short prayer. Before he was sure they had taken off, his bottom felt the reassuring pressure of the saddle, and the gallop proceeded as if there had been no interruption. And after that the jumps were like Atlantic breakers that carried him forward on their crest.

There were checks and delays and false scents by way of contrast. Richard looked for his recent enemy, but he was nowhere to be seen. He had either fallen or dropped out. He had a childish longing to return that stare with interest, having proved himself in the chase. He would not have admitted to himself that he would have liked to have been seen at the five-bar gate. It was incredible what a man can do when his blood is up if he has a brave animal beneath him.

Towards the end of the hunt, the hounds ran into a narrow lane; this led to crowding and confusion because the passage admitted only one rider at a time. Richard chafed at the delay; and, to rub it in, white clouds that had lain like snowdrifts on the edge of the blue began to move, losing their peaceful character in the process; thinning as they spread and turning black. A sour wind whipped up a shower of rain. The light suddenly began to fail; it was time for the harriers to pack it in. The mare appeared to think so; she began to shake her head about, and someone in a plaintive voice asked Richard to control his mount. The waiting transport was several miles away, and to crown the day's sport for the harriers a trail had been laid from where they were now congregating back to the village where they had met in the morning.

Richard had no inkling of this pleasure in store. He had dismounted to rest his mare when he caught a glimpse of the unfriendly horseman of the morning, looking as if neither he nor his horse had taken even the gentlest exercise in the meanwhile. He seemed to be trying to attract Richard's attention. When he was sure he had, he moved off on his horse, indicating by a motion of his head that he expected Richard to follow. He would have gone anywhere to get his animal moving again, even if he might not have cared to admit that he was flattered by this summons. To be noticed by someone who has aroused in one a feeling of inferiority is irresistible to vanity. In every hunt there is an experienced campaigner who insists on taking his own line; Richard assumed that he was being shown how to steal a march on the other riders.

The manoeuvre involved going back a few hundred yards and turning in the open gate of private grounds, an audacity which, judging by the horseman's mien, did not cost him a thought. He rode up to the house—it looked like a rectory —and went round it into a small yard where a wooden gate led into a field. Jumping the gate from a stand, without looking back, he set off at a furious pace across the field, which Richard remembered having passed through during the hunt. But now they were going across their original tracks. They had parted with the rest of the company. This was a *pas de deux*.

The leader was concentrating on keeping in front; Richard had expected him to make some companionable gesture when he saw that his invitation had been accepted. But he hadn't deigned to turn his head, and he was riding a fresher horse. They were now in a long field, at the end of which rose the wall of a demesne. It seemed to ensure an end to their mad gallop. Just as well, Richard decided; he was beginning to worry about the condition of his mare; her breathing was becoming laboured. She had gone gallantly and galloped far. He should not ask her to do much more.

The rider in front, so far from slackening his pace, was using his heels. He had slightly altered course, and the reason soon became apparent. In one place the demesne wall had fallen, and in the gap a bank had been built, an Irish double bank, familiar to anyone who has hunted in the country but to Richard an experience as novel as it was alarming. His mare had carried him so well all day, he must not lose faith in her now. Were she content to scramble over the bank, all might be well. But if she tried to clear it in one leap . . . Fifty lengths ahead, the leading horse took off, landed close to the top, paused, and then jumped clear. How steep was the drop on the far side? Richard would know in a few seconds. Once again he leaned forward and grasped the mane, felt the familiar shudder in her loins as the mare gathered herself to spring . . .

It was quite dark. Where was he? And where had everybody gone? Comfortably stretched out on what his fingers decided was moss spread with autumn leaves, he was wary of making any movement that might discover some injury to his limbs. As if looking for the answer to some intellectual game, he began to piece his recent experiences together. His mare? Where was she? And what had put him down here? As he remembered the picture of a horse leaping off the top of a bank, he looked up and saw what was shutting out the light—from where he lay it could have been the face of a mountain.

His own face was hurting him. Gingerly, he put up fingers and they came away wet. Blood, he realised, when he looked at them. Then, with elaborate circumspection, he clambered to his feet. His head, in contrast to his

limbs, felt marvellously light. Nothing about him felt as if
it was broken; but when he started to walk the left leg
gave an impression of having set up in business on its own
account.

He was in a clearing in a wood, made presumably for
the benefit of the enthusiast who built the double bank. It
was a short distance to the avenue, and out of the trees the
light was better. The sun had asserted itself defiantly at its
going down, and there was an angry glow in the western
sky, wholly appropriate as a background to the ruins of
Ballyorney. That he should be in the Templeton demesne
was not a complete surprise. He had thought of the
possibility when he saw he was approaching some great
house. There were not so many in that part of the country.
What did astonish him—for all the lightness of his
head—was to see that the mansion was no longer in ruins.
The lower rooms were lit up; shining through the fanlight,
the hall lamps made a decorative pattern on the gravel
sweep. There were lights in some of the rooms upstairs.
They beckoned to him. The house seemed to be inviting
him in.

The front door stood open; the hall, he noticed, was lit
by gas; there was nobody to be seen, but through a door
immediately in front of him came the comfortable rumble
of voices and occasional laughter. When he opened the
door, five candle-lit faces turned to see who was
interrupting their dinner. He recognised every one of
them—three girls in very low dresses, all rather alike, and
at each end of the table their parents, looking old in early
middle age. The man, in particular, was as familiar as an old
friend. Richard knew those features much better than his
own father's; and it seemed inevitable and natural when he
rose from the table and came forward with hands
outstretched. "Richard, my dear boy. You have come back
after all."

Before their father could get to him the girls had fallen on Richard like house spaniels. Then one of them shrieked, "Oh, his poor face is bleeding." And there followed an interval while the scratches were being ministered to. While this was going on, the girls' mother, as insubstantial as the numerous veils and ribbons that adorned her person, pressed Richard's face against her thin bosom, murmuring incoherently and suffocating him with the scent of patchouli.

"Look to your mother, Lucy. This has been too much for her. Catherine, you had better lie down. Girls, help your mother up to bed."

Lord Templeton's agitation was extreme; and, certainly, Richard had never seen (except in an old daguerreotype his mother treasured) a face making so fragile a frame for the sad eyes that filled it.

"Now, Catherine, my dear, up you go. Richard will come and talk to you by and by," her husband assured her as she looked back longingly when her daughters were hustling her away.

"I'm afraid you must find your mother sadly failed," Lord Templeton said as he shepherded Richard to the table where an extra place had been laid for him. The servant in livery behind his chair said, "We are all delighted to see you back safe, Mr Richard, sir." Only when he tried to sit down did Richard become aware of his injured leg. It had to be manoeuvred into position.

"Eat up your soup. We were waiting for the main course, but I dare say there will be some confusion in the kitchen at the great news. Have you told them, Rooney?"

"Yes, my lord. Nancy had hysterics, but Mrs Evans threw a bucket of cold water over her. Everyone is delighted that Mr Richard is safe and well."

Richard was guiltily conscious of his host's scrutiny. "Tell me how you got here," he blurted out at last, "and why are you in riding clothes? And why, my dear boy, did you not think of sending a telegram to tell us you were on your way? You haven't changed, I fear. When the gardener's boy came in this morning, roaring his head off—MISTER RICHARD'S COME HOME—I thought your mother was going to faint. We hadn't heard a word from you since your letter came from Varna, and that was months ago. And then, when the household was congregated on the steps to greet you, and you never appeared, I can't tell you how cast down we all were, the women particularly. I felt like strangling the wretched boy with my own hands, but the poor little fellow looked more woebegone than any of us and nothing would shake him. He swore on the Bible and stuck to his story, that he had seen you in riding clothes, leaning on the paddock fence. You didn't look up or seem to notice him, so he ran ahead with the good tidings. What happened to you? Where did you hide yourself? When we were trying to get the truth out of the boy he let out that you looked very sad, which was hardly a compliment to the family."

"I've had a very bad fall, sir. My head feels very light. Could we postpone this talk for the present?"

"By all means. The main thing is that you are home and safe. I can't attempt to describe how your mother has worried over you. The electric telegraph is a marvellous invention; but I wonder are we ready for it. In my view it brings the war very close to home. And on top of our other troubles—the way that elder brother of yours is going on, spending his entire life, it seems, in Paris—Lucy comes begging us to let her go out to the Crimea as a nurse. She may think better of that now that you are home again. Well, girls, how is your mother?" He broke off as the three sisters came in and sat down in their places.

"Quite comfortable," the eldest said. "But I think it would be kind of Richard to go to her as soon as he can. I think she ought to get as much sleep as possible."

"Richard will go when he has finished his dinner. I'm broaching the last bottle of my grandfather's claret. It will be ready when you come down. Dick, you old rascal, I was waiting for the day."

Lady Templeton's condition kept the girls talking while Richard laid in to a succession of dishes, aided by a claret excellent in its way, but only a curtain-raiser to the entertainment to come.

"Tell me candidly, do you notice a great change in her?" the eldest girl enquired when she had an opportunity to talk to Richard by himself.

"She does look very frail," he said. He could hear himself, and he sounded genuinely concerned. He was too interested in the scene to question his own sincerity. He was in the play and watching the play, wholly absorbed by his two roles. Now Lord Templeton was inviting his confidence, lowering his voice so that it increased its penetrative power, and was audible in every corner of the room.

"I have misgivings about Dr Perry's treatment. Bleeding is all very well for my troubles. But for a delicate woman, suffering from chronic anaemia, does it seem sensible to be drawing blood regularly? I don't think so. Perry is a great improvement on his predecessor. Quite gentlemanly, and scrupulously clean in his person, not like that other sawbones, who may have been clever, but I couldn't stand the idea of his putting his filthy paws on your mother. But I wish I had faith in Perry's remedies. He certainly succeeds in keeping her quiet. She doesn't fuss anything like she used to."

One of the girls—Caroline—impatient at being kept out of the male conversation, raised the question of Richard's erratic behaviour. She wanted to know where he had been all day. The park had been scoured in the search.

Papa had driven into the village to make enquiries and
had gone all the way to the station to ask if his son had
travelled down on the morning train. "I know what you
did, you naughty boy. You couldn't delay even to see your
poor sisters. Nothing would do you but to go out with the
Harriers before you had even passed your family the time
of day. And we hadn't seen you for more than two years.
Admit it, you wretch. You could talk about nothing in
your letters to me except to enquire how the building of
the double bank was going on. There were times when I
was so infuriated I said it would be the price of you if you
broke your neck the very first time you tried to jump over
it."

"Caroline! What a horrible, horrible, thing to say," her
sisters exclaimed in chorus.

"I'm sorry," Caroline wailed, and began to cry in
earnest.

"They are all upset," their father explained to Richard.
"You know how it is with women."

There was a general anxiety to get Richard up to the
sick woman's room as soon as possible. When the girls rose
from the table, Caroline came very close to him and
whispered, "I've promised Edward." Before Richard could
think of a reply, she was following her sisters out of the
room. At the door, she turned and put a finger to her lips.

"I'll be waiting for you here. We can stretch our legs out
in comfort and enjoy our wine," Lord Templeton said
when Richard left him alone with the precious bottle. He
was not looking forward to the tête-à-tête upstairs.

The hall was empty; and it was only when he became
aware of this—he had expected to find himself in a flutter
of girls—that he realised he had no clue to help him to
find Lady Templeton's room. The stairs led on to a landing
on which there were six doors. Four, presumably, of the
principal bedrooms; the other two gave, respectively, on

to a passage containing other rooms and a smaller staircase leading to the upper floor. Richard knocked on all the four closed doors, once, gently, on each; and, when no answer came, loudly. There was something exasperating in the absurdity of the situation.

Without much conviction, he went the length of the passage, knocking, as he passed, on each door, not expecting to hear a voice, and not hearing one. Defiantly, he opened the last door and stepped into darkness. A mouse ran across his feet and scuttled into the wainscot. When his eyes became accustomed to the dark he saw that the room was empty. There was no carpet on the floor; the window was shuttered. On returning to the landing, he went up to the first of the four doors, and turned the handle. The full moon stared at him through a hole in the wall. He looked down where the floor should have been and saw a pit. When he stepped back, the door slammed. He stood, waiting for his heart to resume its normal beating, then dragged himself across the landing to the banisters, and used the rail to support a series of kangaroo hops on his working leg down the stairs. There was no light in the hall, and when he opened the dining-room door, where he expected to see Lord Templeton glowing in candlelight, the room was deserted. And someone had removed the furniture. The hall door stood open.

He came out of the dark and was relieved to see all the candles lit in Heaven. He went out through the open door and as before followed the course of the avenue without being conscious of making any decision in the matter. Had his body felt as light as his head, he would not have been surprised to find himself wafted down the drive and over the iron gate at its prosaic end. But he was attached to a deadly weight in his injured leg. He had to drag it along; and his progress was as slow as a snail's. Once he halted and looked back at the house where, a few hours earlier, he had met with so loving a welcome. It had vanished. The black outline of the roofless pile that had taken its place seemed to threaten him. He turned away, but the menace of that transformation cast its shadow over the moon's delight. The magic of the evening had fled, and the stars, when he looked up at them, were as hard as diamonds. They danced, but not for him. He was alone in the night. Or not alone; for he was suddenly gripped by a fear that had been gradually building inside him since he went to look for Lady Templeton. In the distraction of his recent visit he had forgotten the hunt and the devilish rider who had led him into this adventure. No decent member of the Hunt would have let him lie at the bottom of a ditch or allowed his horse to run loose. The wooden-faced girl groom must have been distracted by his failure to report. He was sorry for that.

The genial spell had been rudely broken. There was evil abroad. It leered from the skeleton of the ruined house; it was following him. He was certain of its presence. Behind him? How close? He dared not look back. His spine froze under the intensity of its concentrated malevolence. He tried to go faster, but the effort resulted in a stab of pain in his groin, so exquisite that he threw his head back involuntarily. There was nothing there. Nobody. He could see down the avenue as far as the house and across the fields where patient cattle stood waiting for the dawn to break. He was not threatened by anyone. The silence of the night which had been absolute until then—he knew when a bird moved on its branch from the rustle of a leaf—was shattered by his sudden laughter. It rang across the sleeping fields and echoed in the distant hills. He looked up at the stars; they too were dancing with relief, and now, at last, he was coming close to the trees at the lodge gate. From under their shadow the avenue ran like a ribbon in a bride's hair until it arrived at his feet. He liked that image as it occurred to him, and the soft shadows, after the garishness of the sky, had a peacefulness, a mystery (becoming to a bride). They lay all about the end of the bright path, deepest under the wych elm which hid the lodge from view—the lodge in which his mother was born fifty-five years ago.

The shadows, perturbed by the moon's indecent display, were whispering to themselves, coming gently together for comfort, or stealing shyly away. One he saw distinctly move from the darkest corner and creep into the moon's path where it lay like a dark pool until it came forward, assuming a more emphatic shape. A ship? No. A horse. A horse with a man in the saddle. The illusion was complete until the shadow moved back and merged in the others.

Richard was concentrating so hard on pulling his bad leg along that he had never thought to ask himself what was to happen when he did arrive at the gate, how he was going to scale it, where he intended to go after that. Very soon these questions would force themselves on his attention. Meanwhile . . . He looked up and was startled to see how the shadows had lost their opacity. The lodge was quite plainly to be seen and, beside it, as if on guard, a man on horseback. He must have had Richard under surveillance for the whole of his slow, painful journey. If so, he gave no sign. Richard was not taken in by that. He recognised him at once. That arrogant carriage of the head . . . There was going to be a confrontation now, and Richard welcomed it. He was no longer afraid. His ghosts were laid. Nothing human could frighten him.

The rider moved his horse away from the lodge, bringing it into the full light of the moon. The effect was dramatic. Richard took note of two things: the rider was wearing the uniform of a cavalry officer, with a rent in the tunic where it was discoloured by a recent stain; and only one foot was in the stirrups, the other hung limply by the horse's side. The other thing that Richard noticed was the horse. It was not the one that the stranger had ridden in the hunt. He was seated on Richard's mare.

He suffered Richard's stare without any show of resentment; but, when the examination was completed, rode slowly back towards the trees, pausing to raise a hand in salute. There was no trace of his former insolence in the gesture, and a brother could not have looked on Richard more gently. It was difficult to believe that this soldier and the afternoon's devil were the same person. In trying to reconcile these opposites, Richard was suddenly assailed by an irresistible longing to look once more into the stranger's appraising eyes, for he was convinced that if he were to he would see his own reflected there. He tried to call out, but no sound came from his throat; tried to run forward, but his injured leg fastened him to the ground. The soldier must not be allowed to escape. Richard had a question to put to him, a question that would haunt him to the edge of the grave if he did not get the answer now.

When he arrived at the lodge, the soldier was nowhere to be seen; but the mare was peacefully cropping the short grass under the trees, and looking none the worse for her adventures.

JOYCE CARY

A Private Ghost

As soon as he waked in the morning, Peter, aged eight, felt a difference. Then he remembered that his father and mother were away—they had gone to Dublin very suddenly for the week-end—and that Grand-aunt was also away. His grand-aunt lived close by, and always when his parents had been away she had come to stay and watch over the children. But now she was in a Dublin hospital. No one had come to hear his prayers last night. This was why, he thought, he felt a difference.

His sister Noni, in the next bed, did not notice a difference. As soon as she waked, she proposed to come into his bed, as usual; but he refused her firmly. He was devoted to Noni, and she adored him, but at the moment he did not want adoration. He was preoccupied, listening intently to the household. Noni at six was too young to notice the difference.

Certainly, the household *was* different. It was so different that he could hardly recognise it. The cat next door in the day nursery was miaowing loudly in a despairing voice; it had not been let out yet. Down in the kitchen, below the night-nursery window, someone with a very deep hoarse voice, some old beggar, perhaps, was talking to a dog. And this strange dog was padding round the floor, rattling its claws on the linoleum, and uttering now and then a little whine.

What was stranger still on this strange day was that when Annie the nurse came in five minutes later to get the children up, Lizzie the housemaid came with her. Lizzie and Annie had not been speaking for weeks past. But now they came in laughing, and Lizzie whispered something. Then she ran out of the nursery and shouted down the well of the stairs to the cook, "I told Annie on you, Maggie." Even her voice was a new voice, more like Maggie's when she was drunk. But Lizzie didn't drink.

Breakfast in the day nursery was delayed, and Noni grew impatient. She climbed into her chair and beat on the table with a spoon. Annie, however, was down in the kitchen telling some tale to the beggar, and what was still queerer, she had left the nursery doors wide open. The nurseries, usually so jealously kept aloof, now seemed as public as the back stairs, through which all these peculiar noises were piped direct to the children. Peter sat at the table listening. He frowned. He did not like the difference in the house. He felt a certain nervousness, and he also felt a certain responsibility, but for what, he did not know.

Suddenly he took the spoon out of Noni's hand and said, "Don't do that—it's rude." This was unexpected to Noni. Peter was usually kind to her. She flushed with pain and surprise. Her forehead crinkled and the corners of her mouth turned down; she was about to cry. But Peter's glance daunted her. He said severely, "You're not a baby any more."

Lizzie came in again when Annie brought the tray. The two were giggling together again at something that had happened in the kitchen. And then Lizzie shouted from the window at Mrs Conor, the gardener's wife, slopping past in the rain with a sack over her head and her skirt turned up to the knees. Mrs Conor answered with cheerful yells, and soon she, too, came up to the nursery. She spent the whole morning there, drinking tea and telling stories that made the usually dignified Annie explode through her nose with protesting cries, "Oh, Mrs Conor, you're killing me!"

Mrs Conor stayed all day. After the children's dinner, at noon, all the staff gathered in the day nursery, and there was great laughter when Lizzie was persuaded to ride the rocking-horse—not that Lizzie needed much persuading. She was a pale, high-breasted girl, with big grey eyes and a little round mouth, who was dancing mad, and even when the family were there she would go bouncing through the rooms as if she were late for a ball. When she was on the horse, she laughed so much that she nearly fell off. Then Maggie pushed the horse to make it rock harder, and Lizzie gave a shriek like an engine and began to be angry. But when they all laughed she stopped being angry and proposed a dance.

So Annie played the gramophone. They did not dance, however; they were tired of the idea already. And they began to make much of the children. All of them were devoted to Peter and Noni, and now in the exuberance of their holiday, they were demonstrative, they competed in affection. Lizzie tickled Noni till she laughed herself crimson, and this almost provoked a scene. For Annie, the nurse, taken suddenly jealous, snatched the child away and said, "That's enough." Lizzie turned upon her and laughed in her nose, saying, "You, Annie—" At that moment, Mrs Conor, the hanger-on, who was not quite of the inner household but earned her cups of tea by her good stories and her flattery, made a quick diversion. She lifted Peter to her lap and stroked his hair, which was as pale as flax. "Oh, the pet—the spit of his grandda. And do you know, my prince, that I've seen him? I've seen your grandda with my own eyes."

The maids gazed at her. Annie's breast was still heaving, and Lizzie's little mouth was still pushed out in scorn, but they were attentive. They knew that Mrs Conor had some trick in hand.

"Come now, Mrs Conor," said Annie in her downright way. "The old master is dead this forty years."

"Wasn't that the one that drowned himself in the river?" Lizzie asked.

"Forty-three years," said Mrs Conor, "and that was before I was born, but I've seen him." And looking at the child, she said to him, "And how do you think that was, my pet? How do you think I saw him that was dead?" Peter gazed earnestly at Mrs Conor, and Noni, who had come to lean against her brother, made big eyes round his arm. They knew the question was not meant to be answered; it was simply an introduction to Mrs Conor's story. "It was when I was eight—just your age, my pet—that I saw him walk. He was all in white, and while he walked he kept shaking his hands and the water was dripping from him. And, bless you, I didn't know who he was then, or what it meant. But I was frightened, and I ran to my mother, and it was then she told me about the old master. And she said if I was to see him again I must cross myself."

There was a short silence. All four of the servants were gazing at the two children to see the effect of this tale.

"And they say," said Mrs Conor, "they say that it's only a child has ever seen the old master walk."

"Was it a ghost?" Noni asked in a loud voice.

"Yes, indeed. You wouldn't see him living when he was dead, would you, pet?"

"Ghosts are only stories." Noni said. "Pappy told me."

Peter opened his mouth to say the same thing. But as he glanced up he caught the maids' eyes fixed upon him, and suddenly he was not so sure that they were playing a trick upon him. When Annie or Maggie codded him about potatoes that grew on trees or the man in the moon, they had a laugh in them. They might look grave, but you could feel the laugh. But now there was no laugh, and their grave faces had a different gravity. All at once, he was not so confident of his father's assurances, even about ghosts. Did his father know that things could be so different at home when he was away?

"There aren't such things," Noni said indignantly. But Peter looked at her severely, and she turned red.

"Well, now," Mrs Conor said, "do you tell me I'm telling you lies?"

The children looked at her, and Peter said, "Grandda fell in when he was fishing."

"I wouldn't know that," Mrs Conor said. "But if he only fell in, why would he walk?"

"Why, indeed?" Lizzie said. "And why only for children?"

"Well now," Mrs Conor said, "I wouldn't know that either, but isn't it the same with the fairies? They say it's only children and naturals can see the wee folk. And so you never saw the like of him, Master Peter?"

Peter shook his head, and Mrs Conor looked round at her audience. "If anyone were to see the old master, it would be this one that's so like him." And suddenly she winked. Mrs Conor was a good winker; she could close either eye without the slightest change of expression on the other side of her face. That's why Peter saw only her grave good-natured countenance, while Maggie and Lizzie and Annie had a glimpse of enormous slyness. Mrs Conor once more turned her grave mild face towards Peter. "Yes, my dear, you would be the one, for aren't you the spit of him? It's a wonder that you haven't seen him yet, for it's my belief he crosses that back-yard every day of the week on his way from the water to the cemetery."

"What, Mrs Conor?" Lizzie said. "Every day of the week? I wouldn't like to think that."

"No, indeed," said Maggie, coming into the game. Maggie was old and tired, and slow in her mind, but still she was ready to take her part in a good game. "No, indeed," she said. "Why, I'd be afraid to go into the yard if I thought that."

"But then you wouldn't see him," Annie said. "It would be only Master Peter here that would see him."

"It was about six o'clock in the evening that I saw him," said Mrs Conor. "And they said that was the time that he went into the water."

There was another long pause, and then Lizzie said, "Well now, I wonder, would Master Peter see him if he looked at six o'clock?"

"It'd be a bit dark at six," Maggie said.

"It'd have to be," said Mrs Conor. "You don't think that ghosts will walk in daylight? But there, I'm not saying that Master Peter would see his grandda on any day of week, dark as it might be."

"No," Maggie said "It's only that he might take a look some evening if he wouldn't be afraid."

"It's well he might be," Lizzie said. She gave a deep sigh and gazed into the air with her big grey eyes, imagining the terror of ghosts.

"He would not!" Annie cried. "Would you, my darling? Would you now?"

Peter made no answer to this. He understood the challenge. He had been challenged before, and usually in a trick, as when Maggie had dared him to open a parcel, which, so she said, might have a bomb in it, and it had let out a jumping jack, which hit him on the nose. But he had not really believed that there would be a bomb in a parcel. Who would put bombs in parcels? Ghost were quite another thing. And it was true that his grandfather had died young, and tragically.

"Oh, he's the brave boy always," Mrs Conor said, and Maggie came in hastily, "Sure. There never was any of the family afraid of anything."

"Would you look for your grandda?" Lizzie asked, staring at the boy with her big eyes.

Peter, staring back and wondering at this strange excited Lizzie, answered, "You mean in the yard?"

"You wouldn't have to go in the yard," said Mrs Conor. "You could see from the kitchen window. Aye, it would be better from the window."

"And what better day than today, when themselves is out of it?" Lizzie said.

"It's stopped raining," Peter said, as if he had not noticed Lizzie's suggestion. "Can I go to Willy?" Willy was the garden boy, a close friend of Peter's, but Annie did not always approve of their meetings which, she considered, were often too exciting for Peter and kept him wakeful at night.

"There now," Lizzie muttered. "I knew he'd get out of it."

"Of course you can go to Willy," Mrs Conor said quickly. "He'd be in the cabbages this minute. And I tell you, why wouldn't ye have supper in the kitchen, too—for a treat? I'm sure Annie wouldn't mind just for today.'

"Oh, yes!" cried Noni. "Oh, yes, yes please."

And even Peter, disturbed as he was by the confusion in the house, was pleased by this suggestion. "Oh, do, Annie. I'd like that very much," he said.

"Sure, my pet," Annie said.

"Indeed, and ye shall," said Maggie, winking at Mrs Conor, but so clumsily that Noni noticed and stared at her eye. Maggie was very red, and seemed about to burst.

"And as for ghosts, Miss Noni," said Mrs Conor, "sure your pappy may be right after all. Why, I wouldn't be too sure myself. It's so long since I saw one that indeed your grandda mightn't have been one at all. There now, Maggie, don't I hear your kettle?" And the four rushed suddenly out of the room so violently that they jammed on the narrow back stairs and Lizzie gave a squeak of laughter. Then, below, the kitchen door banged shut behind them.

Peter paid no more attention to their nonsense. He was too pleased with himself for eluding Mrs Conor's embarrassing proposal. Joyfully he hurried off to see Willy in the garden. He even allowed Noni to take his hand and go with him, stipulating only that she should not speak to Willy.

Noni was perfectly satisfied to be beside her darling and listen to his conversation with Willy, while the party moved from the cabbages to the byre, the byre to the pigsty, the pigsty to the pump, where Willy completed his last duty by filling the house tanks, so that, as he said thoughtfully, "You wains have your baths the night."

Peter provided most of the talk, giving, for instance, a full account of the mammoth found in Russia under the ice and explaining that whales were really animals, and had milk. He hadn't had so good a day with Willy for a week, and he started back to the kitchen in the highest spirits. The reason the children loved supper in the kitchen was that the maids, and especially Lizzie, were such good company with their gossip and their jokes. They were always playing some trick on each other and laughing. Last time, Lizzie had pulled Annie's chair away and caused her to sit down hard on the floor. The children had laughed until they could not eat, and Lizzie herself had had to say that they must behave themselves better or they would not be asked again.

They were laughing in recollection of this performance when they came into the kitchen. But what a surprise!

There was no one there but old Maggie, and the table was not by the stove, but pushed into the window embrasure, close against the window itself. And when Maggie had placed them in their chairs, at opposite ends of the table, she made for the door.

"Oh, Maggie," Noni wailed, "I want to have supper with you all." But Maggie muttered something about the storeroom, and went out, shutting the door after her.

Almost at the same moment, there was a moaning cry from the yard, and Peter, who had been put facing the yard gate that led from the front lawn and the river, looked up and saw the ghost. It was just coming through the gate.

The lamp in the kitchen was turned low, and the yard was lighted only by the sky, which was a pale-green colour. The yard, surrounded by barns and stables, by the byre and garage, all in dark-reddish bricks, was paved with dark-blue cinders; these dark buildings and the dark cinders soaked up the light from above. The air in the yard seemed to be without light, so that the whiteness of the ghost was as bright as a swan's feathers on a dark evening. The ghost was all in white; a short thick figure in a sheet, which was pulled over its forehead in front, and which covered its body and fell to the ground so that the creature did not seem to have feet.

When it passed the gardener's shed, it turned towards the kitchen window. And now Peter could see, under the white fold of the sheet, a face as white, except that its eyes were like enormous black holes, and its mouth was grey. This mouth was moving all the time as if crying.

Peter was fixed in such fear, such horror, that he could not take his eyes off this face with its weeping mouth. He got down slowly from his chair and retreated a pace backwards; but this brought him up against the end of the embrasure. And he stood there, fixed, helpless, unable to move, speak, or think.

"What are you doing, Peter?" Noni said, surprised at his getting down from his chair. Then the ghost moaned again, more loudly. Noni looked round, gave a shriek, and ran to her brother. Peter held her tight and drew her to one side—she hid her face against his ribs.

The ghost was now four or five yards from the window. Peter could see long leaves of river weed glistening wet on its shoulders and the water pouring down the white folds to the ground—the eyes were shining palely in the middle of their great black holes. It was staring at him and shaking its hands all the time as if in grief. He thought, "It's crying—it wants to tell me something." He was shivering in terror that the creature would speak to him, and yet he could not run away. He felt he had to wait for the message.

The ghost took one more step towards him and gave another long deep heartbreaking moan. Noni gripped Peter convulsively and uttered shriek after shriek. But the ghost's next move was to its right. With a wavering, wobbling motion, it glided slowly towards the back corner of the house, where it suddenly vanished behind the porch of the scullery.

Almost at the same moment, Annie, Lizzie, and Maggie burst into the kitchen. Peter, mechanically patting and stroking Noni, gazed at them with wide vague eyes as if he had forgotten their existence. Noni stopped screaming and ran towards Annie. "It came—it came—we saw it!" she cried. But the maids were staring at Peter, with eyes nearly as wide as his own—half curious, half alarmed at the child's fearfully white face and crazy expression.

"What—what happened then?" said Annie in a stammering voice.

And now Mrs Conor, rather breathless, came darting into the kitchen from the scullery. She still had some burnt cork under her right eye, but she covered it with her hand, so that the children could not see it. "What's wrong?" she said. "Was that Miss Noni I heard?"

"They saw him, Mrs Conor!" Lizzie exclaimed. "They saw the old master in the yard—did you ever hear the like of that?"

Peter came to himself, walked out of his corner, and took Noni's hand. "It was nothing," he said. And his face turned very red.

"A ghost, nothing?" said Mrs Conor. "Weren't you afeared?"

"We didn't see anything," he said. "It was only Noni being silly. You didn't see anything, did you, Noni?"

Noni stared at him. Then she slowly shook her head. She didn't know why Peter was telling this enormous lie, but she was glad to support him.

He then walked her slowly and with great dignity towards the hall door. The maids parted and let him go. Even Mrs Conor was taken aback by this strangely aloof Peter. He led Noni through the hall into the drawing-room. He seldom went to the drawing-room except on state occasions, in his best clothes. For him, it was a place of ceremony, where grown-up persons of distinction conferred together in quiet tones and a reserved manner upon important matters—births, deaths, marriages, money, family affairs.

As soon as they entered the room, Noni protested that it was a ghost. "I *saw* it." Peter shut the door firmly behind them and cut off the excited chatter of the maids. Then he led Noni to the middle of the carpet and explained to her, kindly but gravely, "Yes, it was grandpapa. But don't talk to them about it. They'd only laugh and he's our own grandpapa."

T. CROFTON CROKER

Teigue of the Lee

"I can't stop in the house—I won't stop in it for all the money that is buried in the old castle of Carrigrohan. If ever there was such a thing in the world—to be abused to my face night and day, and nobody to the fore doing it! and then, if I'm angry, to be laughed at with a great roaring ho, ho, ho! I won't stay in the house after to-night, if there was not another place in the country to put my head under." This angry soliloquy was pronounced in the hall of the old manor-house of Carrigrohan by John Sheehan. John was a new servant; he had been only three days in the house, which had the character of being haunted, and in that short space of time he had been abused and laughed at by a voice which sounded as if a man spoke with his head in a cask; nor could he discover who was the speaker, or from whence the voice came. "I'll not stop here," said John, "and that ends the matter."

"Ho, Ho, ho! be quiet, John Sheehan, or else worse will happen to you."

John instantly ran to the hall window, as the words were evidently spoken by a person immediately outside, but no one was visible. He had scarcely placed his face at the pane of glass when he heard another loud "Ho, ho, ho!" as if behind him in the hall; as quick as lightning he turned his head, but no living thing was to be seen.

"Ho, ho, ho, John!" shouted a voice that appeared to come from the lawn before the house, "do you think you'll see Teigue?—Oh, never! as long as you live! so leave alone looking after him, and mind your business; there's plenty of company to dinner from Cork to be here to-day, and 'tis time you had the cloth laid."

"Lord bless us! there's more of it!—I'll never stay another day here," repeated John.

"Hold your tongue, and stay where you are quietly, and play no tricks on Mr Pratt, as you did on Mr Jervois about the spoons."

John Sheehan was confounded by this address from his invisible persecutor, but nevertheless he mustered courage enough to say—"Who are you?—come here, and let me see you, if you are a man"; but he received in reply only a laugh of unearthly derision, which was followed by a "Good-bye—I'll watch you at dinner, John!"

"Lord between us and harm! this beats all—I'll watch you at dinner!—maybe you will—'tis the broad daylight, so 'tis no ghost; but this is a terrible place, and this is the last day I'll stay in it. How does he know about the spoons?—if he tells it, I'm a ruined man!—there was no living soul could tell it to him but Tim Barrett, and he's far enough off in the wilds of Botany Bay now, so how could he know it—I can't tell for the world! But what's that I see there at the corner of the wall!—'tis not a man!—oh, what a fool I am! 'tis only the old stump of a tree!—But this is a shocking place—I'll never stop in it, for I'll leave the house to-morrow; the very look of it is enough to frighten any one."

The mansion had certainly an air of desolation; it was situated in a lawn which had nothing to break its uniform level save a few tufts of narcissuses and a couple of old trees. The house stood at a short distance from the road, it was upwards of a century old, and Time was doing his work upon it; its walls were weather-stained in all colours, its roof showed various white patches, it had no look of comfort; all was dim and dingy without, and within there was an air of gloom, of departed and departing greatness, which harmonised well with the exterior. It required all the exuberance of youth and of gaiety to remove the impression, almost amounting to awe, with which you trod the huge square hall, paced along the gallery which surrounded the hall, or explored the long rambling passages below stairs. The ballroom, as the large drawing-room was called, and several other apartments, were in a state of decay; the walls were stained with damp; and I remember well the sensation of awe which I felt creeping over me when, boy as I was, and full of boyish life, and wild and ardent spirits, I descended to the vaults; all without and within me became chilled beneath their dampness and gloom—their extent, too, terrified me; nor could the merriment of my two schoolfellows, whose father, a respectable clergyman, rented the dwelling for a time, dispel the feelings of a romantic imagination until I once again ascended to the upper regions.

John had pretty well recovered himself as the dinner-hour approached, and the several guests arrived. They were all seated at table, and had begun to enjoy the excellent repast, when a voice was heard from the lawn:

"Ho, ho, ho, Mr Pratt, won't you give poor Teigue some dinner? ho, ho, a fine company you have there, and plenty of everything that's good; sure you won't forget poor Teigue?"

John dropped the glass he had in his hand.

"Who is that?" said Mr Pratt's brother, an officer of the artillery.

"That is Teigue," said Mr Pratt laughing, "whom you

must often have heard me mention."

"And pray, Mr Pratt," enquired another gentleman, "who is Teigue?"

"That," he replied, "is more than I can tell. No one has ever been able to catch even a glimpse of him. I have been on the watch for a whole evening with three of my sons, yet, although his voice sometimes sounded almost in my ear, I could not see him. I fancied, indeed, that I saw a man in a white frieze jacket pass into the door from the garden to the lawn, but it could be only fancy, for I found the door locked, while the fellow, whoever he is, was laughing at our trouble. He visits us occasionally, and sometimes a long interval passes between his visits, as in the present case; it is now nearly two years since we heard that hollow voice outside the window. He has never done any injury that we know of, and once when he broke a plate, he brought one back exactly like it."

"It is very extraordinary," said several of the company.

"But," remarked a gentleman to young Mr Pratt, "your father said he broke a plate; how did he get it without your seeing him?"

"When he asks for some dinner, we put it outside the window and go away; whilst we watch he will not take it, but no sooner have we withdrawn than it is gone."

"How does he know that you are watching?"

"That's more than I can tell, but he either knows or suspects. One day my brothers Robert and James with myself were in our back parlour, which has a window into the garden, when he came outside and said, 'Ho, ho, ho! master James, and Robert, and Henry, give poor Teigue a glass of whiskey.' James went out of the room, filled a glass with whiskey, vinegar, and salt, and brought it to him. Here, Teigue,' said he, 'come for it now.' 'Well, put it down, then, on the step outside the window.' This was done, and we stood looking at it. 'There, now, go away,' he shouted. We retired, but still watched it. 'Ho, ho! you are watching Teigue; go out of the room, now, or I won't take it.' We went outside the door and returned, the glass was gone, and a moment after we heard him roaring and cursing frightfully. He took away the glass, but the next day the glass was on the stone step under the window, and there were crumbs of bread in the inside, as if he had put it in his pocket; from that time he was not heard till to-day."

"Oh," said the colonel, "I'll get a sight of him! you are not used to these things; an old soldier has the best chance; and as I shall finish my dinner with this wing, I'll be ready for him when he speaks next.—Mr Bell, will you take a glass of wine with me?"

"Ho, ho! Mr Bell," shouted Teigue. "Ho, ho! Mr Bell, you were a Quaker long ago. Ho, ho! Mr Bell, you're a pretty boy;—a pretty Quaker you were; and now you're no Quaker, nor anything else; ho, ho! Mr Bell. And there's Mr Parkes: to be sure, Mr Parkes looks mighty fine today, with his powdered head, and his grand silk stockings, and his brand new rakish-red waistcoat.—And there's Mr Cole—did you ever see such a fellow? a pretty company you've brought together, Mr Pratt: kiln-dried Quakers, butter-buying buckeens from Mallow-lane, and a drinking exciseman from the Coal-quay, to meet the great thundering artillery-general that is come out of the Indies, and is the biggest dust of them all."

"You scoundrel!" exclaimed the Colonel. "I'll make you show yourself"; and, snatching up his sword from a corner of the room, he sprang out of the window upon the lawn. In a moment a shout of laughter, so hollow, so unlike any human sound, made him stop, as well as Mr Bell, who with a huge oak stick was close at the colonel's heels; others of the party followed on the lawn, and the remainder rose and went to the windows. "Come on, colonel," said Mr Bell; "let us catch this imprudent rascal."

"Ho, ho! Mr Bell, here I am—here's Teigue—why don't you catch him?—Ho, ho, Colonel Pratt, what a pretty soldier you are to draw your sword upon poor Teigue, that never did any body harm."

"Let us see your face, you scoundrel," said the colonel.

"Ho, ho, ho—look at me—look at me: do you see the wind, Colonel Pratt?—you'll see Teigue as soon; so go in and finish your dinner."

"If you're upon the earth I'll find you, you villain!" said the colonel, whilst the same unearthly shout of derision seemed to come from behind an angle of the building. "He's round that corner," said Mr Bell—"run, run."

They followed the sound, which was continued at intervals along the garden wall, but could discover no human being; at last both stopped to draw breath, and in an instant, almost at their ears, sounded the shout.

"Ho, ho, ho! Colonel Pratt, do you see Teigue now?—do you hear him:—Ho, ho, ho! you're a fine colonel to follow the wind."

"Not that way, Mr Bell—not that way; come here," said the colonel.

"Ho, ho, ho! what a fool you are; do you think Teigue is going to show himself to you in the field, there: But, colonel, follow me if you can:—you a soldier! ho, ho, ho!" The colonel was enraged—he followed the voice over hedge and ditch, alternately laughed at and taunted by the unseen object of his pursuit—(Mr Bell, who was heavy, was soon thrown out), until at length, after being led a weary chase, he found himself at the top of the cliff, over that part of the river Lee which, from its great depth, and the blackness of its water, has received the name of Hell-hole. Here, on the edge of the cliff, stood the colonel, out of breath and mopping his forehead with his handkerchief, while the voice, which seemed close at his feet, exclaimed—"Now, Colonel Pratt—now, if you're a soldier, here's a leap for you;—now look at Teigue—why don't you look at him—Ho, ho, ho! Come along: you're warm, I'm sure, Colonel Pratt, so come in and cool yourself; Teigue is going to have a swim!" The voice seemed as descending amongst the trailing ivy and brushwood which clothes this picturesque cliff nearly from top to bottom, yet it was impossible that any human being could have found footing. "Now, colonel, have you courage to take the leap?—Ho, ho, ho! what a pretty soldier you are. Good-bye—I'll see you again in ten minutes above, at the house—look at your watch colonel: there's a dive for you"; and a heavy plunge into the water was heard. The colonel stood still, but no sound followed, and he walked slowly back to the house, not quite half a mile from the Crag.

"Well, did you see Teigue?" said his brother, whilst his nephews, scarcely able to smother their laughter, stood by. "Give me some wine," said the colonel. "I never was led such a dance in my life: the fellow carried me all round and round, till he brought me to the edge of the cliff, and then down he went into Hell-hole, telling me he'd be here in ten minutes: 'tis more than that now, but he's not come."

"Ho, ho ho! colonel, isn't he here?—Teigue never told a lie in his life: but, Mr Pratt, give me a drink and my dinner, and then good night to you all, for I'm tired; and that's the colonel's doing." A plate of food was ordered: it was placed by John, with fear and trembling, on the lawn under the window. Everyone kept on the watch, and the plate remained undisturbed for some time.

"Ah, Mr Pratt, will you starve poor Teigue? Make everyone go away from the windows, and Master Henry out of the tree, and Master Richard off the garden wall."

The eyes of the company were turned to the tree and the garden wall; the two boys' attention was occupied in getting down: the visitors were looking at them; and "Ho, ho ho!—good luck to you, Mr Pratt!—'tis a good dinner, and there's the plate, ladies and gentlemen—goodbye to you, colonel—goodbye, Mr Bell! goodbye to you all!"—brought their attention back, when they saw the empty plate lying on the grass; and Teigue's voice was heard no more for that evening. Many visits were afterwards paid by Teigue; but never was he seen, nor was any discovery ever made of his person or character.

MARY LAVIN

The Dead Soldier

When Matty enlisted his mother and his sister Solly went up to Dublin to see him off *en route* for France—and the front. When they got off the train the sun was still to be seen in the alleyways and spaces between the buildings, but by the time they had made their way to the docks it was dark. They stood under a lamp-post so they would be sure to pick him out from the other men as he marched past. When they heard the band in the distance they stood very close together, and when the children came running along in the dark, ahead of the soldiers, the old woman began to tremble.

The soldiers came along four abreast. They came along the quay in dark ranks, advancing steadily, rank after rank, inevitably, like the ranked waves of the sea. And under the lamp-post, where the women stood, the black ranks foamed into faces, for a moment, and then went onward again, rank after rank, into the darkness where the river sirens occasionally wailed.

They knew instinctively when the rank that Matty was in came near, and when his face shone in the light they took the full advantage of their eyes in staring at him.

They smiled and put their hands to their lips. But they couldn't be sure if he saw them.

When they were in the train going home again, the old woman was upset.

"If we ran as far as the next lamp-post we would have seen him again!"

"Now, Mother!" said Solly. "You know yourself that Matty would not have wanted us to do that. He'd only be saying afterwards that we made a laughing stock of ourselves before the other men, running along the street trying to keep up with the soldiers."

"That's like what a daughter--would say," said the old woman. "A son would never say the like of that. A son would never see anything to laugh at in his own mother, no matter what she did."

"All the same," said Solly, "I'm glad we stayed where we were. We might have lost the way if we went any farther from the station, and we might have missed the train." She looked out the carriage window at the strange pattern of the lighted city that was fading against the black sky, and she wondered what got into men that they wanted to go off to fight in a foreign country that meant nothing to them, one way or another. Matt was a real Irishman, if ever there was one, and yet he was one of the first to give his name and go off to France, although the old woman cried and threw herself down on the floor and besought him not to go.

"Women don't understand," was all Matty said, patting the old woman's head.

"Leave the way!" he said to Solly, and he went towards the door.

"Stay where you are, Solly!" said the old woman.

"I can't stop him, Mother, if he's set on going," said Solly, and she had to stand aside and let him pass.

That was only four days ago, and now he was gone; and

in a few hours they would be back in the empty house, making up the fire that had never been let die out before, since the old woman came into the house as a young bride in a blue dress, Solly knew all about the blue dress. It had cerise bows down the front. The old woman was always talking about it. "I suppose she'll never talk about it again," thought Solly. "She'll talk about nothing but Matty now, till the day he comes home again."

The talk about Matty began the minute they got into house. As they made up the fire the old woman told Solly stories about the time Matty was a child, and even when Solly went out to the well she could hear the old woman talking to herself; laughing over some things and sobbing over other things. When she thought of the times she had been hurt and worried when Matty was growing up, she laughed, because those times were gone; but when she thought of the gay times, when he used to bring her home a bunch of cornflowers and poppies from the field, she sobbed, and wiped her eyes with her skirt, because those times were gone as well.

Both the chaff and the grain had gone on the wind, and the barren days had begun. In the house where seven men had sat down, to be served by herself and Solly, there was no one now to sit down but the servers. Matty was the last of the men to leave home, and the force that drove him out to his adventure was beyond the comprehension of women.

Week after week there was no other talk but talk about Matty. The priest called, and he had to stay for an hour and a half listening to an account of the time that Matty played hurley for the county.

When he was going he called Solly out into the yard.

"Let her talk about him all she wants. Don't stop her," he said. "It will be an ease to her mind."

When they got the news that Matty was killed Solly

˙didn't bother to go over to the priest's house, because she knew that he would say the same thing. What else was there to say? And so she went around the house listening to the old woman and encouraging her to talk.

Whenever there was a death in the parish Solly always took the opportunity to console her mother.

"Murty Glynn is dead, Mother. He had a hard death. He was dying for three days and three nights. They said it was agony to look at him. Isn't any death better than that? Isn't a blow of a bullet a grand death compared with that?"

"I don't know," said the old woman. "It's a great thing to die in your bed."

"It's a great thing to die in peace! You wouldn't want to think Matty was lying inside there in the room, writhing in agony, would you? Isn't it better to think of him laughing one minute and lying at peace the next minute?"

"I suppose you're right," said the old woman. "But it's a nice thing to bc able to lay a body out, and see that he gets the best in candles and flowers. It's nice to get a last look at him before he's put down into the grave."

"I think it's not right to talk like that, Mother. It's flying in the face of God's goodness. It's nice to remember him as we saw him last, marching along to the sound of the band, and a smile on his face. I'm glad I don't have to remember him as a corpse. All corpses are alike in my opinion."

"You don't know what you're talking about," said the old woman. "Your father was the most handsome corpse that was ever stretched. People that never knew him when he was alive came from miles just to see him laid out, he looked so handsome. I can see him to this day, when I close my eyes, looking as fine and fierce as a living man, and you'd think to look at his hands that he'd raise up one of them, any minute, and brush away the flies that were flying around the flowers!"

"All the same, I'm glad I don't remember him," said

Solly, "and I'm glad I didn't see Matty dead. I'm glad I remember him alive." She took up a picture from the mantelpiece. It was a picture of two swans, standing in a clump of bulrushes. There was no glass in the picture, and it was framed with engraved steel.

"I was thinking we could take out this picture," she said, "and put in one of Matty."

She took down a prayer book from a shelf under the mantelpiece, took out a photograph, and began to put it into the frame instead of the picture of the two swans.

"Be careful you don't tear it when you're putting it in," said the mother, leaning anxiously over Solly's shoulder and watching her fingers. When she was satisfied that Solly was doing it carefully she picked up the picture of the swans in the bulrushes and put it into the prayer book, and put the prayer book back on the smoky shell.

"Give me that frame," she said. "I'll shine it up a bit." She wiped it in her skirt, rubbing it back and forth, and then looking at it, and wiping it back and forth again, until, apparently, she saw some improvement in it and put it back on the mantelpiece, satisfied. She stared into the eyes of the photograph.

"I often saw him looking just like that," she said.

Solly took the picture and she looked at it. "Isn't it funny," she said, "the different looks a person can have on his face, from one time to another, and yet when you think of him you think of him with the one look on his face? I always think of him the way he looked when he was passing by the lamp-post the night he went away."

"If you were his mother you'd remember every single look he ever had on his face from the day he was born to the last day you looked at him. Do you mean to say you don't remember the way he looked when he came running in with the blood pouring down his face the day he fell on the broken pie dish in the yard and cut his head open?"

"No," said Solly, "I don't remember that day."

"Don't you?" said the old woman in surprise. "Well, surely you remember the day he came racing up the yard with the geese after him, and his face red as the jersey on his back?"

"No," said Solly, "but I remember the way he looked in his uniform the first day he put it on, when he was showing us the map and marking out where France was. He had his cap pushed back on his head, and the track of it was across his forehead in a big red weal."

"It's my opinion that that cap was too small for him," said the mother; "it was too tight across the forehead. It should have been a half-size larger."

"He told you himself, Mother, that they don't look into half-sizes in the Army!"

She smiled into the eyes of the photograph. Matty would be pleased if he was listening to her now, consoling their mother.

But the talk hadn't penetrated far into the old woman's sorrow.

"No matter how many memories you have," she said, "it doesn't make up for not seeing him laid out in his own house. I don't like to think of them burying him in a hurry, along with a lot of other poor young fellows. I think to myself that, for all we know, it may have been night-time, and raining at that, and the place too dark and wet for them to kneel down and say a prayer for him!"

"Now, Mother, stop crying. You may be sure they knelt down and said a prayer for him, no matter how wet or how dark it was, when they didn't know which of themselves would be the next to be shot down."

"I suppose you're right," said the old woman, "and anyway I thought by the letter the officer wrote that he wasn't the kind of man to throw down a spade out of his hands after burying a boy, and not wait to kneel down and say a prayer."

"You may be sure he said many a prayer," said Solly, "but of course, I don't suppose it was the officer himself who buried Matty?"

"He said in the letter that he did! 'We buried him under a little ash tree,' he said. 'I know his mother will be glad to hear that.' I was very glad. I say a prayer for that officer every night after I've said the prayers for Matty and for his father, and for my own poor mother and father; God be good to them. I always say a special prayer for that officer."

"I suppose he was there at the time," said Solly, "but it's likely he got someone else to do the digging for him!"

"I wouldn't give in to that," said the mother. "Matty was a nice lad. Everyone took a liking to him. I never knew anyone yet that didn't take a liking to him, specially when he smiled. He had a lovely smile."

Solly took up the frame and looked at her brother's face again.

"I couldn't get him to smile when I was taking this picture of him. He kept telling me to hurry up all the time. 'Take the picture, can't you, if you're going to take it?' he said. 'I'm not going to stand here all day with the sun in my eyes!'"

"I hope he wasn't lying in the sun when he was wounded," the mother said suddenly. "I heard Mary Mack and Maggie Cullen talking in the shop yesterday about a young lad who was wounded, Maggie's son wrote home to say that the young lad, whoever he was, was lying in the blazing sun for six hours before they found him, and they only got time to pull him over under a bit of a tree or a bush, before the poor fellow died. 'I'm glad I'm not going to die looking up at the bloody sun' was the last thing he said. They stopped talking when they saw I was listening. I suppose they thought I'd feel bad on account of my boy being killed in the war too. But I'd only love to hear them talking. You like to hear about other people's troubles when you have trouble of your own."

"All the same, I wouldn't listen to those old gossipers," said Solly, "they love to talk about people that are dead or dying, just to make themselves important."

"You don't understand. You don't understand," said the old mother. "I was thinking of what they said when I was walking home along the road, and I was wondering what was the last thing our Matty said. The officer didn't think to tell us!"

"I'm sure Matty would be praying," said Solly, "but maybe if the officer wasn't a Catholic himself he wouldn't think to put a thing like that in a letter."

"That's right. I'm sure he was praying. He was a good boy. Still, it's a great consolation for a mother, if she has to lose a son, to see him slipping out of this world with a good grip on the crucifix and his lips moving trying to repeat the prayers of the priest."

"Don't talk like that now, Mother," said Solly. "I've often heard tell that a soldier gets a special grace when he's dying. Many a one, they say, is saved at the last minute, just by thinking of the Judgment."

"That's right. God is good," said the old woman. "I hope I won't have so long to wait now till I'm called myself to meet my dear ones."

"And what about me?" said Solly. "Have you no consideration for me, Mother, that you sit there talking about dying, and not remembering that I'd be all alone then, with no one at all to care whether I get a bit to eat for myself or not?"

The old woman was staring into the fire and she didn't hear Solly. It was getting late and the fire was dying down. Solly took out a candle from the drawer of the dresser. She paid no attention to the fact that the old woman didn't answer her. She didn't expect an answer. Her own remark was an old one, well worn, and brought into use every time the old woman began to talk about dying.

"I think sometimes when I'm half asleep I see his face in the fire," said the old woman, again, after a few minutes' silence.

"Take heed would you fall into the fire some night, staring into it like that, and you half asleep," said Solly. "Will I take out your pillow, Mother, and put it by the fire, for a spell, to take the chill off it before you go to bed? It's getting late."

The old woman looked up.

"Do you know what night it is?" she said.

"Tuesday night, isn't it?" said Solly, looking at the calendar. "Yes, it's Tuesday," she said.

"It's the first of November," said her mother.

"So it is," said Solly. "All Souls' Night."

"My own poor mother, God be good to her," said the old woman, "used to say that the dead come back to their own fireside to-night, and sit down by the hob until the first light comes strealing up through the trees."

Solly went into the other room and came out with the pillow in her arms. "Here's the pillow. Hold it to the fire for a bit, Mother, and then we'll go to bed. Don't be talking about ghosts. Listen to the wind under the door! I wish there was a man in the house to put a bit of cement on the floor, there by the hinge. That's where the wind is coming in."

"My father used to laugh at my mother," the old woman continued, "and tell her that if it was as easy as all that to come back from the grave, there wouldn't be such a dread on people at the thought of going into it."

"That's what I say too," said Solly.

"The old people had strange notions when I was a

child."

"Old people are always the same," said Solly. "I wouldn't wonder to hear that you were thinking of sitting up all night yourself to see if Matty would come back!"

She gave an awkward laugh, and she stood back out of the circle of the lamp so she could look at the old woman. She had an idea the old woman might have a notion of staying up and she wanted to laugh her out of it. The old woman threw a big sod of turf on the fire.

"Why are you putting on turf at this hour of the night, when we're going straight to our beds?"

"It's raking down the fire every night that has this house as damp as it is," said the old woman. "It's no harm to have a good blaze on the hearth during the night in damp weather like this. The wall over there, by the dresser, is dripping wet. The lime is washing down off it. There'll be a hole in it after another winter."

"A man would mix up a bit of plaster for that wall while you'd be looking around you," said Solly. "Is the pillow warm?"

"It is," said the old woman." Light the candle."

Solly stuck a bit of paper in between the red sods of turf on the hearthstone, and when it lit with a pout of flame she held the flame to a candle-butt that she took out of her pocket.

"Are you coming, Mother?" she said, going into the next room and standing the candle in a cup on the table beside the soft tufty bed with its startling white counterpane.

The old woman hoisted herself out of the chair by leaning on the arms and drawing herself up with a jerk.

"Stop that candle from guttering and spluttering," she said.

Solly squeezed the burnt end of the wick with her finger and thumb, and the candle blazed freshly and clearly along the new piece of wick.

"Do you know what it is?" she said. "The moon is so bright to-night you'd hardly want a candle at all!"

Through the small window, the rim of the hill outside the house could be seen against the bright moonlit sky. The light of the candle, the lamp, and the fire, all burning at their brightest, was not strong enough to keep out the light of the moon. Even an odd star, that shone brighter than the other stars, could be seen as clearly from where they stood as if the cottage were in darkness.

"The moon is in full bloom," said the old woman.

Solly stood looking out and listening. The wind had risen and it sounded in the trees, somewhere away off behind the cottage.

"It's odd for the wind to be so high on a moon-bright night," she said.

The old woman went into the inner room. Solly turned down the lamp in the outer room and kicked in a sod that had fallen on the hearth.

"If you feel cold, Mother, be sure to give a rap on the wall, and I'll come down and put another blanket over you." She went up the steps of the loft. "Give a good loud rap," she repeated when she got to the top step.

"I won't want any more over me than I have every night," said the old woman. "Put another blanket over yourself. Young people nowadays haven't as good blood in their veins as we had in our day."

Solly closed the door of the loft. The old woman left her door open and she went on talking softly to herself. Solly listened for a few minutes and then she began to take off her clothes, and she lay down on the trestle bed with her face to the gable window where she could see the bright sky. But she was asleep before a travelling cloud had crossed the bright face of the moon.

Down below the old woman was still talking to herself.

"I don't know why Solly is so cold," she said. "They were all cold, every one of the children, but Solly and Matty were the worst. Perhaps it's because they came last of the family." She sat on the edge of the tufty bed, and it sank down to one side with a creak.

"Matty could never get socks thick enough to suit him." She stood up again and the bed sprang up with a rusty whinge. She went over to the yellow chest of drawers in the corner and pulled out the top drawer. She took out a thick grey sock and another unfinished sock, that dangled out of four steel needles.

"There's no harm in finishing a thing once it's begun," she said. And she went over to the open door that led into the kitchen and listened to Solly's breathing.

"Who knows?" she said. "Matty might come back. There was a lot of sense in the things my mother said. I don't believe that everyone that dies has the power to come back, but a poor harmless boy like Matty, that died so far away from his home, might be allowed to come back as far as the door and step inside for a minute just to please his old mother." She put the finished sock back in the drawer, and then on second thoughts she took it out again.

"He might like to see I was still knitting for him, even after he was gone. But of course it's only nonsense thinking that he'll come back." She put her hand in, under the bolster, and drew out a pair of worn rosary beads that were brightly polished from continual handling.

"Poor Matty!" she said. "Poor Matty! Your old mother would give her senses for one sight of your darling face!" She went out into the kitchen, talking to herself.

"He won't come, I know that. But it's no harm to stay up awhile. I couldn't sleep, anyway. My father was right when he said that people wouldn't get it so hard to leave this world if there was any chance of getting back to it. He had good sayings. He wore my poor mother out with his continual talk, but she cried herself into a fainting fit the day he died. It is a strange thing the way you appreciate a person when he's gone from you. But it's a strange thing too that I never had any hankering to see my father or mother again, once they were gone, nor any of the other children either, the way I hanker to see Matty."

She left the light unlit, finding her way in the darkening and brightening shadows of the fire, and pausing to feel the edges of the furniture almost as a blind person might have done, with gentleness and timidity and yet with a kind of loving gratitude in the touch of her fingers.

"If I had seen him laid out I might have been satisfied," she said, as she sat down by the fire.

For a long time, then, there was no sound, as her fingers went up and down the knitting needles, except when the tips of the needles came together, accidentally, with a little knocking sound. Then a sod fell with a thud, and the bitter smell of smoke threaded the air. She let it burn where it lay until the bitter fumes made her eyes sore. When she stirred in her chair, to lift it, the chair made a harsh sound as it grated on the rough flagstones. She looked anxiously up at the loft to see if Solly had wakened. But Solly slept on.

The clock on the wall seemed to get louder and louder as she listened, and she could barely make out where it was on the wall, because of the way the room was darkening, and because of the way the clouds were passing over the moon every minute. She could imagine that she saw the clock, but she could not possibly have been looking at it, because she imagined it as it was when she was first married. Then the paint was fresh and bright. It was red, with blue and yellow flowers stencilled up the sides, and a fluffy cuckoo that came out on the platform with his beak open and called out the hours. But of course there was no paint on it now. It was as smoky as a pot, and there'd been no cuckoo in it since the day Matty knocked him off with a catapult when he was a little lad. She was very angry with him that day. She was going to raise her hand to him, but he pleaded with her like a little girl.

"I wouldn't have touched him if he was alive, Mother!" he said. "But I knew he was only made of cardboard and feathers," and he picked up the cuckoo and plucked out the feathers to show her the cardboard body.

She put out her hand and groped along the mantel edge till she found the framed photograph, and she lifted it carefully and held it low down near the flames to see the features more clearly.

"If you come you'll find your old mother waiting for you, Matty," she said. "But God is an obstinate man. The dead can never come back. God has his own ideas, but it's very hard on the like of me."

The wind dropped, but it rose again in a gust. Soot loosened in the chimney and fell down on the turf. Under the door there was a thin whistling sound and then the clouds broke and the moon slipped out, like a nut from the kernel. All at once the room was bright, as if a light had flashed in through the window again.

And then there was a step outside the door.

The old woman remained where she was, crouched low over the flames with the steel frame in her hands.

"Good Christ," she said. "Good Christ deliver us!"

She didn't move. The moon was covered again. The steps came nearer. They paused outside the window. They went past the window. They came back. They paused outside the window again.

"Christ and His Blessed Mother," said the old woman. She raised her eyes without raising her head. "I can't be seen from here," she thought. "If I was sitting between the fire and the window it would be another thing; but I can't be seen from here."

The wind dropped. There was no sound.

"Maybe I only thought I heard a step," she said.

Then the steps sounded outside the door.

"The door is bolted. The door is bolted," said the old woman, staring at the door, and as she stared her upper lip raised slowly upwards at the side, till her yellow teeth, and her gapped gums, were seen at each side. Her face looked like a mask with a gap for breathing cut out of the lower part of it.

The hand pressed down the latch.

"Good Christ deliver us! Matty, go back where you belong! Go back where you belong for the love of God and His Holy Mother, and leave us in peace to live out the bit of life that is left to us. Good Christ deliver us! Holy Mother ward off from us all wicked spirits who wander through the night!"

She longed to scream out for Solly, but she couldn't raise her voice beyond a whisper.

The steps went away from the door. They paused again at the window. She could just make out a dark form, indistinctly.

"Good Christ keep the clouds travelling," she implored, and she raised her eyes again as high as she could, without moving her head, till she felt the veins swelling and throbbing at the back of her eye sockets. She saw a great rent coming in the clouds.

"Good Christ! Good Christ!" she said, over and over again, and then the clouds broke and the moon slipped out.

There was no one at the window.

The old woman put her hands over her eyes and ran over to the loft steps, knocking into the edge of the table, and knocking into the bench at the foot of the steps. She didn't feel the pain flash into her dry flesh, in her hurry to touch the warm and living body of Solly.

Solly didn't feel her crawling in across her, but she wasn't surprised in the morning when she found her in the bed.

"I often wondered why you didn't sleep up here," she said. "It's warmer up here than down below. Were you cold? Did you rap on the wall?"

"I didn't rap," said the old woman. "I didn't want blankets. I was lonesome thinking of Matty." She looked at Solly with a sly look, but Solly was drawing on her stockings and didn't appear to notice anything unusual.

"Will I make you a nice cup of tea, Mother, before you put your feet out on the floor?"

"No," said the mother. "I'll get up. What time is it by that clock?"

"It's ten minutes past eight."

"I think I'll go to Mass," said the old woman. "The only way you can help the dead is by praying for them night and day."

Solly looked at her.

"Why are you raising your lips like that, Mother?" she said sharply. "You look as if you saw a ghost!"

"Nobody ever saw a ghost. Stop your nonsense!" said the old woman.

"Last night I was afraid you were going to stay up all night to see Matty," said Solly.

"What would be the use of that?" said the old woman, irritably. "If he came, we wouldn't see him!"

"How do you know?" said Solly, throwing down the broken comb on the chair. She was thinking more of what she had to do than of what she was saying. She had to go to the well and fill the bucket. She forgot to do it last night. She had to fill the kettles. She had to gather a few twigs to blaze up the fire, and she had to put on the pig's mash to boil on the fire as soon as ever the tea was made.

"If Matty came back, and walked in that door," said the old woman, "you wouldn't have the strength to lift your eyes to look at him. It isn't that the dead can't come back, but that we haven't the strength to face them. We don't want them to come back! That's the truth. It all comes to the same thing in the end! They might as well be gone for ever. When they're gone they have to stay away."

"There's no need to shout, Mother, I'm not deaf," said Solly, and she looked at her mother again, more sharply. "Didn't I tell you not to drag your lips back off your gums like that, Mother? It looks terrible. I don't think you ought to go to Mass. It's quarter past eight o'clock already. You wouldn't be down to the chapel before the middle of Mass. Get back into bed and I'll bring you a nice hot cup of tea."

She went out.

Downstairs there was a sound of sticks breaking and a sound of crockery hitting against crockery and a door opening and shutting. There was a sound of a pail being left down on the floor with a clatter and a sound of water splashing into an empty vessel. Then there was a sound of voices in the yard. Soon Solly came to the foot of the stairs leading up to the loft.

"The kettle is beginning to talk, Mother. The tea will be ready in a minute."

The sound of the cup could be heard wobbling in the saucer as Solly came up to the loft with the tea. The spoon was in the cup, sticking up straight because there was so much sugar in the bottom.

"Here it is, Mother, the way you like it, boiling hot with plenty of sugar, and the top off the milk."

The old woman put out her hand and took the cup. She began to drink.

"Don't get the spoon in your eye, Mother," said Solly

looking nervously at the shaking hand.

"Give me the saucer, so," said the old woman, and she poured a thin stream of the tea into the saucer and held it to her lips, holding it with both hands and tilting it like a shallow goblet. "Who was that I heard talking to you below in the kitchen?" she asked.

"It was Packy Reilly. He stepped across the fields to tell me that he was passing here late last night and the cottage was so bright he looked in the window. There was a fire on the hearth big enough to roast an ox, he said. He thought surely there was something wrong, and he tried the latch but the door was bolted. He looked in the window a second time, but he could see nothing. I said we didn't hear him. At least, I didn't hear him myself. Did you hear anything, Mother?"

The old woman stared into the pool of tea in the bottom of the saucer.

"Did you hear me asking you a question, Mother?"

"Go down and drink your own tea. It will get cold while you're standing there talking."

Solly went over to the door leading down into the kitchen.

"Is there anything wrong with you, Mother?" she said, standing over the ladder-hole and looking back at the old woman. She got no answer.

Solly was no sooner at the foot of the ladder than she came running up it again.

"Mother! Mother! Look what I found in the ashes when I was raking out the ash pit." She held out the steel picture frame. It was blackened and twisted from the heat of the fire. "The wind must have blown it off the table," she said.

"It will shine up again," said the old woman, and she reached out her hand for it.

"But the photo of Matty is burnt out of it!" said Solly.

The old woman took the frame. She stared at it. Solly stared at her. Solly stamped her foot impatiently.

"Mother! How many times will I have to tell you to stop drawing back your lips from your gums like that? If you could only see how awful you look!"

The mask broke up at once, but when Solly went downstairs it formed again over the old face, stretching the skin until every wrinkle was flattened out, and giving the face a distorting appearance of youth, more terrifying than the face of death.

AODH DE BLÁCAM

The Ship That Sailed Too Soon

[*The following remarkable story was told by Father Ryan one evening to our fireside circle. Father Ryan is a Gael from Galway, and a travelled man, full of old-time lore, and ever ready with tales of strange happenings by sea and land.*]

I began my clerical studies at Salamanca in the year 18—,when I was a boy of nineteen. During the October of my first year in Spain the effects of overwork took the form of a breakdown in health, and I went to Corunna, a port on the north-west coast, partly because sea air is so medicinal, and partly because that corner of Spain has a particular interest for Irish people. Near Corunna is Brigantia, which is supposed to have been founded by the Milesians when they rested in Spain during their search for Ireland. Often had I heard my father, telling the story of that ancient pilgrimage, relate how Breogan, the father of Milesius, built a famous tower called Tor Breogain, from which Brigantia is said to take its name.

Corunna has a second Irish association. When Red Hugh O'Donnell went seeking an army in Spain, wherewith to retrieve the disaster of Kinsale, it was at Corunna he landed.

With what a strangely-stirred imagination, then, I trod the narrow streets of that historic port, lamenting the ruined hopes of the famous Irish exile. But sad thoughts of the past did not mar my enjoyment of the present, and I found much pleasure in visiting some notable religious houses in the town, the School of Navigation, and the two great forts.

In the evenings I used often to go down to Pescaderia, the lower and modern part of the town, made up of the quays and the buildings that have grown up round them. Here I spent many a pleasant hour practising my Spanish with the fisher-people—in Spain, as in every country, the most sociable and entertaining of men. I also had the opportunity to practise my French, passing a few words with the men of the French schooner *Amèdée*, Kerfriden Louis, Le Mounier Desiré, and the rest. They asked me to call aboard their vessel when their day's work of unbaling goods should be finished, and about twilight on a certain evening I went down to the quays with that intention.

There were several tall cross-rigged ships moored to the long quay, and I guessed that with my indifferent seamanship I should find it not easy to recognize the *Amèdée*. As I was lingering in doubt beside a ship that had moorings some distance from other vessels, a figure on the poop beckoned to me as though I had been expected, and without further hesitation I stepped across the plank from the quayside to the deck.

Here I was not a little bewildered, for the poop from which I had been beckoned rose high above the deck-level, and in the dusk I could barely see the steps by which it was reached. As I moved in that direction I was surprised to notice that a seaman drew aboard the plank by which I had come from the quay, while a knot of men started from some corner in which they had been idling, and busied themselves in the vigorous manipulation of tackle at the foot of the mainmast and also at the bows.

Meanwhile the man who had beckoned me from the poop had come to meet me. What was my surprise to hear, not Kerfriden Louis' courteous French words of welcome, but a torrent of angry Spanish:

"*Como!* is the ship to lose a tide while we are kept waiting for a dawdling boy? Get below and attend to your duties if you do not wish to taste the rope's end."

Then, in no less angry tones, this man, whom I took to be the captain, shouted rapid orders here and there which were obeyed with an alacrity that left no doubt as to his character as a disciplinarian. Sails, I saw, were being hoisted and bent; and glaring, swaying lanterns were lit and hung above the poop and the prow.

"*Mi capitan!—perdone Vd—.*" I tried to engage the captain's attention in order to explain to him the mistake. I caught him by the arm as he was striding past me to direct the unmooring of cables by which the ship was moored.

"*Qué es eso?*" he said impatiently, then paused to look me full in the face.

Even in the tiny pause before he spoke again I half-consciously observed every detail of his person and attire. What strange man was this, I asked myself, dressed in a strange yet picturesque costume that was not that of Spain, nor of any European country I knew, though it slightly resembled the style of old-fashioned Bretons—tunic with leather facings, belt that carried antique firearms, bright knee-boots? His face was of an olive complexion that seemed to add brightness to the swift-flashing brown eyes, in which there glowed fierce expressions of anger and desire.

I knew that I was speaking with a man of no ordinary experience. I could fancy he had seen undreamed-of adventures, and played a part in greater doings than common men dare meddle with. The Spanish in which he addressed me had in it a guttural richness that showed it was not his native tongue, and I found time in that flash of observation to wonder what was his origin, and how he had come to command a Spanish vessel.

All this shot through my mind in the instant in which I was being scrutinized before the order was given to a powerful, piratical-looking man, dressed, as I noticed, in just as strange attire as the captain, and bearing a grim-looking dirk at his hip, to take and confine me in the forecastle. In the midst of such bewildering circumstances I was still surprised to hear the order given in the English tongue.

"I will talk with you later, senoretto," said the captain to me.

Such was the desperate look of my guard, and the stern air with which he was given his orders, that I yielded without further protest, and accompanied him in silence. The seamen, at their various tasks, stared at me with looks of curiosity and wonder as we passed—looks that I returned in kind, such was the unusual appearance of these dusky-featured, giant-like men, all attired in outlandish dress, and often bearing antique cutlasses at their belts.

The forecastle was built in the bows high above the deck level, like the poop over the stern, and the upper deck thus formed was fortified with stockades. Out of the tail of my eye I noticed cannon beside the bulwarks. The impression was borne in on me that the whole build and aspect of the vessel was as strange as the appearance and manner of the crew, and some mysterious stirring of recognition at the back of my memory added to my perplexity. In what book of travel had I seen all this before?

Just where steps ascended to the upper deck in the bows, a door opened on an apartment in the forecastle. My captor led me to this interior, where he proceeded, with a rough kindliness, to arrange for my comfort. Curiosity and the desire for a talk, I suspected, made him slow in his actions.

"You understand English," I began, hopeful of extracting some explanation of the mystery around me. "Tell me what ship this is, and what people these are?"

"Begging your pardon and meaning no offence, sir," said he, "but the captain would make short work of me if I answered the likes of them questions. Under sealed orders we are, in a manner of speaking, and I'm blest if I understand the business myself. Here was I, barely a week ago, snug and cosy, drinking my grog in as nice company as ever I knew —having found a comf'table little inn where they sold good English grog . . ."

"This was in Corunna?" I interrupted.

"Lor' bless you, no, sir, but in them blessed islands down West."

He jerked a black-nailed thumb over his shoulder. Then he sat comfortably in a corner between a kind of bunk and a bench fastened to the wall. He drew out a plug of tobacco, and began shredding it with his knife.

"'Ere was I, 'unting about to find a place w'ere they'd have something better than them furin' wines, w'en I 'appens on this 'ere cosy little grog-shop as I was a-telling you of. Best o' drink there was, and good company, too, and w'en I got into that little bar-parlour, 'Sam Hook,' says I to myself, says I, 'you're in luck.' I tell you I didn't notice time passin' so happy as I was, an' I just thought I was w'ere the good little boys go, as my pore mother used to tell me afore I went to sea. Well, 'ere was I, as I'm a-telling you, so 'appy that I might 'ave been there forever like, and just about tipping a stave, w'en there come a 'orrible knocking at the door.

" '*Is Sam Hook there?*', says a voice.

" '*Ush*,' says I to the landlord, as he was a-opening of the door.

"Well, that blamed fool of a man goes and says yes afore I 'ad time to stop 'm. '*Then tell 'im 'e's got to rejoin the ship at once—cap'n's orders*,' says the voice, and away the messenger goes. 'You're a pretty sort of shipmate,' says I to the landlord. ' 'Ere am I scarcely 'arf a 'our in comf'table quarters w'en you go 'an give me away.' 'You've been 'ere long enough,' says 'e, 'you've been 'ere a precious sight longer than you think,' says 'e—'drinking grog there in the corner, and singing your songs over an' over an' over again till the blessed birds in the trees outside knows the toons of 'em,' says 'e.

"Down I goes to the ship then. 'Look 'ere,' says I to the cap'n, 'I don't want to join ship again so soon, just w'en I found a nice little berth ashore. You get some other man as can pull a rope, an' let me be.'

"Well, 'e just give me one look, an' bless you, I dursn't say another word. 'E's a 'ard man to cross, is the cap'n, an' I just gets back to my dooty as I did w'en first I joined the ship, I dunno 'ow long ago.

"We sailed next day, and the first port we made was this 'ere Corunna. 'Ere we puts in for a day, an' the cap'n sends a boy ashore with some message as I 'eard—accidental-like you know—about some fellow called Don Joon or Agweela, or something. 'Ask if 'e's ready to sail ag'n,' says the cap'n. That there boy didn't come back all day, an' then you come aboard, and the cap'n give orders to sail and no more waitin'. In a mighty hurry 'e seemed ever since we sailed from them there islands (w'ere I found the little grog-shop)—though between you an' me there's *someone* a-'urrying of 'im."

Here Sam winked knowingly. "Whom do you mean?" I asked.

"W'y—there's *someone* aboard, this v'y'ge. Someone very pertick'ler—that's w'at I mean," said Sam. "Mebbe you know 'oo I mean, an' mebbe I 'ave an idea like 'oo it is, tho' I ain't been told, an' you may lay to that. Wait w'ile I get a light."

Here Sam stepped outside to get a light for his pipe, and I had a moment to consider my position. I could not make anything of the story, and now I could feel the ship's motion and hear the clapping of waves that showed we had cleared the still waters of the harbour and were putting to sea. Having listened patiently to Sam's talk, I thought I had ingratiated myself sufficiently to ask him a direct question as to my plight.

He returned bearing bread and a flask of wine. "Cap'n's main angry," said he, "for me staying 'ere talking with you, an' told me to bring you this 'ere grub an' leave you straightaway."

"Just answer me one question," I asked. "Why am I made prisoner like this?"

"Now, now, don't be getting at me like that, sir," said Sam, in a reproving voice that would have been comical had the circumstances been less serious. "I'm not askin' of you whether you're a spy or not—just passed a friendly word like, but I ain't goin' to be got at like that, if I know it."

"Am I suspected of being a spy, then?" I asked. "I came on the ship by mistake. Your captain seems to have mistaken me in the twilight for some messenger he had sent ashore. I don't know who you are or what the ship is, whether you come from Russia, or Turkey, or where . . ."

"Now, now," interrupted Sam, "maybe you came by mistake, and maybe you didn't. I ain't a-goin' to say. Maybe you 'as your ideas about him as is in the state cabin aft, an' maybe I 'as mine. But even if I *am* a poor English sailor man as sailed under the Jolly Roger afore I shipped with this 'ere vessel, I'm a-goin' to do my dooty now, and you ain't goin' to get anything from me. You take my advice, an' don't ask no questions an' we'll get on friendly-like. But don't ferget I'm under sealed orders. Eat this 'ere supper now, and then go to bunk for the night, an' maybe I'll see you again in the mornin'.''

That was all I could get from Sam, so I made a lonely meal, wondering again what was the errand of this vessel on which I seemed to be suspected of spying.

The moon was now high, as I could see from a porthole in my place of confinement, and we were now standing out over the silvery ocean, the land a black streak in the distance. Overhead I could hear the footsteps of seamen engaged in their nautical duties, while the humming and straining of the rigging filled the air with Æolian music.

I was unable to distinguish the speech of the men above me, their words being caught away in the strong sea-wind, so that an indistinct murmur, broken by an occasional laugh, was all I could gain from their voices. After listening intently for some time, I despaired of gaining any further enlightenment till the morrow should come, so having made my night devotions, I wrapt myself in certain rugs which Sam had laid in the bunk for my use, and composed myself to rest.

Despite my natural state of excitement, the rich sea-air had had its effect on my body, and I soon fell into that tranquil state between waking and sleep that usually precedes deep and refreshing slumber. Lying so, I began to dream, and in my dreams I seemed to be back in the Galway of my boyhood, and embarking on some ship of the O'Driscolls, or O'Malleys, or O'Cryans, the stout Gaelic seamen of old days. I fancied I heard the seamen of that ship singing. A familiar Irish air played in my ears, and I seemed to hear the Irish words sung once again as often I had heard them in my father's house:

A ghrádh geal, ná bíodh cás ort
Fá'r éirigh dhuit,
Táid bráithre dhúinn tar sáile
'Gus a d-triall tar muir;
Béidh do phárdun ó Phápa na Róimhe 'guinn
Is céad sláinte a bh-fíon Spáineach
Dom' Rós Geal Dubh

Verse by verse, the famous song in which the northern chieftain is supposed to address Ireland rung in my ears, till the passion of the last stanza broke my half slumber, so that I woke, and seemed to hear the music echoing around me. But, surely, there in very reality, men's voices were lifting the defiant words to the night air—over my head in loud, melodious and unmistakable tones, I heard the last lines sung:

Béidh gach gleann sléibhe ar fuid Éireann, a's mointe, ar crith
Lá éigin sul a n-eugfaidh
Mo Rós Geal Dubh.

Irish sailors aboard this vessel! This startling fact, so strangely revealed, while it added to my perplexities, relieved my anxiety; I knew I could count on some friends at least among the crew. It was good fortune, indeed, they should happen to be Irish speakers, for now I would have a sure means of appeal. I would speak with them, and persuade them to get me released from my absurd captivity.

Then it occurred to me that I would not be able to discover the Irishmen among the crew, even if I should be allowed on the deck next day, so I shouted, my head at the porthole, then and there:

"A *cháirde, éistidh!*"

After I had shouted this two or three times, the conversation overhead ceased, and the men seemed to be listening. Again I cried out: "Listen, friends!"

A voice replied in loud tones: "*Cé tusa nó cad tá uait?*"

I cried out my story—told of my absurd confinement, and begged my hearers, as Irishmen, to go to their captain and appeal for me that I should be speedily taken ashore and released. At the end I heard a consultation in low tones, then another voice —this with the authoritative manner of one used to command—bade me rest till the morrow, when my message would be taken to the captain.

There was nothing to do then but wait the morrow with patience. However, patience was little needed, for the salt air in my lungs made me sleep soundly. In pleasant, romantic dreams, I fancied I was voyaging with Tioboid na Long, or some other captain of the long-distant days when Ireland had her navies that swept the western seas. As I woke, the door of my compartment was open, and I could see on to the sunlit, gently-heaving deck, so that I fancied my dream was real for a while, until, sleep ebbing from my brain, I came back to my nineteenth century self.

I ventured out on to the deck, viewing the amazing scene, and trying to convince myself that I really was awake. Yes, it was no dream. There was the strange stockaded poop in the stern; there were the sturdy masts, with the great painted sails straining overhead. Beside the bulwarks, the quaint wooden-mounted cannon gaped on the rolling waves. Here and there the strangely-attired seamen were busy scouring the boards or knotting cables. On the poop two men guarded the tiller—and beside them, much to my amazement—stood a steel-helmeted figure, carrying a huge gleaming axe.

My eyes rested on this remarkable figure, whom I observed to have mounted the poop by the steps to the main deck. And now he was followed by three other persons.

First came a little brown-habited man, with beads swinging at his belt: a Franciscan friar, to all appearances. Then came a slender-figured young man, covered in a dark, drooping cloak, beneath which a slender sword protruded. Thirdly, the dour-faced captain, who towered over his two companions, mounted the upper deck.

The two seamen and the helmeted man indicated by their attitudes and gestures profound deference as the group passed them, going towards the bulwark. The young man, I observed, walked with a painful limp, yet carried such an air of dignity that I guessed him to be the mysterious personality hinted at by my English friend. Even at the distance, I could perceive an expression of rare pride on his features, which yet had peculiar fascination. The gentleness of his gestures was endearing. He contrasted with the captain beside him, who was pointing northwards over the waters, and talking in what, even by his manner, I could detect to be gruff, short-clipped sentences.

While I was watching these figures on the poop and wondering who the strange personality should be, who was staring with such intent looks over the sea in the direction in which the captain had pointed, the captain himself caught sight of me, and turned hastily to the sentry with an exclamation. The young man also turned, seeming to inquire the cause of the captain's order. The man with the axe was recalled from the steps which he had started to descend. The captain and the mysterious youth appeared to be discussing me.

It was at this point that my good Sam Hook approached me, bringing food.

"Listen," said I, as he set it before me in my apartment, "there are Irish hands aboard this ship. I heard them speaking Irish, which I speak myself. I want you to bring one of these men to me, so that I can speak a few words with him."

I intended to send a message to the captain by such a messenger. I laid my hand on Sam's great paw. With the utmost delicacy and dexterity his palm opened and received the Spanish dollar, or *duro*, that slipped from my fingers. Without seeming to notice this little transaction, my piratical friend replied to my words:

"You speak Irish, do you—and w'y not, I ask? Purty sort o' spy you'd be on this 'ere ship if you didn't, wouldn't ya? W'y, didn't I 'ave to larn some o' that lingo m'self to understand my orders? 'Course you talk Irish. W'y you wouldn't be 'ere if ya didn't, anyone could see that."

"Why should I speak Irish if I should be on this ship?" I asked.

"Now, now, I asked you afore not to try to get at me," said Sam. "W'at are you doing among all these Irelanders if you ain't able to understand their lingo? 'Seems to me, young fella, you ain't got too much sense. If you was lettin' on to be 'ere accidental like, what call 'ad you to let it out you talked Irish? 'Tween you and me, that gives you away, and no error. If you speaks Irish, and 'appens to be found on a Irish ship, well I puts it to you, fair and square—does that *look* like a haccident, eh?"

". . . *On an Irish ship*"

"Yes, on an Irish ship, sonny. No call for you to look so surprised, and no one knows it better than you, that's my opinion. Oh, you may stare. I tell you I'm a Englishman (and proud of it, even if I did sail under the Jolly Roger one time), an' I don't altogether 'old with these Irish. But they treated me fair since I shipped with this company two or three v'y'ges back (afore I found that grog-shop I was tellin' you of), an' I ain't goin' to give 'em away now."

Sam was holding forth in this style, comically trying to appear firm, but all the while obviously delighted to hear himself talk, when heavy steps could be heard on deck, and Sam was called in imperative tones. He left me, and returned in an instant.

"You are to be taken to the cap'n," he said, with a look of commiseration; "I'm sorry for ya, but you ain't no good as a spy, you ain't."

"Indeed, you need not be so alarmed on my account," said I. "I have nothing to conceal, and shall soon make things clear to the captain, if he lets me explain."

"I'm sorry for ya," said Sam again.

I stepped out to where a tall youth awaited me— armed with a scian at his belt and carrying, slung on his shoulder, not a carbine or rifle, but a long bow. I noticed that his hair was matted in a peculiar pattern over his brow, a fact which stirred strange associations in my mind. Without speaking, he led me down the deck towards the poop, and through a doorway to a chamber in which the captain was seated, bending over a table on which maps were spread.

The captain laid down a compass as I entered, and looked up. The youth who had brought me retired with a bow.

Without inviting me to be seated, the dark strange man began to speak, but with my small knowledge of Spanish, I was unable to follow his quick sentences. In the midst of them I caught the words, "His Excellency," once or twice.

"Pardon," I interrupted. "I am unable to follow Spanish easily. I am not a Spaniard, but an Irishman."

"So you tell me," he said, speaking more slowly, but still in Spanish. "I do not know who you are or what your aims may be. When you came aboard I suspected you of being a

Spanish spy. There are Irishmen who are no better than spies, too. When I was told that you were tampering with members of the crew, and addressed them in Irish, I was disposed to keep you in the closest confinement, but his Excellency overheard my order when you stepped on deck this morning, and countermanded it. It is his Excellency's good will to examine you himself, and you are now to go before him. Hush!—no words. I wish to hear nothing from you."

Here the captain rose and passed his strong hands over my vest. "I must ascertain that you have no weapons concealed," he said. "If I had my will, young man, you would not enter His Excellency's presence at all, and as I cannot override his commands, I must at least assure myself on this matter."

Having satisfied himself, apparently, that I was not equipped to effect an assassination, and after silencing me twice when I sought to speak, the captain bade me follow him.

He led me from his room along a passage to a heavily-curtained door, at which stood another helmeted figure, bearing a gleaming axe. This giant guard stood aside, and lowered his weapon from his shoulder, as the captain drew back the curtain and left me. In a moment the captain returned, accompanied by the little Franciscan friar.

"It is His Excellency's good-will to interview you alone," he said gruffly. "Step in."

The monk, who had received my bow with a pleasant recognition, and had eyed me closely, laid a hand on the captain's arm; then addressed that dour personality in gentle Irish.

"*Fan socair*," said he, "O'Driscoll"; and to me: "Have no fear, my son."

So this Spanish-speaking seaman also was Irish! I

passed through the curtains with my mind in a state of dream-like perplexity.

The apartment in which I found myself was large and luxuriously furnished, with rich antique woodwork, chairs and table, and massive hides flung on the ground as rugs. An old-fashioned pedestal globe stood on the table, a round ink-pot holding white quills, and various parchment documents. A silver-worked filigree hanging lamp caught my eye—then a shelf bearing big leather-bound volumes; on the wall to my right hung a fine Spanish Madonna, and at another point a beautifully-graven Crucifix. At the end of the chamber was a network of little windows—built into the bulge of the vessel's stern, through which the sunlit-glistening sea and the ship's white wake could be seen.

But only a glance took in all this, for my gaze was quickly drawn to a figure standing by the windows. He was the young man I had seen on the poop, and now that I was in his presence, my feeling of liking deepened.

He had thrown off his cloak, and now I saw that he wore a rich pleated doublet, with profuse linen at the neck and wrists; silken hose and delicately fashioned mocassin-like footwear. A slender sword in a pale-leather scabbard, and with jewelled hilt, hung at his side. But it was his face that attracted my attention more than his strange and beautiful attire. It was clean-shaven but for a thin moustache, and had a boyish openness, though the firm, sharp chin, and broad intellectual brow, indicated rare personality. Freckles added to its freshness, and to complete the distinctness of the type, he was crowned with bright masses of red-gold hair. When he spoke, the extraordinary sweetness of his voice completed his strange fascination.

"An Éireannach tusa, a chara?"

Thus did he break silence after examining me with piercing grey eyes that seemed to search my mind.

I answered that I was indeed Irish—that I was no spy on this strange ship, but a prisoner by accident. Then I perceived by this young man's gentleness of aspect that my protestations were unnecessary; that his eager gaze had seen the truth in me, and my sentences began to falter.

With sudden words, eager with passion, he interrupted me.

"Oh, how is it with Ireland?" he asked. "Or what are the fortunes of the Gaels?"

He stepped forward and laid his trembling hands on my shoulders as he spoke. "Tell me, tell me!" he appealed.

Then suddenly a wild fancy in my mind turned to conviction, and I fell on my knee before him, kissing his brown sinewy hand. I knew *now* who this strange young man was: "*With countenance so amiable that he captivated everyone who beheld him,*" whose voice "*was like the music of a silver trumpet*"—as one who knew him so long ago had written. Words that sounded to me like a stranger's issued from my mouth:

"O'Donnell, O'Donnell—are you coming home at last?"

"*Eirigh, a mhic,*" he said, stooping to lift me. "Yes, I am coming home at last. How long is it to Ireland since I went away after that terrible day at Kinsale?"

"'Tis near three hundred years," I answered.

"Is that all?" asked O'Donnell. "That was the time that Oisin spent where I have been before he came home to meet St. Patrick. It seemed a little space to him, but to me it has been an eternity of time. Am I remembered in Ireland still?"

"How should we forget you, O'Donnell?"

"Oh, I am glad to be remembered in Ireland," he said, with a voice that thrilled. "Tell me, who is Captain of the O'Donnells now?"

"They have no captain now . . ." I began.

"*What!*"

". . . Neither they nor any other clan have a captain now, for all the clans are mingled together, and there are O'Donnells in every críoch of Eire."

"That is strange, indeed, but doubtless some chief of the O'Neills is Ard-ri over the children of the Gael?"

"No, O'Donnell—Ireland has changed more than you dream of."

"But tell me, at least our people have kept the old tongue?"

"It is as dear as ever to all the true men."

"That is well. But I see there will be much labour before me if I come home. No matter, if there are true men in Ireland we will retrieve Kinsale yet."

"*If* you come home? Are you not sailing for Ireland now?"

"We are sailing for Ireland, indeed, with every span of canvas that can be stretched to speed our journey. We are to reach the Irish waters on Samhain Eve, and if the Samhain fires are flaming on the hills, I shall know the time has come for me to land . . ."

". . . And if not?"

"Ah, if the Good People do not give me that signal, I must sail away again for another weary spell. Three times I have been called, and have come, since Kinsale's day, but the signal was lacking at each of the last two voyages, and I must needs go back to that dreary exile in Tir na n-Óg, or Avilion, as they call it."

"I pray the signal may not be lacking now, O'Donnell."

"Amen to that. But I am detaining you." It was clear that O'Donnell wished to resume the business of which the documents beside him were evidence, interrupted by my interview; but with royal grace, he excused himself on the pretext of inquiries as to my comfort.

"You must be given suitable quarters," he said, "and

pardon O'Driscoll's harshness; an honest fellow but blunt. We shall meet again when you are refreshed."

Here he gave orders to the gallowglass at the door, and a kern was brought who conducted me to a comfortable cabin. The boy retired to bring me materials for my toilet, but in a minute or two Sam Hook appeared in his stead.

"Shiver my timbers," said that worthy, "if you ain't risen in the world, in a manner o' speakin'. I thought you was goin' to swing, so I did, and bless me if you ain't tarned out a real gen'leman. I couldn't 'elp comin' in to speak to ya, so I give that there boy a clout in 'is stern-quarters for not movin' quick, an' brought the stuff ta ya m'self. I was friendly like with you w'en you was a prisoner, so I thought you'd tell me, supposin' you knew, w'ether . . .

"Whether what?"

"W'ether I'm right about 'im in the state cabin?"

"Why, whom do you take him to be?"

Sam edged up close to me, and closed one eye in a clumsy effort at a wink. "Now, then," said he in a whisper, "*Ain't 'e just the Dook o' Mexico that's a-coming to England to court our 'Liza?*"

"'Liza!" I could not guess Sam's meaning for a moment or two. Then I saw it, and laughed.

"Why, Sam," said I, "your 'Liza, if you mean Queen Elizabeth, is dead and gone to never-mind-where these three hundred years. It's a lot longer than you guess since you first sailed in Captain O'Driscoll's ship. The time must have passed without your notice when you were so cosy in that little shop in the mysterious Happy Islands. You are like Oisin or the Children of Lir."

"Never 'eard tell 'o them parties, sir; but do you really mean that 'Liza's dead and gone?"

When I assented, he continued: "Well, bless my 'eart and soul, that's a rum go, so it is. I allus thought there were summat wrong with this v'y'ge. W'y did I allow m'self to

be brought away from that snug little berth I was a-tellin'
you of? This 'ere's a blessed ghost-ship, that's about it. I
oughta 'a' knowed it from them shaddas."

"The what?"

"The shaddas—there ain't none. You come an' ave a
look."

He persuaded me to look out on the deck. There was a
blazing sun in the sky, and the boards shone with dazzling
lustre. But as the sailors moved to and fro on the sunny
deck, they cast no shadow on the sunny wood.
Apprehensively I turned to the bulwark beside me.
Though the two of us were standing together only the
one, my own shadow, was to be seen!

There is no need to describe the rest of the voyage over
the roaming waters until the evening of Samhain Eve
came. When the sun was low in the western sky, I was
standing in the bows staring over a calm sea, northwards
into the autumnal mists, towards which we were driving.
O'Donnell himself also came forward to watch for the first
glimpse of Irish land.

He nodded kindly to me, and seeing me glance
involuntarily at his limping tread, he smiled and said:
"You see I still bear traces of that Christmas night among
the snows on the mountains."

I remembered the frost-bite that had lamed the flying
youth after his escape from Dublin Castle and I was
covered with confusion for having betrayed my curiosity.

"Like poor Red Hugh, you are eager to see Ireland
again?" said O'Donnell, ignoring my embarrassment, and
he, too, strained his eyes towards the haze over the
horizon. Never will I forget those moments, as we watched
in silence; till at last O'Donnell gave a little gasp, and I
turned to see his eyes opened to their widest, his lips
parted, and his hands clenched

"*Buidheachas le Dia, a's le Muire, a's le Pádruig, a's le Colum.*"

He breathed these words, and I, looking again northwards, now saw the faint but unmistakable waving curve of Irish hills rising over the vapours.

O'Donnell shouted gleefully, like a schoolboy, and gave orders. His active kerns ran hither and thither, and in a moment a silken pennon bearing the blazon of a crimson cross ran up to the peak, while a salutation of cannon broke the stillness of evening with thunderous roar. The banner I recognized, remembering how Saint Patrick had marked the shield of Conall, ancestor of the O'Donnell clan, with the sacred symbol, saying: "*In hoc signo vinces.*" So now the historic emblem floated once more over Tirchonaill's lord!

O'Donnell's momentary delight had now passed, and he was watching the clearer outline of the Irish coast with anxious gaze. We could now see the green slopes of the hills distinctly with the purple forms of inland mountains looming behind. Clearer and clearer the vision grew, calm and beautiful—but who can describe the loveliness of the Irish shore seen over the narrowing waters by the returning exile?

The sun was waning fast, and now was magnified as it began to sink behind the mists. Soon it would set, and even now the shades seemed to be gathering. Swiftly in the fresh breeze our vessel clove the waves and hastened on, but faster the day was dying. The sun's shape vanished, and a red glare in the mists told us it had set. The last gold glimmers faded from the peaks ashore, and day dissolved among the high clouds. Night was falling.

All this while O'Donnell hardly stirred. His hands gripped the bulwarks and his body was rigid as he gazed at the darkening land.

Dark had wholly fallen, and the battle-lamps were lit

upon the poop, when we drew near land. Darkness clothed hill and glen, and only a black outline against the stars was visible. Night deepened, and O'Donnell did not stir. In a faint gleam from the lamps I could see his face set firm and pale. I dared not speak. I knew he was waiting—waiting and hoping for the glare of the Samhain fires that should summon him home. I knew, too, that as the night aged, hope was ebbing from his heart, and cold grief flooding in.

All night he watched, while the ship shortened canvas and cruised slowly past the long dark coast; all night, till at last a grey streak in the east broke the darkness, and with the darkness his hopes.

Samhain had come, but not the signal fires!

Then did O'Donnell cast his mantle over his face, and a loud cry of sorrow rose in the night air. The sailors, the captain, and I, too, all who were near him on the upper deck, drew away and left him standing alone, grieving.

The captain led me to the body of the ship, and spoke to me in a whisper—his gruffness all gone, and his face covered with a sadness that I had not fancied him capable of. I now heard him speak Irish for the first time.

"O'Donnell's hopes again are spent," he said, "maybe for an age, and who knows whether he will ever come again? 'Tis in God's hands. But you— you are not of us, and I will have you put ashore. Greet Ireland for O'Donnell, ay, and for me, Felim O'Driscoll. *Beannacht Dé leat, a bhuachaill.*"

He signed to certain seamen, and a boat was lowered, which I entered. A young kern, who seemed to be some sort of officer, motioned me to a seat in the bow before himself taking the helm. Four sturdy rowers urged the little craft swiftly through the water.

The man nearest to me I observed to be no other than my good friend Sam Hook once again. He cast a word or two over his shoulder between each stroke.

"Tame sort of a end for such a v'y'ge, ain't it?" said he. "Seems we're goin' off to them islands again after this. . . . 'Spect you wish you was comin' with us . . . W'y don't you ask the cap'n? I shan't be sorry to get back, an' you may lay to that . . . If I can find that little grog-shop as I was a-telling you of . . . Don't catch me stirrin' again, not likely, not even for Cap'n O'Driscoll . . . Can't un'erstand you Irishers. All this v'y'ge fer nothing like, w'en you can get on so 'andsome in them islands too . . . Don't know 'ow to enj'y yerselves, that's w'at's wrong with you . . . Wait till I gets back to w'ere I was a-tellin' you of, and precious little you'll get me to move ag'in . . ."

At this point in Sam's rejoicings at the prospect of an early return to his "grog-shop" in Tir na n-Óg, the young officer at the helm gave an order, and the rowers backed their oars, so that the boat stopped almost in its own length. I saw that we were now floating close to the beach, in shallow water.

"*Is oth liom é*," said the young man to me. "I fear we must ask you to wade ashore. We dare not touch the soil before the time has come. You remember what happened to Oisin? Like him, we should shrivel up with the age of centuries if we touched the Irish soil before the Samhain fires have blazed."

He stepped forward and shook me by the hand. "Give the love of Niall Óg O'Gallagher to Ulster whenever you go to the North," he said, and then assisted me as I sprang from the boat. I lighted in a mere hand's depth of water and splashed ashore.

When I turned, the boat had already shot several lengths towards the ship. I heard Sam Hook's voice raised in some jolly English catch, till he suddenly fell quiet in the middle of a bar, as if impatiently ordered to be silent. The boat disappeared in the darkness, to reappear near the ship in the glow from the battle-lamps.

After a few moments I saw the ship make sail and begin
to draw away. The lamps cast an unearthly luminance
over the poop, and now I could see O'Donnell's dark
figure, standing there as though to bid farewell to Ireland.
Even at that distance, the figure of the royal exile seemed
bowed with sorrow—and so I watched until at last he
disappeared from my sight, and the luminance was
swallowed up in the darkness.

"Farewell, dear prince," I said. "I see that even the
journey to Tír na nÓg is sad for the royal lover of the
Bright Black Rose."

DOROTHY MACARDLE

Earth-Bound

(FOR R. J.)

"Do you think that people who are not Irish know what homesickness is?" Una said.

"It is harder being away from a country that is in trouble," Michael O'Clery answered, "than from a country that is at peace. It is not homesickness only—it is that you want to be in the fight."

He spoke contentedly. It was his last night in Philadelphia; tomorrow he was going home.

Una's pale little face looked sad in the dying fire-light; the coming and going of Irish friends filled her, always, with joy and pain. Even Frank's keen face grew wistful and, for myself, an unbearable pang of "heim-weh" silenced me.

Una spoke again, after a pause.

"Do you know what I miss more than the people, more than the dear places?" she said. "It is that sense one has everywhere in Ireland—in the glens, and in Dublin—the old squares on the north side, and the quays—of the companionship of the dead."

Frank laughed in brotherly mockery.

"They stay in Ireland, I suppose, sooner than go to

Heaven? Or is it doomed to it they are, instead of Hell?"

But Michael said seriously.

"I believe she's right."

Michael had something to tell us: that could be felt. It was past midnight but Una put coal on the fire.

Three weeks ago Michael had arrived, without a passport, in Philadelphia, on some mission not to be disclosed, and, like most friendly travellers from Ireland had found his way soon to the young editors of the *Tri-Colour*, Una and Frank O'Carroll. Within their hospitable studio his few idle hours were spent.

Nowhere outside Dublin have I known so shabby yet lovable a room. It was perhaps their one treasure, Hugo Blake's glorious "Dawn," that made one seem to breathe there the air of home. That picture is magical. There is nothing painted but the hills of Clare-Galway seen from the water and daybreak in the sky behind, yet it is the dawn of all that Ireland has been waiting for these seven hundred years.

"You could go away from that picture," Michael said once, "and die."

There was little else—brown walls, three uncurtained windows looking down on the Square, at evening all blue shadow and amber lights; faded draperies on the divans and many-coloured cushions around the fire; it was enough, with Frank's iridescent, satirical humour and Una's pleasure in her friends, to create an illusion inexpressibly restful. It was the exiles' oasis of living waters at the end of each arid week.

It was late at night, as now, when all but a guest or two had gone, that the talk would grow full of reminiscences and omens and prophesies and dreams, and strange adventures would be told.

Not one word had Michael said, yet, of the perils that followed his escape, but Una's remark had started some deep train of thought in him. He repeated, in a tone of deep conviction:

"I believe she's right."

"You think they stay—?" I asked.

"Some," he replied. "Some that died for Ireland, thinking more of Ireland than Heaven at the end."

"And they're wanted," he added gravely. "They are surely wanted still."

"Do you know Glenmalure?" he asked then.

I knew it, a deep valley of the Wicklow hills, shut out from life, compelling mournful thoughts.

"They might well be there," I said.

"I'll tell you a thing happened there," Michael went on, "and you can explain it the way you please. It's there Donal and I were on our keeping after we escaped from Mountjoy."

"Donal O'Donell?" asked Frank.

"Yes; he got a life-sentence, you know, and we were to be transferred to Pentonville. My own sentence was only two years, but I was fairly desperate for him. If you ever knew him you'd understand; he'd never been in a city a week together—a long-limbed mountainy lad, the quickest brain I ever met, extraordinarily confident and proud. He'd a kind of thirst for life for its own sake that you don't find often among the boys, yet the death-sentence seemed to give him a kind of joy; 'twas the commutation he couldn't stand—things looked fairly hopeless, you know, then—and Pentonville for life.

We knew 'twould be a desperate chance; he had a damaged foot, he'd be hard to disguise too, with his fiery hair; but 'twas worth any risk and we had Pierce O'Donovan outside—the gaol was never built Pierce couldn't break; we made a plan you'd think crazy and got away.

I'll not forget that night—the sky over us and a grand

wind full of rain and a cruel moon and we driving like fury in an open car, clean through the city and over the hills! Half a dozen times we were halted, but Pierce had licences and all and we got through. He put us with an old couple in the last cottage in the glen—Glenmalure —who welcomed us like their own. We were to stay there till Donal's foot would be well, then we'd be sent for to join the column in the hills.

'Twas a strange land to us both—different altogether from Sligo or Donal's place, Donegal: a steep narrow valley in a wilderness of naked hills, all rocks, bracken and dead gorse, treacherous with spots of bog; the hills are channelled everywhere with torrents—you hear the noise of them night and day. Old Moran was forever warning us: "Many a one got lost here and was never found; the Glen doesn't like strangers," he used to say.

I had no love for the Glen; 'twould be beautiful on the frosty mornings when Lugnacullia had a crest of snow, but in the afternoons—'twas December—when the sun fell behind Clohernagh and the whole place went chill and dark under a vast shadow, you felt drowned . . . I said to Donal it was too like Synge's play. Donal didn't know Synge's play; he never had much use for books; he'd rather be making history than reading it; he loved the Glen: " 'Tis a grand place," he said, "heroic; it remembers the old times."

His foot was better; he could hobble a good way with a stick and we explored the nearer hills on those bright cold mornings—Slieve Moan and Fananieran and Cullentragh. Donal was wild to climb to the Three Lochs, but old Moran made a scare: "There are bog holes you'd sink in and never rise," he said; " 'twould be a good man would do it on a summer day, let alone in the snow"; and not a soul in the valley would guide us, so we gave it up.

One day, though, we followed the torrent to Art's Loch;

it was the longest climb Donal had done and he was pleased; a place like that exhilarated him. The sun was setting and there was a red stormy light on the water lying lost there in its hollow among the great hills. Dead solitary the loch is; I thought there was no life in it at all, but Donal was excited: " 'Tis these places are haunted," he said, "by the old Chieftains and Kings." He looked like one of them himself standing there with the ruddy light on his face; predestined to victory he looked. A song Mrs Moran used to be quoting came into my head, about "The King of Ireland's son" and "the crown of his red-gold hair," but the sun sank and the shadow rose over him and a black thought crossed my mind—"He is the sort England always kills." That place would make you afraid of death.

There was trouble in the glens, we heard; it would likely be after Christmas before anyone would come for us; being ignorant of the country it would be useless setting off by ourselves. We got impatient waiting; maybe we went too freely about the hills; Donal was very heedless with strangers; they'd often stare at him as if wanting to remember his face. Anyway, on Christmas Eve the waiting came to an end.

'Twas a savagely cold day with a wind out of the north and a black sky and folks were staying at home. We sat all the evening with the Morans round a gorgeous fire talking, or rather listening to Donal's talk. He was in one of his keen, inventive moods when he'd plan laws and constitutions and lay out the whole government of Ireland the way you'd tell faery tales to a child. Some of his ideas would startle you, but he'd not let you off till you saw they were sound. He drew a map of Ireland on the bellows with a burnt stick and started planning a military defence; it was a great plan surely that he made. "We could face the nations of the world," he said, "if we had no traitors in our own. Ireland's a natural fortress, the best God made."

"God keep you!" said Mrs Moran fervently: "God spare you, son!"

There was a sharp knock at the door and we stood up; old Moran opened; it was a girl, a neighbour's girl, who worked at the hotel; she was wet and breathless and shivering with cold. The Black and Tans were drinking at the hotel; they had raided Glendaloch and Laragh; they were raiding Glenmalure, "For the two lads escaped out of Mountjoy." She had guessed suddenly and deserted her work to warn us—run all the way. "Beasts and devils they are! My God! if you heard the threats and curses! Into the hills with you," she pleaded, "for God's sake!"

Donal looked at old Moran, "Where will we go?" The old man shook his head wretchedly: "If I could tell you that—" "If you could get to Reilly's at the Three Lochs," the girl said, "they'll not look as far as that; or O'Toole's of Granabeg, or Mr Barton's; but you'll not get so far; you'd have to pass Glendaloch."

Mrs Moran was parcelling up food and sobbing, "My God! My God! the boggy hills and the snow, and he with a broken foot!" Snow was falling, steady and deliberate, out of the leaden sky; Donal looked at it and smiled, the way you'd smile at an enemy; it was better than Pentonville. We thanked brave little Nannie and hugged poor old Mrs Moran and set out, facing north.

There was the ford to cross, then the precipitous face of Lugduff Mountain to scale; by the time we had clambered to the ridge and looked down on Glenmalure again it was night. We saw through the snowfall white lights rushing along the road below, and shots sounding like volleys echoed among the hills.

Our way lay over a rugged moorland, unbroken save for boulders and thwarted trees, a waste of bog and heather, stiff grasses and withered bracken all buried in snow; no light or outline of a house was visible; only the curves of the hilltops against the sky. We knew nothing of these regions; nothing of the direction in which any habitation lay; we could only push straight onward and trust to luck, keeping our faces to the wind.

But there was no luck with us; the snow never ceased falling; not one star shone; each step was a separate labour; the snow drove in our faces; I grew heavy and numb with cold; Donal dragged forward steadily with the help of his stick, but he did not speak at all; I saw his face by the pale gleam of the snow; it was white and grim with pain. He refused angrily to take my arm.

It comes back like a nightmare now: the two of us plodding on towards nothing, labouring up hill and down again, hour after painful hour, the desert around us looking forever the same; we might have been working in a circle for all I knew. At last Donal reeled and clutched my arm, then stood up, breathing through his teeth. I asked if his foot had given out. "If I could rest it a minute," he gasped; "it's only the lumpy ground . . ."

The snow had lightened a little and we could see: a black heaven and a white earth; sharp granite edges thrusting up through the snow; down hill, to our left, a clump of trees.

My own feet were like lead, frozen: I was stupified with cold and could think of nothing to do; I felt a monstrous weight was against us, compassing our destruction: the hills were malignant to us, and the wind, and God. Donal had his senses still; he whispered, "Make for the trees!"

We reached the clump of firs at last and got a respite from the wind; Donal sank down on a fallen trunk, easing the tortured foot; I leaned against a tree, dizzy; I was afraid to sit down. Already that craving was over me that comes so fatally in snow, to abandon the forlorn, dreamlike struggle and lie down in the soft fleeciness and sleep. But Donal had risen, suddenly, as though called: "Come on," he said tensely, "we mustn't rest."

We stood together in the open again, wondering which way to go; one way seemed as meaningless as another; all led to the same end. Donal looked at me for a moment remorsefully: "I'm sorry, Mike," he said, "you could have managed it alone."

I was answering angrily, but he stopped me with "Hush! Look there!" pointing straight in front of him; then he started forward again whispering, "Come on!"

He was following something; I followed him and at last, through the veil of blowing snow, I saw it too—a tall, dark, striding form.

A crazy zig-zag course we made, following that far-off figure which never noticed us, never beckoned us, never turned.

Down a steep rough hillside we went and far along the bank of a frozen stream; up a wooded slope and out once more on a white plain. Dizzied with swirling snow, choked and aching with the cold, we followed—no thought or will left to us of our own.

Donal stopped short now and then for a moment, paralysed by pain, but limped on again; our guide never stopped; we never came near enough to call to him, never near enough to see more than the lithe, tall figure of a boy moving fearlessly through the night.

We were travelling over a difficult, stony hillside, steering towards a black grove of trees, when Donal lurched sideways and leaned on my shoulder, his eyes closed. I saw he was done, exhausted, and I held him, looking for our guide. He had gone; he seemed to have disappeared into the trees. But below us lay the road: it would be easier going; it must lead to houses: hope—the hope of dear life—rose up in me, and Donal opened his eyes. "Come on," he said faintly, standing up and then, with a twisted smile, "I'll have to lean on you."

We had not gone ten yards when the air rumbled with a familiar sound and below us from the right, round the turn of the hill they came driving—those lurching, malignant lights. We were in full view from the road, on the bare hillside, and those were lorries below.

I saw them crashing along and stopping, saw the rutty road splashed with brilliance from the headlights; saw the men dismounting and heard a hoarse voice shouting orders as they scattered to left and right.

I looked at Donal. "Run," he commanded, "I'll follow," and at the first step he pitched headlong and lay on the snow.

On the hillside opposite, the far side of the road, a searchlight from the lorry began to play. To rise, to attempt to drag or carry Donal would have betrayed us both; he was in a dead faint, his face like marble; I lay down, crouched over him in the snow.

Men out of the lorries came swarming up, searching with flash lamps, cursing brutally as they came. Then the searchlight swung over and began to play along our side of the hill. The broad beam came creeping over the slope: I saw the intense black and white pictures leap out of the darkness one by one—saw every boulder, every bunch of stubble as it swept steadily towards where we lay. The searchers crossed it, reeling—they were drunk; they carried bayonets; they were Black and Tans. I pulled my gun out and held it at Donal's head—I meant to fire when the light touched us—God forgive me! what else was there to do?

Then, suddenly, I saw our guide again; down from the cover of the trees he came leaping, between us and the path of light. I heard the triumphant yell of the searchers as the beam caught him full—a tall slim figure with lifted arms. He stood an instant, then ran, swift as a deer, clean across the shaft of light, away from us into the dark again;

volleys of shots and a wild clamour of yells followed him as he ran.

I staggered to my feet, dazed, half-believing I was in a dream; for I had seen him when the light fell on him—the long limbs and the high head and the red wind-blown hair; I would have sworn a hundred oaths that it was Donal, but Donal lay beside me on the snow.

The shouts and firing followed the flyer and the sweeping light followed him over the hill. The lorries were turned and followed, driven madly along the road, and we were left in the empty night. I put my coat over him, chafed his hands and tried to warm his lips with my breath —nothing seemed any good. An awful memory came to me of the story of poor Art O'Neill, fugitive in those glens, frozen to death.

I began to run blindly, for no reason, towards the trees.

Out of the grove of trees a light shone; it was shining from an open door. I stumbled into the light and up the steps of a stone house; a grey-haired man stood there and a girl. "There's a man out there," I told them, "in the snow."

They called servants and ran out with lanterns and a great dog followed them and found him and they brought him in.

It took a long time to revive him, and his foot was lamed with frost-bite, but not much, and, but for that, he was soon well.

We had come, I think, to the kindest folk in Ireland—the O'Byrnes of Glendasan. We must have travelled a dangerous way, they said, through Glenrigh, where King O'Toole is buried, past the grave of poor Art O'Neill—they knew the whole region—it was their own, and its histories, but they knew nothing about our guide.

The Black and Tans caught nobody in the Glen."

Amazed faces were turned to Michael as he ended his tale.

Frank O'Carroll frowned but was silent; Max Barry, who is a rapacious historian, spoke eagerly: "Art O'Neill? . . . Glenmalure! . . . Didn't Aodh Ruadh . . . wasn't it there?" "Yes," Una answered with glowing eyes, "Aodh Ruadh O'Donal!—Red Hugh!"

Michael nodded, "That is what Donal says."

ANNE DEVLIN

Passages

I have a strange story to tell. Even now it is not easy for me to remember how much I did actually hear or see, and how much I imagined. The journey between the shore of memory and the landfall of imagination is an unknown distance, because for each voyager it is a passage through a different domain. This story has a little to do with mapping that passage, but only a little: it is also a confession.

In the summer of '72 I was travelling in Ireland, calling on friends in Dublin, seeing relatives in the West, putting minor touches to my book on Dreams, looking for more folk-tales, and eavesdropping on people's dreams without drawing too much attention to the fact that it was my profession. I have been involved in analysis for several years. I'm not popular with colleagues because they see me as a kind of "pop" analyst—a collector of stories. And in a way that is what I am. On this occasion, while I was staying in Dublin at Sandycove in a house belonging to some friends who had gone abroad for a few months, a girl came to see me.

She had heard I was in Dublin, indeed she knew that I was expected to give a public lecture at Trinity that evening on the subject of my book and so she came to see me because she had a dream to tell me. This is not so strange as it sounds. I had asked several of my colleagues at the university if any of the undergraduates they taught would be prepared to volunteer unusual or disturbing dreams which might help in my research. I was not interested in individual analysis, or the concept of "cure"—I made that perfectly clear: I was interested merely in the content of dream stories as a source for fiction. My earlier publication had been on "History and the Imagination: A study of Nordic, Greek and Celtic Mythology". My next inevitable step was to turn my attention to dream territory. I had advertised and asked for people with particularly unusual, disturbing or prophetic dreams to come forward; I had promised privacy in that I did not wish to know the identity of the people concerned.

An old college friend of mine who was teaching history at Trinity rang me on the morning the girl came to see me. He explained that one of his students had a dream to tell which she did not wish to write down but which she thought might be of interest to me. I agreed to see her at his insistence. This was the girl who came. I was more aware of the dangers of exposing dreams than most others: dreams are very confessional; they offer a power relationship to the hearer in that they ask for absolution. They are a freeing device for the speaker, but the sin has to rest with someone: the priest absolves the sin but he also carries it with him; like the Christ figure he carries the cross that others may be free. This was not a role I cherished or viewed with any great pleasure. I was very wary of people who did invite others to unburden themselves—the result could only be masochism or sadism: the wilful acceptance of suffering or the inflicting of pain: there was no other way. I would either be hurt or hurt in my turn: being human I could not remain neutral. I met the girl with extreme reluctance, and wondered at her motives for wishing to confront me with her story.

Her appearance did nothing to allay my fears; in fact, it increased what I already felt would be a momentous and disturbing meeting. I remember her now as looking very child-like: she had the look of a small elf—which some men find appealing. She was tense and anxious, as though at some point she had taken the decision to hold back. I did not like her much. I find that sort of woman manipulative; full of little betrayals, because of the insecurity of her knowing that she did not rank among the women. Fear was written all over her face.

She looked as if she were on the run from something. And I knew, because I had seen such cases before, that she was haunted. During our opening small talk her utterances came out in jagged phrases, exclamations, sentences begun then abandoned, then taken up with a different subject: she made so many promising beginnings yet never knew quite how to complete them. But in relation to one thing she was utterly articulate: the story she told.

This, then, was how she began:

"When I was thirteen I was invited to spend the long summer vacation at the home of a friend who lived in Dublin. Sheelagh Burke was at school with me, we both attended the Dominican Convent in Portstewart. I was a daygirl; my father owned a newspaper shop in the Diamond in Portstewart. Sheelagh was a boarder; her parents lived in Dublin, where her father had something to do with property investment. I was never very clear. The thing about the upper middle classes even in Ireland is that the source of their income is never very precisely located; it is only a petty bourgeois mentality like mine which would seek to pin people to their incomes."

The girl had a disconcerting habit of standing back and analysing her statements—placing them in a social context, thereby dismissing her own assumptions. Her tutor said she was a natural historian, if only she had the confidence to follow it through. I understood too that there had been some disturbance in her studies of a few years, but was not clear about the nature of this, and had not asked. These thoughts were going through my mind as she continued.

"My parents were delighted at the invitation: this was precisely why they had wanted me to go to grammar school—to make friends like Sheelagh Burke. The Burke house at Sandycove was not far from here, and it was remarkable. It was at the far end of that long stretch of coast road which runs away from Trinity corner in the direction of the Dun Laoghaire ferry terminal, beyond the Martello Tower and still further. I remember arriving there so well. The house formed part of a terrace set back from the main road. There was a small green in front and a gravel path or drive separated the green from the four double-fronted Georgian houses which stood there; the house belonging to the Burkes was the last of the four—that is, the one furthest from Dublin city. Like the other houses it was three storeys high and had a basement, with a separate entrance by the railings outside the front door. The basement was something new in the way of houses to me. In a seaside town like Portstewart there is only the unrelenting parade of low-lying bungalows in wide bare salt-stripped gardens, occasionally relieved by some modern two-storey houses, a row or two of Victorian terraces and of course the Convent itself, a castle of Gothic proportions perched on the cliff face. I had never been in a house with a basement before, and absolutely nothing of the neighbourhood I grew up in equalled the elegance of this fine wide-roomed house, with its brass handles and porticoes, wooden stairways and cornices. A further treat was still to come with that house—the waves of the Irish Sea broke upon the back wall. The garden literally ran away to the sea. From the music-room windows we had uninterrupted views of the sea and the day marked out for us by the comings and goings of the Holyhead ferry.

"I was given a room at the top of the house on the same floor as Sheelagh and Peggy—who lived in—and the view from my window was of Howth Head. I even remember the colour of the room: it was a strong bold rose colour and the walls were full of prints of flowers and birds. The curtains matched the cover on the bed. I recorded every detail of this house, committed it to memory like I did my Latin grammar. I never questioned that this too was part of my general education. After a time it became clear to me why I had been asked to spend the summer with Sheelagh; she was lonely, there wasn't anyone else around. Her parents were remarkable by their absence. Her father, whom we saw fleetingly, flew in and out of Dublin airport with such regularity it made my head spin. Places like Zurich, Munich and New York crept in the conversation by way of explaining these disappearances. I think I met her mother as she was passing through the music-room one day on her way to lunch. And even though she lived in the house and was not flying in and out of the country, we saw even less of her. I recall that she said something like: 'Hello, you're Sheelagh's little friend? How nice of you to come.' The only other inhabitants of the house appeared to be a brother who was a student at UCD, reading Medicine or some suitably middle-class professional subject. Peggy, whom I have already mentioned, was a sort of housekeeper-cum-nanny; her role was never very clearly defined. And as Peggy was slow on her feet and found the stairs too much from time to time, there was a young girl living in also to help. She lived in the basement and was called Moraig. I said that Sheelagh's brother was an inhabitant, that was not strictly true; he had a flat somewhere in the city, and only came home at weekends to eat Peggy's Sunday lunch.

"You can imagine from this that we spent a good deal of time on our own, Sheelagh and I. We played tennis, or went swimming off the rocks at the bottom of the garden; occasionally we took long bus rides into the city and ended up having tea and cakes at Bewleys. I had never had tea in a café before, and certainly not without an adult present. It seemed to me, because of the absence of adults in our lives that summer, that we had in fact grown up; the world was unmoved by our innocence. When we ordered tea in Bewleys it appeared. No one said, as they might have done in a tea shop at home, 'What are you two children up to?' They took us seriously in Dublin. I felt I had entered a newly sophisticated world. In a few short weeks of being at that house, my confidence grew. I discovered that beds left unmade were magically made up. Clothes, even socks, could be hurled around the room with no fear of losing them; they would reappear fresh and clean a few days later. The best china and glass was used without restraint; and, even if broken, was always replaced or renewed without fuss. It put all my mother's restraints and fussy little ways in perspective: 'If you don't pick that up you will lose it; if you don't tidy that away it won't last; we can't use the best china, we might break it.' For the first time I felt I had an answer to her. What did it matter when life could be lived like this? I knew then that something was ruined for me. I have dwelt rather long on this beginning because I wanted to remember what it was like up to the point when everything changed, and not to try to suppress any of the details. Perhaps, though, I have romanticized it a little, but I don't think so. The important thing is this is how it impressed me.

"The music room, as it was called, was a long rectangle running from front to back of the house on the ground floor. It was a very grand room with a marble fireplace, two squashy sofas and a couple of battered armchairs; it had a sanded pine floor and a large indestructible and rather tatty rug—which Sheelagh had said was Indian. This was considered the children's room. It had been abandoned to the Burke children several years before; the smarter apartments and drawing room, which was out of bounds to us, were on the floor above. I never knew why it earned the name the music room, except perhaps it might have referred to the volume of noise emanating from it; because the only concession to a musical instrument that I could see was an upright piano which nobody appeared to play or know how to, standing against the same wall as the fireplace. On the opposite wall to the piano and the fireplace ran row upon row of silent books, and I believe there was a record player somewhere. But I can't quite remember where it was situated. Long small-paned windows filled the short walls at either end of the room so that the light ran right through. From the Sandycove road to the Irish Sea the view was uninterrupted.

"In the evenings when the wind coming off the sea rattled the windows, it was often quite noisy and indeed airy in the music room, even after the curtains were drawn. And it was on one such occasion while sitting in front of the fire with the wind fanning the flames, when Moraig had retreated to her basement, and Peggy was in bed with a cold, that we conceived of the idea of whiling away the evening by telling ghost stories. That is, I would. Sheelagh never told stories. In fact, she could never remember the important details, and she would often have to turn to me and say: 'What comes next? I forget.'

"I began with a favourite of both of us. I was not very original. I often told the same story twice, but usually with embellishments or twists. And Sheelagh was such a good listener and such an awful rememberer that every time she heard the story she said it sounded different. This encouraged me tremendously. I began with a story of Le Fanu's about the expected visitors who never arrive: at one point in the evening the family who are waiting for the visitors hear the sound of carriage wheels on the gravel, they all rush outside and find no one. What I had not allowed for when I was telling this favourite tale of ours, was the fact that right outside the music room was a gravel drive. And, at precisely the part in the story when I started to explain that at the time the family heard the wheels of the carriage on the gravel, the expected visitor had died, at precisely that moment a car drew up very slowly on the gravel drive outside the music room window. Sheelagh took one leap off the carpet where we were sitting in front of the fire and fled out of the room, saying she didn't want to hear any more. I was left in the music room, still sitting in front of the fire, amazed at her alacrity. Normally, I would have been laughing myself sick at my ability to scare her, as I had often done in the past, but the trouble was this time I had scared myself. The massive coincidence necessary to tell an effective ghost story had just occurred. At precisely the time I was explaining the significance of ghostly wheels on gravel as a portent of death—a car drew up. In all my years of telling ghost stories at school, and arranging for bells to ring or doors to open at crucial moments, I had never stage-managed anything so effective as that car drawing up when it did.

"I found myself sitting in the dark of the room with only the light from the fire throwing grotesque shadows on to the walls and the groans of the wind whistling around me as company. I knew then that I could not bring myself to move through the darkness towards the door or beyond into the dark hall and then up three flights of stairs past all those closed doorways and little landings to my bed. I was riveted. So I stayed sitting still with my back to the fire, watching the silent occupants of the darkness, until I calmed down. Once or twice I imagined I saw the handle of the door turning, so I tried to think of something pleasant. But when I looked away to the window all the elements of stories I had told in broad daylight on the beach, or in the gym or the second-form common room, began to reassemble around me. And I wished I hadn't such a fertile imagination. Then, just when I managed to convince myself of my silliness and was beginning to work out how I could make another story out of the incident, something happened which arrested me so completely that I thought my heart would stop. From behind me in the fire I heard a little cry; not a groan, like the wind made, of that I am absolutely clear. It began like a short gasp and became a rising crescendo of 'hah' sounds; each one was following the one before, and getting louder each time. I experienced a moment of such pure terror that I felt my heart would burst with the strain as I waited for the gasps to reach their topmost note. Suddenly, just as the sounds had come to a peak, I felt myself propelled from the room and ran screaming upstairs. I take no responsibility for that action; a voice simply broke from my throat which corresponded to screams.

"In this state, I ran up three flights and straight into the arms of the warm, white-clad and still smelling of sleep Peggy. She had been under sedation all day because of her cold when the screams brought her to the banisters. Sheelagh was standing behind her, clutching Peggy's nightgown and howling like a lost dog. Peggy was furious rather than consoling. She smacked both of us to make me stop screeching and Sheelagh to stop howling, and then asked us what we thought we were up to. 'Bringing the house down like that' was how she put it. Characteristically Sheelagh blamed me for scaring her by telling the story; I blamed her for leaving me downstairs. Peggy resorted to her usual threats of 'Right, Madam. You go straight back to Portstewart in the morning. Do you hear?' And for the first time in the six weeks I had been there I wished she had meant it. I had had enough of the freedom of the place; inside a small voice that I thought I had grown out of was saying: 'Oh Mammy, I want to go home.' Eventually, she got us both back to bed. Calmed, and much scolded, and therefore reassured, I went to sleep.

"I am always afraid to go to sleep. I have been ever since that time, and still have lingering doubts about it. It has something to do with going to sleep with one reality and waking up with another. It was like this on that particular morning. It was late when I woke; the morning boat to Holyhead leaving Dun Laoghaire was already filling the space in the horizon between the shore and Howth Head at the half-way point. I did not wake up myself as I normally do, but was wakened instead by the arrival of Peggy carrying breakfast. She told me to eat up and get dressed and come downstairs when I was ready. There were two men who wished to talk to me. Sheelagh, she explained, was already awake and I could see her after I spoke to the men. She busied herself picking up my clothes and laying things out while I ate breakfast. What surprised me was that she stayed until I had finished and then supervised my washing. I had reached the stage where I was bashful about dressing and wished she would go. But she didn't. When I was ready we went downstairs. I was absolutely convinced now that something momentous had occurred, 'How come Moraig didn't bring breakfast this morning?' I asked, as I reached the foot of the stairs with the tray. Looking back, I am amazed at the ease with which I had become accustomed to being waited upon. Peggy did not answer but said: 'Come and meet the gentlemen who would like to talk to you.' We went into the music room and I have to admit to experiencing a momentary shudder as we passed through the door.

"My suspicions were further confirmed at finding Sheelagh's father there, along with two men. The room looked different in the morning light; below, the boat was slipping past Howth and out to the open sea. On the other side of me I caught sight of a number of cars parked on the green verge; there were some people moving up and down the basement steps. One of the men in the room moved between me and this view from the window. He shook hands and called himself Mr Maguire. He then introduced the other stranger, his friend Mr O'Rourke. I can't recall much of what they looked like except that they were both tall and Mr Maguire was heavier than Mr O'Rourke. But I guessed they were policemen.

" 'We want you to tell us now,' said Maguire, 'what it was that made you scream out last night.'

"I couldn't believe it; I turned to Peggy in alarm. Had she called the police because I had screamed? Before I could reply, Sheelagh's father uttered the first words he had ever spoken to me.

" 'Now don't worry, just tell Mr Maguire what happened. No one is going to hurt you.'

"Peggy squeezed my arm, to encourage me I expect, but immediately I decided that was precisely what they would do—hurt me—and burst into loud sobs. When I stopped crying, they persisted with the questions and so I explained how the ghost story had frightened us. I explained about the wheels on the gravel drive; how

Sheelagh had fled from the room leaving me; how I sat on until I thought I heard sounds coming from the fire behind me.

" 'Voices from the flame?' Mr O'Rourke said, looking meaningfully. 'You heard a voice talking to you from out of the fire?'

" 'Now that's enough Jack!' Maguire said.

" 'Well not exactly a voice talking, more calling out,' I explained. I am quite convinced that O'Rourke felt himself in the presence of a mystic who was in touch with speaking flames. But the other policeman wasn't so sure about the presence of the Holy Ghost in the proceedings, he kept bringing me back to what I actually did hear.

" 'Can you repeat the sounds you thought you heard?' he asked.

" 'I'm not sure,' I said, 'but I'll try.'

"I began to call in the way I thought I had heard the voice call out the evening before. To make the sound I had to take short gasps, and eventually when I was quite breathless I stopped.

" 'Why did you stop?' Maguire asked.

" 'Because I didn't hear the rest,' I explained.

" 'Why?'

" 'Because I was screaming so loudly at the time.'

"And that was all. The interview was over and so was the holiday. Sheelagh and her father drove me to the station later and I did return to Portstewart on that day after all. I would have been glad enough about it except that I felt I was going home in some disgrace, and I was not exactly sure why. Sheelagh spoke very little to me, she seemed very downcast, and told me that she was being sent to an aunt in the West of Ireland for the rest of the summer. 'I hate it there. I'll go mad with boredom,' she said. The last time I saw her she was waving goodbye from the platform at Connolly Station. She did not return to school in September, and she did not write to me as promised. My parents never questioned my early return as I was sure they would. I gave up telling stories after that."

"But what happened?" I asked. I found myself growing impatient. "And what has all this to do with dreams?"

"You're rushing me," she said. "And I have to unfold it slowly. They never told me and I didn't ask because somewhere deep down I already knew it was something profoundly disturbing. Then, one day, when seven years had passed, the truth surfaced to confront me, and this is what happened. I went to Queen's as a first-year history student in '68; the first year of the disturbances in the city. But I wasn't really interested in politics and knew very little about what was happening, except that there were mass meetings in the union, the McMordie Hall and in the streets. It was the beginning of the civil rights movement, when educated Catholics had awakened to political consciousness. Coming from Portstewart I never had any sense of discrimination that Catholics in the city seemed to feel. It never occurred to me that there were official and unofficial histories. Or that Protestants could go through school never having heard of Parnell or the Land League. I always thought that history was simply a matter of scholarship. In the seminars during my first year at university the students were fighting and hacking and forging out of the whole mass of historical detail a theory which made it right for them to march through the streets of Belfast to demand equal rights for Catholics. It was the most exciting year of my life; inevitably I fell in love.

"He was a counterpoint to everything my father, with his little shop and cautious peace-keeping ways, stood for. He was outspoken and clever and courageous; he didn't care who he offended, and he held back for nothing and no one. Until that time I had spent my whole life living on the edge of the kind of respectability that people who run a corner shop find necessary in order to secure a trade and therefore their livelihood. I had heard my father humour the diverse opinions of so many of the customers that I grew to believe opinions were something one expressed but did not necessarily believe in, or indeed act upon. As we ran a newsagent's it became the venue for discussion of current events, particularly on a Sunday morning, when the locals would stroll in to collect the "sundies" and debate the week's news at leisure.

" 'It's about time O'Neill got the finger out over this free-trade business. Why should Lemass do all the running?'

" 'Ah, now, Mr O'Neill's a good man,' I can hear my father interrupt. 'He sends his girl to the convent. Did you know that?'

" 'No, it's not the same O'Neill. You're thinking of the brother.'

" 'It's not a brother; he's the man's uncle.'

" 'That's just the trouble, the government's full of O'Neills; it's very confusing.'

"My father always had a good word to say about everyone. If any politician was criticized he was quick to find some redeeming feature. With the result that I too became something of an apologist when it came to historical circumstances. That is, until I found myself walking en route from the university to the City Hall beside a provoking and thoroughly objectionable undergraduate: John Mulhern. I remember going home for the weekend following some of the first civil rights marches Belfast had witnessed, and finding my father fuming over the early dispatches of the Sunday papers.

" 'Fools and trouble-makers, that's what they are! We have a fine, peaceful little country here. What do they have to go making trouble for?'

"I kept my involvement a secret and refused to be drawn into any of the discussions in the shop which raged during the eleven o'clock Mass. It was a feature of most Sunday mornings that the women went to Mass while the men stayed in the papershop. Then I heard my father say, 'I can't afford a political viewpoint!' as someone tried to draw him out. 'That is a political viewpoint—pure petty bourgeoisie self-interest' was my unexpected reply. It came straight out of the mouth of John Mulhern. I knew I should not have said it (a) because I couldn't justify it, and (b) because I had as good as betrayed my father by taking sides against him in the shop. There was a deafening silence, so much so that you could actually hear the waves crashing along the wall of the promenade some distance down the hill.

" 'That's the stuff! You young ones with your education will tell them boys at Stormont where to get off!' said the man who had provoked the row in the first place. My father, whose anger was all in his face until that point, burst out, 'If that's all the good a university education has done for you, I rue the day you ever went to that place.'

"The conversation was over. I fled into the back of the shop and he followed me. 'Your mother and I broke our backs scraping and saving to give you a chance. If this is how you repay us you can take yourself out of here back to your friends in Belfast with their clever remarks and smart ways; but don't ever come here again, shaming me in front of my friends.'

"We never talked about anything important after that; I withdrew and so did they. I was thrown almost completely on to my friends in the city until I ceased to come home at all. My parents had ceased to expect me to. Occasionally I suppose they would read about this march or that and would guess I was there.

"This is peripheral, I know, but I am coming to the

point. I said the truth about that summer all those years before reappeared at a particular moment. I have given you all this detail because I am a historian and a materialist and somewhere in all these factors an answer may emerge as to why at this particular period in my life the truth, or a perception, should become clear to me.

"It was the sixth of January when we returned to Belfast from Derry after the civil rights march which had taken four days to reach Derry had been attacked at Burntollet Bridge. I remember we, John and I, and two other students who lived in his house, were all feeling very fragile, very tired, and yet strangely elated. Something had been brought to the surface in the façade of political life—the cracks were throwing all sorts of horrors out into the sunlight. I had never slept with John before until that night.

"We had begun to make love and I was lying back in the dark looking at him. I closed my eyes and suddenly I found myself crying out in a way which was strangely familiar: I uttered or heard myself utter a series of small gasps until at the point when the note rose to its highest point I opened my eyes. Then I screamed and screamed and screamed. I imagined that John would strangle me and screamed out in terror. After that the room was full of lights and voices. As soon as the lights came on of course I was no longer afraid of him. The other students in the house thought I ought to have a sedative so a doctor was called. He tried to get me to take a sleeping pill, but I only wanted to rid myself of what I knew. 'She was murdered. Moraig was murdered. He strangled her.' I was rambling on incoherently, as it must have appeared to the onlookers, trying to piece together parts of the story of seven years before. I felt bombarded by signs and images and the meaning of events. They persisted in making me take the sleeping pill and so I gave in. Afterwards I resented having done so, because when I did reawaken I knew that I had passed from that state for ever, and would never arrive at a perception so intensely felt again. With the morning and the new awareness my parents came, and with them a chill. As though they had brought with them the bleak wind which blows in off the Atlantic along the prom and leaves small deposits of sea-salt in the corners of their mouths. I felt the ice kisses on my damp cheek and tasted the bitterness of those salt-years. Before them lay the wreck of a daughter in whom they had invested everything.

"The last communication I had had with my parents prior to that day was a letter from my mother on the first day of January wishing me well for the New Year and informing me of the death of Sheelagh Burke. She had driven off a cliff at Westpoint—near her aunt's house in Galway—a few days before. There is a faint irony in that; her banishment was from Dublin to Westpoint seven years before. It was as though everything had come full circle; some strange mystery had unravelled—wound down. I seem to remember that the tone of my mother's letter was half-reproachful as though in Sheelagh's death was some responsibility of mine. I put the letter in my bag and took it with me on the march; but I lost it somewhere on the road to Derry. I explain this detail again because it may also have been a factor prompting the truth of that evening when Moraig was murdered to the surface of my mind. You see, I too had come to feel that the whole event was the result of some strange invocation of mine. I had called up, or dreamed up, the death just as surely as if I had murdered Moraig."

"But you didn't dream it; you say it happened!" I said, reminding her.

"I haven't told you the rest of the story."

"So far you haven't told me anything original: this is

either Sleeping Beauty or Alice in Wonderland!" I said irritably. "But please go on."

"Haven't you realized that at precisely the moment in my story when I was explaining the significance of wheels on the gravel drive as a sign of death, the car carrying the murderer drew up? I created the event. What is more I later heard a woman making love up to the point of strangulation when I began screaming for her. It was no mystical experience: I heard her cries coming up through the chimney passage. Apparently her bed was right next to the boxed-in fireplace in the basement. When I sat with my back to the fireplace I heard everything. Seven years later when I made love for the first time I re-experienced the earlier memory and found the truth."

"The truth?"

"Yes. When I was making love and I opened my eyes one split second before I screamed out, I saw something. The face I was looking at was not the face of my lover."

"Whose face did you see?"

"I saw Sheelagh's brother. I saw John Burke's face."

We regarded each other openly for the first time, in the way two human beings do when the mask has slipped stripped away either by love or fear—and familiar traces of another remembering show through.

"At what point in the story did you recognize me?" she asked.

"Very early on; but I wanted to hear you out. At one point you almost had me believing you were someone else. I found myself thinking that I was listening to another coincidental story. You changed the names and the house location; that was imaginative. But you rather over-dramatized my sister's death. She did not drive off the cliff at Westpoint. She died of a heroin overdose in a basement flat in Islington. She had become a drop-out a few years before and we lost touch with her. So you see reality is more ignominious. Still, she would have liked your version better—it romanticized her. But then I seem to remember you have a panache for that. Why did you come here with this memory? I find it all very painful."

"Why did I come?"

She had no sympathy for my pain; I had not stopped her but made her angry instead.

"You can ask me that? I have spent three years of my life in a hospital. Did you know?"

I shook my head.

"I can't sleep with the light out; I can't lie in the dark in case I see your face. For three years I took their drugs and their treatments but I kept my secret because I knew the one thing which would cure me was that one day I would be able to confront you with the truth."

"The truth? What is the truth?"

"You killed Moraig."

"Your hallucination of one face on to another isn't proof of a person being a murderer."

"Not proof—truth!" she said emphatically. "The imagination presents or dramatizes as well as intuiting a reality which is nearer the truth than any perception we arrive at through understanding, that is what I believe. And that is what I came here to find out. If I haven't awoken to reality after all this time, then I have awoken to madness. If I'm not through to truth then I'm through to madness. I believe you murdered Moraig because I saw your face."

"Have you told anyone else?"

"No one—not until now," she said. "I need an admission from you—not a denial. I am either sane or mad."

"It's metaphysics. Sanity or insanity," I said.

"It's not metaphysics. It's the difference between truth and lies."

"Let me give you a better explanation of what happened—one you can live with. The car drawing up was a coincidence; it may or may not have had something to do with the murderer's arrival. But two half-hysterical little girls managed to convince themselves that they heard it and so it must be like that. A servant girl, Moraig, was murdered by her lover; and you heard her cries as you said through the chimney passage. Now there is another factor which you haven't mentioned. One of those little girls had a massive crush on her friend's brother. She also knew that he was friendly with Moraig. She knew because she saw them exchanging glances. Isn't it possible that you saw his face when your lover—also called John—was making love to you for the first time because that was the face you wanted to see? You fused the murder of Moraig and the desire to see me into one single incident. And you went to great lengths to say how much you loved this other John—I found it a total diversion, an unconvincing obsession with that part of the story. Was it in case I guessed that you chose him for the resemblance between the names? John's name and mine are the same in reality and in the story. Why?"

"Because I wanted you to remember," she said. "I wanted to see your fear, as you have seen mine. Nothing you have said convinces me that you did not kill Moraig."

"Don't persist with this," I warned her. "I've offered you a way out. You have a strong healthy young mind now—don't pursue this fantasy path any further."

"That is exactly why I came to see you. To find a way back to a path I once knew. I don't want an explanation or a denial but I need an admission of your guilt before I can break out of this . . ." She paused as though she knew the word but could not use it; it came out eventually ". . . nightmare!"

At that point she began to cry.

I watched her very closely and realized for the first time that she was wrong; she did not need an admission; she was already free. In the telling of her story she had changed. She had lost the haunted look: she had confessed. After a while when she was quieter, I asked: "What became of John Mulhern—your lover? You didn't say."

"After that night it wasn't the same between us. He was afraid of me, and I think I was of him. I was taken home for a while to Portstewart and nursed by my mother. A short time after that I was admitted to a sanatorium, as I have already told you. I came to Dublin only this year, to resume my studies. They thought I was better out of the North. He became something in the paramilitary, and is very well known. I heard that he married someone recently, but I don't recall the details."

"He didn't wait for you to heal?"

"No. He didn't wait."

It was that time of day when the Holyhead ferry has passed the tip of Howth on its journey out to open sea; the sun shone on the rocks at Sandycove, and a woman, young, but a woman none the less—faint lines around her mouth marked her out—standing by a window, traced its slow passage forth. There would be many more comings and goings to and from the shore, and many more passages to make as time went by; but at the moment, all her attention was with this one.

I looked away from the window; and found myself alone in the room.

L. A. G. STRONG

Let Me Go

I never saw a ghost only the once, and then I not only saw him; I heard and smelt him. If he'd been a bit closer to me, I could have touched him. He was so natural, I hardly realized he was a ghost, at first. And when I did, the poor fella looked so pitiful, he was so real in his speech and his squalor, so gentle and mild, sure no one could be afraid of him.

It was in the County Tipperary, all of twenty-seven years ago. I have a queer clutch of cousins down there—if they're in it, yet, indeed, for I never heard of them for years now, nor ever visited them saving that one time.

They lived in a great barrack of a place, a kind of a country house come down to being a farm. The rooms were enormous. I was brought upstairs to put my bag in a bedroom big enough for a platoon. Ah, they were a strange lot, the oddest ever, for all they were my cousins.

Three big black-bearded sons, all over six foot, a stout middle-aged sister with rosy cheeks, a thick waist, and the hint of a moustache, a meagre wistful old mother with an empty face and vague eyes, and, until he died, somewhere above stairs, an unseen father with asthma and an invincible objection to visitors. Maybe that was why none of them had married. They were well-to-do farming people, as far as I could see, but there was a depressed queerness about them that I couldn't fathom at all. Fine set-up, presentable, all but handsome, there they sat, the brothers and the sister, and not a word out of them.

The house was dark and cold. It would have been deathly, even in August, only for a huge turf fire in an open stone fireplace, where you could have roasted an ox. Divil a sign of book or newspaper in the place, and, as dusk fell, the smallest lamp on earth, hanging from the rafters on a brass chain, and lighting dimly a wilderness of black hams, sides of bacon, and festooning onions.

We ate in silence, only for the champing of jaws over the food. The table was long, and we sat so far away from one another that each was isolated. I essayed a remark or two, drew nothing but a grunt from one brother, and a faded, absent smile from the mother, and shut up.

When we'd done, the mother disappeared without a word, and the rest of us drew our chairs to the fire and sat in sombre silence. The turf sods smouldered away: now and then one would fall, sending up a shower of sparks and lighting the place far better than the little lamp, which only showed up the gloom.

I'm an adaptable sort of a lad, and was even more so then, so I sat with my thoughts and watched the fire. When one of the men spoke, it made me jump.

"Where have you put our cousin to sleep, sister?"

"Och," says she, "above in grandfather's room."

"Bedad," says black-beard number two, "it must be thirty year since any person slept there."

"Never fear," says the sister, giving me a quite human smile. "There's a jar in the bed, and the clothes on it are hot out of the cupboard."

I smiled and said something or other, but truth to tell I was relieved, for if there's one thing I've a dread of, it's a chill bed. There was another long silence, an hour maybe, and then the sister rose, lit an inch of candle in a heavy old brass candlestick, and gave me it, saying nothing at all.

I took this candle, bade them all good night, and went up the wooden stair that led straight out of the room. At the bend I paused and looked down at them, the three black brothers and the old maid, musing there at the fire as if I had never existed.

I had to go easy on the vast landing, for queer breezes sprang at me from nowhere, and made my candle gutter. At last I reached the room. The big four-poster bed stood in the middle, with the head facing the door. I felt in it. It was warm and welcoming. With the door shut behind me, my spirits rose. I'd be all right here, anyway, and tomorrow I could bid the house and its occupants good-bye, and need never return.

I got into bed, and put out the candle, with fresh pleasure, for it only emphasized the vast space of the room and the height of the ceiling. Now my world was small and warm and immediate. The moonlight that came in the windows fell on a high-backed chair and on the floor. They were tall, eighteenth-century windows, two of them uncurtained. The only curtains were a pair on either side of the bed, reaching perhaps half way along. I made to pull one back, but it was stiff; I thought of the possible shower of earwigs and such I might bring down, and let it be.

For a time I couldn't sleep. My perplexity about the household had made my mind alert and clear. I tried various specifics, from reckoning sheep to trying to remember Scott's "Lady of the Lake". Then I reconciled myself to being comfortable, and fell asleep, as so often happens when one has the sense to relax.

I don't know what hour it was when I awoke, conscious that there was someone in the room: but the moonlight had walked away from the chair to another part of the floor, and a faint additional light came through the windows, as of approaching dawn. I noticed this, for I wasn't in the least bit scared. To this day, the divil nor a bench of bishops will never persuade me but I was wide awake and with all my wits about me.

I turned my head calmly to one side, and there was my visitor, close beside the bed. Did you ever see *She Stoops to Conquer*? You've saved me a deal of trouble, so: for there stood Tony Lumpkin, only a Tony in fear of the bailiffs, maybe, all his jauntiness and joking gone; ay, and most of his loutishness too, poor divil, for there he stood, downcast and miserable. His carroty hair was tied behind with a black bow, and his ruffles were dingy and stained with tobacco, or snuff, or port, or porter—maybe all four. He wore a shabby green velvet coat with breeches to match, and a yellow brocade sprigged waistcoat. He had grey worsted stockings on him, all in wrinkles, and black brogue shoes with gleaming paste buckles.

How did I see all that, all the detail of his clothes, with the room dark but for a faint light from the windows and a patch of moonlight on the floor? I can't tell you, except that I did see it. I have the feeling he sort of generated his own light, or else I was seeing him in another dimension, as it were. But, while at the same time I was perfectly well aware of the room about me, I did in fact see with what I can only call a kind of subdued clearness. I can't explain it.

He had an anxious, monkey sort of a face, reddish and freckled, and a small forehead that suggested he wasn't overburdened with brains. When he saw that I was looking at him, he gave me a poor propitiatory sort of a smile. His teeth were stained and irregular, and he could have done with a shave. I saw his hands then: they were coarse and the nails broken and dirty. He looked for all the world like a small broken fox-hunting squire.

I was wondering what the divil to do, when suddenly he made a gawky bow and scraped his right foot on the floor.

"Sarvint, sir. Sarvint," he said.

The light seemed to get stronger: certainly I could see him more clearly. The metal buttons on his velvet coat shone in a dull sort of way, and he smelled strongly of bacon, turf, and stables. There he stood, pathetic, anxious, grinning at me.

I cleared my throat. "I didn't hear you come in," I said. "Are you—are you staying here?"

"Faith," said he, "I've stayed here this many's the year, and here I'll stay till I'm let depart. Yerrah," said he, "I'm a stranger to this place, for all I've been here so long. Thank God you spoke to me. Do ye know, you're the first man has addressed a civil word to me all the time since I came?"

"Well," said I, raising myself on my elbow and smiling at him, "can I do anything for you at all?"

"Indeed and you can, sir," said the small squire. "I hear tell that once a man's buried with the rites of the Church, he'll be let rest. Well, I amn't buried, sir, far from it, and my bag with a matter of a hundred and twenty-five guineas gone from me all these years. The way it is with me, sir, drifting around and looking on a million faces to find the one kind face, and me not knowing are they living persons or forlorn as I am, yerrah, 'tis the hell of a life, sir, but you'll help me, sure I know you will. You're too fat and too kindly to be mean, and you're not afeard of me, and sure that's everything. It beats me," he said, fumbling apparently for his snuff box, "why folk do be in dread of a man in my state, for we couldn't hurt a flea, even if we wanted to."

"Tell me," said I. "What happened to you?"

"Ay, sir. What happened was this. It was towards the tail-end of August, this very month and, damme, I believe this was the night, though I can't be sure, I'm a bit confused on me dates, so long after. I was sent to Dublin—"

"Hold hard," I said. "What year was it? Do you remember that?

"Seventeen ninety-seven," says he. "There's no doubt of the year, anyway. I was sent into Dublin with a letter and a bag of one hundred and twenty-five guineas for a house in Thomas Street. Number eight. I was to deliver the bag and the letter there to a man who was to give me a receipt for them, and I was to come back without delay to Kilmallock. Them was my orders."

"Who gave you the orders?"

"Mr Ormonde. Ormonde of Kilmallock. I was employed there as a sort of gentleman steward. I'd come down in the world, what with drinking and hunting and other things. Them was my orders. But, sir," his eyes opened wide at me, and his lower lip drooped, "divil a bit I ever set foot in Dublin. I was on a sorrel mare, with a pair of horse pistols," he showed me with his hands, in pantomime that would have been comic if I hadn't been so sorry for the poor fella: I liked him well already—"a pair of horse pistols, a French cloak, and my glazed three-cornered hat without e'er a cockade. It came on to blow and rain close by here, with thunder and lightning. The sorrel was nervous, and I was no better; so, seeing a light ahead, I came to this door below and knocked at it with the butt of my whip. A couple of hounds bayed their heads off in some distant part of the house, and presently the door was opened a few inches by a sulky-looking serving-man with a lantern. I told him how it was with me, and begged shelter for the night for myself and the mare.

"Without a word he came out on the steps and brought the mare away to the stables, at least I suppose he did. Then he came back and conducted me to the kitchen below. It was like a dining-room then. A mighty queer-lookin' fella was seated at the table, a tall man with a black beard on him, a rusty wig, and a dingy black dressing-gown. He was all sorts of a queer fella, for beards didn't be worn, only by philosophers and astrologers and mad lads o' that sort. It gave me a turn, seeing him there, but he up polite enough and asked would I share his supper with him.

"I was sharp set, so I agreed glad enough. The place looked poor, but the food was good and the wine better. It wasn't long before I was blathering, and the lad with the beard knew all about me. He was mighty friendly, I lost all dread of his beard, and after maybe the fifth bottle I was singing and soon fell under the table. I remember the serving-man and another carrying me up to bed, from which I never woke, sir, not in the flesh that is, but as you see me now, and my guineas lost, and with them my soul, or near as no matter."

And the tears began to come out of his comical puckered eyelids and to hang on the stubble of his chin.

I was about to attempt some consoling remark, when there was a jag of bright blue lightning followed by a terrific crashing peal of thunder. Torrential rain dashed at the window, and roared like surf above the roof. I saw my poor friend the squire move slowly and sadly, as if his time was up and he not half done what he wanted to tell me: I watched him move towards the wall on my left, where I was staggered to see an old dark-coloured door I hadn't noticed in my inspection of the room. As I hope to be saved, my friend turned around to me, and he opening the door, and for the first time I took in his petty insignificant features. He was far shabbier and more soiled-looking than I thought him to be at first. He smiled sadly at me, opened the door like any real man, and disappeared through it.

I don't know how long I lay awake after that, and light

slowly filling the room, but when it was broad day and maybe seven o'clock, I turned and looked at the wall, and sorrow the sign of a door could I see in it or any of the walls. I got up and dressed and went down to the big kitchen. The three black-bearded brothers were at the table with their sister at the head, and the old mother at the bottom. All except herself were toying with their breakfast, a few pork chops with a wire basket of boiled eggs and a few gigantic home-made loaves in the middle of the table. I bade them good morning without breaking their grim taciturnity. After a while I took up my courage and, addressing the table in general, I told them of my strange visitor. This evoked no comment, and soon the three black brothers rose and went to their work in the fields. The sister went off to her dairy, leaving me with the old mother, who got her knitting and removed to a window-seat.

The thunder and rain had gone, and the sun shone brightly. Birds sang in the bushes, and I began to feel more like myself. I asked the old dame if I might smoke—she looked all of eighty in the morning light—and she nodded her white head. Emboldened I drew my chair alongside, and asked her what she thought of my experience.

She pushed her glasses up on her forehead, and laid down her knitting.

"Och, there may be something in it. We were always a crossed family here, and we haven't prospered as we might. My poor husband seemed under a cloud all his days, I never knew why. It might be the house, for I remember him telling me when we were married first that as a boy he heard his grandfather say there was murder done in this house."

"When was it, ma'am?"

"Ah, a long time ago. My husband knew nothing about it, only that someone was known to come here one summer night and never seen to go."

"I wonder, ma'am," said I to her, "would your sons ever agree to go with me to my room and see is there e'er a trace of that door? The Lord knows what may be under all those layers of paper."

The old lady rather demurred to this, but my curiosity was up, and with a sort of obstinacy that surprised myself, I put off leaving and stayed till the brothers came in for their midday dinner, when, to my surprise, the mother spoke up and put it to them. I got another surprise when one of the big brothers said, "Ah, what harm would it do anyway? God knows what may be in it, for we all know the sort of fortune we have had in this place."

No sooner was the meal done, than we got a shovel and a couple of crowbars, and we four men went up to my bedroom. I pointed out the exact spot where the squireen had vanished. In a few minutes we had scaled off layers of wallpaper, and there, sure enough, we had the bricked-up doorway.

The job had been solidly done, but it was the work of twenty minutes only for those great stalwart divils to break through. Soon there came a sort of a seeping gush of musty air, faint and frightening. I ran to open one of the two tall windows, but couldn't budge them. The brothers were digging on and taking no notice, so, feeling rather foolish, I slunk back to join them.

Then one used his crowbar like a lever, and tumbled a heap of bricks away the far side of the hole, and we could clamber in. It was a sort of attic or lumber room, with a dull green piece of thick glass a foot square let into the roof for light. In the corner ahead was an old lidless, legless harpsichord with sagging wires. The rest of the furniture was a broken-down chair, a bookcase with no books in it, and a bed. On the bed lay my friend of the night before. He was a mass of cobwebs. He had his green coat on, but ne'er a button—I suppose they had been cut off. His black brogues were on too, but they looked like bits of carved bog oak, and the pastel buckles had ne'er a gleam to them. The grey worsted stockings had rotted, and the green velvet coat looked like moss covering the brown skeleton. At the base of the skull were a few traces still of the carroty hair.

As we stood there in silence, tiny bits of cloth or fluff slowly disintegrated from the bed and softly drifted to the bare boards of the floor. There the squireen lay on his back, with his grisly arms outstretched.

The brothers said never a word. No more did I. We left the room without ever a man looking back. I stayed maybe half an hour longer, and set out for home. I heard afterwards, in a roundabout way, that the poor squire had been decently buried, and the family had taken a better and more prosperous turn.

I never visited them again. Never. I'm not a superstitious man, nor easily scared, but I had had enough of that house. Besides, my job was done. Do you know what gave me the worst turn of all? It wasn't the body. It wasn't even the faint smell in the room, like lilies. It was him saying to me that his host on that fatal evening, the lad he had supper with, was a tall lad with a black beard. That one thing gave me a chill that made it impossible for me to go near the place again. Odd, isn't it, the way things take a man? That's what I couldn't get out of my head. Many's the time I turned over the possibilities. Was the original black-bearded lad an ancestor, and so the curse fell on my cousins? Or did it fall on them because they chanced to have black beards too? And who put it on them? Not my poor friend, not the poor victim, I'm sure. Then who?

Was there a curse? Aye, there was a curse. At least, there was something. I can feel, at this minute, the way it was, going along that landing with my candle. And those big fellas, and the sister—all personable healthy human beings—ah, yes. There was something—and I'm glad to think it's gone.

SEAMUS O'KELLY

The Apparitions of Oul' Darmody

Pa Cloone thought that a Christian never walked through the village of Kilbeg with a heavier heart than he did the day his aunt, Mrs Darmody, of the Lough Farm, turned him out of her house. Pa Cloone some ten months beforehand had come to live with his aunt in high hopes. Mrs Darmody was well-to-do, owner of a fine farm two miles from Kilbeg, a widow and childless. Pa Cloone came to direct the management of the Lough Farm and as prospective heir. His family considered him a very lucky young man. Pa Cloone himself was so elated over his prospects that he proposed marriage to Nell O'Driscoll, of Kilbeg, and was at once accepted. Pa told Nell that there would not be a woman standing Ireland's ground with a more elegant life than herself when he took her over to the Lough Farm as Mrs Pa Cloone, and Nell believed him. The Lough Farm, Pa Cloone declared, had never been worked properly, and when he got the management of it he would show the farmers about Kilbeg a couple of wrinkles. For the first few months after his arrival Mrs Darmody admitted that her nephew, Pa Cloone, was a willing lad enough, if he had not very much method in his work. She was a vigorous, rather taciturn, woman herself, and not given to much intercourse with the people. When, therefore, Pa Cloone became slacker and slacker in his work, and more and more given to carousing in the night, Mrs Darmody promptly sent him back to his mother. Pa wrapped up his belongings in a piece of brown paper, and flung out of the house with all the defiance that might be expected from a high-spirited young man with no earthly prospects whatever. His aunt watched him swing down the road with his head in the air, and then she sent for her cousin, Fintan Gorman, vowing that if Fintan were a better warrant to look after the place he would be the heir.

It will be easily understood from all this that Pa had not a very cheerful mission when he stepped up Kilbeg with his worldly goods wrapped in a piece of brown paper. But he had made up his mind that he was blameless in the matter, and that the presentation of the case to Nell O'Driscoll should be such as would leave no suspicion on his own great integrity. But when Pa Cloone saw the tears welling into Nell O'Driscoll's eyes as he laid his case before her, it dawned upon him that he was, as the Americans say, right up against a difficulty. Without giving himself time for any reflection, he plunged into an explanation which, as it turned out, was the source of most unlooked-for developments.

"Och! What come over you at all, Pa?" Nell exclaimed as she wiped away her tears. Poor Nell could not help her emotion when she felt all the fine castles she had been building in the air come tumbling down about her ears like a house of cards.

"Look here, now, Nell," Pa Cloone said, gallantly, "don't be crying over it at all. I'm just the same thing to you now as ever I was."

"Sure I know you are Pa," Nell answered with just a

note of reservation in her tone. "But what come over you to leave her?"

"I'll tell you that, if you keep it to yourself," Pa said.

"It's not a thing I'm likely to go boasting about," Nell said with some sarcasm.

"Well," Pa Cloone declared, "I was warned to leave her."

"And who was it warned you?" Nell demanded with sudden suspicion.

Pa leaned over and whispered in a hoarse voice, "My uncle warned me."

"Your—your uncle, Pa?" Nell said, unsteadily.

Pa nodded his head. Nell began to pale a little about the lips, for Pa's uncle was some time dead.

"Is it oul' Darmody?" Nell asked at last.

"He's appearing," Pa Cloone said, recklessly and basely. "He appeared to me three nights running. If I didn't leave my life would be taken."

Nell O'Driscoll clung about Pa's neck at the revelation. Pa felt both foolish and false, and was beginning to repent already for the rash words. But there was no turning back now. He was in for it, and should see it through.

"Tell me how it all happened?" Nell O'Driscoll said at last, her natural curiosity getting the better of her fears.

Pa Cloone thought it was as well for him to be in for a sheep as a lamb, and gathered his wits together.

"One night," he began, "I was wakened up out of my sleep. I was hardly wakened when I saw him rising up out of the floor. He was dressed in long, white clothes, and his face was as white as chalk. He just lifted one arm by degrees and pointed a finger— a finger that had no flesh upon it, only the bone—at the door. He said no word, but just looked at me. I was too taken aback to say one word. Then he sank down through the floor again, with the finger pointing to the door again."

"Maybe it was only a kind of a dream, Pa," Nell O'Driscoll exclaimed, a hope seizing her.

Pa Cloone shook his head sorrowfully. "I wish it was, Nell," he said, and meant it. "The next night," he added, warming to his subject, "up he comes again. He come up quicker and pointed to the door sharply. There was anger in his eyes. I knew he meant to get shut of me then. But for all that I wasn't going to give in."

"Oh, Pa," Nell said, "hadn't you the great courage."

"I was thinking of you, and the loss of the place, Nell," Pa Cloone said, shamelessly. Nell threw her emotional arms about his neck again. In the course of some mutually enthusiastic embraces Pa was half beginning to believe in his own story and to regard himself as a bit of a hero. It is hard to resist the sweet things of life.

"Well," Pa went on, with greater enthusiasm than ever, "the third night he made one sudden dart up. He closed his fist and shook it at me. Then he shook it at the door. There was fire in his eyes. He bent down like a cat going to make a spring. I could hear all the joints of his bones grinding in their sockets—"

"Oh, God! don't tell me that part of it, Pa!" Nell cried, half jumping up from her chair.

"Well, if you heard the rest of it, you'd go off in a dead faint, Nell," Pa said, with a set face.

"Well, tell me it all," Nell said, bracing herself for the ordeal, "but leave out about the sockets."

"It isn't at all fit for the like of you to hear," Pa, whose imagination was beginning to fail him, explained. "All I have to say is that I'm a living man after it, but if I stayed another night in that place there'd be a wake and you'd be the chief mourner, Nell O'Driscoll."

This closed the interview with Nell O'Driscoll, and Pa Cloone came away with a feeling that he had scored at a very great cost. Pa Cloone, it will be seen, was a rascal, but would never admit it. If his rascality sounds very terrible to the reader blame not the shanachie, for the shanachie took the people of Kilbeg as he found them, the good and the bad, and sometimes he liked the bad better than the good. Pa Cloone eased his conscience by telling himself that nothing short of the supernatural would reconcile Nell O'Driscoll to the loss of the Lough Farm. He felt a pricking of uneasiness about drawing the ghost of his deceased uncle into the business, but he had also a hope that his uncle would, if he took any interest in worldly affairs, understand that it was through pressure, and in a desperate plight that he belied him. Besides, he had warned Nell O'Driscoll to keep the matter a dead secret. Nell O'Driscoll did honestly intend to keep the thing secret, but much the same circumstances as beset Pa Cloone proved too strong for her. The news got out that Mrs Darmody of the Lough Farm had deposed her nephew, Pa Cloone. Kilbeg discussed the subject with relish. The young girls of Kilbeg whom Nell O'Driscoll had been lording it over as prospective mistress of the Lough Farm—for Nell O'Driscoll was very human—could not resist the temptation—being equally human—of paying Nell back in her own coin. "Well, wasn't it he that had the grand way with him"—"He must have made a terrible bad hand of the job"—"The devil a hand's turn he could do right I'm told"—"Drinking and card playing he was on for, morn, noon, and night"—"You're as well to be shut of him, Nell, if you lose that fine place itself." By such phrases was Nell O'Driscoll stung until, as has been said, the circumstances proved too much for her. She felt that both Pa Cloone and herself should be vindicated at all costs. There was only one way to vindicate them, Nell thought—to tell the bare, naked truth, and have justice done though the heavens should fall. Accordingly, Nell O'Driscoll confided to some of her friends the awful intelligence that Oul' Darmody was "appearing" up at the Lough Farm, and that it was in consequence of that that Pa had to fly the place. Kilbeg literally lapped up the information. It held the boards by every fireside that night and many nights afterwards. Christy Finnessy declared that he suspected long ago that everything was not right up at the Lough Farm, and that it was small blame to the decent boy to be quitting the place of a woman the like of Mrs Darmody. The sour and taciturn disposition of Mrs Darmody—who could never abide the people of Kilbeg—broke in upon the people of the village in a new light. Mrs Finnessy said they were a poor lot of omadauns not to see long ago that she had all the appearance of a woman who was being haunted.

In the meantime Fintan Gorman had come to the Lough Farm and joyfully stepped into the shoes of Pa Cloone. In disposition he was very different to his predecessor. Fintan Gorman was hard-working, conscientious and reticent—qualities well calculated to endear him to Mrs Darmody. And they did. For two weeks he worked steadily on the farm—and then he came into touch with Kilbeg. He took a pair of boots to Christy Finnessy for repairs. Christy was from home, and the woman of the house herself booked the order. Before Fintan Gorman left the house Mrs Sara Finnessy had broached the subject which she was simply dying to discuss with the new arrival.

"There is one thing I have to say of you," she said, admiringly, "you have great heart and courage to spend the night in the Lough Farm."

This led to explanations and revelations. It was startling to Fintan Gorman to learn that it was well known to the people of Kilbeg that oul' Darmody was "appearing" up at the Lough Farm. He took different shapes, Mrs Finnessy declared, sometimes coming in the favourite role of the black dog, and he howling and barking until a lady would be ready to drop with the fright of it. Then again he came in his own natural shape, coughing and barking like a sick sheep just the same as he used before he died. Mrs Sara Finnessy, it struck Fintan Gorman, appeared to be intimately acquainted with all the ghostly activities of oul' Darmody. "Surely he wasn't the only one who was ever known to come back," Mrs Finnessy went on reminiscently. "I knew another man in the part of the country I was brought up as a slip of a girl to do the very same thing. There was a case of an oul' woman there that gave her man such a hard life of it that in the heel of the hunt he dropped on the floor in front of her one day. But if he was dead itself she wasn't shut of him. One night, long after she burying him, she was sitting by the fire when a knock come to the door. 'Who's there?' says she, for she wouldn't open the door after dark for St. Paul, the great apostle. 'A young filly is trampling down your field of oats,' says a strange voice outside. Then she heard the footsteps dying down the road. She opened the door and felt something going in by her like a cold breath of wind, but could see nothing. Then she went to the field of oats; tale nor tiding was there of a filly or any other beast upon four feet. Well (this is as sure as I'm a living woman), when she lay down to her rest that night she heard tappings under the bed. Up she jumps and lights the candle. Devil the taste could she see of man, or woman, child or chick, dog or devil. Very well. When she lay down again the tappings began worse than before. Then the furniture began falling about the same, sir, as if every stick of it got a maygrim in the head. This same work went on every night until the oul' rap had to fly the house. She had the blessing of nobody going with her, and, as I was saying, you have great heart and great strength to pass the night in the Lough Farm."

Fintan Gorman was very thoughtful as he walked back to the Lough Farm, a couple of miles of ground from Kilbeg. He didn't like Mrs Finnessy, he didn't like her story, and he didn't like the way she had for telling it. He didn't believe in ghosts, but he was all the more afraid of them on that account.

Mrs Darmody was more agreeable than ever to him that evening. At bed-time she showed him into the big front room. As she gave him his candle she said, "That will be your room from this out. It was the room himself slept in, and the room he died in, God be good to him! You're welcome to the best I have, Fintan Gorman."

Fintan Gorman didn't like the best bedroom in the house; Mrs Finnessy's story and certain queer thoughts of oul' Darmody kept coming into his mind. A mouse racing across the floor sent the blood pumping through his body. It was some time near daybreak when he fell into an uneasy sleep. He wakened up with a start. He felt something tapping at the bed from underneath. He sat up terrified. The taps were repeated—several more—insistent and distinct taps. He made a leap clear from the bed, grabbed for his clothes, and made for the door. In doing so he knocked over a chair. When he got into the landing outside he heard the old woman moving below. He pulled on his clothes, slipped into his boots, and clattered down the stairs. When he had his hand on the front door the old woman, candle in hand, came out from the room.

"What is it Fintan?" she asked nervously.

"I saw him," Fintan Gorman cried.

"Saw him—saw who?" Mrs Darmody demanded, a gathering cloud about her face.

"The oul' fellow—oul' Darmody," Fintan broke out in his excitement. The candlestick fell from the old woman's hand. He heard her hard breathing in the dark.

"You cur!" she cried. Fintan Gorman threw open the door and stepped out on the road. Thin yellow veins of light were streaking the eastern sky. He breathed freely. He heard the bolt shot fiercely on the door inside, and then he took to his heels down the road. The news of Fintan Gorman's departure created several thrills in Kilbeg that day. The story, as was usual with stories that reached Kilbeg, was inflated to bursting point. It was declared that Fintan Gorman fled the Lough Farm a raging lunatic, driven forth by the ghost of oul' Darmody, who had attacked him with a red-hot poker, and such cursing and swearing was heard that Fintan Gorman thought the roof would light over him. As to the rattling of chains—it was like as if all the ships' cables of the oceans of the world had been gathered into the place.

Mrs Darmody, who knew nothing and cared less about the sensations of Kilbeg, declared, after her experience with Fintan Gorman, that she had had enough of her relatives. She sent for one Thady Cassidy from the mountains beyond Ballinaiske. Thady Cassidy was described in various ways by those who knew him. He was, some said, a decent little man; others referred to him as a clean, discreet little man; more called him a real religious bit of a man. Thady was, no doubt, something of all these things, and he was certainly little. Thady on the first night of his arrival at the Lough Farm was shown, much to his satisfaction, into the front bedroom. Mrs Darmody informing him at the same time that she would have the loft over the kitchen ready for him the following night. He went to sleep early and quite soundly.

But he was wakened up in the middle of the night. He had a feeling that something was walking about the room. He sat listening intently and heard some movements. Then there was a tug at the quilt. He reached out for his coat and struck a match. The room was quite empty. He

lay back on his pillow, pondering over his experience. He
had come rather doubtfully to Mrs Darmody. He did not
care very much for the woman. Her deceased husband he
had often worked for, and held a warm regard for. Then he
remembered suddenly that this was the very room and the
very bed in which he had seen oul' Darmody waked.
There had certainly been something in the room, and he
could not have made any mistake about the tugging at the
quilt; as a fact, it was still hanging a little from the bed.
Thady Cassidy slept no more that night. He rose early and
told Mrs Darmody that he was feeling very sick, and that
he was unable to take on the job. Mrs Darmody lost her
temper and said some stinging things. As has been said,
Thady Cassidy was a discreet, quiet, religious little man,
and he left Mrs Darmody "without as much as giving her
one back answer."

One whole day and night passed before the people of
Kilbeg learned of the arrival and departure of Thady
Cassidy at the Lough Farm. But the delay was fully
compensated for in the knowledge that another man had
had been so promptly disposed of by oul' Darmody.

"Well," said Mrs Finnessy, who was beginning to take
the tone of an authority in the matter of these
supernatural manifestations. "Well, where's the use in
anyone facing the Lough Farm when Thady Cassidy had
to fly? A man that has little or no mind for this world with
the dint of pondering and praying over the next!" Half
way up to and over the hills to Ballinaiske Thady Cassidy
was chased by The Thing, she assured Kilbeg. It was only
when Thady came to running water that The Thing gave
one sudden screech out of it and with that vanished.

Mrs Darmody let a couple of days go over her head
before she made any further adventure with a man for her
farm. She was, in reality, turning the whole thing over in
her mind, and while doing so was engaged in a mental

struggle with her own pride. In the end she had, like many another, to put her pride in her pocket. She consoled herself by reflecting that blood was thicker than water, and that if Pa Cloone had spunk and carried a haughty head he was only taking after herself. She sent word to Pa's mother that she would give him another and last trial.

In consequence Pa once more made up his brown paper parcel, took an ashplant in his fist, and stepped out for the Lough Farm from the home of his retirement beyond Boherlahan. On the road he made many heroic resolutions, for Pa Cloone was, I regret to say, a most consummate liar, and like all consummate liars, he had a partiality for strong resolutions.

Nell O'Driscoll was full of tender misgivings when Pa Cloone dropped in to tell her, on his return journey, that she might as well be leaving her measure for her wedding dress since his aunt, Mrs Darmody, had come crawling to him on her knees to go back to the Lough Farm to save it from wreck and ruin.

"But, Pa," Nell broke out, "you have no business there. What chance have you after oul' Darmody warning you?"

The truth was that Pa had forgotten about oul' Darmody. He had heard nothing of the apparition at the Lough Farm after his departure.

"Well, well," he said, "I'm thinking maybe that he'll have found rest since."

"Indeed he hasn't," Nell O'Driscoll said, "only worse he's getting. Look at the way he ran Fintan Gorman and little Thady Cassidy."

Pa's face expressed the blank of his mind on the affairs of Fintan Gorman and little Thady Cassidy. Nell soon enlightened him. Pa did not know what to think. He cross-examined Nell O'Driscoll, and felt she was not lying. Like all liars, Pa Cloone would not believe that anybody could keep telling the truth all the time. In the end he came to the conclusion that the two men had suffered from delusions, brought about by stories in Kilbeg, for Nell O'Driscoll owned up to giving Pa's secret away.

"I will face him again for your sake, Nell," Pa declared at last. "I'll ask him if he has anything weighing on his mind. Nobody has a better right to ask him that than myself, his nephew. I should try to give him rest, and not be bringing a bad name on the family."

Nell O'Driscoll did not require a great deal of persuasion. She agreed to Pa risking his life once more. The stakes, as far as Nell was concerned, were big. Nell would—let this much justice be done her—have almost risked the thing herself in order to regain the Lough Farm and have the crow over her tormentors in Kilbeg. She did the next heroic thing in encouraging Pa Cloone to face oul' Darmody.

Pa Cloone worked like a Trojan on the farm the first day of his return. He had put the work of two average men behind him by sunset. Mrs Darmody, like the shrewd woman she was, made no comment, but she knew it was a bad sign. Pa felt his bones aching when he lay down to his rest. His aunt took care to treat him fairly. She thought it would give him cause for complaint if he were relegated to the loft over the kitchen and heard that Fintan Gorman, and even little Thady Cassidy from the mountains, were honoured with the front room. Pa sank into the wide feather bed between the elaborate wooden posters with a grateful sigh. He was soon asleep and dreaming a glorious dream that he was successfully cheating a table of card players, with a fat goose for the stake.

Pa Cloone wakened suddenly with a queer feeling. In a semi-conscious condition he realised that something was happening. Something was walking over him. It could hardly be described as walking. The thing, whatever it was, was sliddering and sprawling over him. It groped its way over his stomach as if it were helplessly intoxicated. A tremor ran up through his spine, leaving him stiff and inert in the bed. He felt the thing sidling down and pausing on the brink of the bed. There was silence for a little. Then the most gruesome thing happened. Something fell from the bed to the floor. There was no mistaking the sound. It had the thud of flesh, it fell like a dead body. Then there was a long-drawn inward breath that seemed something of a sigh and something of a sniffle. There was another stagger and a little shuffling on the floor, followed by a long, unbroken silence. Pa Cloone never knew what a coward he was until this hour. He could not move hand or foot if it was to save his life. But his brain was very active. He realised a most sickening lot of things all in one crowded minute. He realised that Fintan Gorman and Thady Cassidy had not been the victims of hallucinations. He realised that the wild stories in Kilbeg were only half the truth. He knew now that his uncle was taking a terrible revenge for the callous manner in which he had used his name. If he had risen up before him, ghostly and frightful, and accused him, threatened him, even attacked him, Pa Cloone thought he could face the ordeal with more bravery. But this horrid thing that had gone on in the dark was only such a revenge as a supernatural intelligence could conceive. It left him a wreck and a coward, lying there as still as the night for the hours that followed. The world seemed to him as if it would never wake again. But it did. A little dim light came into the room, and it encouraged Pa Cloone to turn his eyes in his head, an action which seemed to be a daring and risky deed. He could trace the outline of the furniture in the room, and fixedly watched it become clearer and clearer. He sighed, a little fretful sigh, and mountains of clouds seemed to pass away with that sigh. An inexpressible joy came over him when he heard Mrs

Darmody moving below and then come shuffling up the stairs.

"Pa!" her voice called outside. "Are you wakened, Pa?"

Pa Cloone wiped his dry lips with his tongue before he could answer.

"Yes, aunt," he said at last.

"Are the goslings out? Did I hear them running around?" the voice asked.

Pa Cloone thought his aunt was having a nightmare. "The goslings?" he asked, in a weak voice. The door opened, and Mrs Darmody came in. Pa Cloone thought she never looked so beautiful. For the first time in his life he felt he could embrace her. She stood like a vision in the uncertain light.

"I had a clutch of eggs under a goose in a box under the bed," she said.

She shuffled over to the bed, raised the heavy border that was about it, and went down on her knees. "The time is up for them to-day," she said, and Pa felt her groping at something under the bed. "They're not out yet," she said, grumbling a little and rising. "She's the greatest devil of a restless goose I ever put an egg under. Hard set I was to keep her on them at all. No place would suit her but under that bed." And she shuffled down the stairs again. Pa Cloone lay back in bed thinking hard. His own ghostly experience, the ghostly experiences of Fintan Gorman and of Thady Cassidy were revealed to him. He did not know whether to laugh or to cry. Instead he hung out of the bed, raised the border and looked in. There she sat in the box, right enough, the old goose that had supplied all the thrilling apparitions of oul' Darmody. While Pa Cloone looked at her, the goose gave the bottom of the bed a thwack of her beak, another of the quilled spirit-rappers that bring messages from beyond the Bourne whence no traveller returneth.

It is some time since the apparitions of oul' Darmody stirred hearts among the hills to the core. If you went up to the Lough Farm to-day you would find that Mrs Darmody had long since joined her man, and that Pa Cloone, the rascal, had come into his inheritance. In the parlour of the Lough Farm Pa would show you a very fine stuffed goose under a glass shade. And if you asked him what species of goose it happened to be, he would turn to his good woman, once upon a time Nell O'Driscoll of Kilbeg, now the proud mistress of the Lough Farm, and with a twinkle in his eye tell you that that was the goose that laid the golden eggs.

ERIC CROSS

Saint Bakeoven

I don't pretend to be musical, apart, of course, from knowing a good tune when I hear it—the sort of thing that a fellow can whistle in his bath. It does so happen however, that I was almost responsible for what might have been one of the musical sensations of the century, and, before I forget it, I'd better make some record of it for future generations.

I used to spend a part of each year fishing in Kerry in those days. On one occasion, while I was returning from a mountain lake, I ran into a terrific thunderstorm. Below me in the valley I spotted an isolated farmhouse and I worked my way down to it as quickly as possible. I had barely knocked at the door when it was opened by an old man who ushered me in as though I were the prodigal son returning home. He helped me off with my coat, drew up a chair to the fire for me, and, in general, treated me with even more eager hospitality than you usually meet in Kerry.

"You must find it a bit lonely tucked away back here," I suggested, once the preambles of hospitality were settled.

"Yerra—lonely, is it?" replied the old man, whose name, by the way, was Johnny Quill. "The divil a bit lonely am I ever," he went on. "To tell God's truth, 'tis just the other way about."

"How come?" I quite naturally asked, considering the situation of the place.

"'Tis the fairies," he replied, in a matter of fact way. "Them divils do be at me, pestering and worrying and annoying and bothering me all hours of the day and night. 'Tis only when a Christian, such as yourself, comes along that the sight of him drives them out and I have a bit of peace and ease for myself as it is now. But the moment you'll be gone them divils will be back again with their whispering and their rustling like mice round a corn bin. They have me patience worn out. There should be a law passed against them by those useless people up in Dublin and then put the police onto them. But, oh, no—they're much too busy passing laws to make hens lay eggs by Act of Parliament to have the time to do anything useful. I tell you that the fairies are the plaguiest, most pestering md bewildering form of creation that man was ever burdened with."

"Yes," I agreed, for, after all an old man's fancies break no bones. "I am sure that you must find them a bit of a nuisance."

"Nuisance! Nuisance!" bellowed Johnny. "Why, the divils have me near driven mad. I lambaste them with the handle of a broom. I give them a histe of my boot and a skelp of my tongue, but it's all a waste of energy. A few minutes later and they will be back at their old comether again: whispering hocus pocus; mislaying things and upsetting things on me. There's all classes of them," he continued, "but there is one of them—the plaguiest one of me whole pick of divils, who comes mainly by night. A sort of a foreigner I'd say he would be and a damned bad-tempered one at that. There's some of them all mischief but with this one the game is all music. Whenever he puts his face inside the kitchen the whole house does be filled with the sound of music as though it was the air of the place. Then he tries to be telling me something but I can't make head or tail of the queer language he speaks and that only seems to make him madder and he shakes the great head of him and holds the great fists of him in the air, with the fingers spread out like a dealer trying to buy a beast in a fair for ten pounds from a slow witted man.

" 'Saint! Saint! Saint!' he yells. Then 'Bakeoven! Bakeoven! Bakeoven!' and I can't make sense of that at all for the divil a bit does he look like a saint and the divil a bit do I know what he means by his 'Bakeoven' unless it be one of these newfangled fakes that they have in the towns for the lazy women to bake in."

"To hell with you and your 'bakeoven'," I yell at him, "if it's a 'bakeoven' that you are trying to sell me or persuade me to buy. It was on the cake from the bastable pot that I was reared and on the same I'll finish my days. Then the music starts all over again till my head is like a hive of bees ready to swarm with the sound of it."

"All very interesting," I agreed. "It looks as though the worst of the storm is over. I think that I'll be pushing on." I said goodbye to Johnnny and thanked him, and, as far as I was concerned, that would have been the end of the business, for fairies aren't particularly in my line.

It so happened however, that there was a professor of music johnny, from Oxford, staying in the hotel, collecting "folk music", whatever that may be. Naturally he was a difficult subject for conversation and that night I happened to mention the rigmarole Johnny had told me that day, by way of being sociable.

The professor johnny, whose name was Peterson, pricked up his ears almost immediately and showed more signs of life than I had seen so far in him when I told him the yarn. I went away to bed and naturally had forgotten

all about it by the following morning but it seemed that
this fellow Peterson had, overnight, made a mountain of
the story. He had worked out some crazy notion from it
about a German composer called Beethoven, who had
composed nine symphonies and died before he had
finished his tenth; and he had come back in ghost form to
worry poor old Johnny Quill about it.

Peterson had worked out that Johnny's "Saint" was the
German for "tenth" and his "Bakeoven" was really
"Beethoven"—the composer's name, and the music
Johnny heard, was, of course, the music of the tenth
symphony, now finished. It didn't seem to be dripping
with sense to me.

I happened to go into the bar before lunch for an
appetiser and who should be there but Johnny Quill
himself, celebrating a deal in sheep. We had a drink
together and I left him to it and went off in search of food.
But in the dining room I ran into Peterson, bubbling over
with some new brainwave on Johnny's story. In the hope
of finishing the matter off, as far as I was concerned, I led
him out and introduced him to Johnny himself, the fount
of inspiration. But it wasn't my lucky day, for in spite of his
knowledge of music he could not make anything of
Johnny's accent, no more than Johnny could make of his,
so I had to stand in as interpreter.

I opened the ball with the first round of drinks,
Peterson having lemonade and going straight into action,
instructing me to ask Johnny to describe the appearance
of the ghost or fairy or whatever it was, in detail.

"Tell him," said Johnny, "that he is a stout block of a
bucko with a great stook of hair on his head as though he
is in dispute with the barber—and that might well be, for
he has a fierce, bad-tempered jowl on him. His clothes? . . .
Yerra, he does mostly wear some sort of an ould swally tail
coat with an ould choker round his neck and the knee

breeches they used to wear in the time of the caroline hats."

"Hm!" snorted Peterson, like the man who had found the piece of kidney in the pie, when I translated this for him. "Ask him now what language his fairy or whatever it is speaks."

"The divil be from me but how would I know that," replied Johnny. "Tell the man of the lemonade that 'tis neither English nor Irish but some gibberish makeup of his own and that the only words that I can make out at all are his 'Saint' and his 'Bakeoven', and to hell with him and his 'bakeovens'. I'll stick to me bastable pot."

Peterson was studying Johnny intently as he put him through the third degree. "Ask him now," ordered Peterson, "if anyone else sees this apparition or hears the music."

"Only the divil himself could answer that," snorted Johnny, "but 'tis not likely for ould Bakeoven wouldn't have the time left to be annoying anyone else after all the time that he spends annoying me. He'd scarcely have the time left to wash himself .. . and will you add to that," Johnny continued, "that I will answer no more questions till the gentleman puts away the lemonade and has a glass of whiskey with me like a Christian."

Peterson, in spite of protests, had to yield. Johnny, as the oracle, could call the tune and he called it quickly.

"Would it be possible for me to hear the music and see this ghost if I went along to the house?" was Peterson's next query.

"It might and it might not," was Johnny's answer to this. "But mostly I'd be saying against it for I do notice that when anyone comes into the house to me the music stops and ould Bakeoven goes up the chimney or out of the window. But tell the gentleman that he's welcome anytime and if he can salt the ould divil and take him away with him to foreign parts there will be no man was ever so welcome."

The party spirit was getting into its stride by now. Peterson disappeared for a few minutes and I was hoping that we could adjourn *sine die* but it wasn't to be. He had only been up to his room and he returned with an illustrated history of music. He instructed me to hand it to Johnny and to tell him to look through it and to see if there was a picture in it at all like his "fairy".

Johnny licked his thumb and started to turn the pages one by one. I did not translate all his remarks and comments on the pictures of famous composers he saw, though they were amusing. I had doubts if this Peterson fellow had any sense of humour at all.

After thumbing about half way through the book Johnny let out a yell, putting his finger down on a picture of Beethoven.

"The pesky ould divil himself," he whooped. "The living split image of him! Saint Bakeoven and the great ugly puss of him!" At this Peterson went up in the air. He ordered another round of drinks immediately. Even I began to wonder if there might be something in it after all.

"Ask him now," said Peterson, as pleased as Punch, "if he could describe or remember the music he hears."

"Could I remember the music!" exclaimed Johnny. "Indeed, but it would be the day of the greatest aise to me when the day dawns that I disremember every screech of it. As for describing of it," he continued, after some head-scratching, "will you tell him that it would be beyond the powers of the worst poet yet born to put words to it. 'Tis such a roaring and a buzzing and a banging and a beating: such a twirling of trumpets and a tweaking of flutes and a scattering of the scraping of fiddles that the like of it was never heard before in the history of the world. 'Tis like the bellowings of dumb animals in pain and the howling of infants in divilment and the scolding of women in crossness and in the midst of it all there is this ould divil of a queer one, waving his hands up and down and about in the air as though the sound was all running out of the ends of his fingers, like porter out of a tap.

"Only once did I hear the match of it in my life and that was in the days of the ould militia in the town of Kenmare when someone had treated the band with decency and the band had treated themselves with equal decency and they marched through the town stocious and every man of them doing his best to outblow the other fellow."

Johnny now ordered a round and Peterson replied with another question, asking if Johnny could hum or whistle the music or give some actual idea of it. Johnny was now most ready to oblige.

"I'd give you more than an idea of it, with a heart and a half and good riddance to it," said he, "but that it is a class of music that has no sense at all to it at all at all. 'Tis what you might call a porridge of a music—not like the 'Blackbird' or 'The Coolin' or 'The Wind that Shakes the Barley' or any of the decent civilised tunes that wake a man's heart and set his feet tapping. But I will do the best I can to accommodate the gentleman for he is turning out to be a better class of a man than my first judgment of him. 'Tis something like this that it goes."

With that Johnny drained his glass, threw back his head, fixed his eye on a spot on the ceiling and started to screech and to bawl and to roar and to groan until, after a couple of minutes, even Peterson, with all his interest in music, had had enough of Johnny Quill's version of Beethoven's Tenth Symphony. It was a thirst-provoking effort and Peterson thought the game worth while but demanded a *quid* for his *quo*.

"Ask him if there is any musical instrument that he can

play with which he might be able to reproduce some of the music he hears."

After probing into the nature of Johnny's polite accomplishments, the only thing that I could discover was that when he was young—and that was a long time ago— he had been able to play the bagpipes—but not very well. About here the party broke up.

The following morning, when Peterson had recovered after a good night's sleep, he had worked out a plan of campaign, for there wasn't any doubt now in his mind, on the circumstantial evidence so far produced. He was on the verge of the most amazing musical discovery of the century. The weather wasn't too good for fishing and as there wasn't much else to do I continued as *aide de camp* and general adviser and interpreter.

The first thing that we did was to visit Johnny's house, and we soon found that the fairies were quite definitely allergic to us. Even Peterson did not hear a note. According to Johnny the moment we entered the house both the fairy and his music faded away. Naturally Peterson was a bit hurt about this but he was quite certain that Johnny was speaking the truth and quite incapable of pulling Peterson's leg on his home ground, as you might say.

This meant that we had to fall back on Johnny himself as medium, interpreter or what you will. And that meant that, by hook or crook, he would have to reproduce what he heard by means of the only musical instrument he knew—the bagpipes. Peterson wasn't at all in favour of my suggestion, my quite practical suggestion, of bringing a band along and letting Johnny conduct it. He even suspected that I was pulling his leg and not treating the matter with sufficient gravity.

So the problem, or rather the practical solution to it, was narrowed down to bagpipes. Somewhere in the district there was reputed to be a pair or set or whatever it is of them but when it came to finding them they were as elusive as the end of a rainbow, flitting ahead of us from valley to valley and house to house. At last we caught up with them. Johnny regarded them carefully, seriously and ruefully. With all his native gift of courtesy he could find little good to say about them. There was a whistle or a tweeter or some such vital part missing. One of the protruding flutes or whatever they were was most obviously cracked. More apparent still was a great rent in the windbag. But, with optimism, a dash of glue, some twine and wire, a splash of tar and a bit of an old tyre, Johnny thought that he might be able to make a job of them.

Eventually, with the help of the 'smith and the carpenter and a man who was a great hand at tying a fly and another man who had an uncle in America who, in his day had been a famous piper, so that he had claims to being an expert, one place removed, we got the contraption fixed up. As Johnny tactfully described it— "they worked in a kind of a class of a way." Now all that he needed was a few days' practice to get his wind and fingers into trim.

The appointed night arrived and with it rain in sheets and floods and torrents. This seemed to me to be a warning to let well alone and sleeping spirits lie. It seemed just any other kind of night rather than one to set off into the darkness and the wetness of a desolate mountain valley to hear the first performance of a symphony played on bagpipes—or played any way at all for that matter. Peterson's mind however was made up and I decided that being in for a penny I might as well be in for a pound.

We borrowed the hotel proprietor's car. I took along a bottle of whiskey and a couple of rugs. As luggage Peterson had a wad of music paper. Long before we arrived at the concert hall it was obvious, even above the storm, that Johnny had entered into the spirit of the occasion and was already having a preliminary canter. It seems that somehow the fairy or ghost had got an inkling of what was in the wind and had readily co-operated with the notion. In fact they had already a dress rehearsal and come to a common understanding of the procedure to be adopted. Beethoven would conduct a few bars and while they still lingered in Johnny's ears he would have a skirl or whatever the musical term is for a dash at it and so they would progress from bar to bar.

Johnny himself was by this time so taken up with the idea and the possible hope of ridding himself of his musical lodger, that he was taking the matter almost as seriously as Peterson himself. He wouldn't even have a drink before we started. "Only a dart, now and again, of the purest of spring water," he said, pointing to a bottle at his side, "just for the wind's sake, until the gentleman is satisfied."

Still we were not *personae gratae* with fairies and while we were within the kitchen Johnny said there would not be a note of music. When you think of all the trouble that Peterson was giving himself and other people it did really seem a bit inconsiderate on the part of Beethoven, but judging by the picture of him it was about what you might be led to expect from him. So it meant that we—or rather Peterson—would have to eavesdrop through the window.

I, never having been much of an enthusiast for symphonies or bagpipes, retired to the shelter of the car. I wrapped myself up in the rugs and opened the bottle of whiskey. Unfortunately I was still within earshot of the bedlam which was let loose when the performance started, but as the storm increased the howling of the wind and the lashing rain toned it down somewhat. There would be a squealing and a screeching from the kitchen as though a score of pigs were being slaughtered. There was Peterson huddled up against the window ledge, with the rain cascading over him from the roof, while he scribbled down crotchets and quavers. Now and again he would bawl through the window for a repeat. Now and again there would be a lull in the noise, as Johnny took a swig of the purest spring water for his wind's sake.

Mercifully after a short while I fell into a dose. What woke me wasn't a noise. It was the absence of a noise. came to, conscious that now there was only the howling of the wind and the roar of the swollen mountain torrents around me. There wasn't a sound from Johnny's kitchen. The door was open and Peterson was missing. I made a dash for the house to find Johnny on the flat of his back on the floor, as he would describe it, "stocious". The bottle of the "finest of spring water" lay smashed beside him and from the trickle which was left in it there came a smell which might be mistaken for whiskey. It is not unknown in Kerry where so many improbable things seem to be possible for "the finest of spring water" to have such a smell. Beside the fragments of the bottle lay the corpse of the bagpipes in a heap.

"Busht! Busht and be damned!" were Johnny's last words as he gave himself up to the soundest sleep that ever fell on any man. The description aptly covered all— Johnny, the bottle and the bagpipes. We made Johnny comfortable for the night in his bed. There was nothing more that we could do. The performance was ended. The carriage awaited at the door.

Peterson was quite happy but very wet. There wasn't a doubt now in his mind. It was the true, authentic Beethoven music alright, recognisable even through the medium of bagpipes. A few score nights such as this and he would have the whole thing down in crotchets and quavers. A few months of work on it and it would be ready to astonish the world.

It seemed unfortunate that Peterson developed a high temperature during the night and had to be rushed off to a nursing home the following morning with pneumonia. But all's well that ends well and a few days later Johnny himself had to be taken to the county hospital. The combination of the finest of spring water, the excitement and the strenuous exercises of bagpipe blowing had not been the best treatment for the heart at his age. So, as it turned out, Peterson would not have been able to do anything more, and anyway the bagpipes were quite beyond any further repair.

I had quite a busy time between the two invalids: writing letters for Peterson, when he turned the corner, and doing a few odd things for Johnny. The doctor had advised Johnny to stay on in the hospital and he wasn't at all unwilling. I arranged the settling of his bit of land to a relative so that Johnny would be able to draw the old age pension and so have no further worry.

As soon as Peterson was well enough I drove him over to see Johnny and, needless to say, Peterson had only one interest in the visit.

"Ould Bakeoven and his music? . . . Yerra, thank God that I have neither sight nor sound of him since the blessed day that I came in here—and good riddance, for at last after all these years I have peace and ease for myself and I'm able to call my soul my own."

"But, manalive!" almost shrieked Peterson, "don't you remember the music?"

"The divil a note of it," answered Johnny, puffing contentedly away at his pipe. "The divil a note of it have I heard since I came in and the divil a note of it will I hear to the end of my days for I have handed the place and the cow and the sheep to a nephew of mine and I have no mind to budge from here till they carry me out feet foremost. I'll live the rest of my life like a fine civil servant, at the country's expense, taking my aise like a lord, instead of being at the beck and call of a pack of fairies like a boots in an hotel."

Peterson cajoled, bribed, bullied, pleaded. wheedled and argued but Johnny would listen to no argument and no persuasion. The last thing that he said to Peterson when we came to say goodbye was: "If you should happen to see Ould Bakeoven at any time during your travels will you tell him from me that I did him a great harm and a great injustice and that I am sorry for it, for after all he was right. 'Tis the new-fangled 'bakeovens' that they use in this place for their breadmaking and you never in all your life tasted sweeter or grander or nuttier bread."

BRIAN POWER

The Sixth Figure

I've sketched the thug's face more than twenty times these past few days. About thirty, tall, cleanshaven. A long face, quite handsome. Eyes of winter blue. All the other glittery little eyes around us seemed to worship his. In that dark, nightmare scene I was nothing, he was everything. I am a proud man, I suppose, to have felt that so keenly.

Please do not stay, if you dislike the English, to hear this confession. You are young, perhaps you do not understand that, as we grow older, the world becomes stranger, the pattern more complicated. You'll try to understand? Now, that's a humble answer. Reassuring, I think. No doubt you'll do.

You must not think me fussy. It's a long time since I have *really* made confession and now that I want to do so I feel I have a certain right to demand some reassurance. Living as I've done in an Irish religious house for over twenty years— I'm a Father from Mount Conor, you know it of course—I've had as much as I can take of insulting innuendo about my nationality. You find that surprising? Well, perhaps I *am* too sensitive. People, however, don't have to be conscious of giving offence in order to wound.

It's enough for them to be unconsciously prejudiced—but there. I'm slipping back into paranoia. No future in that, I know.

Perhaps you'll be kind enough, Father, to help me sit up a little straighter against these pillows. That's better. Thank you. No, I wasn't hurt badly. Frightened mainly. But I do seem to have pulled a muscle somewhere at the lower end of my spine when I flung myself at the thug. I failed to stop him shooting the boy and that was humiliating, too. The boy's still upstairs in the intensive care unit, I suppose? I'm sorry about that. If I'd never interfered, perhaps he wouldn't have been injured so badly.

Those are the drawings of the gunman's face, there on the locker. Most of them a good likeness, too. The first ones were the best. Hatred was not quite spent when I was doing them. That's the great sin I have to confess. Not assaulting the ghoul, I don't regret that of course, but hating him. When he pulled the trigger of his revolver, years of pent-up rage exploded in my brain, a blinding fireworks display of unleashed passions. As I made a dive for him, I knew I'd kill him if I could manage it. If I could have laid hands on a knife, a crowbar, anything lethal, I'd have finished him for good and been glad of it.

Does that shock you? The hate I felt, you see, had very little to do with the runny-nosed terrified urchin standing with his bitten fingernails splayed against the wall. He was only the occasion for its exploding. For years I've been suppressing a deep personal detestation of Irish patriots and all they stand for. If I'd had a machine gun that night, I'd have sprayed the thug's entire escort of masked and hooded young ruffians with bullets and enjoyed seeing them writhe, hearing them scream. And if Father Malachy O'Loughlin had chanced to come on the scene, I'd have done for him, too.

I see you are a little shocked this time. Planning to eliminate the second best money-spinner at Novenas of Grace in the diocese! Even the Bishop would find it hard to forgive that. Well, can you imagine how I felt every time Malachy marched into the common room at Mount Conor, entering always as if he were engaged in the storming of the Winter Palace, his red turkey chops quivering in a gloating leer, exclaiming, "Did you hear the latest news, boys? Another British soldier shot!"

Of course, of course. I know the other priests didn't share those precise sentiments. But they said nothing. Nothing! And I said nothing because I am British, too, and reluctant to draw attention to the fact.

The theologians say this is what confession is supposed to be about, don't they? Baring the soul. Facing one's true self. I could say, "Father, I resented remarks passed by a religious confrere." That's as far as I ever got before this. As far as I was prepared to go. Otherwise, I believed the murders and the beatings and the maimings were the problem of the Irish. Let them stew in their own juice, I would have said to myself; it's nothing to do with me.

Until I had this—what shall I call it? Revelation? Insight? Now, that's much harder to describe than mortal sin—a religious experience. Light upon light, serene and joyous, as when the will that moves the eyes together shuts or opens both of them. Strange that it should have been the religious experience that finally led to the explosion of the sin, but looking back I see that was necessary, too. The sin could never have exploded into the light if something else had not first awakened me.

You find this a trifle embarrassing, don't you? You are a young man, it's only natural you are still afraid of the Spirit. Most of my life I have been afraid as well. I could praise the Spirit, pray to the Spirit, tell others of the joys of the Spirit, but the Spirit himself I kept at bay, never allowing him free entry into my soul. I had to keep room there for the hidden sin, the tacit reservation I insisted on making before God that I could love him without loving the Irish among whom I was forced to live. Patrick herding sheep on Slieve Mish must have felt the same way as I did until he escaped, and his return in answer to the voices of children calling was a lifelong reparation for the hate he harboured. I suppose the Provincial sent me here because he regarded me as Liverpool-Irish, not really an Englishman at all. It wasn't so bad before "The Troubles" broke out and after that I stayed more out of lethargy than obedience, accepting with unspoken, seething rancour my lot in this bloody awful little country, with all due respects to you, where two cruel cultures collide to produce unmentionable horrors every time the sun goes down.

It was Bernard, a visiting Father from the Lebanon whose second name I can't pronounce, who was the unknowing instrument of my awakening. He came to Mount Conor last summer to get away for a while from the cauldron of Beirut, if anything an even worse scene of carnage than exists here. That afternoon, before he turned up at supper, I'd been reading in the Bible about how Judas Maccabeus and his small band were attacked at Bethzechariah by the gigantic army of Antiochus the Fifth from which, as it's described, the sunlit mountains caught the glint of bronze and gold so that they gleamed like fiery torches. The Syrians won that battle eventually in spite of heavy losses, but I don't think they could ever claim to have won the war. These things never end so simply. Anyway, I was in the mood to be fascinated by Bernard's account of the origins of the war in the Lebanon and its similarities both with the situation here and the battles in Old Testament times. God invoked as a war lord and all that kind of thing. We got on so well, Bernard and myself, that he came to my room after supper. We had a drink

together and talked and talked; I talked with him as I
could never talk with any of my Irish companions. Finally,
his black eyes distilling an intense desire to share his
whole life's experience with me, he dug out of his travel
bag a few books, they were all about the Lebanon, and he
began to flick through pages here and there, pointing out
passages and items of interest as if time might end for ever
before he could get started.

This is where it becomes difficult to explain. Did you
ever have anything like a mystical experience? Young men
sometimes do, after all, even if young men can so quickly
forget. The only such experience I was ever sure I had
before was when I was a student in our seminary in Rome
long ago, immured in one or those refrigerated rooms built
to withstand summer heat but not winter frost. Perhaps it
could be defined as a sinister rather than a mystical
experience, for it was the embodiment of evil that crept
into my room, not the quintessence of absolute goodness.
Just my luck, I often thought afterwards, that when
mystical experiences were being handed out I should have
been allotted one of the more cussed variety.

Description of an experience of this kind never fairly
reflects the reality. I was lying wakeful one night on my
hundred-year-old mattress, thinking not very deeply about
a coming oral on the De Deo Creante tract, when I
became aware of something lurking in the far corner of my
room, close by the window where my football shorts and
jersey were hanging from a hook in the wall.
Incongruously, I could see my football togs quite clearly
with my natural eyesight even as I gazed in mounting
quiet horror at the shapeless mass which breathed silently
beside them. To say I *saw* this evil form would not be quite
accurate. It loomed there, it was real, but it was some sixth
sense that apprehended the evil nature of it. It was, I must
insist, more real than ordinary seeing. What I actually saw

with my normal vision was too tenuous to be described, yet it was more real than the football gear or the cold of the night or the blanket I clutched tightly as I watched. I was not so much terrified as appalled, for suddenly I knew that evil existed and was close to me. Goodness I had taken for granted, but evil had never seemed so absolutely real and physical before. I knew immediately I could never again discount it.

The following morning, of course, I laughed at myself. Although I knew my experience was no dream, the optimism of youth urged that this was the only sane interpretation possible. I wanted to dismiss it as a dream. The next night, and the next again, however, the apparition, if one could call it that, recurred, each time more vivid and more real. It never returned after that, but I never quite forgot it. You are the first person to whom I attempted properly to describe it. I did begin to tell a friend in the seminary about it. It was on spaghetti day, a Wednesday that always was. I found it impossible to distract his attention from the more absorbing task of conveying twirling fork to open mouth and, anyway, he clearly thought I was raving, so I made some joke and shut up. Don't try to look so respectful. I know you're amused, too. I expected that.

Sorry for the digression. It seemed necessary to get things in perspective. Back to the point, then. As Bernard flicked the pages of one of his booklets on the Lebanon, a page fell open to reveal the reproduction of an old black and white photograph. At first sight there was nothing extraordinary about it. It was a snapshot of a small group of Maronite students and priests, five in number, on an excursion to an ancient monastery. As I looked at it, another more shadowy figure in the foreground arrested my attention, the figure of an elderly bearded monk who seemed to be kneeling among the bushes below the picnic party. Idly the nail of my little finger brushed his features and Bernard said, "Oh, there's some strange story associated with that photograph." Then he turned to another book to quote some statistics about the population of the Lebanon, the Palestinian refugees and who knows what else.

I scarcely heard him. I could not detach my eyes from the sixth figure in the photograph. A peculiar sensation, a kind of peace, descended on me. Even as I stared at the face of the old monk, the habitual pains in my arms and feet, the physical weariness, the tension that always lay around my heart, all flowed away from me and a river of warm blood seemed to stream through my veins. I remember saying to myself, "This is ridiculous, it can't really be happening." I had never prayed, you see, to be relieved of any of the symptoms I mention, for I accepted them as nothing more than the inevitable harbingers of advancing age. I kept rubbing my leg, expecting the dull ache to return any moment. When it became impossible to deny that something astonishing and slightly vexing was occurring, I asked Bernard impatiently, "Who is he?"

Bernard stopped talking, surprised to see me still examining the same page. He answered casually, "Oh, that's Father Sharbel. He was dead when the photograph was taken, they say——"

He broke off as I exclaimed, "Dead?" Then he laughed and proceeded. "There should be only five people in the photograph, they say, but it was claimed that when the photograph was developed a new figure appeared which was identified as Sharbel by people old enough to have known him. There's not much else to tell about him except that he lived and died a hermit at Anaya on top of Mount Lebanon and the local people venerated him as a saint. They say there were thousands of miracles at Anaya—pilgrims flocked there—until the monks built a fine cemetery with the resultant proceeds, and the miracles stopped."

That last bit was not in the book, of course. I have read it through since, and the passage describing the photograph dozens of times. He looks a grouchy enough old character, the sixth figure, but the deep, resolute eyes, whenever I open the page, continue simultaneously to pacify and challenge me. The book, incidentally, was disappointing. Terrible, in fact. The author uses every pious platitude known to hagiography, even going so far as to assert that Sharbel died "in the odour of sanctity".

Meanwhile, my life changed. I looked around me with a new vision to see the world charged with the grandeur of God. I began to read poetry again, and to live it. People seemed different to me. They were no longer the impossible, stiffnecked, hopeless Irish. Each was an unique individual to my eyes, so that I found myself caring what happened to everyone I met. For me the change was thrilling, exciting. How much it affected anyone else I cannot say, nor could I really explain what had happened. After a while I gave up trying to explain it. All I knew was that the strange magnetism of the long dead Lebanese contemplative had bestowed on my life a new peace and direction.

As I listened and observed, I was made acutely aware of the fear and pressure under which people in the houses and flats around us were living. Neighbours who once bade me the time of day and little more began to talk about their anxieties, their divided loyalties. The elderly were afraid to open their doors, even to look out their windows. Mothers fretted about how their sons were spending their leisure time and whom they were associating with. Oh yes, they were often foolish, senselessly doting, condoning what appeared to me to be clear cases of vandalism and aggression. You must know the kind of thing I mean. "Don't throw stones at that car, Johnny. Can't you see the policeman is looking." That type of mentality is rife around Mount Conor. The only crime is to get caught. A good son is defined as one who has never brought the police to your door, not as one who's trying hard to keep the commandments of God or live by some high moral standard. The worry, however, is genuine and the ambivalence largely due to ignorance and a blind tradition. Fair enough, I can see what you mean, there's reason for the tradition and England can't shrug off her responsibility for it. That's another new thing I've begun to learn.

What impressed me most forcefully, as I came to know the people better, was the responsibility each individual carries, whatever his national origin or background, for the continuing reign of terror in our neighbourhood. A handful of savage fanatics, like the thug in those sketches, have been imposing their rule for years upon the locality without a mandate from anyone. And all because people like me, who ought to know better, don't want to know about it. Yes, there are a few who stand against the thugs, mostly by working quietly to build a better community. But who confronts the thugs? Who tries to intercept them on their cruel errands? I didn't exactly say, "Here I am Lord, choose me." But that was the way things began to take shape. People began, you see, to whisper dark secrets in my ear. Once I had made a start there was no going back. I found myself living in a new wide world of defiance. That was why, when an anonymous phone call made it known to me that a boy was to be kneecapped on Tuesday night in the Springvale flats complex, I knew I would have to go down and investigate.

It was close to midnight when I arrived in the courtyard and the place seemed deserted save for the redheaded youth in jeans standing with his fingertips against the wall. Even the sky was cold and empty, the boy might have been praying to an absent God, but when I approached I saw he was shivering with fright. I took him by the arm, he couldn't move or speak, and I assured him, "Don't worry, no one will touch you as long as I'm here."

Somewhere at the back of my mind was a romantic notion that all I had to do was draw a crucifix, brandish it before me, and all demons, whether of the flesh or the spirit, would shrink away from my awesome presence. Instead, out of the shadows crept a dozen or so youths in anoraks, hoods fastened tight about their heads, some wearing stocking masks or scarves across their mouths and noses, all of them brandishing hurley sticks, fine brave upstanding Irishmen all.

"Be off," I shouted. "You ought to be ashamed of yourselves."

They hesitated as I ranted and roared, calling them a gang of cowards, threatening to report them to their parents. The irony of that situation didn't escape me, but it's not easy to know where best to report such misconduct, is it? It was then the thug appeared with his handgun, lurking for a moment in semi-darkness, summoning to mind the phantom of evil that lived in my memory. He waited in the expectation that I would flee. When I didn't, he moved closer and I saw that he was only a thing of flesh and blood after all.

He pointed the gun straight at me and said, "I've come here to do a job and I'm going to do it. Get going."

"You'll do no rotten job while I'm here," I croaked, surprised at how my voice was shaking and thoroughly ashamed of the low level of eloquence which I was able to attain.

"In that case, I'm going to shoot you."

He spoke quite casually, as if shooting a man were of no special consequence. It was this extreme flatness of tone that alarmed me most. Impossible to believe there could be anything particularly heroic in being shot in such a fashion, with no grand gesture, no ceremony, not even a trace of feeling one way or another. I groped for a word of prayer and waited.

It was then that the voice of the people spoke—in the form of an old man hobbling on a stick who emerged from a hallway shouting in an outraged tone, "Don't you dare shoot the priest."

Sharbel, thank God, I thought, irrationally perhaps. Soon the old man was backed by scores of other forms that clung to the shadows of the walls, muttering threateningly or fearfully, both I think. The thug turned his gun for a moment on these intruders, then swung back sharply towards me. From the gathering crowd a woman broke to snatch at his arm. It was that which saved me. I made a rush for the boy, who still had not moved, intending to drag him quickly away. Then the gun exploded and it was the boy who fell. His blood spattered my hands as I tried to help him.

When I saw the blood on my hands, I glanced up at the thug's emotionless eyes and was swept out of my mind by frenzy. I attacked him, but hands seized me and pulled me away only seconds before the soldiers raced into the courtyard and everyone melted once more into the stony wilderness of the estate. While the soldiers stood and knelt watchfully, rifles directed towards overhanging windows and balconies, every nerve taut in their youthful faces, I squatted beside the boy where he lay moaning on the cold concrete and I wept, not for Ireland, not for the scared English soldiers my countrymen, but for suffering wretches from Beirut to Belfast, for the whole enigmatic torture of humanity by humanity. And yet, in the midst of tears, a voice sang inside me and I laughed out loud, so loud that the ambulance men, when they arrived, handled me very gently and humouringly as they helped me to my feet.

"He's a wee bit hysterical," one explained to another. "Shock, you know—the poor bastard."

I see now that Sharbel's mediation must have been, essentially, the same communion with the One True God of Love as I must achieve in this different time and different place. I am glad that he has come to be the singing master of my soul. Almost always, I feel his nearness, though why he should be here, what we could have in common, remains a mystery. Perhaps I am Sharbel? His reincarnation? His purgatory perhaps? Who knows?

Whatever about that, I have confessed at last the persistent sin of my past life. I look forward to finding a new heaven and a new earth, to a lifetime burning in every moment. Old men must be explorers if they are to set a good example to the young.

J. SHERIDAN LE FANU

An Account of Some Strange Disturbances in Aungier Street

My cousin (Tom Ludlow) and I studied medicine together. I think he would have succeeded, had he stuck to the profession; but he preferred the Church, poor fellow, and died early, a sacrifice to contagion, contracted in the noble discharge of his duties. For my present purpose, I say enough of his character when I mention that he was of a sedate but frank and cheerful nature; very exact in his observance of truth, and not by any means like myself—of an excitable or nervous temperament.

My Uncle Ludlow—Tom's father—while we were attending lectures, purchased three or four old houses in Aungier Street, one of which was unoccupied. *He* resided in the country, and Tom proposed that we should take up our abode in the untenanted house, so long as it should continue unlet; a move which would accomplish the double end of settling us nearer alike to our lecture-rooms and to our amusements, and of relieving us from the weekly charge of rent for our lodgings.

Our furniture was very scant—our whole equipage remarkably modest and primitive; and, in short, our arrangements pretty nearly as simple as those of a bivouac. Our new plan was, therefore, executed almost as soon as conceived. The front drawing-room was our sitting-room. I had the bedroom over it, and Tom the back bedroom on the same floor, which nothing could have induced me to occupy.

The house, to begin with, was a very old one. It had been, I believe, newly fronted about fifty years before; but with this exception, it had nothing modern about it. The agent who bought it and looked up the titles for my uncle, told me that it was sold, along with much older forfeited property, at Chichester House, I think, in 1702; and had belonged to Sir Thomas Hackett, who was Lord Mayor of Dublin in James II's time. How old it was *then*, I can't say; but, at all events, it had seen years and changes enough to have contracted all that mysterious and saddened air, at once exciting and depressing, which belongs to most old mansions.

There had been very little done in the way of modernising details; and, perhaps, it was better so; for there was something queer and by-gone in the very walls and ceilings—in the shape of doors and windows—in the odd diagonal site of the chimney-pieces—in the beams and ponderous cornices—not to mention the singular solidity of all the woodwork, from the banisters to the window-frames, which hopelessly defied disguise, and would have emphatically proclaimed their antiquity through any conceivable amount of modern finery and varnish.

An effort had, indeed, been made, to the extent of papering the drawing-rooms; but, somehow the paper looked raw and out of keeping; and the old woman, who kept a little dirt-pie of a shop in the lane, and whose daughter—a girl of two and fifty—was our solitary handmaid, coming in at sunrise, and chastely receding again as soon as she had made all ready for tea in our state apartment;—this woman, I say, remembered it, when old

Judge Horrocks (who, having earned the reputation of a particularly "hanging judge," ended by hanging himself, as the coroner's jury found, under an impulse of "temporary insanity," with a child's skipping-rope, over the massive old banisters) resided there, entertaining good company, with fine venison and rare old port. In those halcyon days, the drawing-rooms were hung with gilded leather, and I dare say, cut a good figure, for they were really spacious rooms.

The bedrooms were wainscoted, but the front one was not gloomy; and in it the cosiness of antiquity quite overcame its sombre associations. But the back bedroom, with its two queerly-placed melancholy windows, staring vacantly at the foot of the bed, and with the shadowy recess to be found in most old houses in Dublin, like a large ghostly closet, which, from congeniality of temperament, had amalgamated with the bedchamber, and dissolved the partition. At night-time, this "alcove"— as our "maid" was wont to call it—had, in my eyes, a specially sinister and suggestive character. Tom's distant and solitary candle glimmered vainly into its darkness. *There* it was always overlooking him—always itself impenetrable. But this was only part of the effect. The whole room was, I can't tell how, repulsive to me. There was, I suppose, in its proportions and features, a latent discord—a certain mysterious and indescribable relation, which jarred indistinctly upon some secret sense of the fitting and the safe, and raised indefinable suspicions and apprehensions of the imagination. On the whole, as I began by saying, nothing could have induced me to pass a night alone in it.

I had never pretended to conceal from poor Tom my superstitious weakness; and he, on the other hand, most unaffectedly ridiculed my tremors. The sceptic was, however, destined to receive a lesson, as you shall hear.

We had not been very long in occupation of our respective dormitories, when I began to complain of uneasy nights and disturbed sleep. I was, I suppose, the more impatient under this annoyance, as I was usually a sound sleeper, and by no means prone to nightmares. It was now, however, my destiny, instead of enjoying my customary repose, every night to "sup full of horrors." After a preliminary course of disagreeable and frightful dreams, my troubles took a definite form, and the same vision, without an appreciable variation in a single detail, visited me at least (on an average) every second night in the week.

Now, this dream, nightmare, or infernal illusion— which you please—of which I was the miserable sport, was on this wise:

I saw, or thought I saw, with the most abominable distinctness, although at the time in profound darkness, every article of furniture and accidental arrangement of the chamber in which I lay. This, as you know, is incidental to ordinary nightmare. Well, while in this clairvoyant condition, which seemed but the lighting up of the theatre in which was to be exhibited the monotonous tableau of horror, which made my nights insupportable, my attention invariably became, I know not why, fixed upon the windows opposite the foot of my bed; and, uniformly with the same effect, a sense of dreadful anticipation always took slow but sure possession of me. I became somehow conscious of a sort of horrid but undefined preparation going forward in some unknown quarter, and by some unknown agency, for my torment; and, after an interval, which always seemed to me of the same length, a picture suddenly flew up to the window, where it remained fixed, as if by an electrical attraction, and my discipline of horror then commenced, to last perhaps for hours. The picture thus mysteriously glued to the window-panes, was the portrait of an old man, in a crimson-flowered silk dressing-gown, the folds of which I could now describe, with a countenance embodying a strange mixture of intellect, sensuality, and power, but withal sinister and full of malignant omen. His nose was hooked, like the beak of a vulture; his eyes large, grey and prominent, and lighted up with a more than mortal cruelty and coldness. These features were surmounted by a crimson velvet cap, the hair that peeped from under which was white with age, while the eyebrows retained their original blackness. Well, I remember every line, hue, and shadow of that stony countenance, and well I may! The gaze of this hellish visage was fixed upon me, and mine returned it with the inexplicable fascination of nightmare, for what appeared to me to be hours of agony. At last—

"The cock he crew, away then flew"

the fiend who had enslaved me through the awful watches of the night; and, harrassed and nervous, I rose to the duties of the day.

I had—I can't say exactly why, but it may have been from the exquisite anguish and profound impressions of unearthly horror, with which this strange phantasmagoria was associated—an insurmountable antipathy to describing the exact nature of my nightly troubles to my friend and comrade. Generally, however, I told him that I was haunted by abominable dreams; and, true to the imputed materialism of medicine, we put our heads together to dispel my horrors, not by exorcism, but by a tonic.

I will do this tonic justice, and frankly admit that the accursed portrait began to intermit its visits under its influence. What of that? Was this singular apparition—as full of character as of terror—therefore the creature of my fancy, or the invention of my poor stomach? Was it, in short, *subjective* (to borrow the technical slang of the day) and not the palpable aggression and intrusion of an external agent? That, good friend, as we will both admit, by no means follows. The evil spirit, who enthralled my senses in the shape of that portrait, may have been just as near me, just as energetic, just as malignant, though I saw him not. What means the whole moral code of revealed religion regarding the due keeping of our own bodies, soberness, temperance, etc.? Here is an obvious connexion between the material and the invisible; the healthy tone of the system, and its unimpaired energy, may, for aught we can tell, guard us against influences which would otherwise render life itself terrific. The mesmerist and the electro-biologist will fail upon an average with nine patients out of ten—so may the evil spirit. Special conditions of the corporal system are indispensable to the production of certain spiritual phenomena. The operation succeeds sometimes—sometimes fails—that is all.

I found afterwards that my would-be sceptical companion had his troubles too. But of these I knew nothing yet. One night, for a wonder, I was sleeping soundly, when I was roused by a step on the lobby outside my room, followed by the loud clang of what turned out to be a large brass candlestick, flung with all his force by poor Tom Ludlow over the banisters, and rattling with a rebound down the second flight of stairs; and almost concurrently with this, Tom burst open my door, and bounced into my room backwards, in a state of extraordinary agitation.

I had jumped out of bed and clutched him by the arm before I had any distinct idea of my own whereabouts. There we were—in our shirts—standing before the open door—staring through the great old banister opposite, at the lobby window, through which the sickly light of a clouded moon was gleaming.

"What's the matter, Tom? What's the the matter with you? What the devil's the matter with you, Tom?" I demanded, shaking him with nervous impatience.

He took a long breath before he answered me, and then it was not very coherently.

"It's nothing, nothing at all—did I speak?—what did I say?—where's the candle, Richard? It's dark; I—I had a candle!"

"Yes, dark enough," I said; "but what's the matter?— what *is* it?—why don't you speak, Tom?—have you lost your wits? What is the matter?"

"The matter?—oh, it is all over. It must have been a dream—nothing at all but a dream—don't you think so? It could not be anything more than a dream."

"Of *course*," said I, feeling uncommonly nervous, "it *was* a dream."

"I thought," he said, "there was a man in my room, and—and I jumped out of bed; and—and—where's the candle?"

"In your room, most likely," I said, "shall I go and bring it?"

"No; stay here—don't go; it's no matter—don't, I tell you; it was all a dream. Bolt the door, Dick; I'll stay here with you—I feel nervous. So, Dick, like a good fellow, light your candle and open the window—I am in a *shocking state*."

I did as he asked me, and robing himself like Granuaile in one of my blankets, he seated himself close beside my bed.

Everybody knows how contagious is fear of all sorts, but more especially that particular kind of fear under which poor Tom was at that moment labouring. I would not have heard, nor I believe would he have recapitulated, just at that moment, for half the world, the details of the hideous vision which had so unmanned him.

"Don't mind telling me anything about your nonsensical dream, Tom," said I, affecting contempt, really in a panic; "let us talk about something else; but it is quite plain that this dirty old house disagrees with us both, and hang me if I stay here any longer, to be pestered with indigestion and—and—bad nights, so we may as well look out for lodgings—don't you think so?—at once."

Tom agreed, and, after an interval, said—

"I have been thinking, Richard, that it is a long time since I saw my father, and I have made up my mind to go down tomorrow and return in a day or two, and you can take rooms for us in the meantime."

I fancied that this resolution, obviously the result of the vision which had so profoundly scared him, would probably vanish next morning with the damps and shadows of night. But I was mistaken. Off went Tom at peep of day to the country, having agreed that so soon as I had secured suitable lodgings, I was to recall him by letter from his visit to my Uncle Ludlow.

Now, anxious as I was to change my quarters, it so happened, owing to a series of petty procrastinations and accidents, that nearly a week elapsed before my bargain was made and my letter of recall on the wing to Tom; and, in the meantime, a trifling adventure or two had occurred to your humble servant, which, absurd as they now appear, diminished by distance, did certainly at the time serve to whet my appetite for change considerably.

A night or two after the departure of my comrade, I was sitting by my bedroom fire, the door locked, and the ingredients of a tumbler of hot whisky-punch upon the crazy spider-table; for, as the best mode of keeping the

> "*Black spirits and white,*
> *Blue spirits and grey,*"

with which I was environed, at bay, I had adopted the practice recommended by the wisdom of my ancestors, and "kept my spirits up by pouring spirits down." I had thrown aside my volume of Anatomy, and was treating myself by way of a tonic, preparatory to my punch and bed, to half-a-dozen pages of the *Spectator*, when I heard a step on the flight of stairs descending from the attics. It was two o'clock, and the streets were as silent as a church-yard—the sounds were, therefore, perfectly distinct. There was a slow, heavy tread, characterised by the emphasis and deliberation of age, descending by the narrow staircase from above; and, what made the sound more singular, it was plain that the feet which produced it were perfectly bare, measuring the descent with something between a pound and a flop, very ugly to hear.

I knew quite well that my attendant had gone away many hours before, and that nobody but myself had any business in the house. It was quite plain also that the person who was coming downstairs had no intention whatever of concealing his movements; but, on the contrary, appeared disposed to make even more noise, and proceed more deliberately, than was at all necessary. When the step reached the foot of the stairs outside my room, it seemed to stop; and I expected every moment to see my door open spontaneously, and give admission to the original of my detested portrait. I was, however, relieved in a few seconds by hearing the descent renewed, just in the same manner, upon the staircase leading down to the drawing-rooms, and thence, after another pause, down the next flight, and so on to the hall, whence I heard no more.

Now, by the time the sound had ceased, I was wound up, as they say, to a very unpleasant pitch of excitement. I listened, but there was not a stir. I screwed up my courage to a decisive experiment—opened my door, and in a stentorian voice bawled over the banisters, "Who's there?" There was no answer, but the ringing of my own voice through the empty old house,—no renewal of the movement; nothing, in short, to give my unpleasant sensations a definite direction. There is, I think, something most disagreeably disenchanting in the sound of one's own voice under such circumstances, exerted in solitude and in vain. It redoubled my sense of isolation, and my misgivings increased on perceiving that the door, which I certainly thought I had left open, was closed behind me; in a vague alarm, lest my retreat should be cut off, I got again into my room as quickly as I could, where I remained in a state of imaginary blockade, and very uncomfortable indeed, till morning.

Next night brought no return of my barefooted fellow-lodger; but the night following, being in my bed, and in the dark—somewhere, I suppose, about the same hour as before, I distinctly heard the old fellow again descending from the garrets.

This time I had had my punch, and the *morale* of the garrison was consequently excellent. I jumped out of bed, clutched the poker as I passed the expiring fire, and in a moment was upon the lobby. The sound had ceased by this time—the dark and chill were discouraging; and, guess my horror, when I saw, or thought I saw, a black monster, whether in the shape of a man or a bear I could not say, standing, with its back to the wall, on the lobby, facing me, with a pair of great greenish eyes shining dimly out. Now, I must be frank, and confess that the cupboard which displayed our plates and cups stood just there, though at the moment I did not recollect it. At the same time I must honestly say, that making every allowance for an excited imagination, I never could satisfy myself that I was made the dupe of my own fancy in this matter; for this apparition, after one or two shiftings of shape, as if in the act of incipient transformation, began, as it seemed on second thoughts, to advance upon me in its original form.

From an instinct of terror rather than of courage, I hurled the poker, with all my force, at its head; and to the music of a horrid crash made my way into my room, and double-locked the door. Then, in a minute more, I heard the horrid bare feet walk down the stairs, till the sound ceased in the hall, as on the former occasion.

If the apparition of the night before was an ocular delusion of my fancy sporting with the dark outlines of our cupboard, and if its horrid eyes were nothing but a pair of inverted teacups, I had, at all events, the satisfaction of having launched the poker with admirable effect, and in true "fancy" phrase, "knocked its two daylights into one," as the commingled fragments of my tea-service testified. I did my best to gather comfort and courage from these evidences; but it would not do. And then what could I say of those horrid bare feet, and the regular tramp, tramp, tramp, which measured the distance of the entire staircase through the solitude of my haunted dwelling, and at an hour when no good influence was stirring? Confound it!—the whole affair was abominable. I was out of spirits, and dreaded the approach of night.

It came, ushered ominously in with a thunder-storm and dull torrents of depressing rain. Earlier than usual, the streets grew silent; and by twelve o'clock nothing but the comfortless pattering of the rain was to be heard.

I made myself as snug as I could. I lighted *two* candles instead of one. I foreswore bed, and held myself in readiness for a sally, candle in hand; for, *coute qui coute*, I was resolved to see the being, if visible at all, who troubled the nightly stillness of my mansion. I was fidgety and nervous and tried in vain to interest myself with my books. I walked up and down my room, whistling in turn martial and hilarious music, and listening ever and anon for the dreaded noise. I sat down and stared at the square label on the solemn and reserved-looking black bottle, until "Flanagan & Co's Best Old Malt Whisky" grew into a sort of subdued accompaniment to all the fantastic and horrible speculations which chased one another through my brain.

Silence, meanwhile, grew more silent, and darkness darker. I listened in vain for the rumble of a vehicle, or the dull clamour of a distant row. There was nothing but the sound of a rising wind, which had succeeded the thunder-storm that had travelled over the Dublin mountains quite out of hearing. In the middle of this great city I began to feel myself alone with nature, and Heaven knows what beside. My courage was ebbing. Punch, however, which makes beasts of so many, made a man of me again—just in time to hear with tolerable nerve and firmness the lumpy, flabby, naked feet deliberately descending the stairs again.

I took a candle, not without a tremor. As I crossed the floor I tried to extemporise a prayer, but stopped short to listen, and never finished it. The steps continued. I confess I hesitated for some seconds at the door before I took heart of grace and opened it. When I peeped out the lobby was perfectly empty—there was no monster standing on the staircase; and as the detested sound ceased, I was reassured enough to venture forward nearly to the banisters. Horror of horrors! within a stair or two beneath the spot where I stood the unearthly tread smote the floor. My eye caught something in motion; it was about the size of a Goliath's foot—it was grey, heavy, and flapped with a dead weight from one step to another. As I am alive, it was the most monstrous grey rat I ever beheld or imagined.

Shakespeare says—"Some men there are cannot abide a gaping pig, and some that are mad if they behold a cat." I went well-nigh out of my wits when I beheld this *rat*; for, laugh at me as you may, it fixed upon me, I thought, a perfectly human expression of malice; and, as it shuffled about and looked up into my face almost from between my feet, I saw, I could swear it—I felt it then, and know it now, the infernal gaze and the accursed countenance of my old friend in the portrait, transfused into the visage of the bloated vermin before me.

I bounced into my room again with a feeling of loathing and horror I cannot describe, and locked and bolted my door as if a lion had been at the other side. D——n him or *it*; curse the portrait and its original! I felt in my soul that the rat—yes, the *rat*, the RAT I had just seen, was that evil being in masquerade, and rambling through the house upon some infernal night lark.

Next morning I was early trudging through the miry streets; and, among other transactions, posted a peremptory note recalling Tom. On my return, however, I found a note from my absent "chum," announcing his intended return next day. I was doubly rejoiced at this, because I had succeeded in getting rooms; and because the change of scene and return of my comrade were rendered specially pleasant by the last night's half ridiculous, half horrible adventure.

I slept extemporaneously in my new quarters in Digges' Street that night, and next morning returned for breakfast to the haunted mansion, where I was certain Tom would call immediately on his arrival.

I was quite right—he came; and almost his first question referred to the primary object of our change of residence.

"Thank God," he said with genuine fervour, on hearing that all was arranged. "On *your* account I am delighted. As to myself, I assure you that no earthly consideration could have induced me ever again to pass a night in this disastrous old house."

"Confound the house!" I ejaculated, with a genuine mixture of fear and detestation, "we have not had a

pleasant hour since we came to live here"; and so I went
on, and related incidentally my adventure with the
plethoric old rat.

"Well, if that were *all*," said my cousin, affecting to
make light of the matter, "I don't think I should have
minded it very much."

"Ay, but its eye—its countenance, my dear Tom," urged
I; "if you had seen *that*, you would have felt it might be
anything but what it seemed."

"I am inclined to think the best conjurer in such a case
would be an able-bodied cat," he said, with a provoking
chuckle.

"But let us hear your own adventure," I said tartly.

At this challenge he looked uneasily round him. I had
poked up a very unpleasant recollection.

"You shall hear it, Dick; I'll tell it to you," he said.
"Begad, sir, I should feel quite queer, though, telling it
here, though we are too strong a body for ghosts to meddle
with just now."

Though he spoke this like a joke, I think it was serious
calculation. Our Hebe was in a corner of the room,
packing our cracked delf tea and dinner-services in a
basket. She soon suspended operations, and with mouth
and eyes wide open became an absorbed listener. Tom's
experiences were told nearly in these words:

"I saw it three times, Dick—three distinct times; and I
am perfectly certain it meant me some infernal harm. I
was, I say, in danger—in *extreme* danger; for, if nothing
else had happened, my reason would most certainly have
failed me, unless I had escaped so soon. Thank God, I *did*
escape.

"The first night of this hateful disturbance, I was lying
in the attitude of sleep, in that lumbering old bed. I hate
to think of it. I was really wide awake, though I had put
out my candle, and was lying as quietly as if I had been

asleep; and although accidentally restless, my thoughts were running in a cheerful and agreeable channel.

"I think it must have been two o'clock at least when I thought I heard a sound in that—that odious dark recess at the far end of the bedroom. It was as if someone was drawing a piece of cord slowly along the floor, lifting it up, and dropping it softly down again in coils. I sat up once or twice in my bed, but could see nothing, so I concluded it must be mice in the wainscot. I felt no emotion graver than curiosity, and after a few minutes ceased to observe it.

"While lying in this state, strange to say, without at first a suspicion of anything supernatural, on a sudden I saw an old man, rather stout and square, in a sort of roan-red dressing-gown, and with a black cap on his head, moving stiffly and slowly in a diagonal direction, from the recess, across the floor of the bedroom, passing my bed at the foot, and entering the lumber-closet at the left. He had something under his arm; his head hung a little at one side; and merciful God! when I saw his face."

Tom stopped for a while, and then said—

"That awful countenance, which living or dying I never can forget, disclosed what he was. Without turning to the right or left, he passed beside me, and entered the closet by the bed's head.

"While this fearful and indescribable type of death and guilt was passing, I felt that I had no more power to speak or stir than if I had been myself a corpse. For hours after it had disappeared, I was too terrified and weak to move. As soon as daylight came, I took courage, and examined the room, and especially the course which the frightful intruder had seemed to take, but there was not a vestige to indicate anybody's having passed there; no sign of any disturbing agency visible among the lumber that strewed the floor of the closet.

"I now began to recover a little. I was fagged and exhausted, and at last, overpowered by a feverish sleep. I came down late; and finding you out of spirits, on account of your dreams about the portrait, whose *original* I am now certain disclosed himself to me, I did not care to talk about the infernal vision. In fact, I was trying to persuade myself that the whole thing was an illusion, and I did not like to revive in their intensity the hated impressions of the past night—or, to risk the constancy of my scepticism, by recounting the tale of my sufferings.

"It required some nerve, I can tell you, to go to my haunted chamber next night, and lie down quietly in the same bed," continued Tom. "I did so with a degree of trepidation, which, I am not ashamed to say, a very little matter would have sufficed to stimulate to downright panic. This night, however, passed off quietly enough, as also the next; and so too did two or three more. I grew more confident, and began to fancy that I believed in the theories of spectral illusions, with which I had at first vainly tried to impose upon my convictions.

"The apparition had been, indeed, altogether anomalous. It had crossed the room without any recognition of my presence: I had not disturbed *it*, and *it* had no mission to *me*. What, then, was the imaginable use of its crossing the room in a visible shape at all? Of course it might have *been* in the closet instead of *going* there, as easily as it introduced itself into the recess without entering the chamber in a shape discernible by the senses. Besides, how the deuce *had* I seen it? It was a dark night; I had no candle; there was no fire; and yet I saw it as distinctly, in colouring and outline, as ever I beheld human form! A cataleptic dream would explain it all; and I was determined that a dream it should be.

"One of the most remarkable phenomena connected with the practice of mendacity is the vast number of deliberate lies we tell ourselves, whom, of all persons, we can least expect to deceive. In all this, I need hardly tell you, Dick, I was simply lying to myself, and did not believe one word of the wretched humbug. Yet I went on, as men will do, like persevering charlatans and impostors, who tire people into credulity by the mere force of reiteration; so I hoped to win myself over at last to a comfortable scepticism about the ghost.

"He had not appeared a second time—that certainly was a comfort; and what, after all, did I care for him, and his queer old toggery and strange looks? Not a fig! I was nothing the worse for having seen him, and a good story the better. So I tumbled into bed, put out my candle, and, cheered by a loud drunken quarrel in the back lane, went fast asleep.

"From this deep slumber I awoke with a start. I knew I had had a horrible dream; but what it was I could not remember. My heart was thumping furiously; I felt bewildered and feverish; I sat up in the bed and looked about the room. A broad flood of moonlight came in through the curtainless window; everything was as I had last seen it; and though the domestic squabble in the back lane was, unhappily for me, allayed, I yet could hear a pleasant fellow singing, on his way home, the then popular comic ditty called, "Murphy Delany". Taking advantage of this diversion I lay down again, with my face towards the fireplace, and closing my eyes, did my best to think of nothing else but the song, which was every moment growing fainter in the distance:—

"'Twas Murphy Delany, so funny and frisky,
Stept into a shebeen shop to get his skin full;
He reeled out again pretty well lined with whiskey,
As fresh as a shamrock, as blind as a bull."

"The singer, whose condition I dare say resembled that of his hero, was soon too far off to regale my ears any more; and as his music died away, I myself sank into a doze, neither sound nor refreshing. Somehow the song had got into my head, and I went meandering on through the adventures of my respectable fellow-countryman, who, on emerging from the "shebeen shop," fell into a river, from which he was fished up to be "sat upon" by a coroner's jury, who having learned from a "horse-doctor" that he was "dead as a door-nail, so there was an end," returned their verdict accordingly, just as he returned to his senses, when an angry altercation and a pitched battle between the body and the coroner winds up the lay with due spirit and pleasantry.

"Through this ballad I continued with a weary monotony to plod, down to the very last line, and then *da capo*, and so on, in my uncomfortable half-sleep, for how long, I can't conjecture. I found myself at last, however, muttering, "*dead* as a door-nail, so there was an end"; and something like another voice within me, seemed to say, very faintly, but sharply, "dead! dead! *dead!* and may the Lord have mercy on your soul!" and instantaneously I was wide awake, and staring right before me from the pillow.

"Now—will you believe it, Dick?—I saw the same accursed figure standing full front, and gazing at me with its stony and fiendish countenance, not two yards from the bedside."

Tom stopped here, and wiped the perspiration from his face. I felt very queer. The girl was as pale as Tom; and, assembled as we were in the very scene of these adventures, we were all, I dare say, equally grateful for the clear daylight and the resuming bustle out of doors.

"For about three seconds only I saw it plainly; then it grew indistinct; but, for a long time, there was something like a column of dark vapour where it had been standing between me and the wall; and I felt sure that he was still there. After a good while, this appearance went too. I took my clothes downstairs to the hall, and dressed there, with the door half open; then went out into the street, and walked about the town till morning, when I came back, in a miserable state of nervousness and exhaustion. I was such a fool, Dick, as to be ashamed to tell you how I came to be so upset. I thought you would laugh at me; especially as I had always talked philosophy, and treated *your* ghosts with contempt. I concluded you would give me no quarter; and so kept my tale of horror to myself.

"Now, Dick, you will hardly believe me, when I assure you, that for many nights after this last experience, I did not go to my room at all. I used to sit up for a while in the drawing-room after you had gone up to your bed; and then steal down softly to the hall-door, let myself out, and sit in the "Robin Hood" tavern until the last guest went off; and then I got through the night like a sentry, pacing the streets till morning.

"For more than a week I never slept in bed. I sometimes had a snooze on a form in the "Robin Hood," and sometimes a nap in a chair during the day; but regular sleep I had absolutely none.

"I was quite resolved that we should get into another house; but I could not bring myself to tell you the reason, and I somehow put it off from day to day, and because my life was, during every hour of this procrastination, rendered as miserable as that of a felon with the constables on his track, I was growing absolutely ill from this wretched mode of life.

"One afternoon I determined to enjoy an hour's sleep upon your bed. I hated mine; so that I had never, except in a stealthy visit every day to unmake it, lest Martha should discover the secret of my nightly absence, entered the ill-omened chamber.

"As ill-luck would have it, you had locked your bedroom, and taken away the key. I went into my own to unsettle the bedclothes, as usual, and give the bed the appearance of having been slept in. Now a variety of circumstances concurred to bring about the dreadful scene through which I was that night to pass. In the first place, I was literally overpowered with fatigue, and longing for sleep; in the next place, the effect of this extreme exhaustion upon my nerves resembled that of a narcotic, and rendered me less susceptible than, perhaps I should in any other condition have been, of the exciting fears which had become habitual to me. Then again, a little bit of the window was open, a pleasant freshness pervaded the room, and, to crown all, the cheerful sun of day was making the room quite pleasant. What was to prevent me enjoying an hour's nap *here?* The whole air was resonant with the cheerful hum of life, and the broad matter-of-fact light of day filled every corner of the room.

"I yielded—stifling my qualms—to the almost overpowering temptation; and merely throwing off my coat, and loosening my cravat, I lay down, limiting myself to *half*-an-hour's doze in the unwonted enjoyment of a feather bed, a coverlet, and a bolster.

"It was horribly insidious; and the demon, no doubt, marked my infatuated preparations. Dolt that I was, I fancied, with mind and body worn out for want of sleep, and an arrear of a full week's rest to my credit, that such measure as *half*-an-hour's sleep, in such a situation, was possible. My sleep was death-like, long, and dreamless.

"Without a start or fearful sensation of any kind, I waked gently, but completely. It was, as you have good reason to remember, long past midnight—I believe, about two o'clock. When sleep has been deep and long enough to satisfy nature thoroughly, one often wakens in this way, suddenly, tranquilly, and completely.

"There was a figure seated in that lumbering, old sofa-chair, near the fireplace. Its back was towards me, but I could not be mistaken; it turned slowly round, and, merciful heavens! there was the stony face, with its infernal lineaments of malignity and despair, gloating on me. There was now no doubt as to its consciousness of my presence, and the hellish malice with which it was animated, for it arose, and drew close to the bedside. There was a rope about its neck, and the other end, coiled up, it held stiffly in its hand.

"My good angel nerved me for this horrible crisis. I remained for some seconds transfixed by the gaze of this tremendous phantom. He came close to the bed, and appeared on the point of mounting upon it. The next instant I was upon the floor at the far side, and in a moment more was, I don't know how, upon the lobby.

"But the spell was not yet broken; the valley of the shadow of death was not yet traversed. The abhorred phantom was before me there; it was standing near the banisters, stooping a little, and with one end of the rope around its own neck, was poising a noose at the other, as if to throw over mine; and while engaged in this baleful pantomime, it wore a smile so sensual, so unspeakably dreadful, that my senses were nearly overpowered. I saw and remembered nothing more, until I found myself in your room.

"I had a wonderful escape, Dick—there is no disputing *that*—an escape for which, while I live, I shall bless the mercy of heaven. No one can conceive or imagine what it is for flesh and blood to stand in the presence of such a thing, but one who has had the terrific experience. Dick, Dick, a shadow has passed over me—a chill has crossed my blood and marrow, and I will never be the same again—never, Dick—never!"

Our handmaid, a mature girl of two-and-fifty, as I have said, stayed her hand, as Tom's story proceeded, and by little and little drew near to us, with open mouth, and her brows contracted over her little, beady black eyes, till stealing a glance over her shoulder now and then, she established herself close behind us. During the relation, she had made various earnest comments, in an undertone; but these and her ejaculations, for the sake of brevity and simplicity, I have omitted in my narration.

"It's often I heard tell of it," she now said, "but I never believed it rightly till now—though, indeed, why should not I? Does not my mother, down there in the lane, know quare stories, God bless us, beyant telling about it? But you ought not to have slept in the back bedroom. She was loath to let me be going in and out of that room even in the day time, let alone for any Christian to spend the night in it; for sure she says it was his own bedroom."

"*Whose* own bedroom?" we asked, in a breath.

"Why, *his*—the ould Judge's—Judge Horrock's, to be sure, God rest his sowl"; and she looked fearfully round.

"Amen!" I muttered. "But did he die there?"

"Die there! No, not quite *there*," she said. "Shure, was not it over the banisters he hung himself, the ould sinner, God be merciful to us all? and was not it in the alcove they found the handles of the skipping-rope cut off, and the knife where he was settling the cord, God bless us, to hang himself with? It was his housekeeper's daughter owned the rope, my mother often told me, and the child never throve after, and used to be starting up out of her sleep, and screeching in the night time, wid dhrames and frights that cum on her; and they said how it was the speerit of the ould Judge that was tormentin' her; and she used to be roaring and yelling out to hould back the big ould fellow with the crooked neck; and then she'd screech 'Oh, the master! the master! he's stampin' at me, and beckoning to me! Mother, darling, don't let me go!' And so the poor crathure died at last, and the docthers said it was wather on the brain, for it was all they could say."

"How long ago was all this?" I asked.

"Oh, then, how would I know?" she answered. "But it must be a wondherful long time ago, for the housekeeper was an ould woman, with a pipe in her moth, and not a tooth left, and better nor eighty years ould when my mother was first married; and they said she was a rale buxom, fine-dressed woman when the ould Judge come to his end; an', indeed, my mother's not far from eighty years ould herself this day; and what made it worse for the unnatural ould villain, God rest his soul, to frighten the little girl out of the world the way he did, was what was mostly thought and believed by everyone. My mother says how the poor little crathure was his own child; for he was by all accounts an ould villain every way, an' the hangin'est judge that ever was known in Ireland's ground."

"From what you said about the danger of sleeping in that bedroom," said I, "I suppose there were stories about the ghost having appeared there to others."

"Well, there *was* things said—quare things, surely," she answered, as it seemed, with some reluctance. "And why would not there? Sure was it not up in that same room he slept for more than twenty years? and was it not in the alcove he got the rope ready that done his own business at last, the way he done many a betther man's in his lifetime?—and was not the body lying in the same bed after death, and put in the coffin there, too, and carried out to his grave from it in Pether's churchyard, after the coroner was done? But there was quare stories—my mother has them all—about how one Nicholas Spaight got into trouble on the head of it."

"And what did they say of this Nicholas Spaight?" I asked.

"Oh, for that matther, it's soon told," she answered.

And she certainly did relate a very strange story, which so piqued my curiosity, that I took occasion to visit the ancient lady, her mother, from whom I learned many very curious particulars. Indeed, I am tempted to tell the tale, but my fingers are weary, and I must defer it. But if you wish to hear it another time, I shall do my best.

When we had heard the strange tale I have *not* told you, we put one or two further questions to her about the alleged special visitations, to which the house had, ever since the death of the wicked old Judge, been subjected.

"No one ever had luck in it," she told us. "There was always cross accidents, sudden deaths, and short times in it. The first that tuck it was a family—I forget their name—but at any rate there were two young ladies and their papa. He was about sixty, and a stout healthy gentleman as you'd wish to see at that age. Well, he slept in that unlucky back bedroom; and, God between us an' all harm! sure enough he was found dead one morning, half out of the bed, and his head as black as a sloe, an swelled like a puddin', hanging down near the floor. It was a fit, they said. He was as dead as a mackerel, and so *he* could not say what it was; but the ould people was all sure that it was nothing at all but the ould Judge, God bless us! that frightened him out of his senses and his life together.

"Some time after there was a rich old maiden lady took the house. I don't know which room *she* slept in, but she lived alone; and at any rate, one morning, the servants going down early to their work, found her sitting on the passage-stairs, shivering and talkin' to herself, quite mad; and never a word more could any of *them* or her friends get from her ever afterwards but, 'Don't ask me to go, for I promised to wait for him.' They never made out from her who it was she meant by *him*, but of course those that knew all about the ould house were at no loss for the meaning of all that happened to her.

"Then afterwards, when the house was let out in lodgings, there was Micky Byrne that took the same room, with his wife and three little children; and sure I heard Mrs Byrne myself telling how the children used to be lifted up in the bed at night, she could not see by what mains; and how they were starting and screeching every hour, just all as one as the housekeeper's little girl that died, till at last one night poor Mickey had a dhrop in him, the way he used now and again; and what do you think, in the middle of the night he thought he heard a noise on the stairs, and being in liquor, nothing less id do him but out he must go himself to see what was wrong. Well, after that, all she ever heard of him was himself sayin', 'Oh, God!' and a tumble that shook the very house; and there, sure enough, he was lying on the lower stairs, under the lobby, with his neck smashed double undher him, where he was flung over the banisters."

Then the handmaiden added—

"I'll go down to the lane, and send up Joe Garvey to pack up the rest of the taythings, and bring all the things across to your new lodgings."

And so we all sallied out together, each of us breathing more freely, I have no doubt, as we crossed that ill-omened threshold for the last time.

Now, I may add this much, in compliance with the immemorial usage of the realm of fiction, which sees the hero not only through his adventures, but fairly out of the world. You must have perceived that what the flesh, blood and bone hero of romance proper is to the regular compounder of fiction, this old house of brick, wood, and mortar is to the humble recorder of this true tale. I, therefore, relate, as in duty bound, the catastrophe which ultimately befell it, which was simply this—that about two years subsequent to my story it was taken by a quack doctor, who called himself Baron Duhlstoerf, and filled the parlour windows with bottles of indescribable horrors preserved in brandy, and the newspapers with the usual grandiloquent and mendacious advertisements. This gentleman among his virtues did not reckon sobriety, and one night, being overcome with much wine, he set fire to his bed curtains, partially burned himself, and totally consumed the house. It was afterwards rebuilt, and for a time an undertaker established himself in the premises.

I have now told you my own and Tom's adventures, together with some valuable collateral particulars; and having acquitted myself of my engagements, I wish you a very good night, and pleasant dreams.

ROBERT BERNEN

Brock

"A small brown dog, the colour of a badger. And you would hear no voice from him. Nor the sheep would not scare before him, the way they will before a black dog, when he was so like the badger, you see, for they'll not scare before the badger neither."

Paddy Rua's kitchen was a mass of irregular stone wall, built long before mortar or plaster was known in the Donegal hills, but smoothed to gentle undulations by generations of whitewash, topped above by the arch of crude roof, the rough-hewn timbers and wattles softened and darkened by equally long generations of smoke from the low stone hearth. The storms that warned of their approach by sending the smoke adversely down the stone chimney to fill the low kitchen had coated the wood with a dark, oily soot and so preserved it from worm and rot. Some thought the soot had preserved the people of the house too with its penetrating astringency, and Paddy Rua, somewhere in his nineties, could still rise from his stool beside the hearth to go out the kitchen door and look over his land and as much of his hill as could be seen, in the ancient manner of farmers scanning the ground to satisfy himself that all was in order, that cattle and sheep were grazing in their accustomed manner and haunts, and that "nothing strange" had interrupted the normal, safe course of animal life on his land. But mostly he sat close to his hearth and its piled turf, turning first one side and then the other to the glowing heat, and recollecting a time before any trace of modern life had been felt in the hills. By agreement Paddy Rua was in his nineties, though some thought he was near the beginning of them, while others put him well further on. A young valley farmer, careless of the nice discretion of the hills, had asked him, and Paddy Rua had thought for a while before speaking.

"Damned if I can mind."

He looked at the fire.

"Damned if I can mind it now. It be to be in the parish register, for Father Cleary there, God rest him, he was there that time, and he looked it out. That was the time the pensions first come to this country, and he looked it out to see when was I baptised and was I the age for the pension. But damned if I can mind what year ago that were."

A long discussion followed, with ample intervals for recollection and consideration, between Paddy Rua, sitting by the hearth, and his wife Mary, a generation younger and ceaselessly shuffling back and forth between hearth and kitchen table as she put bread on to roast above the fire or added fresh water to the kettle or, for want of other work, simply swept the red ashes of the burnt turf back into the hearth, tirelessly interjecting brief affirmative commentaries on Paddy's words—"Aye, caddy, you're right there," was the usual formula, for even at Paddy's great age she still called him "caddy" in sign of approval and affection—and their son Briney Paddy Rua, another generation younger still, the real "caddy" of the house, the human power source for any heavy work. Their voices contrasted by turns, the sound of the wind in Paddy's but the mist and rain in his son's, and in his wife's throat the thin twitter of a bird. But the only conclusion of their deliberations was that "it be to be twenty year or more since the pensions come out first", and nothing more was said about Paddy Rua's age. One thing only was certain, and that was that every trace of the fiery redness of hair that had given Paddy Rua his name had yielded to a perfect, silvery white.

"Aye," he said, going back to his recollection of the brown dog. "Het was a bad winter, you would say, when the snow lay about the streets in wreathes for months and weren't gone from the hills until summer. By Christ the sheep got it hard that year. There was ones lost in the snow in the high hills beyont, and not got at all until spring, and then only the horns got, and bits of fleece. And there would be more lost too, oh loads more, only a man had a good dog to take them to him." To which remark there were more affirmations, both from the wife and the son, who simply shook his downcast head slowly and commented, "Oh, aye, indeed, you want a good dog with the sheep."

A glowing turf on the hearth dislodged itself from the rest of the fire and tumbled on to the flagstones at Paddy's feet. He took up the black iron tongs that stood propped in a corner of the hearth near him and began a delicate rearrangement of the brick-like chunks of turf, until the integrity of the fire had been restored. Then he rose and went to the door, and looked up towards the hills.

"There's a name on every part of the hill. A name in Irish, that a man would know where he was, and if he saw a sheep lost there, or something else like that, he could tell the man that lost it, and him go straight to where it were, and take it with him."

He stood on the "street", as he called the level clay

ground before his house, and looked over the land before him.

"That hill there now, away from us th_er_e, *Cruk Mian* we call that, the Fine Hill. And that big rock you see, that's *Caricka Keena*, the Rock of the Fog, the green fog that grows about the hills. And the high hill there beyont the river, that's *Ben Bwee*, the Yellow Hill. And there above, above the path that we go out and in, that's *Ben Doo*, is the name that's on it in Irish, and in English they call it the Black Spink. *Het's* the bad article."

He looked upwards along the steeply sloping green hill that rose behind his house to the uneven mass of vertical black rock that capped it. High, dark, irregular, a looming shadow of rock crossed by strips of green that attracted sheep and drew them, at times when grass was scarce, by gradual degrees further and further in to the sharp, uneven cliff face, until they found themselves isolated, marooned on a narrow ledge of rock with no way out, none at least that they could find. One who knew sheep could perceive, even from the river-valley five hundred feet below, their near-sighted perplexity as they stood, shifting their stance only intermittently, waiting as though in patient expectation of an opening to appear, of further grazing before them to lead them on, then returning to an examination of the scanty well-picked sward under their feet—but mostly simply standing, expectant, patient.

It happened two or three times a year, this catching of sheep in a natural trap. Almost always it was the year-old ewes—the "yirrols"—that got caught, sheep in the first part of their lives that had not yet learned to be sufficiently wary. And then the sheep farmers looked upwards from the river valley, calm, betraying no anguish or sense of loss. That was felt inwardly, not expressed. To count the loss aloud would only be to add discouragement to damage. But mostly it was hard, or impossible, to get the sheep out again.

"Excepting a man had a good dog could take them out of it," Briney Paddy Rua said over his shoulder as he sat at the small wooden table in the far corner of the kitchen, facing the wall and taking his bread and tea. Above him, in the spaces between the wattles and the earth sods of the roof itself tobacco-darkened clay pipes were wedged, and two pairs of wool-shears hung from wooden pegs, their points downwards. On the floor near the table stood a tall, unpainted wooden churn. Pinned to the wattles of the roof above the hearth was a Brigid cross woven of green rushes. Briney filled his mouth with bread, tearing it off with a sideways forceful motion of his head, and took a sip of tea.

"That brown dog now," he said, "he would take a sheep out of the spink, and do it handy. You would see him handle them quiet, very quiet. You would enjoy to see him do it."

Paddy Rua looked over at his son for a moment.

"Did you know that dog?" he asked. "I thought that dog was before your time. By God, I was only a young caddy myself when I had that dog, younger nor you are now, I doubt."

Briney finished eating his mouthful. "Well, I didn't know him," he said. "But I often hear tell, you see."

"Aye," Paddy resumed. "*Het* was a dog. Brock. That's the Irish on *badger*. You see, when he was so like the badger, we called Brock on him. And he was very biddable, and quiet. It was the nature of the dog, you see, that he would come when you whistle him and walk quiet at your foot. Nor he would not catch any sheep neither, nor do them no harm."

"He was a great dog indeed," Mary interjected, twittering as she poured more tea from an old aluminium tea-pot into Briney's cup. "Aye, caddy, he was a good one."

"Thon was the dog could take the yirrols from the spink," Briney added.

"He could!" Paddy Rua said with emphasis, his eyes beginning to glow with the evoked past.

"By God, there are plenty of good dogs now can do nothing in the spink," Briney went on. "For there is Charley Fetey's big yellow dog that's as good as any dog these parts, would take the sheep to you as nicely"—Briney smiled and held his arm in a gentle, horizontal arc before him—"and put them in the yard for you, and you doing nothing only standing looking on. But if the same dog would come to the spink, you would have work to get him out, you would have to carry him out of it yourself, for he can do nothing in it, only stand. He would be afeared, you see."

"Aye," Paddy said. "I often seen that. But the brown dog was afeared of nothing, and would go in along them wee ledges, and as quiet"—he gestured tranquillity with his hands —"and turn the sheep, the way they would make their way out again, quiet, very quiet. Many's the sheep he took out of that Black Spink. And in that bad winter when the snow lay about the streets in wreathes until spring he was in it four or five times—he was!—and he saved a pile of sheep. You would see the wee brown dog that clear on the white snow. Back and forth, back and forth, until the sheep was out. Sheep that were in it and would be starved with the cold, standing there and nothing to get, they would starve, you see, only he put them out of it. A wee brown spot back and forth on the white snow."

Briney crossed himself rapidly after finishing his tea, replaced his cap on his head with a twist of the peak from side to front that settled it firmly in place, pushed his chair back, and rose from the table. "It's a pity no pup were saved off him," he said. Then he took his stick and walked through the kitchen door, mindful of some routine obligation calling him away. He had heard about the brown dog before, probably more than once, and was too young and vigorous to sit by the fire listening to accounts of what was past when there was present work to do.

Paddy Rua watched him go out, his own eyes watery and slightly dim as they turned from the darkness of the kitchen to the brighter light coming in through the open door.

"No pup," he echoed. "There were no pup saved off him."

The soft rumble of a tractor, the sound rising as though filtered through the hill air from the valley below, caught his attention for a moment. He turned his face back to the fire, to his recollections of the past, of a time when it was a man's work to walk the rough hills in every weather and see to his sheep, and no machine noise, no whine of car or lorry or rumble of tractor, had ever interrupted the natural sounds of the hill valley, nor marred with their exhaust the soft and everchanging smells of the sloping ground. His mind and thoughts went back to those times easily, and he remembered and spoke of a way of life that was gone, of people and of animals that had died half a century before, or longer, and of beliefs that had lapsed. Life had been different then, lived differently, seen differently. Across the hills there had wandered a race of tall, vigorous men who had shared with their half-wild sheep and cattle more than just a habitat, had shared as well a way of being, had shared some of the wildness, even to the wildness of the strange beasts that were unknown only a few miles further west in the tame and disciplined valleys of the dairy farmers: the water-horses, the winged eels, the sword-nosed water-dogs. He had known many things that were hardly and only reluctantly talked of to anyone from beyond the fringe of the hills.

"Everything's away entirely forebyes what it used to be," he commented on his own recollections.

At last his thoughts went back to the brown dog, Brock. The dog had been brought, a pup of a few weeks, over the hills from the glen beyond. He had arrived one night at the farm kitchen in the tweed pocket of a hill farmer's jacket, carried over the hill on the chance that he might be wanted somewhere. Placed on the kitchen flagstones he was looked at carefully and curiously for a few moments, he himself looking back quietly at faces never seen by him before.

"A nice wee pup," was the first comment from one of the group around the hearth.

"Aye," came the reply. "He has a wise look about him."

So, on the ground of his wise look, the "wee brown pup" stayed, and was known as just that, "the wee brown pup," until someone noticed that the sheep never shied from him when he came near them, but always turned away from him slowly, scarcely even interrupting their grazing. "It's because he's like the badger," an old man—a man old when Paddy Rua was young—had pointed out, "for the sheep'll not scare before the badger neither." From that Brock got his name, and had quickly taken to following at Paddy Rua's feet—the brown dog with the red-haired man, as the neighbouring farmers remarked amused at the sight of the small pup following in untaught obedience the tall, thin shepherd. "The dog's hair brown like the badger," one of them said, "and the man's red like the fox."

Paddy Rua made no effort to train the young dog, but when sheep were being moved or brought together his hands and body spontaneously gestured and spoke in the visual language of the working of sheep. The dog learned without being taught, until one day he moved in a long arc away from Paddy Rua's foot, slowly and quietly out beyond the sheep, rounding them up and taking them away from men and dogs and under his own control.

"He went off then," Paddy Rua remembered, "and he took them sheep with him. We were watching to see what would he do, and where would he go. It was the back of *Ben Bwee,* and the dog went away from me and left me on the back of the hill, and I did not see him more until I come down to the house here. And him sitting there, and had the sheep put in the yard and all, and him sitting in the gap, keeping them in. He put them in the yard his self, and kept them there. I knew then I had a good dog."

Paddy Rua soon found that he was right. The dog was a good one, and loyal to the man. Refusing to work for anyone else, he would never leave Paddy's heels. In the worst of storms he stayed with him until all the sheep were seen, or brought together, and when winter blizzard winds blew the snow into deep drifts in the hollows of the northern slopes the dog still remained loyally with the man, leaping and almost swimming his way across or through the drifts, his fur powdered with snow, drops of half-frozen water gathered about his face and nose, blinking into the driving wind, but always staying as long as there was work with the sheep. But most impressive of all was to see the small brown form of the dog climb the snow-covered hill-side that led to the Black Spink, slowly ascend and cross over and above the spink to return, slowly, to the difficult narrow ledges beyond and then, entering one of the ledges, to persuade the trapped sheep to turn and make their way slowly out again.

"Thon was a loyal dog," Mary interjected, as she took the lid from the iron oven that hung above the fire and peered in to see the condition of the roasting bread.

"And a very gentle one," Paddy added. "The only one

thing would put him wild was the thunder. He could not abide it, and when he found the rattle of the thunder he was away, and you would not see him more that day. And another was the gun. If there would be hunters about, the dog was away with the first rattle of the gun, up in some wee holes in the spink, hiding until they be gone, till he would come out again."

"But sure plenty dogs be's that way," Mary interposed.

"Aye," Paddy answered. "Some does."

It was the dog's alarm at thunder and shots that started the trouble. Paddy had a gun himself, a long-barrelled, straight-stocked muzzle-loader, with which he used to shoot rabbits and hares or, when luck brought him close enough, an occasional fox. Seeing the dog's fear he used the gun less often, and when unrest began about the country and it was known that searching raids were being made even on farms in the hills he took the gun high up the sloping hill-side and left it in a low rock cave at the foot of the Black Spink. A veil of glossy dark ivy leaves hid the opening from sight.

But one day the first tractor came to the hill valley and with it a frightening collection of engine noises, louder, more astonishing, than either thunder or gunshots. It was a new experience for the inhabitants, and Paddy Rua was not very surprised to find his dog gone. Nor did Brock return for three days.

"He's up in one of them wee holes up under the spink," Paddy remarked to the old people who had expressed their uneasiness about the dog's long absence. "He'll soon quit that and come down, when he finds the tractor away."

But the absent days were unlucky ones for both man and dog. A few miles down the valley a pack of stray dogs had attacked sheep in fenced inland fields, savaging several and leaving deadly open wounds in their sides and hind-quarters. The brown dog was seen among them and positively identified.

"That dog would do no harm," young, fiery-haired Paddy Rua asserted.

The accuser, a tall shepherd like Paddy himself, shook his head. "You know yourself," he said, "it's the best dogs go to kill sheep the quickest."

It was the fatal defect of the sheep dog. The gathering instinct that men put to work for themselves was descended from savage tactics of survival, from a time when all dogs lived only by their skill in hunting, gathering and killing. All sheep farmers knew that. It was common in their talk, and Paddy Rua could not deny the argument.

For a while he was silent. He looked about the farm kitchen at the faces of the old people sitting near the fire or at the bare wooden table. But they only turned to face the fire or rose and walked through the open door.

"All right," Paddy said at last. "The dog will be put down."

When Brock came back the following morning Paddy Rua tied one end of a piece of brown grassrope around the dog's neck, from long practice and custom carefully knotting it in such a way that it could not slip or tighten on the animal's throat, and then tied the other end of the rope to a thin poplar that grew opposite the kitchen door. He climbed the hill to where he had left his gun behind the curtain of ivy leaves and brought it down with him to the house. As he approached, Brock, lying at the base of the tree, raised his head to watch in puzzlement. In the house Paddy Rua slowly removed all traces of the heavy grease he had smeared on and in the gun before leaving it under the rocks. Carefully he measured out a quantity of black powder and poured it into the gun's long single barrel, following it with a bit of wadding drawn from the shoulder of an old and ragged tweed jacket, ramming it firmly into place with a long willow rod. Then he added small grains of shot, and more wadding, and rammed again. The whole process of loading the gun took him almost a quarter of an hour. Satisfied at last, he took the gun and went out.

The dog was gone. A shred of chewed rope was all that remained trailing from the thin poplar.

Paddy Rua stood for a moment without moving, the long gun balanced in his right hand. Then, without thinking, he raised his eyes to the green slope that rose behind his thatch house, and watched the small brown form of the dog rising slowly upwards, rising and stopping to look back, as he had always done when working sheep, as though this time too he were looking back to the man for gestured instructions, not running impetuously but making his way by slow degrees up the steep hill-side. Paddy Rua stood below and watched the dog ascend until he had reached the spink. Slowly and carefully, as always in the past, the dog rose above the spink, walked along the top, returned down the far side, and walked out onto the narrow ledges, just as he had done so often when turning the trapped sheep out of them. Then he sat.

Paddy Rua started upwards, the loaded gun balanced easily in his hand. He followed the dog's own route, but stopped on the near side of the spink, parallel with the ledge on which the dog sat. Planting his feet firmly into the green sward at the edge of the spink and inclining his tall body slightly forward he raised the gun to his shoulder. For a moment he looked along the barrel until it was steady in his grip, then he fired. The dog collapsed quietly onto the narrow ledge and lay still.

At that moment in his recollections Paddy Rua stopped. A definitive halt in his thoughts intervened. He had no desire to remember or recall any further. A trace of an old man's bitterness and resentment crossed his features. He took off his cap, momentarily revealing the fine white hair that covered his head, and then replaced it firmly with a twist.

"But the other dog were got, you see," Mary interposed.

Paddy Rua looked into the fire again.

"Aye."

He paused.

"It weren't many days after that, there were more sheep tore, and they got the dogs at it. And the brown one in it, it weren't Brock at all. Brock was dead in the spink."

"It weren't Brock at all," Mary echoed. "And then they kilt the ones were doing the killing, but Brock was dead then."

"Aye, Brock was dead," Paddy Rua affirmed. He had ended his story, and he pushed himself up, gently, precariously, from his low stool by the hearth, and went to the wooden table in the corner of the kitchen.

But Mary, pouring tea from the old aluminium tea-pot into a plain white cup, went on.

"Weren't it funny, though, about the sheep after that?"

Slowly Paddy Rua began to eat the bread his wife had smeared with butter for him, softening it in his mouth with small sips of the hot tea. For him the story had ended.

But Briney Paddy Rua, returned from the hill, had heard his mother's last words, and resumed again.

"It were funny," he began. "But there's Brigid Phil across the river and old Jimmy Wee Jack, the next winter after, when the three yirrols came across the hill, driven ahead of the storm, and went into the spink, they were watching that time, and what was it put the yirrols out again?"

"Ones be saying different things," Paddy Rua answered. "You wouldn't know the half of what they be saying."

A reluctance to remember more had come over him, and the story of the brown badger-like dog was at an end, but Mary, as though echoing her husband's last words, revived the smothered recollections.

"Aye," she said slowly, pausing in her sweeping of the flagstones, "one's be seeing different things. You wouldn't know at all what they be seeing."

Paddy Rua's eyes glowed again with memory, and he raised his hand very slightly above his knee.

"I seen it meself," he said, "seen it often after that. And for years more, when the hard winter was in it, there was no sheep lost in the Black Spink, for the wee brown dog were in it still, Brock, to put them out again, a brown spot back and forth on the face of the spink, in snow and all, and the sheep turning and coming out again, quiet, slow, till they be safe."

His raised hand moved in a small arc, a matter of inches, slowly back and forth above his knee, as though recalling, or trying to recall, the back and forth movement of the brown dog. Mary and Briney watched him and looked, as they seldom did, at his eyes, as though trying to see what he saw. Mary, like many others, had seen the sheep come out of the spink in the midst of heavy winter snow, and even in storms. Sometimes, watching, she thought she saw something moving near them, a small dark form putting them out of the spink. She could never be sure.

Word had slowly gone down the river and into the valley below that the Black Spink had lost its power to trap sheep. Sheep went in, but they came out again. Older men and women nodded quietly over the matter and recalled the history of Paddy Rua's loyal brown dog, wrongly accused, that he himself had shot in the very same spink. Younger men pointed out that rocks had fallen from the spink in a spring thaw and that the ledges had probably widened, allowing the sheep to turn and escape. But in the hills, the hill farmers themselves watched from time to time as sheep came out, and sometimes they followed Paddy Rua's intense look, knowing that he saw something in the spink, something that was working the sheep, turning them around, driving them out. Then they looked back to the spink, saw the sheep moving to safety, and tried to see more. It was not certain that any succeeded.

It was certain, however, that the sheep could not have got out of the spink on their own. Every hill farmer knew that, and some had even seen the sheep move—as sheep never moved—into the driving winds and blowing snow.

"But sure," Briney said, "the sheep will always stand with their tails against the storm, never face into it."

But the story was confused. There were some who said that sheep *were* lost in the spink and that it was only Paddy Rua's old ewes, ones that had been in the spink before and been driven out by the brown dog, and so in a manner trained to come out of it—that it was only those sheep that came out of the spink again. Everyone had a different idea of the truth.

Paddy Rua went back to the fire and sat on his low stool.

"There were no sheep lost in it for years," he said. "But then people was talking, saying all kinds of things. Damn, there were no harm in that brown dog that people should take alarm."

"The priest come up," Mary explained. "People were after him to come, I suppose, and he come up to see."

"Aye," Paddy Rua resumed. "The priest come up in his robes and all, a big crowd with him, a *precession*, and up the hill, and beyont, to that lough that's in the hills, and laid him to rest in that lough. That's the wee silvery lough has the trouts in it. Laid him to rest in that lough. That was years ago."

Paddy Rua stood on his street again looking up towards the Black Spink.

"Right there, where you see that bit of white fleece. That's where a sheep went in last winter and never come out again. That's a bit of the wool. Right next to that, that's where the dog was kilt." He stopped for a moment, looking towards the spink, and then added his final comment.

"Thon was a loyal dog," he said.

Later, in the kitchen again, Paddy Rua remembered the gun that had killed the dog.

"Het was the last time ever I used it. I left it then back in the wee cave behind the ivy, and it was only later, after they laid the dog to rest, that I minded the gun, and went up to see about it. And it was there still, but the grease all away off it, and the barrel rusted out. It was rusted out, you see, like fine lace. You would say it was like fine lace. And when I went to lift it out the light went through it like the lace, and it went away then into little bits. Away into tiny bits. Away entirely."

JOSEPH HONE

The Captain in the Pipes

The Mossops had a problem: they were unhappy.

Henry Mossop had seen the Aer Lingus Fly-Drive advertisement in the *Telegraph* Colour Magazine and thought the unusual holiday offered might form a cure to their dumb distress. For that, as he saw it, was their problem: they had ceased to communicate. So he had gone into the travel agent in Plymouth that same day and booked two passages to Ireland forthwith.

The Mossops had never been to Ireland. But Henry, in the course of his career, had known a number of Irish people. They were a lively, talkative race. And this, together with the other friendly attributes of the country generally, he saw as an ideal tonic for their own awkward condition.

There was the change of life to consider, too, Henry thought: or rather, the fact that life hadn't changed. He was nearly forty—and Chief Communications Officer on a Type 42 Guided Missile Destroyer, H.M.S. *Trent*. But his long-expected promotion to the same position on the carrier *Ark Royal* had not materialised and a sense of failure had begun to nibble at the edges of his soul. Their son Giles had been put down in a prep school near

Tiverton; he had two weeks' leave coming up in October . . . Fresh fields, pastures new, Henry Mossop thought, as he left the travel agency.

Sheila Mossop wore fashionable, hexagonal-shaped spectacles but always squeezed the toothpaste from the very bottom of the tube. She too was nearly forty, with thin brown hair, cut short, coming in wisps over her ears—rather a small and decided person, yet not a mousy woman, though latterly she had come to see herself as such. In fact she was bright and forthcoming by nature. But these qualities were largely dormant in her now.

Her problem was not one of communication with her husband. She sometimes thought he talked too much, in fact. She had simply wanted a larger family—something to extend and occupy herself with during her husband's many absences: she had wanted a *proper* family, she had always told herself, a bunch of children growing up like flowers all round her. But Henry, she had long ago realised, lacked adventure in that direction. He had been parsimonious in bed to begin with, afterwards miserly— and finally his lovemaking had become quite bankrupt. She had tried several times to resuscitate the currency with him but without success, for she was shy and inexperienced in such matters. And though she forgot this failure now in her day-to-day affairs, she nursed the hurt obscurely deep inside her.

Henry, on the other hand, viewed the problem differently: he believed that his wife had become frigid. Though he was sensible enough, as he saw it, to regard this as a natural misfortune and not a fault of either of theirs. It was a disability concomitant with the approach of middle age and a flaw in English women generally, he felt.

An old friend and former shipmate of his, who served aboard the QE2, whom he had consulted about the problem some months previously, had tactfully intimated that he should force himself upon his wife. "It's the only way—in the circumstances," he had said, before buying another round of gin and tonics at the local golf club— large ones this time.

Henry found himself thinking about this advice as they drove down from Dublin in their hired car—delayed by a large herd of cows just outside a town called Naas on the main road to Cork. The animals wobbled their udders and jostled their big brown backsides against the side of the car, squeezing past the bumpers. No, Henry thought with disgust—I cannot rape her. His friend's advice, he decided—though possibly suited to some of the passengers aboard the *QE2*—was not a course of action open to an officer in Her Majesty's Senior Service.

They drove on, in silence, across the long rolling countryside, on an almost empty main road, the sun beginning to dip from a cloudless blue sky. The weather, Henry thought, was unseemly for the country and the time of year. It had been a very hot day.

The hotel, a small four-square early Victorian building which had once been a rectory, lay a mile outside Kinsale—on a hill above the small fishing port where black and white terraced cottages ran down to the quay with several smart hotels along it, for the place was a busy and popular tourist resort during the summer season. But now, in mid-October, it had reverted to its ancient ways: a few elderly figures walked the quiet back streets up the hill; a trawler made ready for sea; a family packed up their car in front of the hotel, down from Cork for the day.

The view from the hotel was calm and beautiful in the last of the sunlight. The Mossops, having unpacked and dressed for dinner, sat next to the big bow window in the drawing room sipping Tio Pepe. It was a pleasant room, like that of a private house, with deep chintz armchairs, hunting prints, together with a restrained Russell Flint reproduction over the mantelpiece entitled "Persian Market". They looked out at the long, grey-blue swell of the Atlantic beyond the headland to their right. Calm as a millpond, Henry thought contentedly. He sipped his sherry again and put the glass down carefully. The little round table between them was antique, done in highly polished rosewood.

There was no bar in the hotel. But drinks were readily available to residents, Mrs Jackson, the proprietress, had told Henry on arrival. Meanwhile, the sherry came with the compliments of the house, she had added sweetly.

Henry remembered her smile. It had been a strange thing—warm and full, yet somehow set like a transparency over a sad face. Sixtyish, he thought—genteel Irish with a soft southern burr in her voice and an abundant flow of hair, so healthy-looking that he had been surprised at its complete whiteness, an unnatural white, like a powdered eighteenth-century wig. There was something sensuous and attractive about her, Henry decided. But he couldn't exactly identify it. Perhaps it was the way she walked—very lightly, delicately, like a young woman tip-toeing to bed. And she had deep blue eyes, unclouded still—like a girl's, too—which she looked directly at you with, as if issuing a slightly risqué invitation. He mentioned this fact to Sheila.

"Yes," she replied. "She speaks with her eyes—and listens with them as well. But why Jackson? That's not an Irish name is it?" They sipped their sherry in silence, pondering this fact.

Shortly afterwards they heard brisk footsteps outside on the gravel and saw an elderly, rather angry-looking man stomping past the bow-window. He was dressed in a heavy blue windcheater and stout hiker's boots with plus-fours—though neither the weather nor the ground underfoot merited such accessories. He disappeared from view and they heard the hall door open sharply, the draught flap grating abrasively across the floor.

They were surprised when this brusque entry was not followed by any sound of movement in the hall, nor by the door closing again. The Mossops looked at each other and then out of the window. But the view was empty.

They were startled when they turned back to see the man standing behind them in his stockinged feet, holding his boots in one hand.

He was very small, they noticed now—hardly more than five feet in his socks—his face badly weather-beaten, the skin shrunk against the bones, dark and leathery as the Tollund Man. A large pair of old naval binoculars hung from his neck. His ears were too big for his head and the lobes drooped noticeably: his sparse hair was parted on the left and combed severely sideways in the old fashion. He breathed heavily, his little ferret blue eyes gleaming at them in outraged curiosity. Despite his diminutive size he exuded dominance. It was as if two large men had just come into the room and not one small one.

"Good evening," he said, coming towards them. "You'll be the Mossops." He held his one free hand out. "Captain Jackson."

Henry stood up automatically, as if back on board ship.

"Good evening, sir. Henry Mossop. And this is my wife Sheila."

The Captain took her hand, held it for some long seconds, looking at her appraisingly. "Very nice indeed," he said at last. "Let me join you for a drink as soon as I'm out of these togs." He looked at the sunset through the bow window, the shadows settling gently over the sea and the village below them. "Well below the yardarm," he remarked. Then he turned back to Mrs Mossop. "Going to be a change though. Glass is falling." He looked back out over the bay. "Can't see the Old Head. Always means a change." Then he turned to Henry. "Good trip? From Plymouth—saw from your booking. Needn't ask, need I?—saw it at once. Navy man, eh?"

"Yes, sir. The *Trent*. Communications officer—"

But the Captain had turned away. "Won't be a moment."

Then he turned back. "The *Trent*? Guided Missile Destroyer?"

"Yes, sir."

"Well done. Was with the *Prince of Wales* myself." The Captain left the room.

"The *Prince of Wales*?" Sheila asked.

"Yes. Battle cruiser. The last war. Went down with half her crew off Singapore in 1942."

"How strange."

"Yes. Don't suppose it was his fault."

"No. I meant—him, being married to Mrs Jackson."

"Yes."

They sipped their sherry once more and pondered this fact.

The tapping started that night.

The Mossops' room gave out directly southwards, looking over the rim of the headland straight down to the Atlantic. They had gone to bed early, leaving their bedroom window slightly open, for it had been a warm day and the room still retained a lot of the heat. It was this which puzzled Henry when he woke, some time after midnight—the fact that the central heating had suddenly come on in the middle of the night, in warm weather, for the tapping came from the radiator just beneath the window.

He lay there, half asleep, listening to the confused medley of taps and groans—the water coursing through the system, warming the boards and metal and making them creak, just as his own central heating behaved in Plymouth when it was started up from cold. He drifted off to sleep again.

The tapping noise was louder and more regular when he woke a second time. And since he was warm enough already he decided to turn the radiator off, thus getting rid of the noise at the same time.

He got out of bed and touched the metal ribbing. It was stone cold. And the tap at the bottom was already firmly turned off. Looking out of the window he noticed that a wind was starting to blow strongly from the south-west, rustling the curtains. He could hear the distant thud of waves now, the huge Atlantic breakers falling on the headland in the dark night. The Captain's forecast had been correct: the weather was brewing up. He shut the window and went back to bed.

Just as he lay down he realised something was wrong. His long experience in naval communications alerted him, some sixth sense warning him before he could identify the source of his unease.

Then he recognised it—the tapping coming strongly from the radiator now: three taps, then three with longer intervals; three more short ones. A pause, before the sequence was repeated.

Henry sat up in bed. There was no doubt about it. An S O S signal was coming through the pipes in morse. A Mayday call.

His first thought was that the Captain might be playing some elaborate joke on him—tapping the central heating pipes somewhere downstairs. Henry thought he recognised the sort of man: a retired naval hearty, gone to seed in the wilds of Ireland, up to some prank with an imagined fellow spirit. But as he listened to the continuous cry for help rattling through the pipes Henry began to doubt this. The joke was too elaborate—and too serious. Henry's morse was a little rusty but he soon picked up the drift of the message.

"S-O-S S-S I-N-V-E-R-N-E-S-S L-A-T-5-I.3-4-N L-O-N-8.3-2-W B-O-I-L-E-R-G-O-N-E R-E-A-R-H-O-L-D F-I-L-L . . ."

Henry jumped out of bed and turned his side light on. Sheila woke in the next bed and began to mumble something. But by then Henry was scrabbling about in his jacket looking for paper and something to write with.

"What's happened?" Sheila asked, calmly, in a way that Henry had come to hate.

"Wait—quiet!" Henry got a chair and sat next to the radiator where he started to take down the message. The tapping had become less coherent now, more hurried.

"A-B-O-T T-O A-B-A-N-D-O-N S-H-I- L-A-T-5-1.3-4-N . . ."

"Are you mad?" Sheila went on, sitting up in bed.

"Shshsh," he said. But the tapping stopped just then.

Without thinking, so drawn was he by the urgency of the event, Henry began to tap a message back, using his pen as a morse key on top of the radiator.

"R-E-C-E-I-V-I-N-G Y-O-U A-T K-I-N-S-A-L-E R-E-P-E-A-T P-O-S-I-T-I-O-N A-R-E Y-O-U R-E-C-E-I-V-I-N-G M-E . . ."

But there was silence then. The noises had quite stopped.

"Henry, do get back to bed. What's wrong? What is it?"

"It's a message, don't you see." He turned to her, amazed at her lack of concern. "The ship is sinking."

"Nonsense. It's just the radiator."

Just then it started to go again, but faintly now.

"S-O-S A-B-A-N-D-O-N-I-N-G S-H-I-P L-A-S-T P-O-S L-A-T-5I.3-4-N L-O-N-8.3-2-W S-O-S . . ." The tapping suddenly stopped.

"Do come back to bed," Sheila said rather petulantly. Henry looked at her, his lips quivering with excitement and enmity.

"Just some quirk in the central heating," Sheila said to him next morning at breakfast. "Some bizarre electrical disturbance. The storm last night perhaps—a ship somewhere out there."

"We listened to the Irish news this morning. And the BBC. There was nothing—no reports of any ship sinking. And how can it have been a quirk in the central heating? The heating wasn't on." Henry ate another sausage. He felt nervous, elated—for the first time in years: a feeling he'd last remembered properly when he had read about Gagool the Witchfinder in *King Solomon's Mines* as a child. Henry felt childish suddenly. For of course, on the surface, the whole thing did seem ridiculous and impossible. On the surface. Yet on the other hand he had heard the message, had written it down . . . Henry sipped his coffee silently, thinking. He looked up. Sheila was saying something. He hadn't heard her.

"Do wake up, Henry."

"I'm sorry."

"I said, 'I like it here. It's a lovely place.'" She looked at him with tenderness, for the first time in months. But he didn't notice it.

After breakfast, while Sheila was upstairs getting ready to go out for a walk with him, Henry wandered into the hall. Above a big blue glazed porcelain umbrella stand and next to a large barometer, he found himself gazing at a framed Marine chart, covering south-west Ireland. His eye caught the latitude line of 51 north—and then the longitude 8 west. Allowing for the extra degrees on each line which he had received in the messages the previous night, he made a rough visual transfix on the chart, running one index finger north, the other westwards. The lines bisected each other on a spot about five or ten miles out to sea, directly south of the Old Head of Kinsale. Henry felt the skin around his shoulders prickle. At the same moment he became aware of someone standing behind him. He turned.

The Captain was looking over his shoulder—or trying to, for he was in his stockinged feet again, holding his boots in one hand.

"Morning," he said breezily. "In for a spell of bad weather. Glass's still dropping. Quite a rough stretch of coast, this when it blows. Don't suppose you know it. Navy doesn't come to these parts any more. Though they used to, of course. We had a base in Cobh before the war. Queenstown it was then. Lot of Admiralty dependents still live around here. *Lusitania* went down off the Old Head in 1915. Brought the Yanks in. Lot of wrecks . . ."

"Yes." Henry turned. He decided not to tell the Captain about the tapping in the radiator. It might seem stupid. On the other hand it would do no harm to ask him about the ship itself. The Captain, after all, had given him a natural opening.

"Yes." Henry went on, "I seem to remember a ship—the *Inverness*, wasn't it?—went down near here."

There was silence. The Captain licked his dry lips.

"The *Inverness*? Hadn't heard of it. Not in my time. There was the *Loch Tay* in '37. And a German coaster, the *Bremerhaven*, the same year. And during the war, of course quite a few others. But not the *Inverness*, as far as I know. Why do you ask?"

"Oh, I heard about it—an Irishman on the *Trent*. He had a relation . . ." Henry let the words die away, embarrassed at his lie.

The Captain made a dry, cackling noise, the sound rising from deep within his throat. Henry thought he was laughing. But he was simply trying to coax some phlegm up. The Captain humphed vigorously several times before moving away.

The sky was fairly clear but it was very windy when they went out, with white horses scudding all over the angry grey sea beyond the fishing port. Henry had brought his own binoculars with him and together they walked through the village and up the far side of the valley and along the grassy promontory towards the Old Head. From here, beyond the ruins of what looked like an old army barracks on the cliff, Henry gazed out to sea, swinging his glasses widely over the whole stormy vision. A small trawler was making heavy progress, running against the tide for shelter, riding the waves like a car on a roller coaster, sometimes barely moving at all against the huge swell.

Sheila was cold. "What are you looking at? Let's go back."

"That ship—it must have been like this. Out there."

"Damn that ship. Aren't we having a holiday—away from all that?"

"Yes. I'm sorry." They turned back.

But the mystery of the S.S. *Inverness* continued to hang in Henry's mind like the sword of Damocles all morning. He felt he had behaved unprofessionally about it. Shouldn't he at least have told someone about the messages? Then he reminded himself again that the whole thing was impossible: no ship could communicate through a central heating system; no one would have believed him.

None the less, the incident continued to agitate him. So that, when they stopped for coffee at the Trident Hotel on the quay on their way back, Henry decided to telephone a friend of his, a fellow officer on the *Trent*, whom he knew to be currently on shore leave in Plymouth. He gave the man details of the message and asked him to check with Lloyds Shipping Register in London and call him back at his own hotel that evening if he came up with anything. Sheila looked at him with sour incomprehension when he returned from the telephone booth.

Before lunch, upstairs in the bedroom of their own hotel, Henry saw the Captain standing at the end of the small rose garden, looking over the last of the wind-blown petals, gazing out to sea with his glasses. Getting his own binoculars out again, while Sheila was in the bathroom, Henry followed the Captain's line of vision. But there was nothing out to sea except the tossed spume rising in white drifts from the violent water.

The Captain didn't join them for a drink that evening. He had a fluey cold, Mrs Jackson said, and was trying to kill it quickly upstairs in bed with whiskey and lemon. Mrs Jackson looked tired, her attitude preoccupied, even unhappy. Apart from the few other guests, she had her hands full with the Captain as well, she seemed to imply, hurrying about between the reception desk, the kitchen behind, and their bedroom upstairs.

At seven o'clock Henry's friend in Plymouth telephoned. Henry took the call in a little cabin at the end of the hall, closing the door firmly behind him. His friend had most of the details to hand. He read them out, the line crackling with static, and Henry jotted the information down on a pad supplied by a firm of bottlers in Cork.

". . . the S.S. *Inverness*, a 3,000 ton cargo steamer, launched at Clydeside in 1912, originally owned by the North British Transport and Trading Company in

Edinburgh, sold to the Irish Shipping Lines in 1930—had
sunk with the loss of half her crew on the night of October
9, 1932, five miles off the Old Head of Kinsale, on a
voyage with mixed cargo from Cardiff to Galway. Reports
from the few survivors confirmed the Mayday messages
received at the time: the ship's boiler had sprung a leak in
heavy weather and had subsequently exploded. The boat
had sunk shortly afterwards, going down stern first, the
rear section badly holed beneath the waterline. The
Master of the ship, who had not survived, was a Captain
Patrick Hennessy of Irish Shipping Lines . . ."

When Henry returned to the drawing room Sheila
wasn't there. He found her upstairs crying in their
bedroom.

"I'm sorry," he said, sitting down beside her and trying
to console her. "I won't go on with it all. But I had to find
out about it. Can't you see? I had to."

"*Damn* that ship," Sheila gasped through her tears.
"Damn all your ships." She stood up to get a handkerchief.
Then, in the silence the moment before she blew her
nose, they both turned in horror to the window. The
radiator had started to tap again. Henry went over to it.

"It's all right," he said, smiling at her with relief. "This
time it really is the heating. It's on. The maid must have
done it when she came to turn down our beds. Don't
worry. It's not another message."

But Henry lied. Though the radiator had indeed been
turned on, the tapping was another message. He heard the
first of it: ". . . T-A-I-N H-E-N-N-E-S-S-Y A-R-E Y-O-
U R-E-C-E-I-V-I-N-G . . ." But by then Henry had
shepherded his wife quickly out of the room and down to
dinner.

They shared a bottle of light Beaujolais with their steak
and afterwards Sheila slept more soundly than usual. But
Henry found sleep impossible. The radiator had remained

quite silent. But he was sure it would start up again. And when it didn't he felt disappointed.

Some time before midnight, however—the wind getting up outside and the sea booming strongly again in the distance—he heard a slow drip of water coming from the window. When he got up to investigate he found the tap at the bottom of the radiator was leaking slightly. He put his fingers round it, staunching the drops, and at once the morse started again. It came in spurts but faded right away whenever Henry took his hand off the pipe, so that he had to bind the tap with a handkerchief before he could make any sense of the message. What he heard made his shoulderblades prickle.

". . . he was at Cobh, you see—Jackson, with the Admiralty, in 1931—just after I took over the *Inverness*. Mary and I were living in Cork then . . ." The message began to fade. Henry pressed his fingers hard against the handkerchief and it came back again. ". . . met her at a naval reception—and when she was shopping—came round to see us—he had something . . ." The morse here became confused, almost frantic, and Henry could no longer follow it. Gradually it cleared again. ". . . when I took over the Cardiff-Galway run I knew he was with her—that was the end of . . ." The message became incoherent again, slowly fading. Then, after about half a minute, the original Mayday message came back very strongly: "S-O-S . . . S-O-S . . ." Then there was silence.

Henry took his hand off the pipe. Rain beat on the window above him, the storm gathering strength from the south-west. A window or a door slammed somewhere outside as he crouched in the darkness of the bedroom as if shielding himself from the weather. Jackson, he thought, with the Admiralty in Cobh in 1931: and Captain Jackson with his Irish wife—or rather, as it appeared, with Captain

Hennessy's wife—retired in Kinsale forty-five years later. Was that how it was? And if so, how could he help? What help was there for an infidelity so old and a long-drowned sailor complaining in the night? Henry found himself disbelieving the whole thing for a minute—until he remembered his conversation with the Captain in the hall about the *Inverness*. That was real enough, as had been the Captain's denial that he knew anything about the ship. If the Captain in the pipes was right, Henry thought, Jackson must see him now as some live ghost come to haunt him all the way from Plymouth.

A plumber came from the village next morning to repair the leaking radiator. While the man was in his bedroom Henry—mentioning his qualifications and anxious to look over the system for himself—offered to help him check the central heating installation downstairs: perhaps something was wrong with the electrical circuits in the time switch, for he had explained to the plumber the uneven performance of this mechanism.

The boiler was housed down some wooden steps in a small basement beneath the kitchen. The room smelt of burnt oil and oily tools, like the engine room of a ship Henry thought. There was a neat row of spanners and other engineering equipment above a work bench to one side and some old cabin trunks piled up in one corner. Henry suddenly noticed the white lettering on one of them: "Lt. A. P. C. Jackson, Admiralty Buildings, Section 17/F, Queenstown, Co. Cork, IRELAND."

Together they looked over the time switch above the boiler. Then they unscrewed the cowling next to the chimney and tested the hot water thermostat beneath; finally they removed the igniter and tested it. Everything seemed in perfect order. The plumber went upstairs to check the electric pump in the main hot press, while

Henry remained below to activate the time switch, thus giving the whole system a complete test. On a signal from above he threw the switch and the boiler came to life with a soft roar. It had not been in operation for more than a minute when Henry noticed a small leak in the cold water input pipe. It wasn't much, just a dribble beneath the control tap. But the colour was strange, a red colour. Rust, Henry thought, as he wiped his hands, hearing the plumber coming down the steps again. But it wasn't the plumber. It was Captain Jackson.

"Spot of trouble?" he asked from the stairway, dressed in an old paisley dressing-gown and slippers.

"Not really. Just a small leak in the cold pipe from upstairs. I thought maybe I could help over the electrics— thought the circuits might be out. But they're okay."

"Kind of you to lend a hand." The Captain took a large spanner from above the work bench and came towards Henry, who stepped back involuntarily. The boiler was roaring now and the temperature was beginning to rise in the confined space. The Captain brandished the spanner, enhancing his grip on it. Henry readied himself. But the little man moved away from him at the last moment and bent down to one side of the boiler where he started to tighten— or loosen—the large nut on the input valve.

"Gets clogged up after the summer, not being used," he said. But he failed to make much headway in his work. As he bent down, however, the collar of his dressing-gown pulled back, and Henry noticed a series of neat little red indentations running across his neck. Teeth marks—love bites? Henry wondered.

The Captain stood up. "There. That'll do it."

But he had not done it. The drip continued undiminished.

"Full steam ahead, eh?" The Captain's eyes twinkled in the gloomy light and he looked at Henry mischievously.

Just then, before Henry could make any suitable response, a loud tapping noise came from the input pipe, from the valve which the Captain had been tending. It was morse again, Henry realised at once. "B-A-S-T-A-R . . ." But he lost the rest of it, for the Captain immediately picked up the spanner again and gave the pipe a resounding clout with it. "Bloody pipes," he said, putting the spanner back carefully in its allotted pouch above the work bench. The noise stopped abruptly. But the leak didn't.

It was Sheila's bath late that night which brought things to a head: her scream half way through washing. She was looking at the taps when Henry arrived from the bedroom, sitting bolt upright in the water, rubbing her hands, her face creased with fear and pain.

"What happened?"

"The tap . . ."

Henry moved to put his hand on it. "Don't!" she shrieked. "It's live. It's electric. I just touched it."

"Nonsense, Sheila."

"It *is* you fool. It's live."

"All right. Don't shout. Just get out of the water—*carefully*."

Sheila got out, wrapping a towel prudishly around her. Henry got one of his pipe cleaners from the next room. Then, exposing the metal core at one end and pushing the other into the rubber heel of his shoe, he brushed the tap lightly with the metal. A jagged blue spark sizzled between the two extremities.

"My God," Henry said. "I'll get the Captain. This is crazy."

Turning to leave the bathroom, he heard the cistern above the lavatory warbling gently and the noise of water trickling fast down the sides of the bowl. Then he noticed that, instead of draining away, the level of water in the pan beneath was slowly rising. Sheila followed his glance. She came to him, fearful—the towel dropping away from her, holding to him, embracing him almost.

"Let's get away from here, darling. Right away. There's something wrong. Please!"

He held her for a moment before shepherding her gently into the bedroom. "How can we? It's the middle of the night. We'll get another room."

He didn't push her away. Instead she fell from his arms in disappointment, collapsing on her bed. The moment's reconciliation had been lost.

"I'll get the Captain," Henry said. The weather was blowing up once more outside, another night storm running in from the Atlantic. "Stay here. Don't move. Don't *touch* anything," he said, before going out on to the landing, closing the bedroom door carefully behind him.

The passage-way was dark. The hotel slept. But he thought he knew where the Jacksons' private rooms were—up a small stairway at the end of the landing. He knocked quite loudly on an un-numbered door.

"What is it?" a voice said petulantly after some moments.

"It's Mossop. Can I see you? It's urgent—I'm sorry to—"

The door opened abruptly. Captain Jackson glowered at him, a minute and angry figure in his paisley dressing-gown and stockinged feet. Henry explained. The Captain humphed. "We'll take a look downstairs then. Shut off the electrics. Can you give me a hand? Your line of country."

Henry didn't want to go with him but the Captain was already herding him down the passage-way. In the kitchen he picked up a big torch. The wind was buffeting the windows furiously now, shaking the whole house. But the roar from the boiler immediately beneath them seemed louder still, unnaturally loud. The Captain opened the door to the basement and they moved down the steps. The heat was intense. The metal cowling above the boiler shimmered and there was a large pool of water beneath the main input pipe. The valve was leaking badly now. Henry went forward.

"You'll have to turn everything off," he shouted. "Have you got some candles for upstairs?" He turned. The Captain had disappeared.

The door at the head of the steps was just closing. Henry heard the key turning in the lock as he rushed up towards it. He hammered on it furiously. Then he heard the Captain's voice—vigorous, brutal.

"Two can play at this game, Mossop. Getting me up in the middle of the night with your bloody tricks, are you now? Oh, don't think I don't know what you're up to! Come to plague me about the *Inverness*, tapping out morse on the central heating pipes every evening. And you were down here this morning tampering with the system. Well, now you've messed the whole thing up—you can just stay there with it and cool your heels."

Henry heard him move away. He went back down the steps. The cowling round the bottom of the boiler, where the oil-feed was, had begun to glow and the leak in the input pipe was really running now, the blood-red water seeping across the floor towards him. Henry grabbed the big spanner before running back up the stairs and attacking the stout door viciously with it.

Mary Jackson had woken with the knocking ten minutes before and now she felt cold—the wind and rain whipping at the windows, the full angry force of an Atlantic gale storming the house. She leant over to the side of her high bed and turned her electric blanket on.

A moment after her hand had moved the switch, she arched herself in a fearful spasm, as though the mattress had become a bed of nails. Her head knocked violently against the bed-head as the voltage struck her, coursing through her limbs, making her whole body tremble for a moment, as if at the apex of some great pleasure. Then she lay back, quite still, taking to death like the little death of love.

As the Captain came up the stairs he saw that one of the central heating pipes that ran along the landing skirting board had sprung a leak, the water spraying out in an arc above him, the edges of it spattering his face. He held on to the banisters for a moment, undecided. The house thudded and banged and seemed to move in the big wind, to list and dive in the storm. Then, ducking through the spray, shielding his face, he went purposefully forward.

When he opened their bedroom door he saw his wife looking at him, her head twisted sideways on the pillow, lips slightly open. He thought she was about to say something to him—something angry, for from a distance her expression seemed annoyed. But when he came closer he saw that she had been gazing straight through him with a frozen expression of awful pain.

He thought she might still be alive and could be resuscitated with the kiss of life. He forgot his damp hands and face and didn't notice his wife's arm still lying across the electric cord, so that when he bent over her and put his lips to hers, his whole body shuddered and convulsed, as hers had done, in a brief but violent agony. He fell across her on the bed, joining her inseparably in a last embrace.

In the Mossops' bedroom the lavatory bowl had overflowed and the water by now had risen half an inch over the bathroom floor and begun to trickle out into the bedroom, swamping the fitted carpet. Sheila Mossop sat with her feet up on the bed, as if it were a raft, and watched the water soak across the room, forming a moat between her and the door. She was afraid to move— afraid to step in the water, or to touch the metal door handle and escape out on to the landing. She sat there listening to the fearful wind and, when the lights in the bedroom suddenly went out and some moments after one of the windows blew open in a ferocious gust, she screamed. She stayed where she was for some moments, the wind and rain streaming across the room and the curtains flapping like pistol shots. No one heeded her screams and since there was no water on that side of the bed she put her feet down gingerly and went over to try and close the window.

Walking towards it, pressing against the wind, she put her hand out into the darkness, searching for the window clasp. Instead she touched something damp and soft. The next moment the curtain had wrapped itself round her shoulders, the material slapping viciously about her breasts. She tried to disentangle herself from it. But, before she could do so, the storm grasped her and pushed her backwards into the room—so violently that the curtain was torn from its runners and she fell, hitting her head on the floor.

She lay there stunned for a minute and when her mind cleared she gazed up into the blackness with relief. Henry had come back. She couldn't see him in the darkness but she could hear footsteps. He was walking over by the window, trying to close it, she thought. She propped herself up on one arm, rubbing the back of her head.

"Henry? Thank God. I'm here—by the bed. I fell . . ."

There was no reply. She heard the squeak of some kind of abrasive clothing—a mackintosh or oil-skin—as the footsteps left the window without closing it and approached her.

"Henry?"

Now she was terrified but she could no longer scream. Instead she fought, blindly, as the elements of wind and rain seemed to burst above her now, falling on her, pinning her to the floor. Her nightdress whipped up her legs as she struggled—yet vainly struggled, for what she felt above her, pressing down on her, had no body, no substance—was simply a weightless force which she could not touch, nor rid herself of, yet which possessed her fully and with pain. Her arms and thighs ached with it—and with the struggle she made to escape, turning first one way and then the other. Finally she ceased the fight and gave herself to the strange agony.

When Henry found her she was lying half naked on the floor, the beam of Captain Jackson's big torch spotlighting her like the victim of some hit and run accident, the curtain pulled harshly round her neck and down her midriff. He put the torch on the bed and lifted her up, a bundle of damp flesh, her head lolling back over his arm. He thought her dead. But when he laid her flat and rubbed her body and started to resuscitate her mouth-to-mouth, she regained consciousness rapidly and began to struggle with him violently, pushing him away.

"Get dressed, then," he said rather abruptly. "Quickly, We're getting out." They could hear the few other guests outside on the landing now, moving down the stairs, evacuating the building. Henry managed to get her into her dressing-gown. Then, grabbing a few of their things and shoving them in a suitcase, he helped her across the swamped carpet and out on to the landing. Here it was wetter still and they moved down the stairs after the others through a rainfall of water. It sprayed from pipes above the skirting boards, streamed from radiators, leaked from ceilings, and when they got down to the hall they had to paddle through the water, several inches deep by the reception desk.

"What about the Captain and his wife?" someone shouted from the darkness outside as Henry and Sheila hurried forward, the last to leave as they thought. Henry turned and shone the torch back as they got to the hall door. The water was flowing down the stairs and for an instant Henry saw the Captain standing on the half-landing, an exultant figure in a naval cap and oilskins, holding firmly on to the banisters as though on to a swaying bridge, like a madman happily sinking with his ship. He was just about to go back for him when the explosion rocked him forward, pushing them both out into the night. The boiler had gone up.

Outside, stumbling on to the gravel drive, they saw the back of the building, where the kitchens were, spurt with flame as the fire caught on, feeding on the oil supply. Soon all that part of the hotel was ablaze, rafters and slates falling to the ground, while the front of the house smouldered damply against the flames.

Late next morning, in the Trident Hotel down on the quay, Henry looked from their bedroom window up the hill to where the now completely gutted building smoked like a hulk on the horizon. Sheila lay asleep, under sedation, across the room from him. But her hysterical words, before the doctor had come, remained very much alive in him. "Rape," she had screamed, among many other bitter things, years of repressed resentment exploding in her. "I wonder you hadn't thought of that before."

"But I wasn't *in* the room, Sheila," he'd replied. "It was the curtain—round your neck."

And he had believed this until afterwards, when the detective from Cork had questioned him downstairs, and

told him during the course of their interview that both
Captain Jackson and his wife had been found dead in their
bedroom.

"In an oilskin—and naval cap?" Henry had asked.

"No. Just in his dressing-gown. Why do you ask?"

"Oh, nothing," Henry said.

"Did you see anybody?" the detective went on,
encouraged. "Any stranger in or around the hotel last
night?"

"No," Henry lied. "Why?"

"Well, we have to treat all this as deliberate, I'm afraid.
Arson."

"I don't understand?"

"The Provisionals. The Provisional IRA," the man said
apologetically. "There've been several other cases
recently. Various threats—and attacks on retired British
people living over here. Especially from the forces."

"Oh, yes. I see," Henry said. "It's a bad business."

"Indeed," the detective agreed. "A long, bad business.
I'm sorry for your trouble."

MRS J.H. RIDDELL

The Last of Squire Ennismore

"Did I see it myself? No, sir; I did not see it; and my father before me did not see it; nor his father before him, and he was Phil Regan, just the same as myself. But it is true, for all that; just as true as that you are looking at the very place where the whole thing happened. My great-grandfather (and he did not die till he was ninety-eight) used to tell, many and many's the time, how he met the stranger, night after night, walking lonesome-like about the sands where most of the wreckage came ashore."

"And the old house, then, stood behind that belt of Scotch firs?"

"Yes; and a fine house it was, too. Hearing so much talk about it when a boy, my father said, made him often feel as if he knew every room in the building, though it had all fallen to ruin before he was born. None of the family ever lived in it after the squire went away. Nobody else could be got to stop in the place. There used to be awful noises, as if something was being pitched from the top of the great staircase down in to the hall; and then there would be a sound as if a hundred people were clinking glasses and talking all together at once. And then it seemed as if barrels were rolling in the cellars; and there would be screeches, and howls, and laughing, fit to make your blood run cold. They say there is gold hid away in the cellars; but not one has ever ventured to find it. The very children won't come here to play; and when the men are plowing the field behind, nothing will make them stay in it, once the day begins to change. When the night is coming on, and the tide creeps in on the sand, more than one thinks he has seen mighty queer things on the shore."

"But what is it really they think they see? When I asked my landlord to tell me the story from beginning to end, he said he could not remember it; and, at any rate, the whole rigmarole was nonsense, put together to please strangers."

"And what is he but a stranger himself? And how should he know the doings of real quality like the Ennismores? For they were gentry, every one of them—good old stock; and as for wickedness, you might have searched Ireland through and not found their match. It is a sure thing, though, that if Riley can't tell you the story, I can; for, as I said, my own people were in it, of a manner of speaking. So, if your honour will rest yourself off your feet, on that bit of a bank, I'll set down my creel and give you the whole pedigree of how Squire Ennismore went away from Ardwinsagh."

It was a lovely day, in the early part of June; and, as the Englishman cast himself on a low ridge of sand, he looked over Ardwinsagh Bay with a feeling of ineffable content. To his left lay the Purple Headland; to his right, a long range of breakers, that went straight out into the Atlantic till they were lost from sight; in front lay the Bay of Ardwinsagh, with its bluish-green water sparkling in the summer sunlight, and here and there breaking over some sunken rock, against which the waves spent themselves in foam.

"You see how the current is set, Sir? That is what makes it dangerous for them as doesn't know the coast, to bathe here at any time, or walk when the tide is flowing. Look how the sea is creeping in now, like a race-horse at the finish. It leaves that tongue of sand bars to the last, and then, before you could look round, it has you up to the middle. That is why I made bold to speak to you; for it is not alone on the account of Squire Ennismore the bay has a bad name. But it is about him and the old house you want to hear. The last mortal being that tried to live in it, my great-grandfather said, was a creature, by name Molly Leary; and she had neither kith nor kin, and begged for her bite and sup, sheltering herself at night in a turf cabin she had built at the back of a ditch. You may be sure she thought herself a made woman when the agent said, 'Yes: she might try if she could stop in the house; there was peat and bog-wood', he told her, 'and half-a-crown a week for the winter, and a golden guinea once Easter came', when the house was to be put in order for the family; and his wife gave Molly some warm clothes and a blanket or two; and she was well set up.

"You may be sure she didn't choose the worst room to sleep in; and for a while all went quiet, till one night she was wakened by feeling the bedstead lifted by the four corners and shaken like a carpet. It was a heavy four-post bedstead, with a solid top: and her life seemed to go out of her with the fear. If it had been a ship in a storm off the Headland, it couldn't have pitched worse and then, all of a sudden, it was dropped with such a bang as nearly drove the heart into her mouth.

"But that, she said, was nothing to the screaming and laughing, and hustling and rushing that filled the house. If a hundred people had been running hard along the passages and tumbling downstairs, they could not have made greater noise.

"Molly never was able to tell how she got clear of the place; but a man coming late home from Ballycloyne Fair found the creature crouched under the old thorn there, with very little on her—saving your honour's presence. She had a bad fever, and talked about strange things, and never was the same woman after."

"But what was the beginning of all this? When did the house first get the name of being haunted?"

"After the old Squire went away: that was what I purposed telling you. He did not come here to live regularly till he had got well on in years. He was near seventy at the time I am talking about; but he held himself as upright as ever, and rode as hard as the youngest; and could have drunk a whole roomful under the table, and walked up to bed as unconcerned as you please at the dead of the night.

"He was a terrible man. You couldn't lay your tongue to a wickedness he had not been in the forefront of—drinking, duelling, gambling, —all manner of sins had been meat and drink to him since he was a boy almost. But at last he did something in London so bad, so beyond the beyonds, that he thought he had best come home and live among people who did not know so much about his goings on as the English. It was said that he wanted to try and stay in this world for ever; and that he had got some secret drops that kept him well and hearty. There was something wonderful queer about him, anyhow.

"He could hold foot with the youngest; and he was strong, and had a fine fresh colour in his face; and his eyes were like a hawk's; and there was not a break in his voice—and him near upon threescore and ten!

"At last and at long last it came to be the March before he was seventy—the worst March ever known in all these parts—such blowing, sleeting, snowing, had not been experienced in the memory of man; when one blusterous night some foreign vessel went to bits on the Purple Headland. They say it was an awful sound to hear the death-cry that went up high above the noise of the wind; and it was as bad a sight to see the shore there strewed with corpses of all sorts and sizes, from the little cabin-boy to the grizzled seaman.

"They never knew who they were or where they came from, but some of the men had crosses, and beads, and such like, so the priest said they belonged to him, and they were all buried deeply and decently in the chapel graveyard.

"There was not much wreckage of value drifted on shore. Most of what is lost about the head stays there; but one thing did come into the bay—a puncheon of brandy.

"The Squire claimed it; it was his right to have all that came on his land, and he owned this sea-shore from the head to the breakers—every foot—so, in course, he had the brandy; and there was sore illwill because he gave his men nothing, not even a glass of whiskey.

"Well, to make a long story short, that was the most wonderful liquor anybody ever tasted. The gentry came from far and near to take share, and it was cards and dice, and drinking and story-telling night after night—week in, week out. Even on Sundays, God forgive them! The officers would drive over from Ballyclone, and sit emptying tumbler after tumbler till Monday morning came, for it made beautiful punch.

"But all at once people quit coming—a word went round that the liquor was not all it ought to be. Nobody could say what ailed it, but it got about that in some way men found it did not suit them.

"For one thing, they were losing money very fast.

"They could not make head against the Squire's luck, and a hint was dropped the puncheon ought to have been towed out to sea, and sunk in fifty fathoms of water.

"It was getting to the end of April, and fine, warm weather for the time of year, when first one and then another, and then another still, began to take notice of a stranger who walked the shore alone at night. He was a dark man, the same colour as the drowned crew lying in the chapel graveyard, and had rings in his ears, and wore a strange kind of hat, and cut wonderful antics as he walked, and had an ambling sort of gait, curious to look at. Many tried to talk to him, but he only shook his head; so, as nobody could make out where he came from or what he wanted, they made sure he was the spirit of some poor wretch who was tossing about the Head, longing for a snug corner in holy ground.

"The priest went and tried to get some sense out of him.

" 'Is it Christian burial you're wanting?' asked his reverence; but the creature only shook his head.

" 'Is it word sent to the wives and daughters you've left orphans and widows, you'd like?' But no; it wasn't that.

" 'Is it for sin committed you're doomed to walk this way? Would masses comfort ye? There's a heathen,' said his reverence; 'Did you ever hear tell of a Christian that shook his head when masses were mentioned?

" 'Perhaps he doesn't understand English, Father', says one of the officers who was there; 'Try him with Latin.

"No sooner said than done. The priest started off with such a string of *aves* and *paters* that the stranger fairly took to his heels and ran.

" 'He is an evil spirit', explained the priest, when he stopped, tired out, 'and I have exorcised him'.

"But next night my gentleman was back again, as unconcerned as ever.

" 'And he'll just have to stay,' said his reverence, 'for I've got lumbago in the small of my back, and pains in all my joints—never to speak of a hoarseness with standing there shouting; and I don't believe he understood a sentence I said.'

"Well, this went on for a while, and people got that

frightened of the man, or appearance of a man, they would not go near the sand; till in the end, Squire Ennismore, who had always scoffed at the talk, took it into his head he would go down one night, and see into the rights of the matter. He, maybe, was feeling lonesome, because, as I told your honour before, people had left off coming to the house, and there was nobody for him to drink with.

"Out he goes, then, bold as brass; and there were a few followed him. The man came forward at sight of the Squire and took off his hat with a foreign flourish. Not to be behind in civility, the Squire lifted his.

"'I have come, sir,' he said, speaking very loud, to try to make him understand, 'to know if you are looking for anything, and whether I can assist you to find it.'

"The man looked at the Squire as if he had taken the greatest liking to him, and took off his hat again.

"'Is it the vessel that was wrecked you are distressed about?'

"There came no answer, only a mournful shake of the head.

"'Well, I haven't your ship, you know; it went all to bits months ago; and, as for the sailors, they are snug and sound enough in consecrated ground.'

"The man stood and looked at the Squire with a queer sort of smile on his face.

"'What do you want?' asked Mr Ennismore in a bit of a passion. 'If anything belonging to you went down with the vessel, it's about the Head you ought to be looking for it, not here—unless, indeed, it's after the brandy you're fretting!'

"Now, the Squire had tried him in English and French, and was now speaking a language you'd have thought nobody could understand; but, faith, it seemed natural as kissing to the stranger.

"'Oh! That's where you are from, is it?' said the Squire.

'Why couldn't you have told me so at once? I can't give you the brandy, because it mostly is drunk; but come along, and you shall have as stiff a glass of punch as ever crossed your lips.' And without more to-do, off they went, as sociable as you please, jabbering together in some outlandish tongue that made moderate folks' jaws ache to hear it.

"That was the first night they conversed together, but it wasn't the last. The stranger must have been the height of good company, for the Squire never tired of him. Every evening, regularly, he came up to the house, always dressed the same, always smiling and polite, and then the Squire called for brandy and hot water, and they drank and played cards till cock-crow, talking and laughing into the small hours.

"This went on for weeks and weeks, nobody knowing where the man came from, or where he went; only two things the old housekeeper did know—that the puncheon was nearly empty, and that the Squire's flesh was wasting off him; and she felt so uneasy she went to the priest, but he could give her no manner of comfort.

"She got so concerned at last that she felt bound to listen at the dining-room door; but they always talked in that foreign gibberish, and whether it was blessing or cursing they were at she couldn't tell.

"Well, the upshot of it came one night in July—on the eve of the Squire's birthday—there wasn't a drop of spirit left in the puncheon— no, not as much as would drown a fly. They had drunk the whole lot clean up—and the old woman stood trembling, expecting every minute to hear the bell ring for more brandy, for where was she to get more if they wanted any?

"All at once the Squire and the stranger came out into the hall. It was a full moon, and light as day.

"'I'll go home with you to-night by way of a change', says the Squire.

"'Will you so? asked the other.

"'That I will, answered the Squire.

"'It is your own choice, you know.'

"'Yes; it is my own choice; let us go.'

"So they went. And the housekeeper ran up to the window on the great staircase and watched the way they took. Her niece lived there as housemaid, and she came and watched, too; and, after a while, the butler as well. They all turned their faces this way, and looked after their master walking beside the strange man along these very sands. Well, they saw them walk on, and on, and on, and on, till the water took them to their knees, and then to their waists, and then to their arm-pits, and then to their throats and their heads; but long before that the women and the butler were running out on the shore as fast as they could, shouting for help."

"Well?" said the Englishman.

"Living or dead, Squire Ennismore never came back again. Next morning, when the tides ebbed again, one walking over the sand saw the print of a cloven foot—that he tracked to the water's edge. Then everybody knew where the Squire had gone, and with whom."

"And no more search was made?"

"Where would have been the use searching?"

"Not much, I suppose. It's a strange story, anyhow."

"But true, your honour—every word of it."

"Oh! I have no doubt of that," was the satisfactory reply.

WILLIAM TREVOR

The Raising of Elvira Tremlett

My mother preferred English goods to Irish, claiming that the quality was better. In particular she had a preference for English socks and vests, and would not be denied in her point of view. Irish motor-car assemblers made a rough-and-ready job of it, my father used to say, the Austins and Morrises and Vauxhalls that came direct from British factories were twice the cars. And my father was an expert in his way, being the town's single garage-owner. *Devlin Bros.* it said on a length of painted wood, black letters on peeling white. The sign was crooked on the red corrugated iron of the garage, falling down a bit on the left-hand side.

In all other ways my parents were intensely of the country that had borne them, of the province of Munster and of the town they had always known. When she left the Presentation convent my mother had been found employment in the meat factory, working a machine that stuck labels on to tins. My father and his brother Jack, finishing at the Christian Brothers, had automatically passed into the family business. In those days the only sign on the corrugated façade had said *Raleigh Cycles*, for the business, founded by my grandfather, had once been a bicycle one. "I think we'll make a change in that," my father announced one day in 1933 when I was five, and six months or so later the rusty tin sheet that advertised bicycles was removed, leaving behind an island of grey in the corrugated red. "Ah, that's grand," my mother approved from the middle of the street, wiping her chapped hands on her apron. The new sign must have had a freshness and a gleam to it, but I don't recall that. In my memory there is only the peeling white behind the letters and the drooping down at the left-hand side where a rivet had fallen out. "We'll paint that in and we'll be dandy," my Uncle Jack said, referring to the island that remained, the contours of Sir Walter Raleigh's head and shoulders. But the job was never done.

We lived in a house next door to the garage, two storeys of cement that had a damp look, with green window-sashes and a green hall-door. Inside, a wealth of polished brown linoleum, its pattern faded to nothing, was cheered here and there by the rugs my mother bought in Roche's Stores in Cork. The votive light of a crimson Sacred Heart gleamed day and night in the hall. Christ blessed us halfway up the stairs; on the landing the Virgin Mary was coy in garish robes. On either side of a narrow trodden carpet the staircase had been grained to make it seem like oak. In the dining-room, never used, there was a square table with six rexine-seated chairs around it, and over the mantel-piece a mirror with chromium decoration. The sitting-room smelt of must and had a picture of the Pope.

The kitchen was where everything happened. My father and Uncle Jack read the newspaper there. The old Philips wireless, the only one in the house, stood on one of the window-sills. Our two nameless cats used to crouch by the door into the scullery because one of them had once caught a mouse there. Our terrier, Tom, mooched about under my mother's feet when she was cooking at the range. There was a big scrubbed table in the middle of the kitchen, and wooden chairs, and a huge clock, like the top bit of a grandfather clock, hanging between the two windows. The dresser had keys and bits of wire and labels hanging all over it. The china it contained was never used, being hidden behind bric-à-brac: broken ornaments left there in order to be repaired with Seccotine, worn-out parts from the engines of cars which my father and uncle had brought into the kitchen to examine at their leisure, bills on spikes, letters and Christmas cards. The kitchen was always rather dusky, even in the middle of the day: it was partially a basement, light penetrating from outside only through the upper panes of its two long windows. Its concrete floor had been reddened with Cardinal polish, which was renewed once a year, in spring. Its walls and ceiling were a sooty white.

The kitchen was where we did our homework, my two sisters and two brothers and myself. I was the youngest, my brother Cathal the oldest. Cathal and Liam were destined for the garage when they finished at the Christian Brothers, as my father and Uncle Jack had been. My sister Effie was good at arithmetic and the nuns had once or twice mentioned accountancy. There was a commercial college in Cork she could go to, the nuns said, the same place that Miss Madden who did the books for Bolger's Medical Hall had attended. Everyone said my sister Kitty was pretty: my father used to take her on his knee and tell her she'd break some fellow's heart, or a dozen hearts or maybe more. She didn't know what he was talking about at first, but later she understood and used to go red in the face. My father was like that with Kitty. He embarrassed her without meaning to, hauling her on to his knee when she was much too old for it, fondling her because he liked her best. On the other hand, he was quite harsh with my brothers, constantly suspicious that they were up to no good. Every evening he asked them if they'd been to school that day, suspecting that they might have tricked the Christian Brothers and would the next day present them with a note they had written themselves, saying they'd had stomach trouble after eating bad sausages. He and my Uncle Jack had often engaged in such ploys themselves, spending a whole day in the field behind the electricity plant, smoking Woodbines.

My father's attitude to my sister Effie was coloured by Effie's plainness. "Ah, poor old Effie," he used to say, and my mother would reprimand him. He took comfort from the fact that if the garage continued to thrive it would be necessary to have someone doing the increased book-work instead of himself and Uncle Jack trying to do it. For this reason he was in favour of Effie taking a commercial course: he saw a future in which she and my two brothers would live in the house and run the business between them. One or other of my brothers would marry and maybe move out of the house, leaving Effie and whichever one would still be a bachelor: it was my father's way of coming to terms with Effie's plainness. "I wonder if Kitty'll end up with young Lacy?" I once heard him enquiring of my mother, the Lacy he referred to being the only child of another business in the town—Geo. Lacy and Sons, High-Class Drapers—who was about eight at the time. Kitty would do well, she'd marry whom she wanted to, and somehow or other she'd marry money: he really believed that.

For my part I fitted in nowhere in my father's vision of the family's future. My performance at school was poor and there would be no place for me in the garage. I used to sit with the others at the kitchen table trying to understand algebra and Irish grammar, trying without any hope to learn verses from "The Lady of Shalott" and to improve my handwriting by copying from a headline book. "Slow," Brother Flynn had reported. "Slow as a dying snail, that boy is."

That was the family we were. My father was bulky in his grey overalls, always with marks of grease or dirt on him, his fingernails rimmed with black, like fingers in mourning, I used to think. Uncle Jack wore similar overalls but he was thin and much smaller than my father, a ferrety little man, who had a way of looking at the ground when he spoke to you. He, too, was marked with grime and had the same rimmed fingernails, even at weekends. They both brought the smell of the garage into the kitchen, an oily smell that mingled with the fumes of my uncle's pipe and my father's cigarettes.

My mother was red-cheeked and stout, with wavy black hair and big arms and legs. She ruled the house, and was often cross: with my brothers when they behaved obstreperously, with my sisters and myself when her patience failed her. Sometimes my father would spend a long time on a Saturday night in Keogh's, which was the public house he favoured, and she would be cross with him also, noisily shouting in their bedroom, telling him to take off his clothes before he got into bed, telling him he was a fool. Uncle Jack was a teetotaller, a member of the Pioneer movement. He was a great help to Canon O'Keefe in the rectory and in the Church of the Holy Assumption, performing chores and repairing the electric light. Twice a year he spent a Saturday night in Cork in order to go to greyhound racing, but there was more than met the eye to these visits, for on his return there was always a great silence in the house, a fog of disapproval emanating from my father.

The first memories I have are of the garage, of watching my father and Uncle Jack at work, sparks flying from the welding apparatus, the dismantling of oil-caked engines. A car would be driven over the pit and my father or uncle would work underneath it, lit by an electric bulb in a wire casing on the end of a flex. Often, when he wasn't in the pit, my father would drift into conversation with a customer. He'd lean on the bonnet of a car, smoking continuously, talking about a hurling match that had taken place or about the dishonesties of the Government. He would also talk about his children, saying that Cathal and Liam would fit easily into the business and referring to Effie's plans to study commerce, and Kitty's prettiness. "And your man here?" the customer might remark, inclining his head in my direction. To this question my father always replied in the same way. The Lord, he said, would look after me.

As I grew up I became aware that I made both my father and my mother uneasy. I assumed that this was due to my slowness at school, an opinion that was justified by a conversation I once overheard coming from their bedroom: they appeared to regard me as mentally deficient. My father repeated twice that the Lord would look after me. It was something she prayed for, my mother replied, and I imagined her praying after she'd said it, kneeling down by their bed, as she'd taught all of us to kneel by ours. I stood with my bare feet on the linoleum of the landing, believing that a plea from my mother was rising from the house at that very moment, up into the sky where God was. I had been on my way to the kitchen for a drink of water, but I returned to the bedroom I shared with Cathal and Liam and lay awake thinking of the big brown-brick mansion on the Mallow road. Once it had been owned and lived in by a local family. Now it was the town's asylum.

The town itself was small and ordinary. Part of it was on a hill, the part where the slum cottages were, where three or four shops had nothing in their windows except pasteboard advertisements for tea and Bisto. The rest of the town was flat, a single street with one or two narrow streets running off it. Where they met there was a square of a kind, with a statue of Daniel O'Connell. The Munster and Leinster Bank was here, and the Bank of Ireland, and Lacy and Sons, and Bolger's Medical Hall, and the Home and Colonial. Our garage was at one end of the main street, opposite Corrigan's Hotel. The Electric Cinema was at the other, a stark white façade, not far from the Christian Brothers, the convent, and the Church of the Holy Assumption. The Protestant Church was at the top of the hill, beyond the slums.

When I think of the town now I can see it very clearly: cattle and pigs on a fair day, always a Monday; Mrs Driscoll's vegetable shop, Vickery's hardware, Phelan's the barber's, Kilmartin's the turf accountant's, the convent and the Christian Brothers, twenty-nine public houses. The streets are empty on a sunny afternoon, there's a smell of bread. Brass plates gleam on the way home from school: Dr Thos. Garvey M.D., R.C.S., Regan and O'Brien Commissioners for Oaths, W. Tracy Dental Surgeon.

But in my thoughts our house and our garage close in on everything else, shadowing and diminishing the town.

The bedroom I shared with Cathal and Liam had the same nondescript linoleum as the hall and the landing had. There was a dressing-table with a wash-stand in white-painted wood, and a wardrobe that matched. There was a flowery wallpaper on the walls, but the flowers had all faded to a uniform brown, except behind the bedroom's single picture, of an ox pulling a cart. Our three iron bedsteads were lined against one wall. Above the mantel-piece Christ on his cross had already given up the ghost.

I didn't in any way object to this bedroom and, familiar with no alternative, I didn't mind sharing it with my brothers. The house itself was somewhere I was used to also, accepted and taken for granted. But the garage was

different. The garage was a kind of hell, its awful earth
floor made black with sump oil, its huge indelicate vices,
the chill of cast iron, the grunting of my father and my
uncle as they heaved an engine out of a tractor, the
cloying smell of petrol. It was there that my silence, my
dumbness almost, must have begun. I sense that now,
without being able accurately to remember. Looking back,
I see myself silent in a classroom, taught first by nuns and
later by Christian Brothers. In the kitchen, while the
others chattered at mealtimes, I was silent too. I could
take no interest in what my father and uncle reported
about the difficulties they were having in getting spare
parts or about some fault in a farmer's carburettor. My
brothers listened to all that, and clearly found it easy to.
Or they would talk about sport, or tease Uncle Jack about
the money he lost on greyhounds and horses. My mother
would repeat what she had heard in the shops, and Uncle
Jack would listen intently because although he never
himself indulged in gossip he loved to hear it. My sister
would retail news from the convent, the decline in the
health of an elderly nun, or the inability of some family to
buy Lacy's more expensive First Communion dresses. I
often felt, listening at mealtimes, that I was scarcely there.
I didn't belong and I sensed it was my fault; I felt I was a
burden, being slow and unpromising at school, unable to
hold out hopes for the future. I felt I was a disgrace to
them and might even become a person who was only fit to
lift cans of paraffin about in the garage. I thought I could
see that in my father's eyes, and in my uncle's sometimes,
and in my mother's. A kind of shame it was, peering back
at me.

I turned to Elvira Tremlett because everything about her
was quiet. "You great damn clown," my mother would
shout angrily at my father. He'd smile in the kitchen,

swaying and red-faced, smelling like a brewery, as she used to say. "Mind that bloody tongue of yours," he'd retort, and then he'd eye my uncle in a belligerent manner. "Jeez, will you look at the cut of him?" he'd roar, laughing and throwing his head about. My uncle would usually be sitting in front of the range, a little to one side so as not to be in the way of my mother while she cooked. He'd been reading the *Independent* or *Ireland's Own,* or trying to mend something. "You're the right eejit," my father would say to him. "And the right bloody hypocrite."

It was always like that when he'd been in Keogh's on a Saturday evening and returned in time for his meal. My mother would slap the plates on to the table, my father would sing in order to annoy her. I used to feel that my uncle and my mother were allied on these occasions, just as she and my father were allied when my uncle spent a Saturday night in Cork after the greyhound racing. I much preferred it when my father didn't come back until some time in the middle of the night. "Will you look at His Nibs?" he'd say in the kitchen, drawing attention to me. "Haven't you a word in you, boy? Bedad, that fellow'll never make a lawyer." He'd explode with laughter and then he'd tell Kitty that she was looking great and could marry the crowned King of England if she wanted to. He'd say to Effie she was getting fat with the toffees she ate; he'd tell my brothers they were lazy.

They didn't mind his talk the way I did; even Kitty's embarrassment used to evaporate quite quickly because for some reason she was fond of him. Effie was fond of my uncle, and my brothers of my mother. Yet in spite of all this family feeling, whenever there was quarrelling between our parents or an atmosphere after my uncle had spent a night away my brothers used to say the three of them would drive you mad. "Wouldn't it make you sick, listening to it?" Cathal would say in our bedroom, saying it to Liam. Then they'd laugh because they couldn't be bothered to concern themselves too much with other people's quarrels, or with atmospheres.

The fact was, my brothers and sister were all part of it, whatever it was—the house, the garage, the family we were—and they could take everything in their stride. They were the same as our parents and our uncle, and Elvira Tremlett was different. She was a bit like Myrna Loy, whom I had seen in the Electric, in *Test Pilot* and *Too Hot to Handle* and *The Thin Man*. Only she was more beautiful than Myrna Loy, and her voice was nicer. Her voice, I still consider, was the nicest thing about Elvira Tremlett, next to her quietness.

"What do you want?" the sexton of the Protestant church said to me one Saturday afternoon. "What're you doing here?"

He was an old hunched man in black clothes. He had rheumy eyes, very red and bloody at the rims. It was said in the town that he gave his wife an awful time.

"It isn't your church," he said.

I nodded, not wanting to speak to him. He said:

"It's a sin for you to be coming into a Protestant church. Are you wanting to be a Protestant, is that it?" He was laughing at me, even though his lips weren't smiling. He looked as if he'd never smiled in his life.

I shook my head at him, hoping he might think I was dumb.

"Stay if you want to," he said, surprising me, even though I'd seen him coming to the conclusion that I wasn't going to commit some act of vandalism. I think he might even have decided to be pleased because a Catholic boy had chosen to wander among the pews and brasses of his church. He hobbled away to the vestry, breathing noisily because of his bent condition.

Several months before that Saturday I had wandered into the church for the first time. It was different from the Church of the Holy Assumption. It had a different smell, a smell that might have come from mothballs or from the tidy stacks of hymn-books and prayer-books, whereas the Church of the Holy Assumption smelt of people and candles. It was cosier, much smaller, with dark-coloured panelling and pews, and stained-glass windows that seemed old, and no cross on the altar. There were flags and banners that were covered with dust, all faded and in shreds, and a bible spread out on the wings of an eagle.

The old sexton came back. I could feel him watching me as I read the tablets on the walls, moving from one to the next, pretending that each of them interested me. I might have asked him: I might have smiled at him and timidly enquired about Elvira Tremlett because I knew he was old enough to remember. But I didn't. I walked slowly up a side-aisle, away from the altar, to the back of the church. I wanted to linger there in the shadows, but I could feel his rheumy eyes on my back, wondering about me. As I slipped away from the church, down the short path that led through black iron gates to the street at the top of the hill, I knew that I would never return to the place.

"Well, it doesn't matter," she said. "You don't have to go back. There's nothing to go back for."

I knew that was true. It was silly to keep on calling in at the Protestant church.

"It's curiosity that sends you there," she said. "You're much too curious."

I knew I was: she had made me understand that. I was curious and my family weren't.

She smiled her slow smile, and her eyes filled with it. Her eyes were brown, the same colour as her long hair. I loved it when she smiled. I loved watching her fingers playing with the daisies in her lap. I loved her old-fashioned clothes, and her shoes and her two elaborate ear-rings. She laughed once when I asked her if they were gold. She'd never been rich, she said.

There was a place, a small field with boulders in it, hidden on the edge of a wood. I had gone there the first time, after I'd been in the Protestant church. What had happened was that in the church I had noticed the tablet on the wall, the left wall as you faced the altar, the last tablet on it, in dull grey marble.

> Nearby this Stone
> Lies Interred the Body
> of Miss Elvira Tremlett
> Daughter of Wm. Tremlett
> of Tremlett Hall
> in the County of Dorset.
> She Departed this Life
> August 30 1873
> Aged 18.

Why should an English girl die in our town? Had she been passing through? Had she died of poisoning? Had someone shot her? Eighteen was young to die.

On that day, the first day I read her tablet, I had walked from the Protestant church to the field beside the wood. I often went there because it was a lonely place, away from the town and from people. I sat on a boulder and felt hot sun on my face and head, and on my neck and the backs of my hands. I began to imagine her, Elvira Tremlett of Tremlett Hall in the county of Dorset, England. I gave her her long hair and her smile and her elaborate earrings, and I felt I was giving her gifts. I gave her her clothes, wondering if I had got them right. Her fingers were delicate as straws, lacing together the first of her daisy-chains. Her voice hadn't the edge that Myrna Loy's had, her neck more elegant.

"Oh, love," she said on the Saturday after the sexton had spoken to me. "The tablet's only a stone. It's silly to go gazing at it."

I knew it was and yet it was hard to prevent myself. The more I gazed at it the more I felt I might learn about her. I didn't know if I was getting her right. I was afraid even to begin to imagine her death because I thought I might be doing wrong to have her dying from some cause that wasn't the correct one. It seemed insulting to her memory not to get that perfectly right.

"You mustn't want too much," she said to me on that Saturday afternoon. "It's as well you've finished with the tablet on the wall. Death doesn't matter, you know."

I never went back to the Protestant church. I remember what my mother had said about the quality of English goods, and how cars assembled in England were twice the ones as those assembled in Dublin. I looked at the map of England in my atlas and there was Dorset. She'd been travelling, maybe staying in a house near by, and had died somehow: she was right, it didn't matter.

Tremlett Hall was by a river in the country, with Virginia creeper all over it, with long corridors and suits of armour in the hall, and a fire-place in the hall also. In *David Copperfield*, which I had seen in the Electric, there might have been a house like Tremlett Hall, or in *A Yank at Oxford*: I couldn't quite remember. The gardens were beautiful: you walked from one garden to another, to a special rosegarden with a sundial, to a vegetable garden with high walls around it. In the house someone was always playing a piano. "Me," Elvira said.

My brothers went to work in the garage, first Cathal and then Liam. Effie went to Cork, to the commercial college. The boys at the Christian Brothers began to whistle at Kitty and sometimes would give me notes to pass on to her. Even when other people were there I could feel Elvira's nearness, even her breath sometimes, and certainly the warmth of her hands. When Brother Flynn hit me one day she cheered me up. When my father came back from Keogh's in time for his Saturday tea her presence made it easier. The garage I hated, where I was certain now I would one day lift paraffin cans from one corner to another, was lightened by her. She was in Mrs Driscoll's vegetable shop when I bought cabbage and potatoes for my mother. She was there while I waited for the Electric to open, and when I walked through the animals on a fair day. In the stony field the sunshine made her earrings glitter. It danced over a brooch she had not had when first I imagined her, a brooch with a scarlet jewel, in the shape of a dragon. Mist caught in her hair, wind ruffled the skirts of her old-fashioned dress. She wore gloves when it was cold, and a green cloak that wrapped itself all around her. In spring she often carried daffodils, and once—one Sunday in June—she carried a little dog, a grey Cairn that afterwards became part of her, like her earrings and her brooch.

I grew up but she was always eighteen, as petrified as her tablet on the wall. In the bedroom which I shared with Cathal and Liam I came, in time, to take her dragon's brooch from her throat and to take her earrings from her pale ears and to lift her dress from her body. Her limbs were warm, and her smile was always there. Her slender fingers traced caresses on my cheeks. I told her that I loved her, as the people told one another in the Electric.

"You know why they're afraid of you?" she said one day in the field by the wood. "You know why they hope that God will look after you?"

I had to think about it but I could come to no conclusion on my own, without her prompting. I think I wouldn't have dared; I'd have been frightened of whatever there was.

"You know what happens," she said. "when your uncle stays in Cork on a Saturday night? You know what happened once when your father came back from Keogh's too late for his meal, in the middle of the night?"

I knew before she told me. I guessed, but I wouldn't have if she hadn't been there. I made her tell me, listening to her quiet voice. My Uncle Jack went after women as well as greyhounds in Cork. It was his weakness, like going to Keogh's was my father's. And the two weaknesses had once combined, one Saturday night a long time ago when my uncle hadn't gone to Cork and my father was a long time in Keogh's. I was the child of my uncle Jack and my mother, born of his weakness and my mother's anger as she waited for the red bleariness of my father to return, footless in the middle of the night. It was why my father called my uncle a hypocrite. It was maybe why my uncle was always looking at the ground, and why he assisted Canon O'Keefe in the rectory and in the Church of the Holy Assumption. I was their sin, growing in front of them, for God to look after.

"They have made you," Elvira said. "The three of them have made you what you are."

I imagined my father returning that night from Keogh's, stumbling on the stairs, and haste being made by my uncle to hide himself. In these images it was always my uncle who was anxious and in a hurry: my mother kept saying it didn't matter, pressing him back on to the pillows, wanting him to be found there.

My father was like a madman in the bedroom then, wild in his crumpled Saturday clothes. He struck at both of them, his befuddled eyes tormented while my mother screamed. She went back through all the years of their marriage, accusing him of cruelty and neglect. My uncle wept. "I'm no more than an animal to you," my mother screamed, half-naked between the two of them. "I cook and clean and have children for you. You give me thanks by going out to Keogh's." Cathal was in the room, attracted by the noise. He stood by the open door, five years old, telling them to be quiet because they were waking the others.

"Don't ever tell a soul," Cathal would have said, years afterwards, retailing that scene for Liam and Effie and Kitty, letting them guess the truth. He had been sent back to bed, and my uncle had gone to his own bed, and in the morning there had begun the pretending that none of it had happened. There was confession and penance, and extra hours spent in Keogh's. There were my mother's prayers that I would not be born, and my uncle's prayers, and my father's bitterness when the prayers weren't answered.

On the evening of the day that Elvira shared all that with me I watched them as we ate in the kitchen, my father's hands still smeared with oil, his fingernails in mourning, my uncle's eyes bent over his fried eggs. My brothers and sisters talked about events that had taken place in the town; my mother listened without interest, her large round face seeming stupid to me now. It was a cause for celebration that I was outside the family circle. I was glad not to be part of the house and the garage, nor to be part of the town with its statue and its shops and its twenty-nine public houses. I belonged with a figment of my imagination, to an English ghost who had acquired a dog, whose lips were soft, whose limbs were warm, Elvira Tremlett who lay beneath the Protestant church.

"Oh, love," I said in the kitchen, "thank you."

The conversation ceased, my father's head turned sharply. Cathal and Liam looked at me, so did Effie and Kitty. My mother had a piece of fried bread on a fork, on the way to her mouth. She returned it to her plate. There was grease at the corner of her lips, a little shiny stream from some previous mouthful, running down to her chin. My uncle pushed his knife and fork together and stared at them.

I felt them believing with finality now, with proof, that I was not sane. I was fifteen years old, a boy who was slow and backward in his ways, who was all of a sudden addressing someone who wasn't in the room.

My father cut himself a slice of bread, moving the breadsaw slowly through the loaf. My brothers were as valuable in the garage now as he or my uncle; Effie kept the books and sent out bills. My father took things easy, spending more time talking to his older customers. My uncle perused the racing pages; my mother had had an operation for varicose veins, which she should have had years ago.

I could disgrace them in the town, in all the shops and public houses, in Bolger's Medical Hall, in the convent and the Christian Brothers and the Church of the Holy Assumption. How could Cathal and Liam carry on the business if they couldn't hold their heads up? How could Effie help with the petrol pumps at a busy time, standing in her Wellington boots on a wet day, for all the town to see? Who would marry Kitty now?

I had spoken by mistake, and I didn't speak again. It was the first time I had said anything at a meal in the kitchen for as long as I could remember, for years and years. I had suddenly felt that she might grow tired of coming into my mind and want to be left alone, buried beneath the Protestant church. I had wanted to reassure her.

"They're afraid of you," she said that night. "All of them."

She said it again when I walked in the sunshine to our field. She kept on saying it, as if to warn me, as if to tell me to be on the look-out. "They have made you," she repeated. "You're the child of all of them."

I wanted to go away, to escape from the truth we had both instinctively felt and had shared. I walked with her through the house called Tremlett Hall, haunting other people with our footsteps. We stood and watched while guests at a party laughed among the suits of armour in the hall, while there was waltzing in a ballroom. In the gardens dahlias bloomed, and sweet-peas clung to wires against a high stone wall. Low hedges of fuchsia bounded the paths among the flower-beds, the little dog ran on in front of us. She held my hand and said she loved me; she smiled at me in the sunshine. And then, just for a moment, she seemed to be different; she wasn't wearing the right clothes; she was wearing a tennis dress and had a racquet in her hand. She was standing in a conservatory, one foot on a cane chair. She looked like another girl, Susan Peters in *Random Harvest*.

I didn't like that. It was the same kind of thing as feeling I had to speak to her even though other people were in the kitchen. It was a muddle, and somewhere in it I could sense an unhappiness I didn't understand. I couldn't tell if it was hers or mine. I tried to say I was sorry, but I didn't know what I was sorry for.

In the middle of one night I woke up screaming. Cathal and Liam were standing by my bed, cross with me for waking them. My mother came, and then my father. I was still screaming, unable to stop. "He's had some type of nightmare," Cathal said.

It wasn't a nightmare because it continued when I was awake. She was there, Elvira Tremlett, born 1855. She didn't talk or smile: I couldn't make her. Something was failing in me: it was the same as Susan Peters suddenly appearing with a tennis racquet, the same as my desperation in wanting to show gratitude when we weren't in private.

My mother sat beside my bed. My brothers returned to theirs. The light remained on. I must have whispered, I must have talked about her because I remember my mother's nodding head and her voice assuring me that it was all a dream. I slept, and when I woke up it was light in the room and my mother had gone and my brothers were getting up. Elvira Tremlett was still there, one eye half-closed in blindness, the fingers that had been delicate misshapen now. When my brother left the room she was more vivid, a figure by the window, turning her head to look at me, a gleam of fury in her face. She did not speak but I knew what she was saying. I had used her for purposes of my own, to bring solace. What right, for God's sake, had I to blow life into her decaying bones? Born 1855, eighty-nine years of age.

I closed my eyes, trying to imagine her as I had before, willing her young girl's voice and her face and hair. But even with my eyes closed the old woman moved about the room, from the window to the foot of Liam's bed, to the wardrobe, into a corner, where she stood still.

She was on the landing with me, and on the stairs and in the kitchen. She was in the stony field by the wood, accusing me of disturbing her yet still not speaking. She was in pain from her eye and her arthritic hands: I had brought about that. Yet she was no ghost, I knew she was no ghost. She was a figment of my imagination, drawn from her dull grey tablet by my interest. She existed within me, I told myself, but it wasn't a help.

Every night I woke up screaming. The sheets of my bed were sodden with my sweat. I would shout at my brothers and my mother, begging them to take her away from me.

It wasn't I who had committed the sin, I shouted, it wasn't I who deserved the punishment. All I had done was to talk to a figment. All I'd done was to pretend, as they had.

Canon O'Keefe talked to me in the kitchen. His voice came and went, and my mother's voice spoke of the sheets sodden with sweat every morning, and my father's voice said there was terror in my eyes. All I wanted to say was that I hadn't meant any harm in raising Elvira Tremlett from the dead in order to have an imaginary friend, or in travelling with her to the house with Virginia creeper on it. She hadn't been real, she'd been no more than a flicker on the screen of the Electric Cinema: I wanted to say all that. I wanted to be listened to, to be released of the shame that I felt like a shroud around me. I knew that if I could speak my imagination would be free of the woman who haunted it now. I tried, but they were afraid of me. They were afraid of what I was going to say and between them they somehow stopped me. "Our Father," said Canon O'Keefe, "Who art in heaven, Hallowed be Thy Name . . ."

Dr Garvey came and looked at me; in Cork another man looked at me. The man in Cork tried to make me talk to him, telling me to lie down, to take my shoes off if I wanted to. It wasn't any good, and it wasn't fair on them, having me there in the house, a person in some kind of nightmare. I quite see now that it wasn't fair on them, I quite see that.

Because of the unfairness I was brought, one Friday morning in a Ford car my father borrowed from a customer, to this brown-brick mansion, once the property of a local family. I have been here for thirty-four years. The clothes I wear are rough, but I have ceased to be visited by the woman whom Elvira Tremlett became, in my failing imagination. I ceased to be visited by her the moment I arrived here, for when that moment came I knew that this was the house she had been staying in when she died. She brought me here so that I could live in peace, even in the room that had been hers. I had disturbed her own peace so that we might come here together.

I have not told this story myself. It has been told by my weekly visitor, who has placed me at the centre of it because that, of course, is where I belong. Here, in the brown-red mansion, I have spoken without difficulty. I have spoken in the garden where I work in the daytime; I have spoken at all meals; I have spoken to my weekly visitor. I am different here. I do not need an imaginary friend, I could never again feel curious about a girl who died.

I have asked my visitor what they say in the town, and what the family say. He replies that in the bar of Corrigan's Hotel commercial travellers are told of a boy who was haunted, as a place or house is. They are drawn across the bar to a window: Devlin Bros., the garage across the street, is pointed out to them. They listen in pleasurable astonishment to the story of nightmares, and hear the name of an English girl who died in the town in 1873, whose tablet is on the wall of the Protestant church. They are told of the final madness of the boy, which came about through his visions of this girl, Elvira Tremlett.

The story is famous in the town, the only story of its kind the town possesses. It is told as a mystery, and the strangers who hear it sometimes visit the Protestant church to look up at the tablet that commemorates a death in 1873. They leave the church in bewilderment, wondering why an uneasy spirit should have lighted on a boy so many years later. They never guess, not one of them, that the story as it happened wasn't a mystery in the least.

JOHN McGAHERN

The Wine Breath

If I was to die, I'd miss most the mornings and the evenings, he thought, as he walked the narrow dirt-track by the lake in the late evening, and then wondered if his mind was failing, for how could anybody think anything as stupid: being a man he had no choice, he was doomed to die; and being dead he'd miss nothing, being nothing. And it went against everything in his life as a priest.

There was still the lake, the road, the evening, he tried to count, and he was going to call on Gillespie. Gillespie was sawing. Gillespie was always sawing. The roaring rise-and-fall of the two stroke stayed like a rent in the evening. And when he got to the black gate there was Gillespie, his overalled bulk framed in the short avenue of alders, and he was sawing not alders but beech, four or five tractorloads dumped in the front of the house. The priest put a hand to the black gate, bolted to the first of the alders, and was at once arrested by showery sunlight falling down the avenue. It lit up the one boot holding the length of beech in place, it lit the arms moving the blade slowly up and down as it tore through the beech, white chips milling out on the chain.

Suddenly, as he was about to rattle the gate loudly to see if it would penetrate the sawing, he felt himself (bathed as in a dream) in an incredible sweetness of light. It was the evening light on snow. The gate on which he had his hand vanished, the alders, Gillespie's formidable bulk, the roaring of the saw. He was in another day, the lost day of Michael Bruen's funeral nearly thirty years before. All was silent and still there. Slow feet crunched on the snow. Ahead, at the foot of the hill, the coffin rode slowly forward on shoulders, its brown varnish and metal trappings dull in the glittering snow, riding just below the long waste of snow eight or ten feet deep over the whole countryside. The long dark line of mourners following the coffin stretched away towards Oakport Wood in the pathway cut through the snow. High on Killeelan Hill the graveyard evergreens rose out of the snow. The graveyard wall was covered, the narrow path cut up the side of the hill stopping at the little gate deep in the snow. The coffin climbed with painful slowness, as if it might never reach the gate, often pausing for the bearers to be changed; and someone started to pray, the prayer travelling down the whole mile-long line of the mourners as they shuffled behind the coffin in the narrow tunnel cut in the snow.

It was the day in February 1947 that they buried Michael Bruen. Never before or since had he experienced the Mystery in such awesomeness. Now as he stood at the gate there was no awe or terror, only the coffin moving slowly towards the dark trees on the hill, the long line of the mourners, and everywhere the blinding white light, among the half-buried thorn bushes, and beyond Killeelan on the covered waste of Gloria Bog, on the sides of Slieve an Ierin.

He did not know how long he had stood in that lost day, in that white light, probably for no more than a moment. He could not have stood the intensity for any longer. When he woke out of it the grey light of the alders had reasserted itself. His hand was still on the bar of the gate. Gillespie was still sawing, bent over the saw-horse, his boot on the length of beechwood, completely enclosed in the roaring rise-and-fall of the saw. The priest felt as vulnerable as if he had suddenly woken out of sleep, shaken and somewhat ashamed to have been caught asleep in the actual day and life, without any protection of walls.

He was about to rattle the gate again, feeling a washed-out parody of something or other on what was after all nothing more than a child's errand: to tell the Gillespies that a bed had at long last been made available in the Regional Hospital for the operation on Mrs Gillespie's piles, when his eyes were caught again by the quality of the light. It was one of those late October days, small white clouds drifting about the sun, and the watery light was shining down the alder rows to fall on the white chips of the beechwood strewn all about Gillespie, some inches deep. It was the same white light as the light on snow. It was as simple as that. As he watched, the light went out on the beech chips, and it was the grey day again around Gillespie's sawing. It had been as simple as that. The suggestion of snow had been enough to plunge him in the lost day of Michael Bruen's funeral. Everything in that remembered day was so pure and perfect that he felt purged of all tiredness and bitterness, was, for a moment, eager to begin life again.

And, making sure that Gillespie hadn't noticed him at the gate, he turned back on the road. The bed wouldn't be ready for another week. The news could wait a day or more. Before leaving he stole a last look at the dull white ground about the sawhorse. The most difficult of things seem always to lie closest to us, to be always around our feet.

Ever since his mother's death he found himself stumbling into these dead days. Once crushed mint in the garden had given him back a day he'd spent with her at the sea in such reality that he had been frightened, as if he'd suddenly fallen through time; it was as if the world of the dead was as available to him as the world of the living. It was also humiliating for him to realise that she must have been the mainspring in his days. And now that the mainspring was broken the hands were weakly falling here and falling there. Today there had been the sudden light on the bits of white beech. He'd not have noticed it if he hadn't been alone, if Gillespie had not been so absorbed in his sawing. Before there must have been some such simple trigger that he'd been too ashamed or bewildered to notice.

Stealthily and quickly he went down the dirt-track by the lake till he got to the main road. To the left was the church in a rookery of old trees, and behind it the house where he lived. Safe on the wide main road he let his mind go back to the beech chips. They rested there around Gillespie's large bulk, and paler still was the line of mourners following the coffin through the snow, a picture you could believe or disbelieve but not be in. In idle exasperation he began to count the trees in the hedge along the road as he walked: ash, green oak, whitethorn, ash, the last leaves a vivid yellow on the wild cherry, empty October fields in dull wet light behind the hedges. This, then, was the actual day, the only day that mattered, the day from which our salvation had to be won or lost: it stood solidly and impenetrably there, denying the weak life of the person, with nothing of the eternal other than it would dully endure, while the day set alight in his mind by the light of the white beech, though it had been nothing more than a funeral he had attended during a dramatic snowfall when a boy, seemed bathed in the eternal, seemed everything we had been taught and told of the world of God.

Dissatisfied, and feeling as tired again as he'd been on his way to Gillespie's, he did not go through the church gate with its circle and cross, nor did he call to the sexton locking up under the bellrope. In order to be certain of being left alone he went by the circular path at the side round to the house, the high laurel hedge separating it from the graveyard and church. There he made coffee without turning on the light. Always when about to give birth or die cattle sought out a clean place in some corner of the field, away from the herd.

Michael Bruen had been a big kindly agreeable man, what was called a lovely man. His hair was a coarse grey. He wore loose-fitting tweeds with red cattleman's boots. When young he had been a policeman in Dublin. It was said he had either won or inherited money, and had come home to where he'd come from, to farm and to prosper.

He had a large family, and men were employed. All around, the yard and its big outhouses with red roofs rang with work: cans, machinery, raillery, the sliding of hooves, someone whistling; and in off the yard was the enormous cave of a kitchen, the long table down its centre, the fireplace at its end, the plates and pots and presses along the walls, sides of bacon wrapped in gauze hanging from hooks in the ceiling, the whole room full of the excitement and bustle of women.

Often as a boy the priest had gone to Michael Bruen's on some errand for his father. Once the beast was housed or the load emptied Michael would take him into the kitchen.

He remembered the last December evening well. He had driven over a white bullock. The huge fire of wood blazed all the brighter because of the frost.

"Give this man something," Michael had led him.

"Something solid that'll warm the life back into him."

"A cup of tea will do fine," he had protested in the custom.

"Nonsense. Don't pay him the slightest attention. Empty bags can't stand."

Eileen, the prettiest of Michael's daughters, laughed as she took down the pan. Her arms were white to the elbows with a fine dusting of flour.

"He'll remember this was a good place to come to when he has to start thinking about a wife," Michael's words gave licence to general hilarity.

It was hard to concentrate on Michael's question about his father, so delicious was the smell of frying. The mug of steaming tea was put by his side. The butter melted on the fresh bread on the plate. There were sausages, liver, bacon, a slice of black-pudding and sweetest grisceens.

"Now set to," Michael laughed. "We don't want any empty bags leaving Bruen's."

Michael came with him to the gate when he left. "Tell your father it's ages since we had a drink in the Royal. And that if he doesn't search me out in the Royal the next Fair Day I'll have to go over and bate the lugs off him." As he shook his hands in the half-light of the yard lamp it was the last time he was to see him alive. Before the last flakes had stopped falling, and when old people were searching back to "the great snows" when Count Plunkett was elected to find another such fall, Michael Bruen had died, and his life was already another such poor watermark of memory.

The snow lay eight feet deep on the roads, and dead cattle and sheep were found in drifts of fifteen feet in the fields. All of the people who hadn't lost sheep or cattle were in extraordinary good humour, their own ills buried for a time as deep as their envy of any other's good fortune in the general difficulty of the snow. It took days to cut a way out to the main road, the snow having to be cut in blocks breast-high out of a face of frozen snow. A wild cheer went up as the men at last cut through to the gang digging in from the main road. Another cheer greeted the first van to come in, Doherty's bread van, and it had hardly died when the hearse came with the coffin for Michael Bruen. That night they cut the path up the side of Killeelan Hill and found the headstone beside the big yew just inside the gate and opened the grave. They hadn't finished digging when the first funeral bell came clearly over the snow the next day to tell them that the coffin had started on its way.

The priest hadn't thought of the day for years or of Michael Bruen till he had stumbled into it without warning by way of the sudden light on the beech chips. It did not augur well. There were days, especially of late, when he seemed to be lost in dead days, to see time present as a flimsy accumulating tissue over all the time that was lost. Sometimes he saw himself as an old man that boys were helping down to the shore, restraining the tension of their need to laugh as they pointed out a rock in the path he seemed about to stumble over, and then they had to lift their eyes and smile apologetically to the passers-by while he stood staring out to sea, having forgotten all about the rock in his path. "It's this way we're going," he felt the imaginary tug on his sleeve, and he was drawn again into the tortuous existence of the everyday, away from the eternal of the sea or the lost light on frozen snow across Killeelan Hill.

Never before, though, had he noticed anything like the beech chips. There was the joy of holding what had eluded him for so long, in its amazing simplicity: but mastered knowledge was soon no knowledge, unless it opened, became part of another, and what did the beech chips do but turn back to his own death?

Like the sudden snowfall and Michael Bruen's burial his life had been like any other, except to himself, and then only in odd visions of it, as a lost life. When it had been agreeable and equitable he had no vision of it at all.

The country childhood. His mother and father. The arrival at the shocking knowledge of birth and death. His attraction to the priesthood as a way of vanquishing death and avoiding birth. Oh, hurry it, he thought. There is not much to it. Many have it. There is not enough room. His father and mother were old when they married, and he was "the fruit of old things", he heard derisively. His father had been a small farmer. His mother, a seamstress. He could still see the needle flashing in her strong hands, that single needle flash composed of thousands of hours.

"His mother had the vocation for him", perhaps she had, perhaps all the mothers of the country had, it had so passed into the speech of the country, in all the forms of both beatification and derision, and it was out of fear of death he became a priest, which becomes in its time the fear of life, and wasn't it natural to turn back to the mother in this fear: she was older than fear, having given death as well as life. There was then his father's death, the father accepting it as he had accepted all poor fortune all his life long, as his due. refusing to credit the good.

They had sold what they had together, and his mother had come to live with him, and was happy. She attended all the Masses and Devotions, took messages, and she sewed, though she had no longer any need, linen for the altar, soutanes and surplices, his shirts and all her own clothes. Sometimes her concern for him irritated him to exasperation but he hardly ever let it show. He had the outside duties of a priest. The fences on the past and future were secure. He must have been what is called happy, and there was a whole part of his life that without his knowing had come to turn to her for its own expression.

He discovered it when she began her death. He came home one summer evening to find all the lights in the house on. She was in the living room, in the usual chair. The table was piled high with dresses. Round the chair was a pile of rags. She did not look up when he entered, her still strong hands tearing apart a herring-bone skirt she had made only the year before.

"What on earth are you doing, Mother?" he caught her by the hands when she didn't answer.

"It's time you were up for Mass," she said.

"What are you doing with all your dresses?"

"What dresses?"

"All the dresses you've just been tearing up."

"I don't know anything about dresses," and then he saw there was something wrong. She made no resistance when he led her up the stairs.

For some days she seemed absent and confused but, though he watched her carefully, she was otherwise very little different from her old self, and she did not appear ill. Then he came home one evening to find her standing like a child in the middle of the room, surrounded by an enormous pile of rags. She had torn up every dress or article of clothing she had ever made. After his initial shock he did the usual and sent for the doctor.

"I'm afraid it's just the onset of senility," the doctor said.

"It's irreversible?"

The doctor nodded, "It very seldom takes such a violent form, but that's what it is. She'll have to be looked after."

She recognised him when he visited the Home during her first year there, but without excitement, as if he was already far away: and then the day came when he had to admit that she no longer knew who he was, had become like a dog kennelled out too long. He was with her when she died. She'd turned her face toward him. There came what seemed a light of recognition in the eyes, like a last glow of a match before it goes out, and then she died.

There was nothing left but his own life. There had been nothing but that all along, but it had been obscured, comfortably obscured.

He turned on the radio.

A man had lost both legs in an explosion. There was violence on the night-shift at Ford's. The pound had steadied towards the close but was still down on the day.

Letting his fingers linger on the knob he turned it off. The disembodied voice on the air was not unlike the lost day he'd stumbled into through the light on the beech chips, except it had nothing of its radiance—the funeral during the years he must have carried it around with him had lost the sheltered burden of the everyday, had become light as the air in all the clarity of light. It was all timeless, and seemed at least a promise of the eternal.

He went to draw the curtain. She had torn up all her clothes before she left the house. She had made the red curtain too with its pale lining but hadn't torn it. How often must she have watched the moonlight on the still headstones beyond the laurel, as it lay evenly on them this night. She had been afraid of ghosts. Old priests that had lived in this house, who through whiskey or some other ill had neglected to say some Mass for the dead—and because of the neglect the soul for whom the Mass should have been offered was forced to linger beyond its time in Purgatory—and the priest guilty of the omission could himself not be released until the living priest had said the Mass, and was forced to come at midnight to the house in all his bondage until that Mass was said.

"They must have been all good priests, Mother. Good steady old fellows like myself. They never come back," he remembered his own idle reply as he drew the curtain, lingering as much over it as he had lingered over the turning off of the radio. He would be glad of a ghost tonight, be glad of any visitation from beyond the walls of sense.

He took up the battered and friendly missal, that had been with him all his adult life, to read the office of the day. On bad days he kept it till late, the familiar words that changed with the changing year, that he had grown to love, and were as well his daily duty. It must be surely the greatest grace of life, the greatest freedom, to have to do what we love because it is also our duty. Even here he wasn't able to read on this evening among the old familiar words for long. An annoyance came between him and the page, the Mass he had to repeat every day, the Mass in English. He wasn't sure whether he hated it or the guitar-playing priests more. It was humiliating to think that these had never been such a scourge when his mother had been alive. Was his life the calm vessel it had seemed, dully setting out and returning from the fishing grounds? Or had he been always what he seemed now? "Oh yes. There you go again," he heard the familiar voice in the empty room. "Complaining about the Mass in the vernacular. When you prefer the common names of flowers to their proper names," and the sharp, energetic, almost brutal laugh. It was Peter Joyce, he was not dead. Peter Joyce had risen to become a bishop at the other end of the country, to become an old friend that he no longer saw.

"But they are more beautiful. Dog rose, wild woodbine. buttercup, daisy . . ."

He heard his own protest. It was in an hotel that they used to go to every summer on the Atlantic, a small hotel where you could read after dinner without fear of a rising roar from the bar beginning to out-rival the Atlantic by ten o'clock.

"And, no doubt, the little rose of Scotland, sharp and sweet and breaks the heart," he heard his friend quote maliciously. "And it's not the point. The reason that names of flowers must be in Latin is that when flower lovers meet they know what they are talking about, no matter whether they're French or Greeks or Arabs. They have a universal language."

"I prefer the humble names, no matter what you say."

"Of course you do. And it's parochial sentimentalists like yourself who prefer the *smooth sowthistle* to *sonchus oleraceus* that's the whole cause of your late-lamented Mass in Latin disappearing. I have no sympathy with you. You people tire me."

That had taken care of that annoyance, as its simple logic had once taken his breath away, but he was curiously tired after the vividness of the recall. It was only by a sheer act of will, sometimes having to count the words, that he was able to finish his office. "I know one thing, Peter Joyce. I know that I know nothing," he murmured when he finished. But when he looked at the room about him he could hardly believe it was so empty and dead and dry, the empty chair where she should be sewing, the oaken table with the scattered books, the clock on the mantel. And wildly and aridly he wanted to curse. But his desire to curse was as unfair as life. He had not wanted it.

And then, quietly, he saw that he had a ghost all right, that he had been walking around with for a long time, a ghost he had not wanted to recognise—his own death. He might as well get to know him well, he would never leave now. He was in the room, and had no mortal shape. Absence does not cast a shadow.

All there was was the white light of the lamp on the open book, on the white marble; the brief sun of God on beechwood, and the sudden light of that glistening snow, and the timeless mourners moving towards the yews on Killeelan Hill almost thirty years ago. It was as good as any, if there ever could be a good day to go.

And somewhere, outside this room that was an end, he knew that a young man not unlike what he had been once stood on a granite step and listened to the door bell ring, smiled as he heard a woman's footsteps come down the hallway, ran his fingers through his hair, and turned the bottle of white wine he held in his hands completely around as he prepared to enter a pleasant and uncomplicated evening, feeling himself immersed in time without end.

ACKNOWLEDGEMENTS

The editor and publishers are grateful for permission to include the following copyright stories in this anthology: Robert Bernen: "Brock", copyright © 1977 by Robert Bernen, reprinted by permission of the author. Elizabeth Bowen: "Hand in Glove", copyright © 1952 by Elizabeth Bowen, reprinted by permission of Curtis Brown, London. Joyce Cary: "A Private Ghost", from *Spring Song and Other Stories* (Michael Joseph, 1960) copyright © 1960 by Joyce Cary and reprinted permission of the Estate of Joyce Cary. Eric Cross: "Saint Bakeoven", copyright © 1978 by Eric Cross, reprinted by permission of the Estate of Eric Cross. Aodh de Blácam: "The Ship that Sailed Too Soon", copyright © by Aodh de Blácam, reprinted by permission of the Estate of Aodh de Blácam. Anne Devlin: "Passages", copyright © 1986 by Anne Devlin, reprinted from her collection *The Way Paver* (Faber, 1986) by permission of the author and Anthony Shiel Associates Ltd. Joseph Hone: "The Captain in the Pipes", copyright © 1977 by Joseph Hone, reprinted by permission of the author. Mary Lavin: "The Dead Soldier", copyright © 1943 by Mary Lavin, reprinted by permission of the author. John McGahern: "The Wine Breath", copyright © 1977 by John McGahern, reprinted from his collection *Getting Through* by permission of the author and Faber and Faber Ltd. Dorothy Macardle: "Earth-Bound" copyright © Dorothy Macardle, reprinted by permission of the Estate of Dorothy Macardle. Brian Power: "The Sixth Figure", copyright © 1980 by Brian Power, reprinted by permission of the author. L.A.G. Strong: "Let Me Go", copyright © 1952 by L.A.G. Strong, reprinted by permission of Peters Fraser and Dunlop Group Ltd. William Trevor: "The Raising of Elvira Tremlett", copyright © 1977 by William Trevor, reprinted from *Lovers of Their Time and Other Stories* (The Bodley Head) by permission of the author.

BIOGRAPHICAL NOTES

ROBERT BERNEN: Born in Manhattan, he worked around the New York beaches in his teens and then won a scholarship to Cornell University where he studied Latin and Greek. He subsequently did graduate work at Harvard and in 1970 settled with his wife as a sheep-farmer in Donegal. They returned to live in the U.S. in the early eighties. His sojourn in Ireland resulted in two best-selling collections of short stories, *Tales from the Blue Stacks* and *More Tales from the Blue Stacks*.

ELIZABETH BOWEN: Born in Dublin, in 1899, she was educated in England, where most of her life was spent. The family estate was Bowen's Court, in Co. Cork, which she inherited on her father's death in 1928 and in which she lived from 1952 to 1960. Ireland provided the material for one of her best novels, *The Last September*, and for many short stories. She wrote in all ten novels, over seventy short stories, many works of non-fiction, and over six hundred reviews and essays, and was acknowledged as one of the leading English-language authors of her time. She died in London in 1973.

JOYCE CARY: Born in Derry, in 1888, he was educated in England, though most of his boyhood summers were spent in Inishowen, Co. Donegal. He studied art for a few years and then read Law at Oxford, graduating in 1912. He served in the Red Cross in the Balkan Wars and subsequently joined the Nigerian political service, fighting with the Nigerian regiment in the Cameroons in World War I. He was invalided home in 1920, when he settled in Oxford and devoted the rest of his life to writing. He produced sixteen novels and many short stories, much of his work being based on his experiences in Africa. He died in Oxford in 1957.

CONALL CEARNACH: Born in Connemara in 1876—real name Frederick O'Connell—he was educated at Trinity College, Dublin, and ordained for the Church of Ireland in 1902. He was appointed rector of Achonry in 1907, later lectured in Celtic at Queen's University, Belfast, and became Assistant Director of Radio Eireann when it was formed. He died in 1925 as the result of a street accident.

T. CROFTON CROKER: Born in Cork in 1798, he was the first of the great collectors of Irish folklore. In 1818, after the death of his father, he moved to London, working as a clerk in the Admiralty until he retired in 1850. He produced many books of legends and fairy tales, the most celebrated being *Fairy Legends and Traditions of the South of Ireland*, which was translated into German by the brothers Grimm. He died in London in 1854.

ERIC CROSS: Born in Newry, Co. Down, in 1903, he was a scientist, chemist and inventor as well as a writer. He was the author of only two books, *The Tailor and Ansty*, the celebrated classic about the Tailor of Gougane Barra, and *Silence is Golden*, a collection of short stories. He died in 1980.

AODH de BLÁCAM: Born in London of Ulster parents in 1890, he worked on the *Enniscorthy Echo*, was a member of Sinn Fein, and was interned in 1922. After a spell on the staff of the *Irish Times* he became editor of the *Standard* and later joined the *Irish Press*, his daily feature under the pen-name of "Roddy the Rover" gaining countrywide popularity. He was active in Fianna Fail, which he left to join Clann na Poblachta, but he failed to win a Dail seat in the 1948 election. The author of a number of books, many of them on the lives of Irish saints, he died in 1951.

TERENCE de VERE WHITE: Born Dublin, 1912. A graduate of Trinity College, Dublin, he entered the legal profession but gave up law in 1962 when he was appointed Literary Editor of the *Irish Times*. Between then and 1977, when he retired, he built up a reputation as one of Ireland's most distinguished men of letters. He has published many novels, short stories, biographies, an autobiography, histories, and other works of non-fiction.

ANNE DEVLIN: Born in Belfast in 1951, she lived in West Germany for a time before moving to Bristol and then, in 1984, to Birmingham. Her first short story, which won her a Hennessy Literary Award, was published in the *Irish Press* in 1982, and her collection, *The Way-Paver*, was brought out by Faber in 1986. She has also gained much acclaim for her television and stage plays, winning the Samuel Beckett Award for the best first play on television, the Susan Smith Blackburn Prize, and co-winning the George Devine Award in 1986.

JOSEPH HONE: Born in London 1937, he was educated at Kilkenny College and St. Columba's, Dublin. He was a producer with BBC Radio before joining the UN Secretariat in New York, after which he returned to live in England in 1968. He has written two novels and a volume of autobiography.

MARY LAVIN: Born in Walpole, Massachussetts, in 1912, she has lived in Ireland since the age of 10. Educated at U.C.D., her early writing was greatly encouraged by Lord Dunsany, who wrote the foreword to her celebrated first collection of short stories, *Tales from Bective Bridge*. She has written two novels, but it is her many collections of short stories that have won for her a world-wide reputation as well as a number of prestigious Awards, including two Guggenheim fellowships.

J. SHERIDAN le FANU: Born in Dublin in 1814, he was educated at Trinity College and called to the Bar in 1839. He left law for journalism, but after the death of his wife in 1858 he became a recluse and devoted the rest of his life to writing. He published fourteen novels and many short stories, and is considered to be one of the great masters of suspense.

DOROTHY MACARDLE: Born in 1899, her father was Sir Thomas Macardle, head of the Dundalk brewing family. Educated at University College, Dublin, she became a teacher at Alexandra College, where she was arrested by the British because of her involvement with the republican movement. Her experiences in Mountjoy and Kilmainham were the basis of much of her creative writing—plays, novels and short stories—but her major work was *The Irish Republic*, a massive history of the Revolution, concentrating on the political aspects of the years 1921-1923. After World War II she was mainly concerned with the cause of displaced and refugee children. She died in 1958.

JOHN McGAHERN: Born in Dublin, in 1934, he was raised in Coothall, Co.Roscommon, where his father was a police officer. His first novel, *The Barracks*, won him a Macauley fellowship in 1964, and he has since published four further novels and three collections of short stories. He has lectured widely in Britain and the U.S.A., and at various times has lived in Spain, the U.S., andEngland. He now lives and writes in Co.Leitrim.

SEAMUS O'KELLY: Born in Loughrea, Co.Galway, *c* 1875, most of his working life was spent as a journalist on Irish provincial papers. He wrote two novels and a number of plays, some of which were produced at the Abbey Theatre as well as in Britain, but his best work was done in the short story. He died suddenly of a heart attack in November, 1918, as the result of a raid on the office of *Nationality*, a Dublin periodical of which he was editor, by British forces celebrating the end of World War I.

BRIAN POWER: Born in Dublin in 1930, he was a clerical officer with the E.S.B. before entering Holy Cross College in 1951. Ordained in 1958, he is a graduate of U.C.D., and of Boston College. His first short story was published in the *Irish Press* in 1971 and won him a Hennessy Literary Award. Since then he has published two collections, *A Land not Sown* and *The Wild and Daring Sixties*.

MRS J.H. RIDDELL: Born Charlotte Elizabeth Lawson Cowan in Carrickfergus, Co.Antrim in 1832. Her father was High Sheriff for the County, but following the breakdown of his health the family fell on hard times. He died in 1853, when Charlotte and her mother moved to London, Charlotte having to support both of them as best she could by writing. In 1857, after her mother's death, she married Joseph Hadley Riddell, a civil engineer, and soon became one of the most popular of Victorian writers, author of over forty novels and a similar number of short stories. Her husband died in 1880, leaving heavy debts which she spent the rest of her life paying off. This, and the decline of her popularity due to the changing taste of the reading public, rendered her penniless, and she died of cancer in 1906.

L.A.G. STRONG: Born in Plymouth, England, in 1896, of Irish parents, he spent much of his childhood in Ireland. He won an open classical scholarship to Oxford and took his B.A. there in 1920. He taught until 1930, when he decided to devote all his time to writing. Highly prolific, his work included many novels, short story collections (one of which won the James Tait Black Memorial Prize), plays, children's books, school books, detective stories and much literary criticism. He died in 1958.

WILLIAM TREVOR: Born in Mitchelstown, Co.Cork, in 1928, he studied History at Trinity College, Dublin. Before turning to writing he had a growing reputation as a sculptor. His novel, *The Old Boys*, won the Hawthornden Prize in 1964 and since then he has gained many awards, including the Whitbread. A prolific author of novels, short stories, and TV plays, he was made an honorary C.B.E. in 1978. He now divides his time between Italy and his home in Devon.

THE SECRET ARMY

J. Bowyer Bell

The Secret Army is the definitive work on the IRA. It provides an absorbing account of a movement which has had a profound effect on the shaping of the modern Irish state. J. Bowyer Bell, a specialist in the problems of unconventional war, terrorism, risk analysis and crisis management, has been a research scholar at Harvard and MIT and at the Institute of War and Peace Studies, Columbia University. He is now President of the International Analysis Centre in New York. He has written more than a dozen books, including *Assassin! The Theory and Practice of Political Violence* and *The Gun in Politics: An Analysis of Irish Political Conflict 1916-1986.*

POOLBEG

Terrible Beauty

Diana Norman

Constance Markievicz was the most remarkable Irish woman of her generation. Renouncing her Protestant Ascendancy upbringing, she threw herself wholeheartedly into the struggle for independence which dominated Irish politics in the first two decades of this century. A dedicated feminist, she campaigned for equality and suffrage for women, viewing these aspirations as part of the nationalist issue. An ardent socialist, she was committed, alongside Connolly and Larkin, to the cause of Labour and the freedom of workers.

Imprisoned several times by the British authorities and sentenced to death for her part in the Easter Rising of 1916, Constance Markievicz went on to win election in 1918 as the first woman member of parliament, and then the world's first woman Minister of Labour in the first Dáil Éireann. Her courageous action and politial achievements earned her the respect and affection of ordinary Irish men and women.

Diana Norman has written a warm and sympathetic biography, in which her subject's personality is shaped by the threefold influences of resurgent nationalism, feminism and socialism. Believing her to have received less than her full due from previous biographers, Diana Norman here restores Constance Markievicz to a pre-eminent position not just in Irish history but in the history of women in the twentieth century.

POOLBEG

THE CIVIL WAR 1922-23

Eoin Neeson

Using material scrupulously culled from contemporary sources (newspaper, archival, eye-witness accounts, interviews, field dispatches), Eoin Neeson's now-classic narrative history of Ireland's Civil War appears revised and updated since its first publication in 1966.

Step by tragic step, we witness the unfolding drama and birthpangs of Ireland's nationhood: the Truce ending the War of Independence and the Treaty negotiotions of 1921; the Dáil debates and widening split between Republicans (anti-Treatyites) and Free Staters (pro-Treatyites); the fall of the Four Courts, opening salvoes, and alignments of Church, Press, Industry and Army; the summer campaign in the field as the war front moves south from Dublin to Wicklow, Wexford, Waterford and Tipperary, to the fastnesses of Cork, Kerry and the 'Munster Republic'; the tragic death of Michael Collins, the descent into guerrilla skirmishing, executions and their legacy — all are skilfully documented and assessed.

No understanding of Ireland's contemporary history and politics is possible without a knowledge of the crucial events of the Civil War years. The detail and clarity of Eoin Neeson's masterly appraisal make Civil War 1922-23 a compelling and riveting read.

POOLBEG

The Poolbeg
Golden Treasury of
Well Loved Poems

Edited by Sean McMahon

The *Poolbeg Golden Treasury* is a delightful
anthology of everyone's favourite poems. There are
pieces to be recited aloud, others to be savoured in
solitude. The book brims over with patriotic odes,
romantic lyrics, stirring ballads, poems evoking a
far-off time and place. It ties together the strands of
different traditions into a garland of well-loved
verse.

POOLBEG

IRISH SAGAS
AND
FOLK TALES

Eileen O'Faoláin

Here is a classic collection of tales from the folklore of Ireland. It begins with the heroic sagas, the ancestral tales of men and gods — *The Children of Lir*, *The Fate of the Sons of Usnach*, and the magnificent *Cattle-Raid of Cooley* (the story of the Táin). Then comes the noble tales of Finn and the Fianna, Oisin in the Land of the Ever Young, and the Pursuit of Dermot and Grania. Finally there are the chimney-corner tales of the Little People — *The Black Thief*, *The Bird of the Golden Land*, and many others. Throughout the book, Eileen O'Faoláin maintains a fine command of beautiful, flowing language and captures the heart of Irish story-telling at its enchanting best.

POOLBEG